THE DREAMER.
THE EA

WHOSE

It's the early years of the Twenty-First Century. Without the guidance and values long championed by the old guard—Superman, Batman, and Wonder Woman—a younger generation of super heroes is ravaging the world. But when the Man of Steel returns from self-imposed exile, his very presence could be the catalyst that pushes us all into Armageddon.

Seen through the eyes of Norman McCay, an aging minister who embarks on a disturbing odyssey of revelation with an angel known as the Spectre to guide him, KINGDOM COME is the story of what defines a hero in a world spinning inexorably out of control . . . of the mighty beings who adapt to that changing world, and those who can't . . . of personal battles fought with inner demons, and the final war that will determine the fate of our planet.

KINGDOM COME™

"Solves many puzzles from the original series . . . the pleasure is in the little details."
—*Cleveland Plain Dealer*

"Full of vivid characterizations, gripping action scenes, and notions of pure whimsy."
—*Publishers Weekly*

"A wonderful breathlessness . . . an improvement upon the very entertaining source comics. . . . KINGDOM COME will remind you why these heroes have made such an impact on pop culture for the past sixty years."
—*Science Fiction Age*

"While your adult half ponders the sociological and philosophical concepts raised in the story, the kid in you can get a bang out of seeing your favorite super heroes flying around, doing what they do best. And, so help me, I can't think of a better way to spend my reading time."
—*Mobile Register* (AL)

"Gives depth and characterization not possible in the comic book series."
—*Bookman News*

ACCLAIM FOR THE AWARD-WINNING CLASSIC COMIC BOOK MINISERIES

"A masterpiece."
                    —*New York Daily News*

"Rich, involved storytelling."
                    —*Chicago Sun-Times*

"If you want a think piece on the place of moral people in an amoral world, I'd happily recommend *Kingdom Come*."
                    —*TV Guide*

"An all-time classic."
                    —*Wizard*

"A magnum opus."
                    —*Comic Shop News*

"I can't recommend *Kingdom Come* enough."
                    —*Tripwire*

KINGDOM COME™

Elliot S. MAGGIN

based on a story by Mark WAID
and Alex ROSS

illustrated by Alex ROSS

ASPECT®

WARNER BOOKS

A Time Warner Company

All titles, characters, and related indicia are trademarks of DC Comics © 1998. The stories, characters, and incidents featured in this publication are entirely fictional.

Grateful acknowledgment is given for the use of "Ode to a Dream" by Mark A. Semich © 1993 by Mark A. Semich. All rights reserved. Reprinted with permission.

Aspect® name and logo are registered trademarks of Warner Books, Inc.

Warner Books, Inc.
1271 Avenue of the Americas
New York, NY 10020

Visit our Web site at
www.warnerbooks.com

 A Time Warner Company

Printed in the United States of America

Originally published in hardcover by Warner Books
First Paperback Printing: September 1999

10 9 8 7 6 5 4 3 2 1

Kingdom Come *type design by Todd Klein and Alex Ross*
Cover illustration and design by Alex Ross
Book design and composition by L&G McRee

To Julius Schwartz

He gave me, the boy, a gift of dreams;
then he taught me, the man, to share it.

—ELLIOT S. MAGGIN

To Brian Augustyn,
who hired me when no one else would,
without whom today I would be asking not,
"What will the Flash do this month?" but rather,
"Would you like fries with that?"

—MARK WAID

For my father, Clark Norman Ross,
the real McCay and the true inspiration for
all of *Kingdom Come*.

—ALEX ROSS

For a moment, he stirred and remembered.

He caught a glimpse of a great fortress
in the frozen wastelands of the north.
Of a lost paradise on a distant world.

He saw a time when he had no blood on his hands,
and never would.
When the violence of hatred and mistrust,
the temptation of moral compromise,
could no more overcome him
than a droplet of water could conquer the sun.

But then the memory slipped away
like the dream it was.

—MARK A. SEMICH
Ode to a Dream, 1993

There came a time when the old gods died!
The brave died with the cunning! The noble
perished, locked in battle with unleashed
evil! It was the last day for them! An ancient
era was passing in fiery holocaust!

—JACK KIRBY
The New Gods #1
DC Comics, 1971

ACKNOWLEDGMENTS

~~~

Legends pass from one hand to another, from one mind and set of premises and prejudices to the next, and sometimes back again. I must pay homage, in roughly reverse chronological order, to a number of fabulists and philosophers who—knowingly or not—worked to make what follows possible: Julius Schwartz and Mortimer Weisinger; Orson Scott Card and Isaac Bashevis Singer; Jerome Siegel and Joseph Shuster; Robert Montana and Stan Lee; Jack Kirby; Otto Binder and William Moulton Marston; Joseph Campbell and Edgar Allan Poe; Walter Elias Disney and Samuel Langhorne Clemens; Thomas Jefferson and Benjamin Franklin; Terence Hanbury White and Thomas Malory; Solomon, Isaiah, Jeremiah, Ezekiel, and John; Aristocles and Homer; and those whose hands and minds have contributed and passed the legends along, and many of whose names we have never heard.

Thanks first of all to Alex and Mark for noticing and for telling the whole world.

To Mike Barr for lunch and for Xu'ffasch. To Bill Finger, Sheldon Moldoff, and Bob Kane for Batman and Robin. To Denny O'Neil and Neal Adams for making me notice that it's possible to do this stuff well. To Curt Swan, Kurt Schaffenberger, and Murphy Anderson for Superman. To Carmine Infantino and Gil Kane, the favorite artists of my youth, whose work I came to appreciate properly only after I grew up. To John Broome, Gardner Fox, and Mart Nodell for Green Lantern and the Flash. To Matt Wagner for the Sandman. To Mark Evanier for his contribution to much of the source material. To Clark Ross for being a significant example of the source material. Alfred Bester, of course. Cary Bates and Jeph Loeb for long nights over coffee and cereal and long years of seeing the world as it ought to be. Charles Kochman and Dan Raspler, among the stalwarts of DC Comics—the former for recognizing self-indulgence when he sees it, either in the form of verbosity or dessert; the latter for appreciating a good turn of phrase and a steak. Betsy Mitchell—The Rock—and Wayne Chang of Warner Aspect, and Dana Brass, Chris Eades, Rob Simpson, and Elisabeth Vincentelli of DC Comics.

Wayne and Alice King, keeping the heat on in New Hampshire. Hoyt Robinette and Joanne Edvvard. Pam, my patient wife, and Jeremy and Sarah, our obstreperous but inspiring children. Thanks to John Matthews, Gordon Fellman, Max Lerner, and Philip Slater, especially for the time they spent at Brandeis. Mom and Dad and chapter five. Rabbi Aaron Kriegel, who told me to read Andrew Greeley. Alan Moore, especially for "Whatever Happened to the Man of Tomorrow?" and the dignity it made me feel. Larry Ganem for saying I should do it and acknowledging that he said it for all the wrong reasons. Thanks to Suzanne Fix and to Justin Alexander for being astute. Thanks to my Confirmation students, for listening. To my second-funniest friend and support system, Karen Maurise. To Richard Narita and Irene Yah-ling Sun for New Year and *feng shui*. To David Weiss, still looking over my shoulder, for the cigars.

Jeez, after all that, I hope you guys like it.

ELLIOT S!
The Big Valley

PART I

Our Mission Is Clear...

CHAPTER 1

City of Dreams

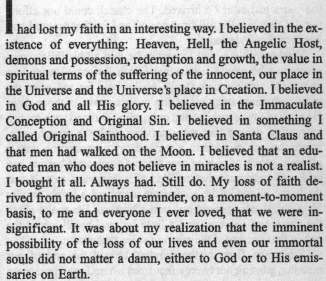

I had lost my faith in an interesting way. I believed in the existence of everything: Heaven, Hell, the Angelic Host, demons and possession, redemption and growth, the value in spiritual terms of the suffering of the innocent, our place in the Universe and the Universe's place in Creation. I believed in God and all His glory. I believed in the Immaculate Conception and Original Sin. I believed in something I called Original Sainthood. I believed in Santa Claus and that men had walked on the Moon. I believed that an educated man who does not believe in miracles is not a realist. I bought it all. Always had. Still do. My loss of faith derived from the continual reminder, on a moment-to-moment basis, to me and everyone I ever loved, that we were insignificant. It was about my realization that the imminent possibility of the loss of our lives and even our immortal souls did not matter a damn, either to God or to His emissaries on Earth.

It was a world without a Superman.

Ω Ω Ω

It began with an ending: that of Wesley Dodds, my friend. Wesley was challenging and smart and the kind of man I hoped to be someday. He was much older than I and was most of the reason I'd come to Metropolis a little over ten years before. It was thanks to Wesley that I took the part-time position in the pulpit of the old Presbyterian church on Jefferson Avenue and Fifty-Fourth Street.

The century was young in those days. It amazed me how short a time it took for the notion of living in the Twenty-First Century to become passé. I took on this job after I ostensibly had retired to collect my pension and enjoy whatever golden years God held in trust for Ellen and me. The congregation was down to just a few dozen families, though that number worked its way as high as a hundred again for a brief time in the years just after I'd arrived. The church could not afford, nor did they need, a full-time pastor, and for that matter I was not even Presbyterian.

Wesley told me, and I suppose he told all his fellow congregants who would listen, that Dutch Reformed was close enough to suit my new flock. Wesley was far and away the most influential member of the congregation in those days. He praised my preaching and counseling skills to such an embarrassing degree that my interview with the search committee was no more than a perfunctory conversation with a pleasant group of people over tea and fresh strawberries in a midtown apartment that smelled of mildew and rust. It was the home of one of the committee members, a lovely man in his eighties who passed on soon afterward. We spoke about the change of seasons, and a little bit, as I recall, about the comet that decorated the evening skies that month.

Superman flew by the window toward the end of our meeting, passing not twenty feet from where I sat. He seemed close enough to touch. He was more floating than flying, not at all in a hurry to get wherever he was going. His body language, even in flight, said, "I have power and glory to spare."

Of course I had seen people fly before at one time or another. That was not uncommon in America after all, even in those days, but it was the first time I'd seen *him*.

"Gee," I think I said.

My interviewers looked out the window and somebody said, "Oh," catching on to the fact that someone from out of town might be in awe of this sight.

"I've heard that Metropolitans consider it good luck when he flies by," I said.

"It's good luck if the windows hold up," someone said, and laughed. "But don't you worry about luck, Reverend McCay. You've got the job already if you want it."

"Norman, you might have noticed"—Wesley grinned, leaning toward me as we gathered up our fellowship and carried it out of the search committee meeting—"that the average age of the congregation is dead."

It was an amazing church nonetheless. It took up the entire ground floor of the LexCorp Building, which had risen at the height of the city's last great building boom. The company founded by Lex Luthor, the industrialist and sometime felon, had acquired the square block containing three large pay-by-the-hour parking lots and an old Presbyterian church. It had not been a historic building by any means; the church had burned or fallen in or decayed and been rebuilt half a dozen times in the previous two hundred years. The congregation went back to the Eighteenth Century on that site, and there was always someone or other paying homage to the Creator on that corner.

Luthor had gotten tired of waiting for the last of the congregants to give up or die. One day at a news conference on the street outside the old church, he'd made a big show of promising that if the elders gave the go-ahead, he would build a finer church on that site than Metropolis had ever seen. The congregation—those awake enough to know what they were voting on—had said sure, and Luthor proved good to his word. The new church had opened for worship even as LexCorp's skyscraper-in-progress had risen above it, and construction crews had adjusted their schedule to accommodate that of the Presbyterians of Jefferson Avenue.

The church was more than thirty years old by the time I came to take my job as part-time pastor, and it was by any measure the finest building in which I'd ever served. It was marble, granite, and steel, like the rest of the building above it, but with hardwood paneling inside. The main floor of the sanctuary sat about a story and a half below ground level so that a battery of large stained-glass windows decorated eye-level on the Jefferson Avenue side for passersby. It had a stunning pipe organ like none I had ever seen or heard elsewhere, taking up the eastern wall and reaching up the entire three-story height of the sanctuary. A balcony and a choir loft sat around ground level, with doors to classrooms that we used only for storage. I do not think that in the time I was there we had a single regular congregant under sixty, and certainly none of Sunday School age.

People around the country—as well as the local municipal boosters—still called Metropolis the City of Dreams in those days. A fellow named Ellsworth once had lost an attempt to get reelected Mayor using "City of Dreams" as a campaign catch-phrase. The Mayor had gone the way of all historical footnotes, but the catch-phrase grew roots. The City of Dreams was where the Man of Steel made his life and found his friends and his enemies and forged his legend, but it was more than that. Metropolis was the image people all over the world held of America. Metropolis was the city Americans envisioned when they thought of the future. This was where ideas were born and where trends started their sweep across the culture. Finally, it was where the ruination of it all began.

When my wife, Ellen, and I came to Metropolis, Magog— the self-styled heir to Superman's mantle—had already made a few appearances. It was clear to everyone, it seemed, except Magog himself, that Superman was above such sophomoric balderdash and was hardly in the market for a successor. Magog was young and brash and wore a golden horned helmet and carried a sceptre through which he focused his superpower the way rock music stars of my youth carried their hair and their attitudes. Superman, by contrast, was well into middle age by then. The veteran was enormously accomplished and enjoyed the admiration of all but his most irredeemable enemies. Enjoy it he did, too. Swimming through the air on patrol in the evenings, he grinned as boyishly as the blood brother of the wind could grin. A local news outlet had once caught footage of him scooping a woman with a carriage of twins up from in front of a bus racing a yellow light through an intersection. He saw to the mother and children's health and gravely delivered a gentle rebuke to the contrite bus driver. Then the camera had caught him unloading a bit of a laugh at his own solemnity while retreating up into a cloud. When we all had seen him last, Superman was graying around the edges and looking a little weathered, but he was more powerful than he had ever been before and cut an astonishing figure across the sky.

We loved him. Even my congregant who complained that the Man of Steel rattled the windows when he breezed by loved him. Even those whose petty fantasies of confidence and criminality he thwarted, and whose reform he inevitably embraced and championed, loved him. Even those of my colleagues who saw his enormous temporal power as rivaling their monotheistic teachings, and who then heard with what eloquence he accounted for himself—especially to the children—loved him. It seemed the right thing to love him. God seemed to love him so.

Then something must have happened in his life. For a little while no one saw him smiling or laughing as he went about his never-ending battle. And finally he took offense at us—for good cause, but, after all, we mere mortals had certainly offended him in the past and he'd never made a pretext before of folding in upon himself—and this time he was gone. And he did not return.

Soon afterward I lost Ellen in the most useless of accidents. Perhaps Superman could have prevented it. Perhaps if he had not left the city, the public carelessness that had brought it about never would have caught her. Perhaps not. Nonetheless, I thought all the world was gone to gray and stillness and death, but I was wrong. It was only the City of Dreams that had died. The world throbbed on relentlessly, and the city where dreams withered continued to scream, as cities do, at the top of its marble, granite, and steel bellows. It was different, is all.

Ω Ω Ω

I was afraid toward the end of his life that Wesley Dodds was suddenly a little unbalanced. By the time he left us I had no doubt of it. But after he had gone, it became clear that he was the sanest man I ever knew. Yet that was not how it started. This was how it started:

"So the question of truth in the Bible thus becomes irrelevant," I put forth to the congregation, and most of them listened and nodded as they always did. Or slept. The big sanctuary had about thirty people in it this Sunday morning, more than I was usually getting these days. The only one who had any particular reaction at all to what I was saying was Wesley, and I perceived his reaction only because he was my friend.

"In the context of the Scriptures," I went on, "the most important element, I feel, is the way the story is told. This is not to say that events as the Scriptures describe them are not literally true. I expect that generally they are. But the real value of the Scriptures is in how we understand them. The metaphorical truth of the Scriptures is absolute. Often, art is a lie that tells the truth."

With this, Wesley eased over the edge.

"Woe unto them," Wesley said, almost under his breath.

I ignored him at first.

"Woe unto them!" he said louder.

"Excuse me?" I asked from the pulpit.

The other folks sitting near Wesley shushed him, but he got up to his feet—stiffly, as though against his will—and with an almost embarrassed expression on his face, declaimed, "No no no, Norman. This is not metaphor. This is not apocrypha. Moses did not scale Mount Sinai to receive the Ten Suggestions. This is truth, unconditional and immutable. There is a right and a wrong in the Universe, and that distinction is not difficult to make. Woe unto them that sow iniquity with seeds of vanity, and sin as it were with a cart rope." Then he sat down. He was in his nineties by then, and never before had I seen him spring up and down with such agility. "Excuse me, Pastor," he mumbled into his prayerbook, and after a moment both he and I gathered ourselves, and I finished my sermon.

That was the first time.

Wesley was the sort of fellow one would expect to live to outlandish maturity. We had met at the exercise club in Wilmette where Ellen and I used to go twice a week. He'd been in town for a chemical industry convention; he'd finally retired, I think, when he hit ninety. He bought a weekend pass to the gym to keep up his regimen, his custom for out-of-town trips lasting more than a few days. Ten minutes of stretches to warm up; ten or fifteen repetitions of moderate calisthenics alternating muscle groups on the various iron and chrome weight gadgets that in my previous experience only the washboard-bellied young people had dared tackle; a brief rest, and then twenty minutes of light aerobics on the rowing simulator, the step machine, or the treadmill. A performance with which I probably could have kept up on a good day. Then again, I was nearly two decades younger, and by all accounts the elderly Wesley had done it every day. The first time I'd seen him do this, I retreated to the sauna, which served the purpose of making me sweat enough to fool my aging body into believing it was sufficiently exercised for the day.

After some minutes the hairless old man with the pale skin and the thin but dense chest had appeared in a towel in the sauna and struck up a conversation. I told him I was a minister, and he told me, laughing, he was a retired super hero who had gotten impatient with the competition and gone into the drug trade. The rub was that this was the absolute truth. We'd gotten into a long conversation about Nietzsche and Gnosticism, in the course of which the sauna dehydrated me, and I lost track of the time. He helped me out, staggering, leaned me against a tile wall for a shower and a cup of water, and laughed some more. Wesley Dodds had laughed all the time—just like Superman—even through the bad times. He'd sat me down on the bench in front of the women's locker room, and when Ellen came out, startled, he told her just to pour lots of that Glacial Milk mineral soft drink down my gullet. Ellen and I had invited him over for a home-cooked meal that evening, and, from that day until fifteen years later when I buried him, we were friends.

"There were voices," Wesley said, "and thunderings, and lightnings, and an earthquake. And there followed hail and fire mingled with blood."

He lay propped up on the bed at Saint Clare's now. Doctors had removed him from the intensive care unit, saying it would do him no good at that point. The most intensive care he could get now consisted of attention and comforting, they told me. Wesley suffered three strokes and two heart attacks, and only the enormous investment he'd made through the years in individual health insurance kept his doctors from issuing a "do-not-resuscitate" order. Years into the Twenty-First Century, enormously heroic measures for extending the period of a person's dying were available to anyone like Wesley who insisted on emerging kicking and screaming into the next world like a babe in birth trauma.

I was familiar by now with Wesley's recurring visions. He kept talking about the eagle carrying the golden lance, contending in the sky with a giant sucking bat as doom approached from out of sight. There were torrents of green fire, flashes of red lightning. Wesley spoke of a legion of the mighty drowning in a great lake of heat waves and burning sand, and over and over again of the American flag in the shape of a man, tattered and torn, struggling to emerge through a wall of fire.

He described all this again, ignoring my pleas to rest. He said, "There fell a great star from heaven, burning as if it were a lamp. And I beheld, and heard an Angel saying with a loud voice, 'Woe woe woe to the inhabiters of the Earth.' "

Wesley used to call himself the Sandman during his youth. No one to my knowledge ever gave him a genetic test, but he was probably a metahuman the same as Green Arrow the archer and Wonder Woman the Amazon Princess and—who knows?—Joe DiMaggio and Muhammad Ali. The current thinking in scientific circles, or the thinking that was current the last time I read the latest journal report, is that the capacity to rise to what we call super heroism is genetic. Estimates are that the metagene is in the cellular structure of 12 to 16 percent of the current human population. It appears to be a highly dominant trait.

Back before I was old enough to be conscious of such goings-on, the Sandman had been all over the tabloids, one of the first—or maybe the very first—of the modern wave of masked adventurers with a solid sense of public relations. His "costume" had been rudimentary: a trench coat and, to hide his face, a World War One mustard gas mask that he'd found in a trunk in his grandfather's attic upon the old man's death. He'd skulked through the night solving mysteries, righting wrongs, sandbagging bad guys. It had been a lot of fun, he insisted, until he found he was developing arthritis in his joints as a result of all the rooftop-leaping, window-crashing, and thug-tackling that came to be expected of a super hero on a day-to-day basis.

"It was all my fault I had to quit," Wesley had mused over a glass of Bordeaux he'd brought to share with Ellen and me one evening back in Wilmette. "I demanded too much of my body. Much too much. Who knew what super heroes were supposed to act like before I decided how I would act?"

"What do you mean?" Ellen asked him.

"Well, my pop was a major-league pitcher for a few years, you know."

"Really?" My ears perked up; I'd been an enormous Cubbies fan all my life, up until the day Darkstar and the Manotaur rumbled out the last World Series back in '02. "What club was he with?"

"The Tribe mostly," Wesley said, "and I spent most of my childhood in Cleveland. He was the guy on the mound when the Babe pointed up in the bleachers and sent a home run where he'd pointed."

"You mean that really happened?" I said, astonished. "I thought it was apocryphal."

"Most stories are apocryphal and true at the same time, but that one's real to boot," Wesley told us, taking another sip. "I was there. Yankee Stadium. Independence Day weekend. Way back. Pop was none too happy with that pitch, and the skipper took him out of the lineup after that inning. I sat in the visitors' dugout with my father's teammates because he didn't trust me to the New York crowds. Can you imagine that? A father feeling it was unsafe for a young boy alone in a crowd of baseball fans even back then? Ah, me."

"What did Babe Ruth and Yankee Stadium have to do with the Sandman?"

"I'd grown up around super heroes," he said, pouring Ellen and himself another half-glassful, "or around the closest thing we had to them. I used to resent sports figures being called heroes in the press. Then I realized the Sandman was taking all his signals from them. You couldn't be effective as a costumed adventurer in the Nineteen-Thirties and Forties without owing a lot to Babe Ruth and guys like him."

"Are you telling me Babe Ruth was a metahuman?"

"I don't know about the science," Wesley went on. "Genetics is voodoo to me. I just knew that the Babe was my idea of what a super hero was supposed to be like. Strong. Unrelenting. Incredibly generous of spirit."

"And apparently unable to grow up," Ellen observed, with Wesley nodding.

"Same as me." He smiled. "Still."

"So why'd you stop, really?" I asked him.

"The competition in the super hero biz got to be hell." Wesley had laughed, Ellen and I laughing with him—not because it'd been funny, but because Wesley had seen fit to laugh.

Then he stared at his glass, rolling it back and forth over the fingers of his left hand so the good wine draped viscous liquid curtains over the inside of the crystal. "And one day," he said, "I realized it was the life of a super hero that killed the Babe, and I didn't want it to kill me too. I loved life so much back then that just those memories'll keep a man going for a long time after."

Ω Ω Ω

I looked out the window of the hospital room that housed my friend Wesley's deathbed, and the night sky was peppered with dark, darting creatures. They perched on gargoyles and spires. They traced the lines of the roadways like low-flying planes. They hovered here and there, conferring and congregating high above the rooftops. They were mutations and accidents and biochemical experiments gone awry. They were the children and grandchildren of heroes and villains and retired victims of circumstance of a simpler age. They were heirs to a lost time of right and wrong in the Universe, when that distinction had not been difficult to make. They had a dimension beyond that which the rest of us possessed, and, more than the skyline itself, they dominated the spirit and identity of this city.

When Superman had dropped from sight, so had most of his generation of higher-minded warriors. He'd been the most powerful and, paradoxically, the most human of them. He'd also seemed unbound by the infirmities that age brings, those troublesome little stiffenings of the soul that we like to cover over with a cosmetic we ironically call "dignity." I guess we supposed that guys like Batman and Green Lantern and the Flash and Hawkman simply had receded into the scenery the way stage and film stars did, in favor of younger players better able to take the same roles. Those of us who wondered some more, however, soon noticed that the roles had become different. Heroism was no longer about inspiring human achievement. Suddenly it was about belittling it.

Wesley told me that. It was around the time he first interrupted my sermon.

It was not only Metropolis' sky that was different. On and under the ground, things were going unfixed. Battles over the landscape left cars and buildings a shambles, and the asphalt and concrete of the byways themselves lumpy and misshapen like an ill-tended throw rug. For all the burst pipes and water mains, water pressure was so depressed that it usually took most of a day to fill a bathtub, and showers were a luxury available only at out-of-the-way spas. Commerce was next to impossible in the general vicinity of where these young super-folks contended or simply showed off, and Midtown alone— from the old Union Station up to the Park—averaged two rumbles a day. That was what the set-tos among these highly hormoned types were called: rumbles. I understand that Cal Tech has begun measuring rumbles seismically and giving them ratings on the Richter scale.

By this time I'd lost track first of most of the costumed folks' names, and then of who were the good guys and who were the bad guys altogether. Apparently I was not the only one. The popular culture as well twisted to the shape of this new self-image that humans were growing around themselves. Wesley called me early one morning about a year before his death, all excited over the new theme restaurant called Planet Krypton on the far side of Governor's Plaza.

"Come on," he barked through the phone line and my morning haze. I had not found my glasses or the coffee maker yet, and he was saying, "Get your holier-than-shit ass out of the kip, Padre, and I'll meet you in your lobby at seven forty-five. That's fifteen minutes by most of my clocks."

I did not mind his swearing; it seemed to fit the context of his personality. But I hated it when he called me "Padre," and I was not sure why. "Is there life at this hour?" I asked him.

"Only metahuman life," he said. "This place has an under-twenty-buck breakfast special. My treat for a change," and he hung up.

The subways in Metropolis were continually being repaired. The taxis were uniformly rusted-down, cannibalized, homemade jobs that as often as not leaked exhaust into the interiors and onto the passengers. Buses were a joke, and the phrase "bus schedule" was a contradiction in terms. No one kept a car in Metropolis unless it was up on blocks in some secured location, and no one drove into town in a car built since the turn of the century except to get an insurance settlement on it. The only reasonably reliable means of transportation around town were feet and hovercraft. Rich corporate executives used the prohibitively expensive vehicles. Hovercraft were good because if they got caught up in a rumble, they were not bound by roads, rails, or gravity. They could generally recover their stability through shock waves much like a sailboat, unless they took a direct hit from one of the "heroes."

Congress was forever passing laws in an attempt to nullify the economic hardships that metahuman activity imposed on individuals and communities. Most insurance companies had a special high-priced category of rumble coverage. The award of benefits for rumble insurance was based on rules and assumptions similar to those governing "acts of God."

Highly active metahumans learned early on that the best career path for them, despite or perhaps because of their enormous earning power, was to get whatever they needed through whatever means they could manage, and stay as broke and unlitigable as they could. Whatever got in their way—buildings, walls, asphalt, people, irresistible forces, immovable objects—would crumble, and they did not have to pay for anything no matter what laws Congress passed. All the President's horses and all the President's men still could not figure out how to squeeze water from a stone or reparations from a wild-eyed impoverished super hero.

So Wesley met me in the lobby of the old LexCorp Building, where I lived in a little apartment adjoining the upper floor of the church, and we walked the several blocks downtown. Wesley counted vehicles with handprints, footprints, or what he thought were dents from body slams somewhere in their hulls before we reached the Plaza. I was increasingly hesitant to walk with him through town, the scenery upset him so. At the Plaza the police stood waving their arms mechanically, moving pedestrians along. Behind them strips of yellow tape cordoned off what used to be the eastern exterior wall of the big old Metropolitan Radio Corporation building. Some sort of flying craft three stories high hung partly in and partly out of the sixth floor where, I knew, they were usually broadcasting the morning's installment of *The Daybreak Show*. At least it looked like a flying craft, with its curved aerodynamic chassis twisted into itself along lines that traced where the building walls once were. Later, I realized it was actually the remains of the statue of Odysseus that had stood in the nearby square for decades, all twisted and stretched so it reminded me of some weird science-fiction artifact.

"Move along," the middle-aged policeman said to people who were, by and large, already moving along. "Move along," he repeated as his arms waved, and the people on the sidewalk ignored both him and the spectacle.

"Hey, son." Wesley tried to get the cop's attention.

"Move along," the cop said, and didn't notice Wesley was talking to him.

"Excuse me. Officer?" Wesley persisted.

"Yes, sir?" the man answered, a little bit surprised as he continued to wave his arm back and forth as though a little motor in his shoulder were forcing him to do so.

"Ever miss the concept of human achievement?" Wesley asked the cop.

I rolled my eyes and yanked Wesley by the jacket sleeve, but he locked eyes with the Metro cop long enough to see the man tilt his head like a pet dog who did not understand what you were trying to tell him. Then he gathered up his officiousness and said, "Move along," some more. "Move along."

Wesley counted body-slammed cars numbers seven, eight, and nine in the remaining block before we made it to the restaurant and slipped inside.

$$\Omega \quad \Omega \quad \Omega$$

It was the Twentieth Century again at the Planet Krypton restaurant, sort of. For most of the latter years of the last century the building on this site had been called The Hippodrome. Years ago it had been a multiple-level parking garage and apparently had done a good business holding cars for commuters during workdays and for revelers at night and on weekends. People used to come into Metropolis to revel a lot. There was no longer much use for multilevel parking garages in this city of biologically propelled ground and sky traffic. The restaurant developers had hollowed out the big garage, and on its roof was a rotating model of Krypton—a wobbly green planet caught in the act of exploding. Continents hung by thick rods off the meridians of the doomed world. A proportionally planet-sized spacecraft of an oddly art deco style revolved around it in permanent escape mode. The battlements of the building were decked out with cartoony baby pictures of some of the most familiar masked faces of a bygone time: the Flash from Central City; Wonder Woman with big hair; the crisp young dawn-of-the-space-age fellow who used to wear the Green Lantern uniform ex-

tending a hand, his ring glowing and spewing fumes as if of
dry ice; and more. They all looked so wholesome and quaint
up there, even the villains. I guess that was the idea.

The interior of Planet Krypton had all the charm of a barn.
Sound bounced off the walls and fixtures in an unsettling din. At
the end of the century, I remembered, there had been a trend
toward gutting old industrial spaces in Midtown and turning
them into sandwich-and-martini houses with themes. It was a
throwback in form as well as content.

Wesley covered his face with a wary mask when a maître
d' in an ill-fitting Green Lantern suit stepped briskly up to the
two of us. The kid did that officious heel-off-the-ground
"ahem" and said, "Good morning, citizens. How may I serve
you?"

"What the hell—" Wesley said.

"Two for breakfast," I interrupted my friend.

It was important to Wesley that the costumed champions
of whom he was the first—and of whom Superman was
perhaps the last—be remembered for the values they had
brought to their chosen fights. It was important to him that the
world remained aware of the generations of metahumans who
had advanced human achievement rather than stomped on it.
Thus, his excitement upon hearing about this silly little
restaurant. He should not have been surprised that the antici-
pation outshone the reality.

As Green Lantern showed us to our seats, Wesley snarled
at a strawberry blonde waitress in a Wonder Woman outfit,
and then commented with a sniff at our emerald warrior,
"Well, at least they got a guy with the right color hair."

"Did they? Yeah, I guess so." The boy in green grinned ef-
fusively. "So what do you think? Not a bad job on the tights,
huh? They tell me I make a pretty good Green—what do you
call him?—Arrow," he noted mistakenly, and then he scurried
off to greet some more "citizens."

Booster Gold's original costume—that is what the plaque
read, at any rate—hung over a mannequin in a clear cylin-

drical case on the restaurant floor. I heard later that the former Justice Leaguer was a partner in this enterprise, and that there were franchises going up in Keystone, Midway, Gotham City, and South Coast within the year. A little red-haired girl in green sunglasses and a Robin costume waited on us. The Martian Manhunter, with buck teeth and freckles showing through the green facial makeup, carried a tray of glasses. Catwoman and Lobo, both bulging a bit in the midriff, bused tables. All sorts of ticky-tack reproductions peppered the big room. Aquaman's trident sat on a shelf propped on a green power battery. A golden Amazon tiara hung from a hat rack next to Captain Marvel's cape and the original Flash's winged helmet. A plaster fist wearing a tight blue cuffless sleeve protruded from a hole in a wall. A scale model of something that looked like the first Bat-Plane anyone had ever seen hung in a power-diving position from long wires in the ceiling. Episodes of an old cartoon series called *Super-Tots,* about super-powered babies in costumes of the original Justice League members, played on a multiple-screen complex at an angle connecting the ceiling to one wall. A golden eagle-beaked head mask straddled a Twelfth-Century European mace and a Sixteenth-Century pair of Asian nunchuks. Wesley even noticed a mustard gas mask, circa World War One, peeking out from behind a holographic display of famous front pages from the defunct *Daily Planet,* but he did not seem flattered or even impressed.

"I had no idea it was already this bad, Norman," Wesley told me as he rearranged the scrambled eggs in his pentagonal plate with the S-emblem embossed across it.

"It's not so bad," I said, guilty about so enjoying the American Way on White I scooped off my round plate. Under my sandwich a graphic of a yellow lightning bolt slashed the ceramic face of the plate.

"It is," Wesley said, "and worse."

"What do you mean?"

"I've been seeing visions, Norman." He leaned forward to

whisper to me, as if anyone else could have heard him over the general chaos. "I've been hearing voices."

"I have bad dreams, too."

"No, not dreams!" he said, pounding the hilt of his fork on the table and hurting his hand. "Visions like I had when I was the Sandman."

Ω   Ω   Ω

"Read to me, please, would you, Norman?" Wesley asked me as he pressed the heat-sensitive button that propped up the head of his hospital bed. I think that little outing to Planet Krypton over a year before had been the last time Wesley and I'd come close to having fun together. He was out of breath from his latest screed, which rendered him unconscious for a few minutes and caused me to wonder whether he was already gone from us. "Read from *The Revelation of Saint John the Divine,* would you, Norman?" Weakly, he pressed the little cloth-bound Bible into my hand. "How about Matthew, or Micah," I suggested. "You don't need to hear all that apocalyptic stuff with the—"

He waved his arms and opened his mouth as if to yell. Only short bursts of breath came out, but I agreed to read what he told me to read just to keep the peace, such as it was. He was frail. What was left of him was just the frame of what once had carried my friend Wesley Dodds, that great civilized beast of a man.

He recited with me as I read: " 'Seven thunders will utter their voices. And it was given unto him to make war with the saints.' "

Wesley gathered up a surge of energy and madness and said, "Babylon falls, Norman. Be the one who listens to me," and twisted around his finger the tube of the intravenous drip that was bypassing his tortured throat to feed him through his forearm. He gave the tube a yank and slid it out from under his flesh. Only a drop of blood oozed from the indentation where the tube had fed his vein. "The sands run out and I can do nothing but wait in my own filth for sleep finally to claim me. Will someone act when I can't?"

"Wesley, please"—I tried to ease him back down onto his bed—"take comfort. There is peace awaiting."

"Of course there is, Norman, for me," and he thundered in a voice that, now that I think on it, could not have come in any natural manner from a man so near the end, "but not for you! You're the poor, pitiful dreamer who comes next." A nurse in the hall looked in and called for a doctor, then the two of them shoved me away to tie his wrists to the bedposts and resecure the IV drip.

"I'm sorry," I said over and over, maybe to the doctor and the nurse, who looked through and beyond me with not even the personal regard they accorded their patients. "I'm sorry," but for what I was not sure.

"Hear me, Norman. I owe you much, but I have nothing to leave you except insight. 'And I will give power unto my two witnesses,' Norman, do you hear me?" he demanded. "It is yours to be one of those two. Be my witness, Pastor. It's all in the words of God. It's all there. The end is near! Read the book!"

Eventually the doctor and nurse calmed Wesley down and did not think to throw me out, so I picked up the Bible again and read some more from *First Corinthians,* a book that was a little less incendiary:

" 'Now this I say, Brethren, that flesh and blood cannot inherit the Kingdom of God. Behold, I show you a mystery; we shall not all sleep but we shall all be changed . . .' "

And Wesley did in fact find sleep and somewhere in the night made the change. I officiated his funeral three days later. There were no relatives, only a few of the good people of the church.

That night, I dreamed.

CHAPTER 2

Vision Quest

Wesley died on a Friday. The world ended the following Monday. In my dreams.

Something in my body was afraid to go to sleep. It was not because of Wesley's funeral, though he was a close friend. I have spent altogether too much time at funerals in the course of my career for them to affect me one way or the other. People's lives move me, not their deaths. Ellen used to say that the lifestyle of a minister to an aging congregation gave me a dark sense of humor. I was relieved to find that my poor, deluded wife thought I had a sense of humor at all.

Monday afternoon we buried Wesley out on the Island in a plot that he'd bought long ago. He'd come to the church questioning what there was to believe in; I wish I could have offered him better answers. Certainly, thankfully, he had them now. I went out there on a rented hoverbus with some of the folks who came to the funeral, but I felt a little off-balance afterward and I did not want to be around my congregants, so I took the commuter train back as far as the outer boroughs of the city. The train—at home in a rail yard far from Metropolis—was clean and spiffy, and the ride was as smooth as the devil's sales pitch, as my grandma Imogene used to say. My long compartment floated eight or ten inches above the smooth concrete gully that traced the old railroad line as far as the Metro County East Hub. Three city administrations had promised over the past ten years to complete construction in the tube from the Hub under the river into Union Station. The ongoing project had furnished designer shoes and Havana cigars for scores of manufacturers of optical-fiber-laced concrete forms all up and down the Eastern Seaboard for a decade. No one knew how much rubble really existed down there or how much it would cost to clean up and rebuild the tube, even if the rumbles had suddenly stopped.

The ride along the south coast of the Island was fairly safe and generally peaceful nonetheless. Metahumans tended to be city folk. There were only about a half dozen others in the car making their way into town as the line geared up for the rush period of commuters going back out to the suburbs. So I sat by the window and watched the train make a blur of the Atlantic coast.

There is a twilight area just before sleep. It is the point at which you begin to put together the disparate visions of your unconscious and see the edges of your dreams. When you find yourself in this twilight area, you have about a minute to put down your book and find a comfortable position. Sometimes you try to finish the paragraph you are reading, and invariably the light stays on all night and you dream about doing calisthenics and you have a stiff neck in the morning. At least that is my experience. I thought I found the twilight as I sat in the train and watched out the window as an enormous golden eagle rose from the oceans dripping water and rising on the wind. It left a wake in the air of pale red, gold, and blue as it powered upward into the sky in the direction of a gargantuan hairy bat that hovered on the wind currents of the stratosphere. We all see things like this in our dreams as a matter of course, so I closed my eyes and put down the copy of an old book by Mort Sahl called *Heartland*.

I did not sleep. The skin of my arms was all tingly and electric against the inside of my jacket. My heart beat hard enough for me to hear it as I lay my head against the cushion of my seat. I suppose I was not sleepy, and it occurred to me that the scene I witnessed over the water outside my train window might be real. I pried my eyes open and scanned the horizon, but there was no giant bat, no drenched eagle leaving a primary-colored contrail against the clouds. The few others in the car with me either dozed or played at cards or stared glassily at the scenery. No one reacted to anything untoward. There was no reason to panic. This was interesting.

Then I slept.

Ω   Ω   Ω

Sleep was green and white, and the white felt like blood. I have never been very good at remembering my dreams. This time, however, they must have floated somewhere near the edge of my consciousness. I saw a flowing green curtain all the way around me, shielding me from something. I saw through the occasional breaks in the curtain a fire of white-hot flame, like the sun. I saw glimpses of a sea of bleach-white human bone scattered over a desert. I saw patterns of ash in the shape of bone crumbling to dust. And there was the American flag, hovering in the sky, flying in my direction— sadly but slowly, as if it had power and glory to spare. As the flag approached me, it began to take the shape of a man.

"Are you all right, mister?" somebody said.

"How doth the city sit solitary, that was full of people!" somebody else said in a familiar but foreign voice. "How is she become as a widow!"

"What is he babbling about?" one of the people around me asked.

"Just sounds. Nonsense. Gibberish," another said.

"Mister, you're scaring me," yet another voice said. "Please wake up."

"She that was great among the nations," that other voice continued, louder now.

"His eyes are open," someone said.

"But is he awake?" someone else wanted to know.

"And princess among the provinces, how is she become tributary!"

There were six or seven people standing around when I realized I was awake and coming out of a dream, and it was my voice that reverberated down the train. I went to pull my voice back but I still heard myself say:

"She weepeth sore in the night, and her tears are on her cheeks . . . She hath none to comfort her," I said before I could stop; I realized I was not speaking in English.

"It's not gibberish," a dark-eyed boy said. "I think it's Hebrew."

It was Hebrew, I realized. I heard the end of it. It was from the book of *Lamentations,* in the tongue in which the prophet Jeremiah originally wrote it.

"I'm all right. Thank you," I told the good people around me. "Really," I said, wiping the spittle from my mouth as they went back to their seats.

We were coming into the Madison Heights section at the easternmost edge of Metropolis. We would slip underground and be in the Hub in a few minutes. Then would come the long walk across the bridge into Midtown. I wondered if I had suffered a seizure of some sort, and repeatedly made a fist with both hands to make sure my strength was sufficient. I felt fine physically. I looked behind me to see the dark-eyed boy, the one who had recognized the language I was speaking, sitting two seats behind, and I waved to get his attention. Apparently everyone else in the car was keeping an eye on me. Three people rose halfway from their seats to see if I needed help—or perhaps to protect the boy—then sat back down warily.

"Sonny? Did you hear all I was saying?"

"No, sir. Well, maybe. I don't know."

"Was it all in Hebrew?"

"I'm pretty sure. What I heard, that is."

"Did you recognize anything I was saying?"

"No sir. Just a word here and there. I don't really speak it. I can just read it when there are vowels."

"What do you mean, when there are vowels?"

"Well, Hebrew doesn't really have vowels. You just kind of put them in as a temporary guide for people who are learning the language. Kind of like accent marks." The boy thought a moment, then asked me, "Don't you know that, sir?"

"No," I told him, and I sat back in my seat facing away from him as we entered the darkness of the tunnel. "I don't understand a word of Hebrew."

ת   ת   ת

So now I was speaking in tongues. I had lived in mild fear of this since boyhood.

Really.

My maternal grandmother had spoken in tongues. She'd been a suffragette in her early days, but once women had gotten the vote, she no longer had a cause to champion, so she had taken to the evangelical circuit, at first as an audience shill: On a signal, she would go into paroxysms of ecstasy and roll on the ground with the preacher's summoning of the Spirit upon the crowd; or she would come into a tent meeting on crutches, and then throw them off and walk at the appropriate time. Soon, however, she graduated to preaching, becoming quite well known in evangelical circles. "Reverend Imogene Arcane, First Lady of the Holy Witness," was how she billed herself. She had gone off on her own and pitched tents and presided over revival meetings all over the South and Midwest in the Depression and the War years. When she had no cripples to heal or heathens to convert, she'd spoken the words of the Scriptures and lost texts in the original languages, or so her roadies and retainers had claimed. It is very difficult to make up nonsense words and sounds and string them together, so they *seemed* to be from an unfamiliar language. If that, as I suspect, was what Grandma Imogene had done, then she'd marketed her skill very ably.

My father's oldest brother, Billy Pring McCay, may have been a better preacher even than Grandma. He'd been an advocate of something he called "Spiritual Expansion." He'd taught people that they could learn new things and acquire altogether-new abilities—things like skiing or playing the trumpet or speaking dead languages—from meditating on the ability for extended periods. He would go to little towns to "wake up" the missing talents in people whose lives needed a little nudge here and there to make them interesting. He'd cured a lot of cases of math anxiety over the years, and quite a few cases of hysterical blindness. We were all convinced that he'd been the model for the character in that musical comedy about the small-town con man. Uncle Billy had actually been tarred and feathered and deposited on a freight car once when he claimed to be able to train a boys' marching band in a little town in northern Iowa.

My great-aunt Rebecca, Grandma Imogene's older sister, had been a witch, the recognized matriarch of a number of covens of the exponents of the ancient Wicca faith, who danced naked in the forests of the upper Midwest. Rebecca had been far less public about her talents and influence than some of the other extraworldly seekers and scoundrels of the family, and for good reason. Among all of us, Rebecca seemingly had been the one with the most money. She'd lived in a big home with little gargoyles decorating the window panes and lots of animist paraphernalia around its dark interior. Instead of a lawn she had an extensive herb garden, and little flower pots growing sprigs of all sorts of unfamiliar flora had hung near all the entrances and exterior walkways of the big old place. Toward the end of her life she'd become interested in *feng shui*, the Chinese art of harmonious furniture arrangement, writing one of the first English-language books on the subject, which sold quite well. Before her death she'd told my older sister, Minerva, that she was passing the mantle of her responsibilities on to her. Minerva, a mother of two who had served as an Army nurse in the War in Europe, and active in her local chapter of the Jaycees at the time, had been horrified. To this day, Minerva says, she is forever turning away from her door potential acolytes who appear looking for poultices and cures and blessings.

None of my generation—neither of my sisters and none of my cousins—seems to have carried on the McCay family tradition. I am the only one who pursued a career in the clergy, but I am sure my ancestors would consider me the wettest blanket of all. I turned out to be a liberal. My ministries have always leaned toward urging couples to make potentially good marriages work, prompting the sick to follow the advice of their doctors, encouraging parents to allow their children to follow their bliss. I marched for civil rights in Selma and in Washington. In the Eighties I went to the old Soviet Union to meet with a delegation of Refuseniks and to South Africa to petition the minority government to release Nelson Mandela from prison. I have spent a lot of time in prisons, mostly as a freelance chaplain but occasionally as a protester engaged in civil disobedience—against segregation when young and against the forcing of metahuman children out of public schools when old. My life has been conventional: a quiet rebellion, I suppose, against the immoderation of my heritage.

Almost midway through my seventy-seventh year, a widower with few surviving friends and a handful of aging congregants dependent upon me to be their spiritual shepherd, I became a seer of visions and a speaker in tongues.

On my walk across the Outerborough Bridge I saw a giant checkered clown rising from the river below, but nobody else seemed to see it, so I walked on. I saw the cable of the Governor's Island Tramway overhead fraying and breaking, with a hundred passengers flying into panic, but no one on the bridge reacted, so I suppressed my urge to run and walked on woodenly until, inevitably, the vision passed and the real tramway continued along its sturdy cable. As I walked the several blocks to my apartment, I heard myself muttering, in the Latin, the fifth chapter of the book of *The Revelation of Saint John the Divine,* though I had neither read nor spoken any Latin since my days in graduate school. Besides, I'd long suspected that Saint John had been quite as mad as my grandmother while writing that book, and it was included in the New Testament for reasons largely political.

I was seeing things that, evidence suggested, were not there at all. When I was young they used to call that "tripping." Back at home I thought about Wesley, and stared for a little while at the picture of Ellen that sits on my night table. I considered calling the Dutch Reformed Ministry Family Services Association to ask if they could recommend a good psychological counselor. A behaviorist, I thought I would specify. Then I decided against it. I was old. Maybe I would die before anyone really noticed.

Ω Ω Ω

I spent a lot of time that week walking through Metropolis. I walked all over much of the town, from Central Square to the Financial District.

Down near the old ferry port I saw where George Washington had hidden out before taking command of the Continental Army in the first months of the American Revolution, and I saw, plainly and clearly, a young officer in no uniform but buckskin handing him the hilt of a long sword. Washington looked over the blade, scraped off a trace of tarnish with a fingernail, and slipped it into the scabbard at his side, and he allowed a bit of a patrician wince as his troops broke attention to whoop and holler their approval. I suppose people passing by thought I was a bit daffy as I stood there watching and listening and occasionally smiling at what seemed to be nothing in particular. A little daffiness in a decorous, neatly dressed man is tolerable in Metropolis these days.

On the lower west side I saw a score of British clipper ships—circa the Seventeenth Century—docking secretly. The armed men who unloaded from them made their way undetected through the forests of Indian country to breach the flimsy wall of the first Dutch settlers who founded the city, to declare it a British Crown Colony.

Along the east side where today a shining steel and concrete garrison houses the New United Nations, that great urban fortress fell away like the cities that H. G. Wells saw rising and tumbling from his time machine. And across the water that came visible as the seat of the world body vanished, there was a long Viking ship, cracked abeam on a sandbar, and a brace of men at oars drowned in its hold, and one enormous glowing figure of a man, unaware that he was still alive, washed on the shore. The man wore tattered furs of animals that had surrendered their skins halfway across the world, and a throwing hammer hung from a leather belt slung on his waist. The man, damp and muscular, got to his feet, and he actually looked at me in the face. My mad vision addressed me with a glare and grunted. Then he walked off into the forest primeval to join a local tribe and lay the foundation for the Iroquois Federation, the first republic to stand on the North American continent.

I believe in visions. I think we have them, all of us. As a teenager experimenting with meditation and second sight, I always had thought the tip-off in the battle of dreams from my unconscious versus communications from elsewhere was whether a vision provided something I could not have made up myself. Once, in something seeming to be a dream, someone had told me a joke and I'd laughed. The joke had been new to me. Then upon opening my eyes, I could not remember the joke. My casual experimentation with the paranormal had ended with divinity school.

My lately acquired psychosis—that is how I still thought of it, even as I alternately enjoyed and was horrified by it—allowed me to remember what a historic place, what a center of life, my adopted city was. I am sure that had I been allowed simply to wander the city looking at its past indefinitely, I would have seen an allosaurus making a meal of a pteranodon; a curious sea creature dragging itself ashore and giving birth to amphibians; the sea reclaiming the land; the glacier reclaiming the sea; the mantle of lava reclaiming the ice; the void reclaiming the dust. I might even have heard the magic words He spoke at Genesis. Yet, my dementia did not allow me to indulge my passion for the past. The future arrived too soon.

Ω   Ω   Ω

Friday, there was a rumble. In midtown, not far from my church, a flash of yellow-orange light blew past me, and I walked on. Surely it was a blast from another time, and I was not in the mood. I looked both ways before I crossed the street to try my luck waiting for a bus and noticed a few people turning to run from something I could not see yet. Then a bus rose from the ground and hurtled in my direction.

The sky was full of screaming colors. This could only be a vision; I could not make this up. Then when a howling little girl popped out a window of the bus as it slammed to a stop against a curb and fairly flew into my gut, the third alternative occurred to me: This really might be happening.

According to the word of God, the meek will someday inherit the Earth. Someday. But God never accounted for the mighty.

Like dust devils coalescing from the tightening air, a handful of colorful figures suddenly appeared in the sky, on the ground, on the walls and roofs of the buildings. Who knew what the conflict was about, or to whose standard to flock? A mortal could only follow the ancient rhythms embossed on genetic memory and run for safety.

I snatched up the terrified little girl and retreated with her into the recessed doorway of a mattress shop. I nearly dropped her because she was so wet—I still do not know whether with tears or perspiration. We huddled in the doorway, and I wrapped her as well as I could in my body, careful to let her see as little of the terror in the sky above as I could. But as dense, flying hardware and flying bodies that were even harder slashed by close enough to slice gashes and footprints in the very wall against which we sought shelter, I could not look away.

They were beautiful. They were perfect. Their skin was unblemished, the movements of their muscles like the dance of continental plates. Most of them were in their teens and twenties, after all, but the older ones were likewise beautiful. Costumes hugged their bodies like paint and rolled over their musculature as they contended and flexed.

Probably the most stunningly beautiful creature I have ever seen—I learned later that she went by the name of Nightstar, the daughter of an alien princess and a circus acrobat turned freelance adventurer—rose in a reverse parabola above the street and left a contrail of violet light and flowing hair. From her fingertips she shot bolts of rippling heat to slice through the hull of a big horned robot creature that somehow offended her.

A golden woman wearing apparently no clothing other than long jagged golden spikes covering her head and limbs rose over the wind currents. Her name, it turned out, was Lightning. As I looked more closely at her, I realized that she was like a photographic negative. Shadows and highlights reversed on her body. Just looking at her was quite unsettling. She seemed to vanish like the center of a spiral, then reappear in place whenever she moved. She unleashed doglegging white streams of static charges at a hulking, body-armored, furry longhorn bison who walked on two legs and wielded an enormous gun in a pair of heavily muscled suede arms. I realized it was the Manotaur, an accident of a cloning experiment of years ago. He'd begun life as a cause célèbre in the tabloids, a creature who ought to be allowed to come to term, people had insisted. Now he spent his life ripping the other works of humanity apart.

A thinning shaft of dry blue heat, navy at its edges and shifting between baby blue and strands of blinding white in its thick core, slithered past us, sunburning us as it went. His circulatory system shone through translucent skin. Nuculoid was the stretchable being's name, and I'd read that a medical research facility had certified that the bionuclear power he generated was noncarcinogenic, but I huddled around the child with my body as he whipped by nonetheless.

An elephant-eared figure wearing a full body covering of dark steel—Tusk, he was called—ran on clattering flexjoints across the boulevard, carrying a turreted multi-snouted weapon that looked as though it could level a large state.

A woman encased in some other type of metal—somehow this "person-of-steel" look with jagged and vented bodily features had become a kind of fashion declaration among metahumans during the past generation or so—stood morphing on the arch of a street light. The metal of her back flowed down and outward, dropping into tear-shaped extensions that rose and hardened to the shape of wings. Trix was her name, I learned later, the child of a S.T.A.R. Laboratories expatriate who'd decanted her biological components directly into the alloy shell he had built for her. She would never grow physically but then she was about nine years old, and I wondered whether and how she might ever reproduce. I stopped wondering when the door against which we pressed rattled like a salt shaker.

This vibration was not due to the antics of the flying, pounding, shooting, and slashing people on the street. A truck driver did it. Or rather his truck did when he saw his eighteen-wheeler headed into the middle of the rumble and realized he could not brake before the vehicle passed under the path of the slowly descending Trix. He jumped out and left the truck to the elements. It smashed through the window of the mattress store that gave us our shelter. I told the little girl not to worry, it was just a thirty-ton truck, nothing dangerous, and she took comfort in this. Then the temblor began.

Trix blasted the Manotaur with an extrusion of metal that

flew out—who knew how far? maybe forty feet?—to jolt the big bull on his reinforced chest and throw him spine-first through the many-paned window of a jewelry store. The arm retracted into itself as quickly as it had flown out. The ground rolled like an ocean wave.

The robot on the street, the one that Nightstar attacked with bolts of energy, was sliced in pieces and seemed to be stalled in place. This did not stop the others from attacking or defending it. I could not tell, for the most part, who was doing what. The machine was of some sort of malleable ceramic. It flowed over the ground, looking for its disconnected pieces whenever a blow dismembered it. The device was evidently the focus of the conflict, though I have no idea how such a conflict—once its participants whip themselves up in a hormonal frenzy—finds a way to wind down. One gathered that these street gladiators had done this dance before from every angle. Those who fought today might have been allies yesterday and would rejoin or plot against one another tomorrow as the fancy took them.

The Earth shook with every blow. Could the earthquake that had leveled Anchorage the previous spring and permanently covered two islands in the Cook Inlet have been any more intense? There was a crack, and then the Earth moved. A smash and another motion below our feet. A roar and another. Soon the sound itself caused our bodies to react in terror, anticipating the shudder to come. We stood on liquid concrete and were unable to swim.

"Your mother," I said to the quivering little girl wrapped in my arms. "Where is your mother?"

"There," she whispered, "with Calvin," and pointed at the crumpled wreckage of the city bus from which she had emerged. It now lay like a pile of laundry, twisted around a fallen light pole and an erupting fire hydrant.

"Calvin. Your father?"

"My little brother."

Who knew where the child's mother and little brother were now?

Wesley Dodds had loved his heroes. He loved the legacy of heroism and sacrifice that, through his own career, he'd helped to define for them. The world of the children and grandchildren of Wesley's heroes, though, was a shaky place. They numbered in the nameless thousands, these progeny of the past, moving through the world under color of the legends of those who'd come before. They no longer fought for the right. They fought simply to fight; their only foes were each other.

The superhumans boasted that they had all but eliminated the supervillains of yesteryear.

Small comfort.

They moved freely through the streets, through the world. They were challenged but unopposed. They were, after all, our protectors.

This too shall pass, I told myself. As long as their world existed, then humans had the chance to reclaim what they had built. In the face of superhuman might and superhuman odds, time still had not run out on humanity, I insisted to myself.

The rumbling stopped. The blows of air and Earth suddenly dissipated. I looked up and saw them vanishing in a handful of flashes in the direction of Planet Square, where the day's headlines walked around the triangular tower and advertising displayed itself on a jumbo monitor that people could see clearly for half a mile uptown. Regular people—business people and shopping people and walking-around-town people—popped their heads out the doorways and windows and crevices of the street like prairie dogs. As if with a hive mind, they too ran off in the direction of Planet Square. There was a buzz in the air. Everyone was talking to everyone. I ignored it. Good riddance, I thought, as the child and I scurried in the direction opposite the intersection and the pile of twisted steel and ceramic that used to be a bus.

"Mama?" the child called, at a loss to figure a way to enter or deal with the wreckage.

I held her back, determined myself to crawl inside alone, but there was a sound. A baby cried.

"Oh for Heaven's sake," I muttered, and found a slit that, when it was wider, had held a window. I slithered in like a caterpillar.

I felt the girl tugging on my cuff as I made my way in, wondering suddenly how I might find my way out again, or what I would do at all if there was a recurrence of the rumble.

"Are you all right, mister?" she wanted to know. "You're barely moving."

"I'm fine, child. Just making my way in."

I heard a sigh, and the baby cried some more. It whimpered, actually, but at least sounded healthy.

Once I got past the fallen seats that were embedded in the distorted wall of the vehicle and blocking my way, I found myself in a chamber like a cave. Glass was all over the floor like granite crystal, and in a far corner huddled the shivering figure of a woman. I went to her and touched her, and she jumped. She did not jump far; I learned later that she had broken one leg in two places and the other in three, and her spleen had been punctured by a shard of window glass that got her from behind. But she was wrapped around her baby, Calvin, as an added layer of protection. It worked.

Inside the wreckage of the bus I splinted the woman's legs with broken metal from the dismembered seats and strips of cloth I took from the jacket I was wearing. I had never liked that jacket much. The little girl—her name was Vanessa—was able to call a rescue unit with a cell phone she found in the wreckage outside, and firemen came to cut the three of us out. My little girl's brave mother would be hospitalized for several weeks, but she would recover. She would carry an artificial spleen for the rest of her life.

No one asked any questions. Everyone wore dour faces. Even the firemen walked strangely, stiffly, through their rescue work, like zombies.

Then my visions mingled with my surroundings again.

The enormous television monitor on the triangular tower in the Square was blowing out nonsensical images. The people in the Square, and all throughout the city as I made my way home, wore the expressions of the dead. They looked like those stricken figures of the damned that Michelangelo had painted on the chapel ceiling, slapping their faces and pounding the pavement and wandering the streets in a fog.

KANSAS IS GONE, the superscript over the big public television monitor said.

Preposterous, I told myself, even as I saw again the images in my mind's eye of the golden eagle and the giant bat rising above the clouds to meet a hurtling ball of fire.

Statistics and diagrams flashed across the screen for the brief moments I watched it—for the length of time it took to convince me it was a manifestation of my own mind lying to me some more. There were phrases like EQUIVALENT THROW WEIGHT and GROSS MEGATONNAGE and GENERAL NATIONAL ALERT and a dozen other collections of words whose import was meaningless to me, just like the visions on the lenses of my eyes.

It was Friday and I had a sermon to write and I needed to get started on it, I supposed. It would take me more than a day, I expected, to get my thoughts coherently onto paper with these visions assaulting my senses and these snatches of apocalyptic Scripture tumbling unbidden from my lips.

My visions were seeing visions. Amid searing jolts of flame and white heat and metaphorical suggestion, the city now took on the aspect of the dream. Nobody wore any discernible expression beyond the range from horror to blankness. There were no advertisements among the flashing lights of the Square, only dire news of the loss of the world's Breadbasket that could have come only from my own nightmares. This was not my city. This was not a fit place for humans to live. This was a projection from my unconscious onto the very images among whom I walked. I believed nothing I saw or heard.

At home I did not turn on a television or radio, and when I flipped on the computer I ignored the flashing light of the Netservice News. I had work to do, and the world could go hang for a day.

There was hubbub on the sidewalks. I shut my streetside windows. I sat down to write and fell asleep at my desk. Again I dreamed:

A giant basket of bread and corn and vegetables sat on an enormous flat verdant plain. A great golden crow circled the basket and cawed menacingly, then dove into the bread and tossed it about so not a crumb or a seed remained. And the sun rose and burned the land even unto the roots of the grass.

CHAPTER 3

Bleeding Kansas

There seemed to be no time at all, after the boot-up of the new Millennium, between an event and the general worldwide awareness of that event. If the Secretary-General of the United Nations sneezed in Metropolis at noon, the Singapore Commodities Exchange did a plié before close of business. If a fire burned a microchip plant in Senegal overnight, the price of Random Access Memory got boosted at Fry's Electronics in the San Fernando Valley before the store opened that morning. If a tree fell in the Amazon Rain Forest and the Netservice News did not report it, then it probably did not really happen. This time the news reached me a day later than it reached everyone else. Alone on the planet, I was absent for the final sign of the Apocalypse. When the news came over the wires I had already rejected the evidence of my own senses. How much more rejection, therefore, did I have to heap upon these journalistic heralds of doom?

I love the story of Joseph. Technically, I have always felt, it is the best-constructed story in the Bible. It's the one about the young son of the Patriarch Jacob, the eleventh of twelve boys, who has prophetic dreams of personal glory. His jealous brothers sell him into slavery and tell their father he was torn up by beasts. Years later, in time of famine, his brothers travel to a far country to ask its mighty Prime Minister to sell food to their family. The mighty Prime Minister turns out to be Joseph, once enslaved but having grown up to make good. As it happened, it was Joseph's talent for understanding and interpreting prophetic dreams—the personality trait that his brothers found so objectionable—that gave him the opportunity to rise from slave to Prime Minister. I shuddered to think that such a kingmaking talent now devolved from Wesley—whom I believed, when dying, to be mad rather than prophetic—to me.

Once upon a time a prophet's brothers would sell him to a band of traveling nomads. But what people do to prophets nowadays is truly frightening.

My real fear—rather than of being burned at the stake like Joan of Arc or shot in the head like Martin Luther King, Jr.— was of people taking notice of this power I acquired late in life and making me President. Certainly Americans these days— those old enough to remember, anyway—are nostalgic for the likes of Reagan and Clinton, happy warriors stomping merrily through the halls of the White House, delighted with who they were and where they found themselves. Deep in their bellies, most Americans long to make someone President who actually wants the job. They do not, however, care enough for their leaders' sensibilities to elect a complete incompetent, and that is the only kind of person who would be glad to hold the position these days. The hangdog image of that office's unhappy occupant at the time of Wesley's death finally alerted me to the fact that my latest relentless dream about the golden crow laying to waste the basket of bread was true. It was tied so closely to the course of historical events that I did not recognize the reality even when it slapped me across the face.

Ω Ω Ω

Having fallen asleep at my workstation, I woke to find myself having somehow made my way to bed. It was a little past five in the morning, and I was interested in nothing else but finishing the following morning's sermon and perhaps doing a little shopping when I was done. I did not remember any dreams, but that did not mean there had been none. My joints were achy and my body was stiff in all its vulnerable places. Maybe I could get through the day—or at least, God willing, through my sermon—without suffering an attack of the Holy Rolls.

Up in the corner of my computer screen an icon I never had seen before began to flash, and I could not double-click it off. My glasses had fallen off my face and broken sometime during the rumble the previous afternoon, and I could not make out the shape of the offending flasher in the corner. I squinted. It was the little face of an attractive middle-aged woman framed by short-clipped blonde hair and wearing a morose expression. It was a few moments before I realized it was President Capper's face beaming into my workspace along the Netservice emergency break-in system. Evidently the President had given—or was still delivering—an address to her public on a matter of some importance. Reluctantly, I left my sermon to tap my fingernail on the President's touch-screen icon and chose REPLAY from among the choices on the little roll-up menu that appeared.

My writing on this sermon had begun to crank along, finally, and I did not appreciate the interruption. I was expounding on the story of Joseph. There would be no mention in this sermon of the rubbish that leaked from my unconscious. No soaking wet clowns in checkered pants flying through the sky. No visions of the Norse conquest of North America. No Jeremiads spewing forth in pre-Biblical Hebrew. No devastated Breadbasket on an incinerated prairie. I was just writing a hopeful parable for my little Sunday morning flock about how sometimes dreams come true.

On my monitor there appeared the Seal of the President of
the United States, an eagle clutching an olive branch in one
talon and arrows in the other. In big type with jagged serifs a
headline read:

Holocaust in Kansas
▲ ▲ ▲
President Jennifer Capper
Addresses the Nation

Holocaust? A politically loaded word, I thought. What
ever could have happened to prompt such a . . . But before I
had a chance to wonder about the conclusion of my clause,
the President came onscreen.

"My fellow Americans," she said, "and my fellow citizens
of the world," she went on.

Uh-oh. I had a bad feeling about this. American Presidents
had gotten out of the Kennedyesque habit of flaunting their
position as titular emperor of the non-American regions of the
planet back around the time they had started naming their
former National Security Advisors to run the United Nations
Secretariat.

"As I broadcast this via all the available satellite and
groundlink communications networks, it is a little bit past two
in the morning Washington time. The National Security
Council in the past few minutes has been able to confirm
much of what has been reported and speculated upon concerning the critical events of yesterday afternoon in the
American Midwest. We have determined that indeed a high-
yield nuclear device ignited yesterday at ground level within
ten miles of the city of Abilene, Kansas, at five twenty-one in
the afternoon Central Standard Time. Seismic calculations in-
dicate a force well in excess of a forty-megaton concussion.
The initial shock wave spread as far as Topeka to the east,
Wichita to the south, and the Nebraska border to the north.
With prevailing easterly winds, in the flat topography of the

agricultural plains, some damage continued far to the west, with winds and heat as far as the Colorado state line. The tapering sweep of the initial wave stopped only at the foothills of the Rocky Mountains in eastern Colorado, and the glacial permafrost on the peaks of many of those mountains has melted for the first time in several hundred years. Satellite and aerial reconnaissance, which has been exhaustive and thorough during the past six hours, has found significant reduction in signs of life—human, animal, and vegetable—in a two-hundred-mile radius centered on Kansas. A secondary concussion continues to radiate from the explosion site in the form of fallout and grossly unseasonable heat."

She spoke in a monotone. Never before had I seen her so without passion.

President Capper had never held elective office. She'd been the national chairman of American ETI, "Education and Training Initiative," an organization raising money and building schools in Third World countries. One Sunday morning she'd appeared on the news beating the bushes for an exchange-student program involving a kind of metahuman Peace Corps. Give the superkids a mission they could get their steely fingers around, and benefit the rest of the world in the process. The idea was that young superpowered Americans would go to various places around the world to share their gifts and special skills to build up the physical and intellectual infrastructure of underdeveloped areas. At the same time, selected students from these participating countries would come to stay with families in the United States and study here. She'd mapped out the whole plan, drawn up schedules, prepared special events and spreadsheets before presenting a word of it to the public. She'd done her homework. The idea had caught the public's fancy, and so had its messenger.

As President Zachary King's second four-year term sludged to a halt, the Chief showed the wear of the office far beyond his years; there had been no one of any substance on the horizon to succeed him. Jennifer Capper had gotten caught up in the celebrity grinder before knowing it, so it seemed, and the New Federalists had nominated her in absentia. At the time of that breaking news, no one had had any idea of the candidate's whereabouts until a foreign correspondent for Galaxy News tripped over her at an education conference at an obscure university in Sri Lanka. She'd been genuinely startled by the reporter's news of her nomination as a Presidential candidate, but she'd risen to the occasion with a brilliant, self-deprecating acceptance statement delivered, off the cuff, into the reporter's hovercam from the floor of a hot and crowded auditorium. Ms. Capper ran no campaign, hired no consultants, and publicly repudiated the several hundred independent organizations that had sprung up in communities and on the nets advocating her candidacy. She was obviously a very thoughtful, brilliant, and passionate woman and appeared honored to be nominated for President, but she had not anticipated much chance of ever actually holding the office.

"What would be the first thing you'd do as President?" a reporter had asked Jennifer Capper one October afternoon during lunch in a little dive on Dupont Circle in Washington down the street from her office.

"Demand a recount," she told him, and the reporter dutifully sent this statement far and wide along the Netservice News.

"Assuming you were elected and there was no getting out of it," the reporter continued, "how would you deal, for example, with the Southeast Asian trade deficit?"

At this, the reporter's wide audience saw Ms. Capper apologize to her female lunch companion, apparently a colleague, place her napkin on the table in front of her, and steeple her hands to think for a moment. The camera recorded her few moments of thought. Then she turned to the reporter and his lapel microphone and launched into a detailed account of how joint ventures between sister communities in opposite corners of the world could benefit both economies and, by extension, the economy of the world. She went on for twenty minutes, spouting statistics and tossing around brand-new ideas like confetti as the reporter's eyes grew buggier and buggier. In response to his request for a position paper, she said maybe she would send one along when she got around to writing all this stuff down.

"You mean you just made up all this stuff here?" the journalist asked. "Over your soufflé?"

"Yes. As I say, that's my job at American ETI. We take what used to be called the Great Unwashed all over the world, all those huddled masses yearning to breathe free, and we turn them into consumers and taxpayers. It's a pretty good trick, I think. Now if you'll excuse me, my lunch is getting cold."

That was how the campaign had gone until, to the surprise of no one on Earth except Jennifer Capper herself, she'd been elected President. She'd reported to her job running American ETI until the morning after Election Day, a morning she fought her way through a crowd of reporters and admirers to the lobby of her office building only to find there a phalanx of Secret Service agents, who tripped her into an enormous black hoverlimo with flags waving from its shoulders. They whisked her away to the Old Executive Office Building across the street from the White House, where a crisp and spiffy young man in a suit whose corners did not bend had handed her a list of fifty-five hundred high-level jobs she would have to fill in the two months before the day of her inauguration.

Her Presidency's first casualty was the metahuman Peace Corps project, going the way of the dodo and the great auk. There simply was going to be no time for it.

Throughout her career, Jennifer Capper had taken pride in her creative approach to management, but the White House has never provided an environment conducive to reflection. There is just too much to do, and not enough information to be sure of how to do it best. She often would long for the simple up or down decisions the Presidents of her youth—en-

cumbered only by Cold War and hostile Congresses—had had
to make, like whether to annihilate a foreign city or two.

Ω   Ω   Ω

I tapped a finger on the voice icon at the corner of my
screen and said, "Freeze-frame." I interrupted President
Capper in midsentence and called up the news index. It was
no surprise that virtually every headline that unrolled from
the master index had something to do with the disaster that I'd
dreamed and then slept through:

World

KANSAS FALLOUT CLOUD HEADS FOR NORTH PACIFIC

UNITED NATIONS WORLD FOOD SUMMIT WARNS OF FAMINE

BRITISH PRIME MINISTER RESTRICTS AMERICAN GRAIN IMPORTS

RUSSIAN PARLIAMENT PASSES METAHUMAN SANCTIONS

National

RELIEF TEAMS SCOUR KANSAS IN PROTECTIVE GEAR

FOOD HOARDING NATIONWIDE LEAVES MARKETS BARE

KANSAS REFUGEES' STORIES: ROCKY MOUNTAIN HORROR

METAHUMANS HOUNDED FROM SHOPPING MALL IN INDI-ANAPOLIS

Local

METRO AIRPORT CANCELS 92% OF CROSS-COUNTRY TRAFFIC

INTERSTATE 95 CLOSED FOR NATIONAL SECURITY ACCESS

GREAT EASTERN SUPERMARKET CHAIN ANNOUNCES MASS SHUTDOWNS

CITY COUNCIL PROPOSES METAHUMAN CURFEW, SANCTIONS

Then as I watched, that last headline under local news got bumped off the list and the top line moved down to make room for

MAGOG STRONGLY SUSPECTED IN KANSAS CATASTROPHE

Magog. I never even liked the sound of that guy's name.

$$\Omega \quad \Omega \quad \Omega$$

I switched back to the President's speech, which I'd left suspended in midparagraph. She spoke about the implications of the effective sudden loss of an entire state, about the value of Kansas to the world economy and to the culture. She talked about the loss of the birthplace of one of her heroes and predecessors, Dwight Eisenhower. Impatient, I fast-forwarded to the conclusion.

"Please do not make unwarranted assumptions or act outside the law," President Capper told the world. "The first impulse of many of us, in an uncertain condition of this sort—"

I wondered when there ever had been a condition of this sort and how she might know people's typical reactions to it.

"—is to assign blame to the most convenient scapegoat available, from foreign governments to powerful individuals to groups with whose philosophy you may disagree. This is not about philosophy, my fellow citizens. It is about survival and sovereignty.

"We have a lot of scapegoats and even a few suspects. Be assured that every agency of this government is up late tonight, along with the displaced people of the Midwest and the worried people of the world. Through the grace of God and the prudence of our leaders, nuclear weapons have not ignited in anger or war since before most of us were born. That is an admirable record for a technology that is now nearly a century old. We, your duly elected leaders, will find those responsible for this horror, and we will bring them to justice.

But until we do, it is the job of all of us to help one another and to begin to rebuild. That is work enough for everyone.

"Thank you, my fellow citizens, and good night."

Ω   Ω   Ω

I wrung my hands, rattled my cheeks, enjoined my word processor back to work, and tried to see if I could salvage any of my sermon for Sunday morning. I could save a phrase or even a paragraph here or there but not much: things like "How nice it is to see so many faces this morning," and "Why don't we all pick up our hymnals and sing," and other innocuousness. Anything substantive no longer appeared to apply. So I would have to start from scratch. I still had a few hours, and on the morning after the greatest man-made disaster in recorded human history I was lucky enough to have a roof over my head, a word processor that worked, and a job to do.

That was a good place to start, I thought. My sermon could open by citing the luck we had left. Then that icon reappeared in the upper-left corner of my monitor, and I could get nothing done with the sullen countenance of President Capper flashing at me like a traffic sign. I checked to see what the commotion was, and now there were half a dozen gray-suited, gray-faced people sitting in a row at a long table. They were lined up in front of the big Presidential seal, so I supposed they were down at the White House in the Press Room. I caught them in the middle of a live broadcast of their presentation. I recognized most of them: the Director of Central Intelligence, the Attorney-General, the Secretary-General of the United Nations, the FBI Director.

"—if you encounter this individual, whether you are metahuman or not, please do not attempt to apprehend him," Secretary-General Wyrmwood was saying. "Withdraw from the scene. If necessary and at all possible, withdraw your family and any other innocent persons from whatever premises in which you find him. Magog is a powerful and dangerous fugitive. This warning applies not only to the suspected felon Magog but to any remaining members of the so-called Justice Battalion who were involved in its vigilante attack on the late criminal known as the Parasite."

And the camera angle widened to include the President standing aside the table where her chiefs of the law enforcement and intelligence communities sat. On an easel next to her was a poster-sized photograph of Magog, his scarred face nearly the same golden color as his helmet and its trumpet-shaped horns. His look was blank and without concern for anything external.

Once, long ago, Superman had warned us of the danger Magog posed. The Man of Steel had brought his putative successor to trial in the death of a desperate criminal whose demise had left no one missing him. When the jury had voted not in the name of justice but of what they'd felt was the community's self-interest, Magog had become Superman's successor in fact, the new hero of Metropolis. The Last Son of Krypton was nowhere to be found after that.

Now, an arduous decade after his ultimate public triumph, here stood Magog—his allies now probably as dead as the hapless Parasite—having rendered himself, in the space of moments, one of the most accomplished mass killers since the beginning of time.

CHAPTER 4

Hellfire, Damnation, Spin Control

~~~

There were voices, and thunderings, and lightnings and an earthquake," I said, "and the seven angels which had the seven trumpets prepared themselves to sound.

"The first angel sounded," I said, "and there followed hail and fire mingled with blood.

"And they were cast upon the earth," I said, "and the third part of trees was burnt up, and all green grass was burnt up.

"And the second angel sounded," I said, "and as it were a great mountain burning with fire was cast into the sea: and the third part of the sea became blood.

"And the third part of the creatures which were in the sea, and had life, died," I said, "and the third part of the ships were destroyed."

I did not mean to say it, but I said it. It just came out. I forgot where I was. I forgot before whom I stood. Norman McCay was in his pulpit, and all was faulty with the world.

When I'd been a student considering the ministry as a vocation, I'd thought the least attractive aspect of the job was the public speaking. Every once in a while in those days, a survey would come out showing that the thing people most feared—more than drawn-out illness or being fired from their jobs or death—was the prospect of having to address a large group of people. And those who quoted these surveys generally supposed that it would be surprising for their audiences to hear this. Quaint, I thought, that in those days there had been people believing the most fearsome thing ought to be death. But whenever I stepped into a church, whenever I faced a crossroads, whenever I wished for something, whenever I woke up in fear of a dream I could not remember, I was standing before God. Humans, even superhumans, never seemed so fearsome again. I took up my mantle when I realized that.

But now I stood in the center of people's frames of vision in the sanctuary of this splendid church in which, through my twilight years, I have been able to serve. I stood before perhaps eighty frightened people, the largest Sabbath morning crowd that my congregation had been able to muster in years. Now they were all here because of the dread events of the past days, and this was the only place they had to turn. And now instead of the comfort for which they had come, I was spouting forth what I had long believed to be words from a dying fever dream of Saint John the Divine. In those days the apostle had lain hallucinating through the last days of his life, banished to a desert island by a frightened king, scribbling or dictating these words of the most horrifying unfulfilled prophecy in the Scriptures.

I had no time to think, as my mouth dribbled on, that perhaps I should reevaluate my regard for Saint John. Because if Saint John was mad, then Wesley had probably been mad as well. And if Wesley was mad, then certainly I, his successor, was also mad. I had no time to think this until my dismayed flock in the sanctuary thinned. I was too busy trying to get my mouth to stop.

"And the third angel sounded," I continued against my will, "and there fell a great star from heaven, burning as it were a lamp, and it fell upon the third part of the rivers, and upon the fountains of waters."

Mrs. Watters in the third row started to weep. Her son, I knew, was an agronomist who lived with his family in southern Nebraska. Surely she had been unable to communicate with him since the disaster. It was altogether likely that he, so far from Ground Zero, was fine, but Mrs. Watters did not know that for sure. Church was where she came to seek—in vain—the comfort she required until she did know. I was ashamed, and it was my shame that finally stanched the intemperate words of the inconsolable Saint John.

"I spoke of metaphors some weeks ago," were the first words I dragged, kicking and screaming, from my conscious will. I tried to change the tone of my voice to convince my congregants that the whole unsettling episode was my effort to make a point. "The metaphors of John the Apostle in the book of *Revelation* concern events similar to the trial we and our families experience today."

Murmuring. I was losing my congregation. My blathering had lasted too long. I needed to pull them back with rationality before I could offer them the comfort for which they were here.

"In *Revelation*," I continued gamely, "Saint John describes a dream of grasslands turned to desert and stars raining fire on the Earth and rivers and oceans turning to blood. It is a greater hardship, in its way, than even we have suffered these past few days."

They were starting to look at me again. I had eye contact with seven or eight of the people in the pews. Mrs. Watters quieted down. Slowly, they were coming around.

"*Revelation*, from which I quoted when we began, is a vivid dream that its author left to posterity. To us. And what have we learned is the purpose of dreams? Dreams are our rehearsal for adversity. They are our self-education, a way for us to face our fears before we have anything to fear. We do not have to have degrees in psychology to know that it is our dreams that keep us sane. And literature, storytelling, is our collective dream."

Nodding. I saw nodding. It was slight scattered nodding, but nodding nonetheless, with open eyes. The members of my flock were with me again, I was sure.

"In His wisdom, two thousand years ago the Lord sent Saint John a dream to keep us sane. A time capsule that foresaw nuclear power and metahuman frailty. In the book of *The Revelation of Saint John the Divine* we have a precedent to follow even in the case of what seems to be a devastating apocalypse."

Yes! I recovered it. Mrs. Watters smiled up at me through red eyes. I found a point to make, and I made it. I brought it full circle. I was ad-libbing the most delicate sermon of my career and making it work. I could do anything. I could prophesy, for Heaven's sake.

"The most apocalyptic tale of the Scriptures recommends that in answer to our ordeal we do this: We must say, loudly and clearly, 'Fear God, and give glory to Him; for the hour of His judgment is come: and worship Him that made Heaven, and Earth, and the sea, and the fountains of waters.'"

Now I was declaiming like the pipe organ that rattled the walls of this room, the way Isaiah once must have caused the walls of the court of King Hezekiah to clatter. And finally I was saying what I wanted to say at the same time as I was letting words that wanted to be said fall from my mouth.

"His judgment is come," I said, and meant to pause. But instead I said, "And there followed another angel, saying, Babylon is fallen, is fallen, that great city, because she made all nations drink of the wine of the wrath of her fornication."

Oh for Heaven's sake, what was I talking about?

"And the third angel followed them, saying with a loud voice, If any man worship the beast and his image, and receive his mark in his forehead, or in his hand . . ."

Mrs. Watters had *her* forehead down in her hand again. Mr. Steeplegarde crinkled his brow in a way I had never seen him do before. Several lucky folks toward the back were eyeing the doors and clearly wondering how to slip between them without making them swing open and shut. My congregants dropped their faces into prayerbooks or the weekly church bulletin or counted the number of pipes on the organ. And again I could not stop and certainly could not explain.

". . . The same shall drink of the wine of the wrath of God, which is poured out without mixture into the cup of his indignation; and he shall be tormented with fire and brimstone in the presence of the holy angels, and in the presence of the Lamb."

Mr. Tarlow, toward the rear pews, found a way. He looked at his watch, feigned alarm, and, smiling apologetically at nowhere in particular, padded out the door appearing for all the world to have someplace terribly important he realized he had to be.

"And the smoke of their torment ascendeth up for ever and ever: and they have no rest day nor night."

Then finally, my witness exhausted, my voice was mine again. I let go of whatever was in my hands, pages of Scripture I must have torn from my prayerbook in a preaching frenzy. "Forgive me," I said. "This isn't what I wanted to . . . Forgive me."

And so it went.

Ω   Ω   Ω

As I always did, I greeted my people—those who politely stayed through my uncertain benediction—as they left the church. I did not get much eye contact even then. A minister measures the value of his day by eye contact. What few eyes I did see were angry or sullen or blank, shying from my gaze.

My congregation had trusted me for years, and this day I betrayed them. In mourning, unable even to fathom the news that stopped the world, they came to me seeking encouragement that I could not offer.

Ω   Ω   Ω

I went through the empty church looking for discarded papers and the prayerbooks that remained on the seats, but by the third row I could not stand any more. Holding a retrieved prayerbook, I folded myself into a seat and slowly tumbled sideways until my head rested on the pew and my eyes gently closed, seeking a dreamless sleep. All I could do was clutch my hands open and shut, tense my muscles, and deny myself a succor I surely did not deserve.

There was a rustling of the air. I wondered where I might have left a window open. I ignored this sound that sought to shorten my brief rest. Who knew, if I allowed myself to sleep, when some dream would presage an even bleaker future? Who knew, if I kept my eyes open, when some vision would tease my wits with symbols of a catastrophe that I was neither smart nor creative enough to decode? Let the phantom wind rustle the currents of this big airtight room. Let the ghosts of the million gone in Kansas come and carry me away with them, too.

Then I had to open my eyes. My body made me. I opened them in time to see a big stained-glass representation of a lion lying down beside a lamb, fluttering as though it were cloth. I did not believe this was happening. I had been prepared by the dire visions of these past days and weeks—both Wesley's and mine—to greet the unlikely and the unwieldy with skepticism and disdain. When the fluttering began to take the form of the sort of robe that might wrap a monk and began to flow through the stained glass as though emerging from a pool, I rose from my pew and turned my back to leave this vision. But there arose in my pathway a shrouded human figure, very far larger in its proportions than any dweller among men. And the hue of the skin of the figure was of the perfect whiteness of the snow.

"What do you want from me?" I asked this spectre, and, to my surprise but not delight, it answered me.

"The visions you have seen," the figure said, "the witness

you have borne, they are real, Norman McCay. I am real. Are you somehow not yet convinced of that?"

"I am convinced of it," I replied. He was an enormous man in a green robe that constantly flapped around him as if with the wind. His face seemed bleach-white, but I could not for the soul of me make out his features or find even his eyes. And quietly, without resistance, I added, "I am not convinced, however, that you and the other visions are worth paying attention to."

"I have need of you, Norman McCay."

I have gone mad, I told myself. Now my visions talked to me. They addressed me by name.

"You are not mad, Norman McCay," the figure said, and I did not even realize he was addressing my thoughts rather than my words before I answered.

"I would far rather go mad than continue to walk through the tribulation I have lived and witnessed already." Now I knew why so many prophets die insane. It is a welcome respite from the certainty that afflicts them. I turned my back on the figure again and walked toward the side entrance . . .

. . . where he greeted me, materializing in a moment out of a ruffle of rolling air that turned green, then white, and collected into the massive figure.

"It is your sanity that I count on, Norman McCay."

"What are you? A vision that talks back?"

"I am the spiritual continuation of one that has been of your kind. And yes, a vision of sorts. Those of your plane who know me, call me the Spectre."

Could this really be a supernatural figure standing before me? I wondered. Did I have a better explanation? A rational explanation? And was rationality an option for me right now? I had to think. I turned away again.

"Even as I stand before you," he said, suddenly standing before me again, "an act of unspeakable evil has begun to manifest. Armageddon is fast approaching."

This was too much for me to consider all at once. I just

stood there, feeling the skepticism melting off my face to make way for realization and wonder. The apparition shot out a hand that first touched my forehead and then touched nothing at all as it moved into my head and rested there as if I were thin air.

"But you know this, Norman McCay, do you not? After all, you have the dreams."

"You . . . what?" I said, fumbling over the words. "You see into my mind? In my soul?"

"Yes."

"What are you? An angel?"

"Of a sort. A higher power has charged me with the duty of punishing those responsible for this coming evil."

"Coming evil?" I wanted to know. "What coming evil? What do we do to stop it?"

"That is not my mission."

"Not your mission?"

"I need you, Norman McCay."

"For what?" I suspected we had a divergence of missions. "If you want me to do some good, then I will. Who is responsible for the Kansas Holocaust?"

"Long ago I would have judged swiftly, with clarity," this angel in green said, "but my faculties with regard to temporal affairs are not what they once were."

"You were human, you said?"

"Once I wore the name James Corrigan and reveled in the deliverance of justice. That was lifetimes ago, and what humanity remains in my nature is inadequate. Now I must anchor myself to the soul of a mortal who seeks justice."

"But I don't—"

"You will."

"My business is redemption, Ghost. Justice has always been a mystery to me."

"You will come to understand many mysteries," he said.

He drew his face close to mine when he said that. It was all I saw: not really even a face but a pasty haze of white. The rest of the world seemed to melt into darkness for a moment. His aspect shifted, as though he could not determine himself into a space where he fit.

"Then, these delusions I have been suffering—"

"Visions," he said.

"They're . . . what? Real?"

"The limits of human language do not allow me to characterize them adequately," he said, "but their validity is the reason I have sought you out."

"You didn't send them?"

"Certainly not."

I realized that if ever I really believed in angels—and I supposed that I did—then it was curious that I experienced none of the terrible swift ecstasy of which my forebears incessantly preached. Nor was there fear or terror; what I perceived to be my encroaching madness accounted for far more horror than the mere arrival of an angel could effect.

Then he said, "I came too late in search of the dreamer Wesley Dodds. He saw tomorrow with a power he did not understand, but passed to you nonetheless."

"Wait a minute." I strained my intellect to grasp the concept. "What you're saying is that this . . . this capacity of mine is the product of our own will? Wesley's and mine?"

"Do not yet dismiss the concept of human achievement."

And thus I knew he had been watching both Wesley and me for some time.

"Now your dreams will guide us both. In order for me to fulfill my mission we must both witness the events that will lead to Armageddon."

"If you are truly a being of great power," I insisted, "how can it be that you have no way to avert this catastrophe?"

"That is not my task."

"Then, whose task is it?"

"Among your kind, there are those of great power. Once these souls might have stemmed the tide of destruction. But as you will see, they are no longer the solution. They are, in many ways, the problem."

I did not want to hear that. I did not want to hear much of this, not even the fact that my visions were an extension of reality. I had hoped lately to spend my twilight growing comfortably senseless.

He reached a hand toward mine and said, "Come with me."

"No," I said. "I cannot simply leave. My congregation depends on me. They look to me for—"

And he directed my sight to a Book of Common Prayer, lying on the floor between two pews. It was the book that I clutched in my hand when I had tried to sleep on the pew, a handful of pages ripped from it as if not by a distracted elderly pastor but by teenage hoodlums who had ransacked the sanctuary. "Need you?" he gently challenged. "For what?"

Vulnerable enough for the moment at the sight, I dropped my hand into his and the air began to swirl slowly around me and my lovely church faded. If I had thought about his proposition for another moment, I surely would have turned him down.

CHAPTER 5
Cincinnatus

~~~

When I saw the endless fields of wheat and alfalfa waving in the breeze, the first thing I did was cry. My initial reaction to news of the Holocaust in the Heartland had been simply to try integrating it into what I was already doing: helping my congregants to deal with the world as it was. When I finally walked out among the people abroad in the city of Metropolis, fully a day after the disaster, there seemed to be two populations: the terribly sorrowful on the one hand, and on the other hand the numb, like ghosts. These were the extremes, and there was no middle ground. Here in the wheatfields, wherever it was that this apparition—this Spectre—had carried me, I finally joined the ranks of the sorrowful.

What I saw when the world re-formed from haze into firmament were amber waves of grain stretched over the countryside as far as the eye could see. Off in the distance a sturdy post-and-beam barn rose over the rich healthy loam; outside the barn, unbound by corral or fencing of any sort, horses and goats and dogs—and a monkey, I thought I saw—bounded and leapt through a clearing. A colt grazed under the watchful eye of a mare who stood between it and her spirited stallion.

A little white terrier yipped and howled at the enormous old pig that ignored the dog to chew on a rawhide bone.

I imagined the fronds of wheat brushing the tears from my cheeks as I walked like a spirit toward the barn. In the distance was a mesh corncrib and, beyond it, a field of corn as high as an elephant's eye. I mourned for the Heartland of America and wished for the answer I wanted to hear as I asked my impassive keeper:

"Have you taken me to the past? Or can such a thing as this be in our world's future?"

The Spectre actually hesitated a moment and reached to place a chill hand on my head before he said, "We have not broached the barriers of time, Norman McCay. Time passes here as it always has in your experience."

"Then how is a place like this possible? I thought—"

"It is gone, make no mistake. The place whose grain has been the staff of the lives of billions and whose corn has fattened mountains of livestock is lost. Its earth is irradiated. Its productivity is truncated. But this is another place. Look farther."

That I did. From the direction of the barn I heard the tapping of a hammer. I walked the distance—it seemed about a quarter-mile, but I covered it in little time—and looked in the wide door. Inside, a man was inspecting the new shoes that evidently he just had affixed to the hooves of an enormous dray horse. He cleaned the dirt from the bottom of the horse's feet with a metal hook he held by a handle between two fisted fingers, and put the animal's leg down. It was not until the horse walked by me, mane flowing, the fur of its fetlocks blowing like flags, that I saw that this animal's withers were quite higher than my head, and I realized how enormous a man the animal's master must be. The man was of human proportion, no doubt—not like the form my ghostly guide affected—but nonetheless huge and imposing. His arms were thicker than my thighs. He was shirtless, in a bibbed denim coverall whose cross-straps strained against his back as he bent over to lift an arm-wrenching anvil from the ground and carry it out after the horse as though it were a hammer or a screwdriver. Then I realized I saw no hammer here, though I had heard the tapping of one. There were no tools here at all other than anvils of various shapes on a few workbenches, and a large bucket of silver horseshoes and nails. A tractor perched against a wall alongside the open doorway.

The man's hair was long, tied back in a ponytail that was jet black on the top, but as he walked I could see that its underside was gray like the temples of his dense, tight head of hair. The full ragged beard was nearly white. His face was weathered somehow, but not with the sort of weathering that comes with age. Those lines come only from life. Certainly he was vigorous and strong in a way I had not seen before in a man whose eyes were so knowing. I envied this man the grace with which he carried his years.

"Do you know this person?" the Spectre asked in a voice only I could hear as he appeared silently behind me.

"The farmer looks familiar," I whispered, "but no. Should I know him?"

"There is no need to lower your voice. Even he can neither see nor hear us. You have never met, but yes, you should know him."

I watched him produce handsful of oats from the pockets of his overall to feed the horses and goats. He gave long bone-shaped biscuits to the pig and the dog, who stood diligently by his heel unmindful of the horses' hooves.

"So who is he?" I asked the Spectre.

My companion did not answer. In fact, he seemed as unaware of my presence as did this man.

The man looked out across his wheatfield as he patted the little dog. Then he went into the barn and came back out carrying the tractor balanced on one hand over his head. He set the machine down facing the edge of the wheatfield and went inside again for the thresher attachment.

"He came to Earth," my guide told me, "with powers and abilities far beyond those of mortal men."

"Oh my dear Lord," I said. "It's Superman."

"Yes," the Spectre answered finally, "a name he has not used since he began his self-imposed exile ten years ago."

Ω Ω Ω

After some moments it occurred to me to wonder: Where was the sun? The air was bright, the sky was a uniform deep azure that faded to a lighter shade of blue only around the extremes of the horizon. Shadows did not cast, but fell in puddles around the bases of objects, as if light came from all directions at once. Yet light seemed to come from nowhere, just the air. There was no light source in the sky.

"We're not on Earth, are we?" I quizzed this dour angel. "He left, I remember. There was a trial, a sense of inevitability. Everyone says he felt driven from the planet, that he's off saving worlds somewhere else. That is where we are now, right?"

The Spectre resumed his silent impassivity. Superman rode the saddle of the tractor as he cut and threshed the acres of grain behind him. One would think he could do it faster, and that the only reason he might do it this way was personal enjoyment. He did not look like a man who enjoyed much, however. He looked like the farmers of my rural southern Illinois youth: content but not particularly happy.

"So what planet are we on? Have I ever heard of this place?"

"Earth," the Spectre said.

"Some terraformed world he's renamed Earth."

"Earth," the Spectre said. "The world of your birth."

"Why did this part of the Heartland not get destroyed in the Holocaust?"

The Spectre looked at me, then looked at Superman on his

tractor, threshing away. I wondered which of us confused the spirit more.

"Where is everybody?" I asked him. "He's so alone."

"Not always."

"Is that what he wants? Is that what any man wants? To live with anvils and animals?"

"There are others sometimes," the Spectre said, looking up into the distance.

His raised head prompted me to look in that direction, beyond the barn where Superman rode and threshed. There, walking through the waving grain, was a tall woman, a tiara holding her hair and wearing a tunic of red, blue, and gold.

"Hello, Clark—" she said when she was closer, then corrected herself. "Kal."

"Diana, welcome. What brings you to the farm?"

"The vain hope that you're not still here," she told him.

"What happened to him?" I asked the Spectre. "Is that Wonder Woman? Why hasn't she aged at all? What are they to each other? Where is this place?" I just kept asking the same questions over and over and added one or two when they occurred to me, in the hope that occasionally I would get an answer to something. "Why is it that even in a noncorporeal state I still feel like a man in his seventies?"

"You are a man in his seventies," the Spectre finally allowed.

"I was hoping . . ." I said. Somewhere in a corner of my heart I suppose I had hoped coming with this dour spirit might leave me younger. Now I dismissed that, another discarded fantasy of an old man.

"It's been months, Kal. But haven't you heard?" the Amazon asked him incredulously. Evidently I had been the second-to-last person on the planet to notice the latest sign of the Apocalypse.

"What do you mean, Diana?" The big man climbed down from his tractor, stepping back when she offered him a kiss on his mouth. Then he straightened up and kissed her cheek, and she ran a hand along his waist. She was strange to him, and he felt like a teenager for a moment, discovering the eyes of a girl for the first time.

Then the moment broke.

"You're needed, Kal."

"Right. The harvest is almost in."

"Back in the world, I mean. You're needed."

"Um-hm."

"Kal-El," she said. "Kansas is gone."

"What are you talking about?" He looked back at her, expressionless. "My Kansas?"

"Your Kansas, Clark."

"Don't call me that."

"I mean Kal. Gone."

"Who's Kal?" I asked the Spectre, who did not answer. "Who's Clark?"

"I've got more important things to do," the farmer told the Amazon and climbed back up to the saddle of his tractor.

"I said *Kansas*. Listen to me, dammit!" she hollered at him, losing her composure. "This is bad news, Kal. It's shaken the world. It ought to rattle you just a little. Didn't you pick up the seismic disturbance here?"

"Day before yesterday?"

"Yes. Day before yesterday."

"I felt something. Figured it for about a seven point six somewhere in the Badlands. Don't get inside much to check things out this time of year."

"Well, you were a few states off. And several orders of magnitude. Kal, it was Magog."

"What do you mean it was Magog? Is he shooting nukes out of that joystick of his now?"

"No, it was his gang. They call themselves the Justice Battalion these days. Or did. We think, except for Magog himself, they're gone now."

"Justice Battalion," the big man said almost under his

breath, with enough disdain to tar a regiment. "Look, I don't want to have anything to do with these people anymore. These are my roots. Here."

"You can't live in solitude forever."

"I'm Superman. I can do anything."

"Except, apparently, face your fear."

"I'm not afraid of him," the man snapped.

"I didn't mean Magog. I meant . . ." and she paused, wondering what she meant, or how to tell him. "Kal," she began again, "you've lost so much since I first met you. But you've gained so much, too."

"Gained? Earthlings die. You know that."

"They were your parents, Kal. And she was your wife. Don't call them 'Earthlings.' "

"I have work to do, Diana." And he turned away from her. "Here things grow."

"Kal, Magog's out of control."

"I tried to tell them that ten years ago."

"And they didn't listen, I know. Stop punishing them."

"I'm not interested."

"That's not really Superman, is it?" I turned to the Spectre, who nodded. "What happened to him?"

"What happened to you, Kal?" the woman asked him just as I had done. "I've known you most of your life, and I still don't understand what happened to you. What happened to your code, Kal? What did you used to call it? Your torah?"

"Gone. Like a childhood fantasy."

"Truth, justice, and the American way, right? We all repeated that like a mantra under our breaths when we were up against it, do you know that? Even those of us who weren't Americans."

"I don't care about—"

"What's the last thing you did care about?"

"Lois."

She closed her eyes, turned her back on him as if she were counting to ten, and turned to face him again.

And I asked the Spectre, "Who's Lois?" but he did not answer.

The tractor began to move slowly, but she darted in front of it and stood with her hands on her waist. "At least come inside and take a look at what's happened."

He stopped the machine before its grille would certainly have flattened against his lady friend, and he said, "I've got animals and crops, Diana."

"This to your animals and crops," and she emitted a shrill whistle on a clear steady tone, and suddenly half the wheat-field vanished and the sky blackened, and there was a neighing and a barking and a bleating.

We were under an enormous dome, and now the illusion of bucolic fields as far as the eye could see was gone. It was winter on the Tundra.

"You spooked the livestock."

"I remembered the frequency code. At least I provoked a reaction in something."

"Last time I share my secrets with a girl."

"A girl?" And her face went dark like that of a barbarian warrior. She scrambled to the foothold aside the tractor and delivered an open-handed slap to the face of the man. He laughed and rolled over backward from his saddle, tumbling through the air parallel to the darkened ground and landing softly on his feet. She comforted her reddened slapping hand in the crook between her chest and her opposite arm.

This was Antarctica. He'd come to live in the last place on the only world he'd known, where humankind did not scatter cities like grass seed or impose foibles like dogma. Now that Diana had retracted the illusion, the starry sky hung revealed with only the barest hint of sunlight below a fringe of the northern horizon—and from this place every direction was north. The wheat and corn crops that stretched for a fair distance were real, but, beyond the acreage under the solar-radiated dome where this man took his succor, the great glacier rose in steps on all sides. He walked over to what was now clearly the wall of the dome. Rather than whistling, he pressed a panel that a moment ago was a reflection of waving wheatfields, and the illusion returned along with the composure of his livestock.

"Truth, justice, and the American way, Kal," she said again. "You always had a way with words."

"Comes of writing for a living."

"Nice turn of phrase, but you can't have forgotten completely what it meant to us. There's no one else to lead us."

"Who do you think I am? George Washington? I'm done."

"For how long? Another ten years? Until the radiation cloud reaches down here?"

"Come on, Diana."

"Come on, Clark."

He shot her a look through narrowed eyes.

"Kal. I'll help you with the baling. Or chaffing. Or whatever it is you do. It'll be great. Just like back on the farm. But first come inside and look at the news. Look what Magog has let happen to the world, that's all I ask. And steel yourself."

"Don't humor me. I don't need humoring."

"It's all I can think of to do." She stared at him soulfully, and, through the laconic detachment of a man too long alone, he smiled.

He walked to her and nudged her gently with his shoulder, then walked toward a spot where there was a door in the side of the dome. She followed and took his hand like a schoolgirl.

"Men lose themselves in women," I told the Spectre.

"Clarify that, please," the apparition demanded, and I was gratified that he did.

"This is a brave and mature man," I said, "an accomplished man. But this woman is not the one who was to be his life's companion. There was another one, wasn't there?"

"Yes," the Spectre told me, "but how could you know that?"

"I'm a minister," I told him.

"Your presence here, Norman McCay, is necessary for your insight."

"Then share yours. Tell me about Lois."

"You know of her," he said. "She was called Lois Lane."

"Lois Lane? The journalist? Wasn't she a married woman? To . . . to the last editor of the *Daily Planet,* right?"

"Clark Kent."

"Right. Clark." And in my slow, plodding fatbag of a human brain a peg fell into place. "He's Clark. The writer. Weren't both killed by the one whom Magog killed?"

"Only one of them was really killed. Longer than he was Superman, he was Clark."

"Oh, for Heaven's sake."

Ω   Ω   Ω

For decades, there had been legends of the Fortress of Solitude, the apocryphal home of Superman. Some of the stories held that it was in the Amazon Rain Forest or in a grotto deep in a Pacific trench or below the sewers of Metropolis. Some said that it was in a "pocket universe" tucked away in the big globe that rotated atop the old *Daily Planet* building, or that its entrance was through a crater on the far side of the Moon. A disoriented dogsledder competing in the Iditarod once had reported seeing a huge golden key north of the Arctic Circle that might fit into an enormous door camouflaged in the side of a glacial mountain, but the "key" had turned out to be a directional marker for pilots traveling the great circle routes among the northern continents. I had always thought it made more sense for Superman to live on an isolated farm in the Midwest or in one of the anonymous beehive cubicles of apartments in Metropolis, rather than in some hidden imperial citadel far from mortal perceptions. What I saw here with the Spectre beneath the Antarctic Tundra reminded me of my conviction that every fable of humankind's collective consciousness is, in some sense, true.

The interior of the Fortress was decorated like the den of a giant packrat, with an occasional piece of shiny booty hanging in a corner or from a wall. It was the least luxurious and most unlived-in domicile I have ever seen a sentient being occupy. What most struck me was the matter of scale. But instead of the occasional agate marble or tinfoil gum wrapper or dismembered doll's head that one might find in the packrat's hole, here was a metal-jacketed book twelve feet high with several hundred pages of etched galvanized steel, casually leaning against the dirt-and-stone wall of a narrow room with a forty-foot ceiling. A pair of statues, in some sort of enamel over granite, of a stern-looking man and woman in alien dress and headgear. A fully grown tyrannosaurus, unearthed perhaps in the course of building this nest from its frozen preserve. Down an unlit hall was a clear chamber of some sort, like a bottle on a small stand, stuck with a Post-it Note full of scrawlings in a language I did not recognize. While I was looking at the chamber, an open box with a kind of flower— an extraterrestrial thing, maybe—materialized on a small stand beside it. And in the room where Superman walked with Wonder Woman was a crazy-quilt collection of monitors and receivers, piled on top of one another and scattered over the floor. The rock-and-permafrost ceiling here was higher even than the one in the room with the book. The screens upon screens and numerous projection devices reached to the ceiling.

"On," he said, and crossed his arms over his chest. He casually floated up halfway to the distant ceiling to get a better view of everything.

And the flood of light and sound suddenly flew through my senses and then shut me down like a shot of 120-proof whiskey. A hundred screens lit a hundred images, and two hundred speakers spoke in as many sounds and voices, and the only clear message that rode the chill air was Kansas.

Magog was at fault, all right. Satellite monitors caught the whole thing. Every broadcast facility in every corner of the

Earth, it seemed, even the specialized subscription services that normally put over the airwaves only old films or documentaries on fishing or contemporary musical performances, spread this word. Humanity and its superhuman "protectors" over the years had leveraged Earth's life support systems out to the edge, and now someone had pushed all of us over it.

Here were images of the Justice Battalion: Captain Atom, who could loose the nuclear energy of his own body; Judomaster, who was lethal at using her opponents' weight and inertia to her own advantage; Thunderbolt, who ran as fast as the old Flash in his youth—when he'd been a bit slower, after all—and ran these days with Magog; Peacemaker, the misnamed weapons-smith who went after purported lawbreakers with nervous-system homogenizers and brainwave scramblers; Nightshade, the otherworldly maniac who could summon a liquid darkness to the brightest of days; and Alloy, the sentient biomechanical organism who was the faceless amalgam of an old sophisticated club of robots called the Metal Men.

And in the center of it all was a little old man named Maxwell Jensen whom a reporter once had named the Parasite, and the name had stuck. His skin was disfigured; his manner was one that reflected only terror and panic.

Jensen was a kind of idiot savant, a timid little cipher among the brotherhood of supervillainy. He could duplicate the abilities of people with whom he came in physical contact, and he'd thought at one time to put this talent to work to make himself rich. The Parasite could touch a philosopher and explain Kant; touch a dog and bark; touch Superman and fly. Years ago he'd tried out his capacities on a few banks and a jewelry store or two. His problem was that when he got up in the morning, he was not very bright, and with every ability and power he added, his plan changed. His might have been an effective power in the hands of someone with a little foresight or genuine ambition. All Jensen started out with, however, was envy. All he finished up with was regret, but, mercifully, it probably lasted only a moment.

With a history of arrests like his, all poor Jensen needed to do was put on his silly little skintight costume that hugged his old jailbird's wrinkles where it was not ripped and worn, or show up somewhere someone recognized him, or have a mild psychotic incident to attract the attention of Magog and his storm troopers. He did all of those things, apparently, and there he was on the enhanced audiovisual file from the reconnaissance satellite duking it out with the Justice Battalion in Saint Louis.

Magog in his gold breastplate and twisted-horned helmet and power sceptre was just looking for a fight, and he bulldogged his buddies to do the same. The Parasite, with his unpredictability, always gave them a good workout and ended up gibbering in a prison cell for resisting arrest. All he ever did, though, when the "heroes" came spoiling after him, was panic. It was never clear that this was a criminal offense.

He shoved someone and picked up the ability to fly. He stumbled against someone else and accumulated relative superspeed. He led the Battalion on a merry chase that ended up somewhere in central Kansas and left a trail that looked like that of a tornado in the wake of the brawl. And all along, the audio file kept sending back evidence of the Parasite trying to surrender.

"Leave me alone. Leave me alone!" he insisted.

"I'll go quietly, just don't touch me, okay?" he pleaded.

"No, don't use your power near me, I won't—" He cut himself off.

The visual image clearly showed Captain Atom hurtling across a corner of a field of grain with a fist extended at the little man. In a maneuver worthy of the Judomaster—from whose talents the Parasite's capacity to do this certainly came—Jensen escaped Captain Atom's blow and shoved against his chest as the Captain flew toward the ground . . .

. . . and the Parasite literally split the Atom.

As the Parasite sucked up Captain Atom's power in such close proximity to him—mingled like strong drink with the powers of the others—all the undigested energy behaved like a horrible wail of feedback reverberating between a pair of runaway audio speakers. Captain Atom's chest, where the Parasite had touched him, emitted a blast of white light. In the image delay and enhancement we could see Alloy stretching his malleable body over that of Magog, his leader—to protect him, one would presume—then the entire image vanished in the expanding shock wave.

Our technology allowed us to be witnesses to our own demise. There was no more visual or audio record discernible from the reconnaissance satellite, but sonar readings in the immediate region of the blast detected one figure moving through it all. It was an individual the size of a man with a pair of blunt protrusions extending from its head. The speculation was that because of Alloy's protection, Magog survived Ground Zero. In fact, when high-level radiation inspectors and rescue crews dropped on the scene less than a day later, they found remains—eroded teeth and bone, ash impressions of figures, shards of durable costuming, pulsing white-hot slabs of Alloy, that sort of thing. These remains suggested that all on the scene were vaporized except for Magog himself and possibly Alloy as well.

Magog was nowhere to be found. Neither was most of Kansas.

Superman learned this here among his cacophony of broadcast equipment piled up in this room of the Fortress, two days after it had happened. I learned the details with him.

Immediate casualties hovered at a million as the dying Captain Atom's radioactive energy swept millions of acres. Kansas was an irradiated wasteland, as were parts of Nebraska, Iowa, and Missouri. The sterilization of the agrarian culture of America's Breadbasket threw the world economy into near-collapse in the face of global famine.

"Off," Superman said when he'd had enough, and the din silenced.

Ω   Ω   Ω

"Nothing to be done now anyway," he said.

"Excuse me?" she wanted to know.

"It's over. What is there left to do?"

"Lead us back."

"Me?"

"Who else?"

"I don't believe in leaders."

"Since when?"

He shrugged and walked back out into the hallway, toward the door that led into his domed wheatfield.

"Kal, please." She took his arm, and he stopped to listen for a moment. "Our generation takes its lead from you. We always have. You must face this. If you don't, neither will the rest of us. And it just goes on."

He stood still for a moment, looking at her. He seemed confused about what to say or whether to say anything.

The moment was long enough for her to say, "Kal?"

"Open," he said, and a whoosh of wind rushed through the sliding metal plates of the doorway that emptied into his Antarctic farm. As he stepped out he said, "There's nothing I can do from here. Go back to your island, Diana. You're safe there." And the doorway clapped shut behind him.

"Safe?" she asked no one in particular, and then again, louder, "Safe?"

And the Spectre and I rematerialized high above the South Pole, where the Amazon Princess breasted the cold air in flight through the curtains of the Aurora Australis and twisted north in the direction of the distant Mediterranean.

" 'The rest of us'?" I asked the Spectre. "Who are 'the rest of us'?"

"Indeed," he said, "there are those who, a decade ago, felt the crush of Superman's inability to perceive himself as the inspiration he was. The shock of seeing Superman abandon his never-ending battle took an immeasurable toll on his contemporaries, his peers."

"I see," I replied, but I did not yet.

CHAPTER 6

Where Are They Now?

~~~~~

Ω Ω Ω

ere is where they have gone," the Spectre said, and again he pulled aside the Aurora that hung like a curtain over the sky.

Ω Ω Ω

Where once the great forests of the Pacific overgrew a national border, now stood a large wooden structure with a corrugated aluminum roof thirty feet over its floor. It was a weekend, and, at the main field mill of Mercer Bainbridge Paper Products, only the company's executives met over brandy and cigars to consider a strategic business plan for their future. Log steps led up to a genuine sawed plank deck at the entrance of this building. In the days before my life had begun—not long, in fact, before my time—a building of wood might have appeared to be a poor person's structure. Then during my young adulthood, it had been the fashion among many of the more affluent to build and live in constructions of such a design, out of nostalgia for the vanishing rusticity of the past. Now, with the loss of the world's virgin forests and the wide use of ceramic and plastic to substitute for real wood in building materials, only the fabulously wealthy had even sheet-wood paneling. This building put mere paneling to shame. It had an actual log-and-beam frame and exteriors of piled logs with diagonal tongue-in-groove pine interior walls. Inside, on a loft that served as a conference room overlooking a battery of enormous saws and pulping vats, the board of directors considered the problem of setting the prices that wholesalers would pay during the next year.

The paper business had been good to them. Their graphs and projections showed them precisely how much of the forest to slice away and at what rate to allow for adequate timber growth. By their definition, "adequate" growth meant the forest would replenish itself long enough so that the board could take the company bankrupt and leave the shareholders, employees, and pensioners with as little as possible. This would still allow each of the nineteen men in this room to parachute away with enough cash to see them and their families through the next century in spite of any natural or artificially induced disasters that might assault the world or its economy. Now that the world's Breadbasket was gone, however, their options suddenly expanded.

Mercer Bainbridge held millions of acres of pasture and enormous herds of cattle on land that once had been forest, from the Amazon River Valley to the Canadian Klondike. Cattle pasture was the major by-product of deforestation, which was actually the principal activity of the Mercer Bainbridge Paper Company. A few days before, there had been quite enough cattle in captivity to render the natural protein market effectively saturated. Part of this group's plan was simply to unload the land and herds in the course of liquidating the company's assets when the time came. Now, however, there was chaos in the markets for all forms of food.

Always, there was profit in chaos.

Then a big chunk of the profit came careening through the corrugated ceiling and tumbled along the diagonal through the inside wall before it smashed down on the floor of what once was riverside forest land. The wall splintered. Beyond it, among the stumps of what once was the Pacific Northwest Rain Forest, settled the twisted metal of one of the backhoes that had been dredging the banks. Impossibly, the big hunk of machinery had come crashing from above.

"What's going on here?" the President of Mercer Bainbridge Paper demanded because he felt he should.

And a cast-iron, spiked mace the size of a watermelon came riding a clattering chain through the hole in the ceiling to smash into the mill's biggest pulping vat and instantly transformed it into an impressionistic sculpture.

No one asked any more questions. The nineteen members of the Board of Directors of Mercer Bainbridge Paper Products scrambled out of the big wooden building—some through the doors, some through the walls that were no longer standing. Only then did they see him, meticulously dismantling their paper mill. His wings extended, their tips pulsing rhythmically against the air like a swimmer treading water, he hung in the sky:

Hawkman.

He was a man the size of an ox, with golden wings three times as wide as he was tall. With cabled arms he held the mace as with the wings he held the sky. What looked like a feathered helmet came down over his face, but there was no gap between what seemed to be a decorative hooked beak and his chin. Then the beak opened and out of it came the loudest, shrillest, most horrendous cry ever to crease an Earthly sky. The aquiline beak was no decoration, these men realized. This strange visitor from another planet, this Thanagarian policeman, identified more closely with the birds who lived on Earth's natural skin than with the humans who meant to tear it away.

Hawkman was taking it back.

Like an angry angel, I thought, solemn and splendid. He looked far more like an angel than the angel who led me through this little adventure. As the nineteen cigar-puffing, brandy-sniftering directors looked on, the enormous winged man slammed his mace over and over again into and through the building. He crushed and splintered the wood of the structure itself on the forest floor, and the metal ended up twisted into small chunks, like steel rocks. It was comical to watch the silly suited men caught with their dignity down in mid-wheel and dirty-deal. This large fellow had wings growing out of his back, and feathers so thick on his chest and legs, they could be fur. Perhaps in some small way he could put a stop at least to this corporate carnage, I thought. Perhaps not. At any rate, he would continue to try.

Slats came free of posts and splintered on the ground.

Steel saws fell apart into loose teeth that the rushing waters of the river would file and make dull.

Papers, desks, skitters, and heavy vehicles and equipment went flying and scattering into loose parts and tumbling into the water.

Piece by piece, the works of Man by this riverbank were being reclaimed by the Earth. This flying alien who rode the wind was feeding it back with Man's own ancient weaponry.

Beside the deconstruction of the mill flowed the Chumash River, wide and deep and filled with the waste and foam of the belching mill. Once, before the coming of Hawkman, this river had been puzzled by the taming effect of a complex of dams. They were gone now, and the Chumash was wild again. The wood that had made up the Mercer Bainbridge building would break down on the forest floor, enrich the insulted soil, and perhaps give birth to new forest. The steel rocks were now the final waste material of the mill, and, with a savage wind from the flapping of his great wings, the man-bird swept these into the river to pile across the bed and slim the pitch of the water at this point.

Hawkman used the nonbiodegradable waste of the mill to rearrange the river itself, making a patch of whitewater here. Adventurous canoers passing through this place in days to come would call it "Papermill Rapids." Certainly with the new behavior of the Chumash River, this no longer would be a place suitable for the alluvial wastes of such a mill.

The man-bird treading the sky spread his wings to their enormous span. And the onlookers calmed themselves and stared like field mice in the path of an eagle. He loosened a cry from his throat that shattered the din of confusion over who ruled this place.

Hawkman fought the lonely battle against the despoilers of the planet and specifically the Northwest of this continent. He shattered logging equipment. He destroyed buildings and building materials in the dwelling places of his winged brothers and sisters. He smashed dams and made the stone and metal of their structures part of the new environment he left behind. It was a lonely battle, and, in truth, he was losing it.

Once more the thunderstruck and stranded men who had made an enemy of Hawkman saw him draw down those great wings. The air that single motion harnessed propelled him high above the nearest cloud and sent a wave of wind to tumble the nineteen men over and into one another like tenpins. I stood, myself a wraith, detached from the plane of existence wherein that wind blew, but I do swear it chilled my blood.

$$\Omega \quad \Omega \quad \Omega$$

"Look at your watch," the Spectre said.

I looked. It was not moving. Imperiously the Spectre swept his hand over my wrist, and the watch worked again. Who knew what sort of physics applied here in this nether-plane? Certainly not a physics that supported biological clocks or even wristwatches. But now my watch temporarily ticked away, approximating the snail-like pace of the time-keepers of the corporeal world.

We descended to a city: slick narrow towers, glistening fa-cades, little civic art, and virtually no vegetation on the streets and sidewalks. This was not a Nineteen-Thirties Deco city like Gotham or a City of the Future That the Future Left

Behind like Metropolis. This was a city of the Seventies, full of monolithic Philip Johnson skyscrapers and people in wide lapels and polyester.

"Note what your timepiece says," the Spectre urged.

"Seven thirty-two," I said, accurately, I thought.

"It measures time in seconds, does it not?"

"Yes."

"What, then, is the time?

"Seven thirty-two," I said, then added, "and eighteen seconds. Now."

I was not done saying that last word when the most remarkable sensation came over me. I was frozen stiff. I was not cold or in pain or at all uncomfortable, but suddenly I was no longer moving and felt somehow incapable of moving. Space careened by me at some unutterable speed, and I was in the city itself and in my line of vision was—beyond the watch on my arm that I was unable to drop to my side—the blur of a human figure in scarlet. In the moment suspended between the eternity of now and the next second, I knew that this was the Flash and this must be Keystone City.

He had been wholly out of sight for years. Maybe his speed was the reason.

The walls and barriers of the city sped through my vision, but this hazy being—slipping in and out of dimensions and frames of reality as if the continuum and all Creation were a singularity—stayed in the frame of my sight.

He raced up the side of a building to catch a falling cat and deposit her behind a window high on the fifty-seventh floor, and then closed the window behind him.

Racing over the top of the building, he straightened six loose or cracked tiles in the perimeter of the roof, seeing to the safety of anyone who in the future might be walking below.

Through all this the Flash stayed clearly—as clearly as such a blurry and indistinct fellow could stay—in my line of sight, along with my watch, on the arm I seemed unable to lower. My senses were speeded up but my reactions, even though I was unbound by physical reality, did not catch up. I suspect I was too tied up with my humanity—still—to manage such a dislocation of my conventional perceptions. Yet I could not turn back the tide of lightning-fast sensation that poured through my line of sight as, beyond the figure of the Flash, the city of Keystone became a smudge over the landscape.

He breezed into a firehouse where an alarm was about to clap on. Sixteen firefighters sat around the hall doing pull-ups, playing video games, doing clerical work. At least that was what the virtual statues of firefighters I saw seemed to be doing. Meanwhile, the Flash slowed just enough to see the pixels on the dispatch monitor spell out an address . . .

. . . across town. We were there in the same instant, where licks of flame made a colorful still picture from an upper window of a tidy little two-story house on a tree-lined street. Standing still—or, rather, suspended between two moments— a fire is not a coherent thing. It is a thousand little sparks of red, yellow, and green, making a fading chiaroscuro pattern against the sky. Light slowed as we approached, to let its brother fire through.

Up the facade of the house and through the breaking wall and broken window we went, through the fire too fast for the heat of the flames to make an impression. Into the fiery room we went, and my red-streaking quarry lifted a child trapped by a wall of flames at her bedroom door and tucked her under his arm. And through the flames he took her, down a hall into a playroom, and he whipped another terrified child, an older one, into his other arm. He skittered down an "obstructed" stairway—obstructed only if you moved slowly enough to be concerned that it was falling to pieces and some of the steps were little more than charred splinters. In a collapsing living room the frantic mother, unaware of her immediate danger, stood with a phone to her ear, wearing a rictus of horror on her face as she strained to see beyond the conflagration. She was yet unaware that the Flash had safely brought her children to her side. Kids still under his arms, he ran around the mom and swept her up in the wake of his passing.

Frozen in position—with her now-empty hand still grasping for a phone at her ear—she followed in a stream of wind as he carried the kids out to the front lawn, deposited them gently on the ground, and caught her as she flew by, stopping her progress so that she would not break any bones on landing. He placed her down next to the kids, who, in the next moment when the Scarlet Speedster was already far gone, would realize they were safe.

Now the Flash was at the fire hydrant on the curb a few doors down the street. He unscrewed the hose nozzle with a million persistent little nudges of his hands, and twisted on the spigot the same way. It was bone dry in there as far as I could see, of course, but water simply did not blow out of a hole that fast. And he was off again.

Back at the fire station across town the sixteen men and women were in precisely the same positions they had been before. The alarm was still about to ring. They were all—though they could hardly have known it—about to turn to look at the address forming from lazy little pixels on the dispatch monitor. The Flash snatched up paper and pencil from under the face of a man filling out a time sheet and scratched out a message on it in graphite that would not fall off the trail of the pencil or affix to the page until the Flash again was gone from this place . . .

The message, when someone glacially turned his head to read it—just as the alarm sounded—would read, LATE AGAIN, BOYS.

. . . and back across town to the house afire and the mother and two kids still prone in odd positions on the ground. Neighbors and pedestrians in the area were statues in position just beginning to gather and watch the disaster. The slow-motion torrent of water came inching out of the spigot of the hydrant where the Flash began worrying it upward like a sculptor pressing on clay—

—and I was suddenly back in real time, and the water-spout flew up at the sky, in a snaking pattern through the limbs of an old tree, then winding around an electric line and up above the house. Every drop rained down on the fire to quench it as I lowered the wrist that held my watch from in front of my face.

The Fastest Man Alive was nowhere to be seen.

"What time is it?" the Spectre asked me.

"Oh," I said, raising the watch again. "Seven thirty-two," and I paused too long before I said, "and twenty-one seconds."

"It took you two seconds to say that," the Spectre observed.

"So all that we watched," I said in wonder, "took place in the course of a second?"

"A little less," the Spectre said, as I heard the fire hissing away and watched the train of water from the hydrant falling off to a trickle. "That is the way it is in Keystone City."

"He must feel like a very old man," I said, "years and years of experiences crammed into every day of his life."

No one ever saw him, but everyone knew he was there.

Ω Ω Ω

In high Earth orbit, 22,300 miles above the planet, a large imposing man at least my age but looking quite a bit younger sat watching the sky. It was just high enough that the planet might be standing still if the great green satellite orbited on an equatorial path, which it did not. Alan Scott, Earth's first Green Lantern, stood guard against a planetary invasion, and had fewer visitors even than Superman had when he spent his time plowing up the frozen Earth beside his Antarctic Fortress.

He sat and watched the skies in great black projections of light on the green walls of this city-satellite. He walked from one pod through a tunnel to another, carrying a sword of verdant light that projected images of the skies on the walls wherever he walked. He must be quite mad with isolation, I thought.

Then I saw him watering his plants and talking to his laboratory animals, and was sure he was as insane as I once thought Wesley was.

And finally he dictated a dispatch that typed itself on a screen and went directly to Earth as he talked: "Zero-gravity research into zinc alloy cell growth retardant is inconclusive but promising. Cancer cell remission in rhesus monkeys continues in eighty-eight percent of the cases. Standing by."

He sent the message to Nevin Scrimshaw, a prominent nutritionist at MIT whom I happened to know. Nevin had been on the cover of every news magazine in the country when he'd reversed lymphatic cancer with vitamin and mineral supplements. Evidently Green Lantern spent a lot of his time functioning as Scrimshaw's graduate assistant. Mad or sane, whether or not he was needlessly preoccupied with guarding against an alien invasion, Green Lantern was still fulfilling that oath that once was synonymous with his mission: "In brightest day, in blackest night; no evil shall escape my sight. Let those who worship evil's might beware my power—Green Lantern's light."

I have no idea why I remembered that, but I did—like every schoolchild.

Ω Ω Ω

On a Rapid Transit car underneath San Francisco about a dozen and a half people were growing increasingly worried. At opposite ends of the car, there slowly collected handsful of costumed teenagers, and neither the group at the fore end nor the group at the aft end looked as though they liked the other group very much.

"We've got Rapier," a large, thick-muscled boy of perhaps seventeen said through enormous white teeth. As he said this, another dangerous child—a thin and quick little mongoose of a boy—spirited through the aft end door of the moving car to join his group.

"So, we got Automag," a similarly large fellow at the fore end said, throwing open his car door and pulling in a humanlike creature four feet high, four feet wide, and four feet thick.

The two groups glared across the car at each other some more. The train was an express, barreling along the center track through one station after another. Moving at breakneck speed along the center rail, the two groups stared each other down. They called each other names. They brandished their weaponry and occasionally levitated something or tossed an energy pellet of some sort or melted something with a glance. The only ones intimidated were the passengers stuck between, sinking lower in their seats, digging deeper into their reading material, more and more concerned with seeming less and less concerned. Then unexpectedly the train was on the rightmost track and came to a stop in some station where hardly anything ever stops, and every civilian on the train stormed the sliding doors and poured out onto the platform as soon as the doors could release them.

Only a small blonde woman boarded. She carried the exaggerated figure of an old-time movie star, but crow's-feet betrayed the fact that she'd traversed a crucial hill lately and might not be aware of it yet. No matter, into the conveyance she bounced, and, heedless of the nonsense collecting at the extremes of the car, she found a seat in the empty center and opened up a trashy magazine.

A few kids noted the ample proportions and slatternly appeal of the car's sole civilian passenger. With a shove or a look from a crony, though, any curious hormone bag got a reminder of the passenger's apparent age—certainly well over thirty—and evident cluelessness.

Then somebody—on who-knew-which side—said, "Rampage!" and the subway rumble was on.

The first kid to blow out of his corner leapt across half the length of the car to grab a vertical pole and swing once around it, extending his legs together as he swung up some momentum . . .

The passenger put up a hand—late—as if to wave away his swinging legs, and pursed her lips for a moment.

. . . and the kid swung off in a crazy direction, slamming his feet into a shatterproof plate glass window and his head onto a plastic seat back. He was out of commission.

Two came from the other end. As they approached the center of the car, the pair slipped and fell on their butts as if they were old-time slapstick players.

One flew across the space and touched down nose to nose with the leader of the opposing gang . . .

The woman glanced up from her magazine, then back down.

. . . and as the rumbler put a hand on the commuter bar above him to posture and huff out his territorial ultimatum, he suddenly yanked his hand away, blew on it, shoved it between his legs, and squeezed it, trying to weather intense pain and heat.

And it went on like that. A comedy of errors afflicted every sniveling little metachild who arrogated himself into position to threaten another. Finally the express train came to a real stop where there were travelers who actually wanted to get on and go somewhere. By then, the troublemakers were tired of their troublemaking, and all got off to trudge home.

At the following stop the slatternly blonde got out of her seat and left the useless magazine in a trash bucket. Fluffing out her lovely hair and shaking her body—constricted by the illusion of the unfashionable—like a dog hopping out of a pool, she bounced up the subway stairs into the San Francisco sun.

"Power Woman," I said to the Spectre, who nodded. "I thought I recognized her."

Ω   Ω   Ω

"No problem," Ray Terrill said. "I'm a colorful guy."

It was a hospital in the eastern foothills of the Colorado Rockies, a little town called Smoky Hill. Here people still picked up the mail at the Post Office in the morning, and cowboys carried six-shooters, and traveling software salesmen kept their palmtops in their saddlebags and communicated from horseback with the home office in Sunnyvale. The nearest big city was Arapahoe. But it was here, in a valley bounded on the east by a pattern of three big calderas and a butte, where a hospital stood shielded from the fallout and ash of the Kansas explosion. It was the "clean" location closest to Ground Zero, and here was where Ray Terrill volunteered as a triage assistant tending the burned and sick refugees of Kansas.

"But it's such a nice jacket," the mother said. "We can't take it. We may never see you again."

The jacket he wrapped around the shivering boy was leather, with one yellow and one red sleeve and an orange collar. This was Ray's speed. He was lost in adolescence, though he approached fifty.

"I've got six years to go in my forties, and I swear my thirties lasted longer than this," Ray insisted to the shivering little boy—victim of vicious third-degree burns over 70 percent of his body. The burning was the least of it.

Ray might have thought twice about alluding to his advanced years, considering the prognosis for this child. Mom had been away in Kansas City at the time of the blast and escaped unhurt. Dad, two sisters, thirty head of cattle, and the family dog all had died. No one could figure how this boy had made it, but his mother found him the day after the blast, huddled under a heat blanket in the barn. Who knew how Mom had gotten past the authorities into the burn zone so quickly, either. They were new arrivals here at the hospital, and both would have to undergo radiation testing—especially

Mom, who'd gone into the zone with only the piecrust roof of her Jeep hovercraft to protect her from ravening gamma rays.

Ray Terrill leaned over the boy—he did not even ask the kid's name; there were so many, he would never remember, and mostly it did not matter—and pretended just to muss the hideously burned child's sparse hair to distract him. What Ray actually did was suck up every iota of dormant radiation poisoning from the child's system with that one sweep of his hand. He did the same thing to the boy's mother—a recent widow and, he thought as he did it, something of a babe too—and felt even more radiation leave her and disperse through his own system.

Ray told the mother that he was sending her son to the burn ward and that she should expect his recovery—assuming he was clear of radiation poisoning, which had yet to be tested—to last a little more than a year. She looked at her son, his persistent smile, his crusted skin, the colorful leather coat over his quaking frame—and she was actually relieved to hear this. They were two of the lucky ones. They would make it, Ray knew.

By the time his shift was over, Ray secretly had rebuilt the radiation-tainted DNA patterns of fourteen people and dissolved dormant but potentially carcinogenic free radicals from the bloodstream of thirty-seven more. He pulled sheets over the faces of four who'd died on arrival.

Ray Terrill then fired up the Sturm und Drang of his remarkable physiology, poured himself into his shiny golden body suit, and flew off unseen over Kansas to clear the land of radiation poisoning. Ray Terrill was the Ray, the walking, breathing, high-flying anthropomorphic lightbeam. He was a solid mass not of cells but of photons, an energy being living among humans. He could sense and change the nature of matter at its very molecular level.

Kansas, however, was a job and a half. If only he were getting paid by the acre.

Ω Ω Ω

Where were the rest of them? The Amazons, I learned, still lived on Paradise Island, a remote cay with no fixed location. The mermen and -maids still swarmed deep in the Atlantic and mostly made their homes in the sunken ancient city of Atlantis that settled askew on the floor of the Chronus Trench. The Legionnaires of the Thirtieth Century occasionally appeared here and there, mostly with futuristic historians in tow to gather around historic events and document them. There would be none of these latter on Earth in the coming months, however. This time, according to the Spectre, was a rippling labyrinth of probability fields, and no time traveler in his or her right mind would give it anything but a wide berth.

Ω Ω Ω

"There was someone else," I told the Spectre.

"There are many more," he said.

"No, I remember another one," I said, "whose real identity we all learned some years ago and who dropped from public view like a discredited character witness. He made his home in Gotham City."

"Yes."

"What has become of the Batman? Of Bruce Wayne?"

"You will see him soon enough."

"When?" I asked the Spectre, not sure whether I really felt the need to know, or whether it was simply morbid curiosity.

Suddenly, I was in a very dark place. I saw nothing. All I heard were rhythmic irregular tappings and the murmurs of a whispered icy voice.

"Maneuver twelve," the voice said, clearer now, and gradually a figure materialized in my line of vision.

Broad metallic shoulders shifted back and forth against a high-backed chair on top of a platform.

"Variation D-sixteen," the voice said, and the light shifted.

Beyond the figure was a monitor, and on the monitor was the dim image of a man with a gun looking upward in fear. It was a robbery, aired on this monitor. Then I saw that it was a battery of small monitors, maybe ten of them, each trained on the gunman from a different angle. He dropped the gun. Surrounding him were a company of twelve-foot-high robots, each with a black bat stenciled on its chest. The Bat-Knights. One robot held out a hooked arm to the frightened gunman.

Eventually, the man gathered enough presence to pick up the dropped weapon and hang it by its trigger guard from the hook of the fearsome robot's extended claw.

"Vehicular mishap on Gotham Bay Bridge. Dispatch ten," the Batman said, and on the monitors I saw all the robots but the one with the gun take to the air.

"What is he?" I asked the Spectre. "An android?" There were metallic frames all down his arms, legs, and shoulders. His neck was in a brace, yet he moved with the agility of a twenty-year-old.

"He abused the gift of his body for decades," the Spectre said, "and now needs artificial means to support his muscu-lature."

"You mean he *used* his body," I corrected. I was always in awe of how the Batman moved, even deep into middle age. I could not be anything but jealous still of the sensation in that man's bank of memory. His hair was white and finally thinning just a little. His muscles seemed well exercised, de-spite or perhaps because of the metal framing. And he wore what seemed to be a perpetual sardonic grin on his face.

"What is he doing here?" I wanted to know. "Isn't he as alone as Superman was in the Tundra?"

"No," the Spectre said, "not as alone, but more confident than Superman of his own counsel."

"Quiet night, then."

"In Gotham City all the nights are quiet now. Batman has his city under control."

"Maneuver nineteen, units three and four," Batman said, and, one would presume, the flying Bat-Monitors complied.

"Why?" I wanted to know.

"It makes him happy," the Spectre said.

Ω Ω Ω

"Confident of his own counsel," was how the Spectre described this aged Batman. I wondered what that meant. My mission—the Spectre's mission, really—demanded that I too be confident of my own counsel. I had never been. Always had I questioned my premises. Always was I looking at the Devil's side of every argument. Why not ask the Batman along on this quest? He was used to judging. He was one well acquainted with the approaching night.

"Have faith, Norman," Ellen used to tell me whenever I woke up in the middle of the night wondering about a decision I had made, or doubting the efficacy of the advice I'd given someone.

"Faith in what?" I always asked her.

"God, of course," she always said.

"It isn't God's judgment I doubt," I always replied.

And always, she smiled—an indulgent smile a lot like Bruce Wayne's smile, now that I think on it—and kissed me and rolled off to sleep while I was stewing. It was not as though I did not know what advice Ellen would have given me. It just would have been comforting, in this most perplexing moment of my life, to hear it again.

CHAPTER 7
Scrooge Me Not

I don't think so," I said.

And he said, "Pardon?"

"Include me out," I said.

And he wanted to know, "Do you consider that a serious option?"

For a moment we hovered over Gotham City, then that dark city faded to nothingness, and only the shimmering lights of the Aurora surrounded us.

As a boy I'd gone to Minneapolis with my father and seen the flickering curtains of light in the night sky for the first time on a road in the middle of nowhere, with no city lights to obscure our view. We'd stopped and stood out in the cold, shivering, and I would not leave until my father finally had started the engine again and flipped on the headlights to overpower my sight. Even then I'd begged him to drive with the lights off so I could watch out the window until oncoming traffic had begun to build and blot out the sky. The little collection of electrostatic patterns in the night there was the most beautiful thing I had ever seen.

As a teenager I'd decided with certainty, because of those lights, an age-old issue filled with doubts and questions:

whether there was a God. Even then I'd known only a hand like His could so casually have arranged ionic matter and rogue electrons in a pattern that would look to those below like a curtain in the sky.

The big eyes on butterflies' wings are to ward off predators. The colors and patterns of flowers are to attract bees who could spread their pollen. The mane of the male lion is there to attract the attention of the female lion and perpetuate the mane-bearer's genetic line. But the Aurora hangs in the sky for no practical survival purpose at all. It's there only to be beautiful, and can be nothing but the gift of a loving God. I'd come to that conclusion during a callow, self-involved adolescence. I suppose I know it still.

But as surely as He has given us the Aurora and the stars in the sky, He sent this dark-edged angel to impress me into his oh-so-vital service, and I was not sure I wanted any of it.

The Spectre pulled back the comfortable blanket of Aurora that surrounded me when we "traveled," and below us was the Outerborough Bridge, the old span that linked midtown Metropolis with the two counties east of the river.

How long had it been since he plucked me up from my church after Sunday morning services? Had all our travels and sightings fit into a moment? Or had it been years? I had no sense of time now, the way I had always imagined the sensation of living as a spirit to be. But as we descended gently through the sky to the foot of the bridge, and my apparent size contracted from that of a continent to that of an ordinary, rather diminutive man, I felt the smell of my body coming back to me. I was still a wraith, like the Spectre, but to be surrounded by this familiar place, so few blocks from my home, was to be almost corporeal again.

"That's all?" I asked. "That's all you have to show me?"

"That disturbs you?"

"I have a problem with the job description," I told him. "I did not understand my duties to include standing idly by while the world went down the nearest drain."

I think this perplexed him. He did not respond. As for me, it was the opportunity of my dreams. I was negotiating ethical policy with a duly constituted representative of the Creator of the Universe. Like Abraham arguing over the disposition of Sodom. Like Jonah begging off the warning to Nineveh. Like Jeremiah pleading ineptitude at his call to prophesy.

I would have done better if I had gone to law school.

"What were your words, can we recall?" I nudged this grim spirit. "You want me to help you to 'seek justice'? To 'guide' you in determining who is responsible for the destruction of . . . of . . . whatever is about to be destroyed?"

"That would be the world as you know it," the Spectre said as we touched down on the sidewalk below the tramway that traced the course of the Outerborough Bridge.

"Define your terms," I persisted. "What world? Worlds die all the time. Lives end. Hopes perish. Dreams crash and burn. Yet your very existence is a testament of hope. A declaration that God hears prayer, that the spirit is eternal. You're an angel. That makes you a messenger of hope. Where's my hope, Spectre?"

"At no time did I promise you hope."

Around us the city milled. Pedestrians passed through our incorporeal forms. Above us the tram emptied of commuters from the Governor's Island housing development and filled with shoppers on their way to the big mall on that little island in the river. The occasional flying person ambled through the edges of the sky. Buildings loomed. Traffic snarled. It seemed a usual day, unsullied by the insult to the biosphere or by what the Spectre so quaintly referred to as the impending "end of the world."

"A greater power sent you," I said. "Your very existence is testimony to the viability of faith. Yet all you have to tell me is that those who could save us, won't?"

I paused, but not for effect. Were I corporeal, I certainly would have needed to catch a breath, and I paused because habit told me I needed to do so.

"Then it is my judgment," I said, "that the guilty is he who denies hope. Punish yourself and the horse you came in on."

"Horse?"

"But first be so kind as to return me to my life, please."

The angel drew himself up to an imposing height and stood over me and said, "That is not an answer."

"That is rather not the answer you solicit," I said. "If your preconceptions rule you, then you have no need for me. My life, please. I understand that I have affairs to get in order."

"What are you, man?"

"I have no idea," I snapped. I was on a roll now. "You're the one with the eternal truths, aren't you? But I do know a few things that I'm not. I'm not a pushover. I'm not a slave. I'm not an angel encumbered with divine imperatives. I'm not some Dickensian clown you can intimidate with Victorian guilt. And I'm not biting. Home, please. I quit."

"You cannot quit," he whispered. "Do you have a mission assigned you by the Author of Creation? Have you stood face to face with God in the inmost chamber of the continuum? Have you been told by the Lord of the Universe what is expected of you?"

And I remembered the seeking of my youth. And I remembered the exultation and then the wave of sudden peace enveloping me when I chose my vocation. And I remembered to whom I answered when I sat in my house and when I walked and when I lay down and when I rose. And I thought of the still, small voice I heard from before I myself could talk and continued to hear; the voice that came from my head or my heart or from somewhere untouchable in my being. And I answered:

"Yes . . .

". . . I . . .

". . . have."

I had not felt so alive since my Ellen had stood at my side to remind me.

CHAPTER 8
Portents and Imperatives

The Spectre, enormous and imposing, slowly faded from my line of sight even as I regained my own physical form right there on the sidewalk in front of a hundred drivers and passengers and passersby. If anyone noticed my rematerialization, the only indication was that they might have jagged in their path to go around rather than through me. No one registered alarm or even surprise at seeing a little man in a white beard and a navy blue cardigan appear out of thin air. Not much could rattle a Metropolitan.

Here was something that did:

A florid woman in whiteface and the checkered costume of a clown dropped from the superstructure of the streetside tramway station onto the roof of the tram as it pulled out toward the bridge. Throwing her head up at the sky, she called out, in as shrill and loud a voice as I had ever heard, apparently at a monstrous many-jointed robot that descended toward her from somewhere above a cloud.

Before the robot could fall to light on the roof of the tram by her side, all hell broke through the nervous calm of the city afternoon.

I learned later that the woman called herself "the Joker's

Daughter," though she was no relation to that deluded clown who'd died on a Metropolis street almost ten years before. The robot was named N-I-L-8—a play on words when you say it out loud—and responded to the voice commands of those who knew the code. And out from below and behind them—from inside the cable car itself, I supposed—climbed a third figure: a man in heavy boots and a cowl and an armored gray chest-plate with a kind of shield over it that said, in red block letters on a field of yellow, FAIR PLAY. I learned his name later on, too. He called himself "Mr. Terrific."

The three of them, woman, man, and robot, faced down four opponents—Thunder, Swastika, Trix, and Manotaur—who seemed to materialize out of nowhere and then crouched on the bridge plying their powers. I was as acutely aware of the play-by-play of this rumble as I had been of the one in the street days earlier, the one that had begun with the tumbling of the metro bus, and for the same reason. I was in imminent danger here. No sooner had I dismissed the Spectre and his proposal out of hand than I found myself in this life-threatening situation. So I studied these terribly powerful children, studied their every move. It seemed to me, for example, that I'd seen the man-bull—Manotaur—and the biomechanical morphing person—Trix—in that very same rumble in the street, but whereas they'd fought against one another previously, they contended on the same side this time. I should not even have noted it as something odd; it was not. This was a game to them, these children who played fast-and-loose with our lives.

Trix, Swastika, and Manotaur's "powers," at that moment, appeared to consist of being able to hold and fire large automatic weapons. That seemed to be precisely what the Joker's Daughter, Mr. Terrific, and even the robot N-I-L-8 were doing, just shooting. To be fair, the ordnance N-I-L-8 possessed was actually built into the machine, and was thus quite a bit bigger and heavier than that of any of the others. No one but those of us on the ground and the footpath of the Outerborough Bridge seemed to mind, and certainly we did not count. Only Thunder, the young African-American child—he could not have been older than twelve, I judged—was using anything resembling a "superpower." He shot tendrils of static electricity, stylized lightning bolts, from his hands.

I wondered what actually constituted a "superpower" these days. Was it merely, as this sociopath Swastika illustrated, the ability to deform your body and engage in spontaneous public warfare? Swastika's "superpower" appeared to consist of the willingness to undergo a full-body tattoo. That is, his entire body was tattooed that dull blue graphite color, except for the bare flesh that formed the shape of a swastika in its negative space. Was his superpower his ability to withstand the pain that this process involved? Or was it his ignorance of history? Surely, somewhere along the line of his short life, this young man had taken a genetic test—you could buy them in drugstores—and upon seeing the blue color generated by the little yellow stick, he'd determined that he was one of the one-in-seven who had the metagene. So he had manufactured an identity for himself and dubbed himself superpowered. Still, these "heroes" never seemed to get hurt, even in this deadly game, even when it appeared they meant to hurt each other.

Surely the metagene imparts to its possessor a measure of initiative and ability, even when it does not manifest any "powers" per se. Would that it imparted sensibility as often.

I was in the line of fire between Joker's Daughter on the roof of the tram and Trix hanging from a cable of the bridge. I dropped flat on the surface of the bridge, quivering with the knowledge that suddenly I was again sufficiently corporeal to die. I rolled where I could and crept like an inchworm where I had to, to get as far from the danger as possible. That was not very far. The weapons fire went on for what seemed days. Playing it back in my mind, I realized it could not have lasted longer than thirty seconds. The tram cable kept moving, and through the rumble it traveled only from several yards outside its station to the edge of the bridge itself: a distance equiv-

alent to crossing a wide street. It was time enough for mothers
to yank their children to what appeared to be safety behind
stopped cars or under cover of bridge pillars. It was time
enough for the gunfire itself to be drowned in the screaming
of terrified motorists and pedestrians. It was time enough for
a disaster to strike out at the dozens of folks innocently riding
home, encased in the see-through peapod of the cable car.

Either through the contrivance of those firing at the
woman and the man riding the roof of the tram, or just from
the weight of the robot N-I-L-8, who covered their passage
with weapons fire, the cable guiding the tram frayed and
unwove. Its track snapped. The car full of people slid off its
groove, and the dozens of helpless souls within were caught
like a panicky herd of cattle trapped in a sudden roll of lava.
There was a bullet hole in the window of the tram, and I could
see that at least one person inside, a young bearded man in his
thirties, was injured and bloody. As one, the passengers
creased back their lips to object with their howls of despair.

I was on the walking path leading to the bridge. There
were others around me, along with a railing on either side.
There was no getting away from this spot as broken cable
snaked by my face on its way to the river below. The listing
tram pointed in my direction to begin its fall.

"We don't need judgment," I hollered at no one in particular as disaster reared up from the lapping river below. "We
need hope!" I screamed at whoever, unseen, could have been
listening. If the Spectre, invisible to me now, was truly gone,
and my weak voice was lost among the rumble of this scene,
then surely God heard. But did He care?

For a moment my head reeled. I saw the vision again, the
smoky angel plunging through red licks of flame. That was
what Wesley had seen and what I was seeing. The destruction
of Kansas was just the beginning of the end. Those who called
themselves heroes shared a silent guilt. I looked and saw how
they dealt with it: worse than before. Not out of boredom did
they act; rather, they acted with abandon. "And the third part

of the trees was burnt up and all green grass was burnt up and the sun and the air were darkened."

I realized I was speaking aloud. Then I shook it off, and it was gone.

Without warning, a streak of primary-colored light whispered along the edges of our sight. This was no illusion. This was real.

There was a wind. But it was not a wind. It was a blur of motion that creased the air. And when the blur passed, it left behind twisted and broken weapons and startled combatants. Now the tram full of people tumbled end over end toward me still.

And a whirlpool rose from the river below, chasing the disaster that had preceded it. It was a twister of water that bent sideways from below our feet to angle around the bridge, then upward toward the sky. It caught the falling tram on a pillow of roiling liquid and deposited it—not softly, but no more roughly than the good landing of a plane—on a suddenly cleared portion of the bridge only yards from where I stood.

The folks in the tram settled in their places and the whirlpool receded back onto the river, and the doors of the vehicle slid open to let the riders, rattled but intact, step out to safety. Those who'd brought about this furor, whose abandon would casually snuff who knows how many lives, gathered their wits and the remaining pieces of their ordnance and looked around with caution bordering on terror. Where would it materialize? Would they ever see its face before it brushed by them again?

We all knew. Those who'd grown up here, and those who'd adopted this city, did so knowing that such things once happened here with regularity and might happen again one day.

He changed the course of a mighty river. He bent steel in his bare hands.

Many of us, empowered by the vacuum that despair suddenly left behind, rushed to help the tram riders, some of them grinning widely and bleeding here and there at the same time.

Even before the bystanders freed themselves of the cable car, they knew. We all knew, and we remembered.

"Look!" someone said.

"Up in the sky!" someone else said, louder this time.

"It's a bird!" It was not a bird.

"It's a plane!" It was a song, a chorus, a refrain grown more beloved for its absence during these years.

Floating stately from above came the Man of Steel. The Last Son of Krypton. The Eternal Hero. The Man of Tomorrow. The hope, at last. The never-ending battle had a champion again.

"It's Superman!"

He held the dismembered slag of N-I-L-8, the combat robot, in one hand, and dangling from the other by their respective trousers were the clown woman and the FAIR PLAY man whose artifice had invited the chaos of this day. Superman opened both hands, and his burdens fell ungracefully to the surface of the bridge as he hovered there still.

He looked great. No more white beard, and his hair was short and gray against the nape of his neck. The uniform was as of old, but the emblem was a little simpler, the red now a slash of an S against a pentagonal field of black rather than gold. Gold was the color of the rival whose intrigues and disasters had soured him on this city once upon a time. Was it the darkness of his visage that had moved him to alter the emblem, or was it simply a desire to repudiate his presumed successor? Magog, the golden prince, was the one who'd brought the disaster that brought Superman back to us.

. . . brought Superman back to us.

He had not turned his back on us forever, after all. He'd reversed himself, and so could I. There he stood in the sky, faith rewarded.

But the imperatives of my unconscious mind gripped my voice and sight again.

I looked up at him and, in a vision the likes of which I had not suffered since the Spectre pulled me out of church to press our doleful journey, I saw him screaming through the red licks of flame. I saw Superman, in the sky and in the future at the same time. Here, above the heads of those he'd saved, he was grim and potent. There, in my vision, in the same place, he mourned all he ever held close. He mourned at the top of his lungs and the limits of his moral strength. The smoky figure of my crimson vision suffered in fire, in physical pain, in blinding heat and of woeful countenance. The threat of Armageddon was alive. It had just begun.

Dear God, I thought, you have sent your true angel back to us to bring us peace, but you decree that this is destined to bring only loss.

Dear God, you and I must talk.

CHAPTER 9
Prayer

God stopped talking to people, by my reckoning, between twenty-two and twenty-five hundred years ago, during the heyday of the Hebrew prophets. Humankind, though they could not have known it at the time, would embark on a new phase.

Here is the difference between men and angels: Angels know everything and can do nothing about it; men know nothing and can do whatever they want. Absolute certainty about anything is anathema to the human condition; free will is unknown to the angelic.

Jeremiah was one of the last prophets of whom we know who actually had conversations—arguments sometimes— with God. The first one came when Jeremiah was just twenty-one years old. Jeremiah tried to convince God that he was too young and callow for the burden of prophecy. And God said that He had known Jeremiah since before he was a glimmer in his parents' eyes, that God had grown and fashioned Jeremiah to this mission the way an artist fits a shape to its landscape. I do not know of an instance when Jeremiah won an argument with God, but I suspect that the experience of verbal combat with His creations was one that the Deity did not relish. The prospect of losing the debate—especially given God's plans, at the time, for the human race—loomed.

Maybe He does talk to us once in a while. People say they hear from Him, and we dismiss them as deluded or we ascribe ill intentions to them for saying so. Maybe on a rare occasion He does say something here and there, but because of the rarity we cannot be sure, even if He does, and perhaps that is the point.

If we knew for a certainty that God was looking down over our shoulder, how could we be other than perfect? How could we make decisions, moment to moment, on grounds other than that they were right to make? How could we decide to be good if such a decision were foregone? And how would we know whether we were doing good for the light within us or out of respect and fear for the Light peering over our shoulder? How could we grow?

We would all be doomed to be angels.

If God were to come down and say, in that stentorian voice of my imagination, "Norman McCay!" I think that alone would make my day. Even if He had no more to say than that, I would be delighted. Even if He said it in a squeaky off-key voice. In a cracking adolescent voice. I could go with that for a while. I still would be unsure, even self-doubting, the way I was when Wesley's visions first began to assault my sensibilities. But if God were to talk to me, and I could know it was He, I would willingly, happily go mad for the remainder of my days and wish them to be long.

Meanwhile, I must content myself with our ongoing one-way conversation.

Ω   Ω   Ω

"I'm very angry with You, You know. Of course You know.

"I apologize for being angry. Which is not to say I'm not angry still; I am. But I apologize for being angry, and when I stop, if I stop, I'll probably apologize for having been angry.

I know it isn't a healthy or productive emotion. I have come, over the years, to look upon health and productivity as admirable things and always supposed You did as well.

"Then there came the imminent end of the world—whatever that means—and we stopped talking for a little while. That is, I stopped talking. I stopped talking when You took Ellen, but I started again soon. I stopped talking when I was a kid and my little dog ran off to do whatever it was You wanted her to do instead of make my life fuller, and I started again after a while. Now I'm talking again and I hope You've noticed. This doesn't mean I think things are any better; they're not. I just didn't want the world to end while we weren't on speaking terms, so this is only on a contingency basis. I hope You've noticed anyway.

"Listen: I'd appreciate it if the world didn't end. I know it's a stretch to change Your plans. All the retooling and rethinking and paperwork. Well, maybe You don't do paperwork, but there must be something like paperwork involved or else You wouldn't plan in such long terms.

"Your lackey the Spectre told me that the course is set and it's just a question of placing blame, and all I've got to do is figure out whose fault it is and let him take care of the rest. He was unclear, by the way, whether it was You or he who decided this would be my job. I'm not sure how closely You micromanage his performance. Don't get me wrong, I do appreciate the fact that You—or even he—saw fit to make me a part of all this. I still wonder why me, but I won't quibble.

"What I wonder, and I don't expect You to tell me now, especially while I'm still a little angry—make that really angry, since I can't see a reason yet to be less angry than I was when I first heard about all this stuff—what I wonder is whether You could see Your way clear to give me a little more flexibility here. The way You did for Ishmael's mother.

"You remember Ishmael's mom, Hagar, right? To appease his jealous wife, Abraham sent Hagar and little Ishmael into the desert to fend for themselves. To die, it seemed. And at some point when things looked bleakest, You opened her eyes so she could see a well full of water. I read that carefully, and found it was worded very precisely. You didn't plant a well there or crack a rock open to create a spring, or say, 'Let there be water,' and there was water. You caused her to see, is all the book says.

"No retooling. No rethinking. Probably a minimum of paperwork; maybe just a requisition form or something.

"What I'm asking You to do, if You would, is—when the time comes—just to open my eyes. Okay? No big miracles. No abrogation of Your laws of physics or chemistry. Just if there's a way through it—the narrowest way through it—and nobody else sees it or thinks to go there, just open my eyes. Give me the sight. Give me the magic words. Give me the desperation, whatever it takes. Just open my eyes. Please.

"I know I said I was angry with You, and I probably am, but I love You.

"And Ellen, too, she should know.

"Amen."

Ω Ω Ω

I was sitting in the church. It was dark. There was no heat on. I was in the front pew facing the altar, and, for all I knew, no one had set foot in this place since I left with the Spectre, however long ago that was.

Huddled in my sweater and hunched over in my seat, I finished my prayer, such as it was, unloaded my head from my right hand, and opened my eyes as I rose to my feet.

"I am told to ask you again to accompany me," the voice from the back of the room said as softly as such a voice could say anything.

The tall white figure wrapped in the green cloak and hood stood slightly bent at the shoulders. Was that humility I saw in his stance? No, Norman, I told myself, don't ascribe human habits to the divine—or even to the minor functionaries of the divine.

"I have reconsidered my decision, yes," I said.

I walked purposefully up the aisle and, like Scrooge accommodating the Ghost of Christmas Yet to Come, grabbed up a swatch of that thick robe in my hand. It felt like the curtain of the Aurora must have felt.

"Let's go," I said, and we were off.

CHAPTER 10

Seven Angels

"Where have you taken me? I no longer have any sense of time or place."

"Time has little meaning where we walk, Norman McCay. We move freely from moment to moment. Guided by your visions I show you only that which we must see. You are disoriented?"

"Enormously. I wasn't really asleep, but I saw the man in the flag and the eagle rising in the sky. I was dreaming again."

"Were you?"

Ω Ω Ω

"America's not as big as it used to be," the man in the red-white-and-blue paraphernalia hollered from the crown of the Statue that symbolized liberty to the world. "For Heaven's sake, Kansas is gone."

The big blue-vested caricature of a man with the golden eagle collar and mask called himself the Americommando. He declaimed from two hundred feet over the heads of the huddled masses assembled on the little island in the harbor. To either side of him stood the colorfully costumed, heavily armed figures of his handful of allies, those he called his Minutemen. He spoke of himself in the third person.

"For long years the Americommando and his Minutemen have protected these shores from the threat of foreign powers. In our zeal, we have overlooked the most insidious foreign threat of all."

Until not long ago, the United Nations had stood in its great vaulted complex in New York City. But given the clandestine terrorism in those days, both from within and without, the danger there came to be too great. Years ago there had been a great explosion at the UN when someone—no one ever had figured out who, though it was probably someone who'd died that day as well—had driven a rented station wagon off an elevated sidewalk through a hurricane fence and smashed the car nose-first onto an ill-patrolled courtyard. Windows had flown from the surrounding buildings and walls had cracked, killing and maiming people. The New United Nations headquarters was a fortified complex on the east side of the fabled city of Metropolis where, at the time the international community had chosen the site, superhuman heroes used to keep their home safe. Now the threat was no longer clandestine; it came plunging through the skies in colorful costumes.

The Americommando vaulted the rail of that weathered crown, tumbling downward toward the crowd.

The Statue, the gift of a foreign ally, had deteriorated to a shadow of her former self. The tines of her crown were broken and ragged. A hole gaped through the penny-thin copper of her chest. The old hairline fracture of her right arm now collected tributaries that looked like swollen capillaries. The sheet metal walls of her relatively new torch were riddled with pinholes, and at night the light glared through in blinding specks. Impact dents and handprints punctuated all of her features. She was first a convenient meeting point for superhuman business, and then a frequent flashpoint for rumbles. Scaffolding for repairs reached only to her waistline and toppled with regularity. It was a wonder that this sacred lady was recognizable at all these days.

In light of this little harbor island's diminished status as a tourist destination, President Capper had the admirable idea of organizing an immigration checkpoint in the Statue's base: a barracks in Metropolis Harbor for East Coast immigrants, to function the way Ellis Island once had done. She appointed a new Undersecretary of the Interior to retool the facility, and the project grew into an ambitious ongoing plan to restore the neglected historical sites and national monuments all over the country.

On this day, at the foot of the Statue, masses of would-be Americans teemed, yearning to breathe free. They were of every hue from ebony to sun-sheltered pale. They wore all manner of clothing that any of them might have considered suitable for a long sea or air journey and still consistent with a respectful appearance at the desk of a Department of the Interior intake official. All of them lost and caught again a breath and a heartbeat when first they saw the embattled lady who loomed over the harbor. In her latest guise of a tempest-tossed ancient ruin, she still imposed.

There were too many of them, it is true. Always there were more of them than anyone expected. As a boy I'd learned that in the enormous wave of immigration from 1850 to 1920, the number of people annually seeking a nesting place in the American family topped a million for a few years. I recall a seventh-grade social studies teacher laughing, saying that certainly we could never reach such a figure again. Before my middle age, a new tide brought twice that many every year as a matter of course. Through feast and famine, through peace and war, through serenity and dislocation, through the wiping away and redefinition and abandonment and substitution of one structure of values and politics and sociology after another, they came. Sometimes they said it was for religious freedom. Sometimes for political asylum. Sometimes for economic opportunity. Sometimes just for safety. Lately, with the demise of governments across the globe, they'd come less to avoid the excesses of their rulers than to evade the ineffectiveness of those rulers. The only reason they ever really came was the reason my great-grandfather had given to his son— my grandfather—the first McCay of our line to be born an American: for a home where their daughters and sons could feel free to stay, no more and no less.

In this most unlikely of American moments, these hopeful antecedents crammed waist-to-elbow around the pedestal from whose heights this sacred lady had greeted each sunrise for a century and a half. And a madman, wrapped in nativist misapprehension and wielding an automatic weapon, hurtled into their orderly spiraling line.

"Today the Americommando declares war on the wretched refuse!" he declared as his star-festooned jackboots hit a cleared patch of premium ground and made it shudder. "We can't house you now. We can't feed you now. Still, you force yourselves upon us."

Dozens of the refugees—some because they could understand English, and others because they had seen the body language of tyrants and killers before—took his words as a cue to pitch themselves and their children into the harbor in desperate search of sanctuary.

"At the command of the Braintrust," the Americommando ordered, "my Minutemen will cleanse America's shores."

And at a hidden signal, one presumes from whatever "Braintrust" to which the maniac referred, the others on the crown leapt over its parapets and opened fire, along with their leader below, on the crowd at the Statue's base.

It got worse.

Out of the southern sky came flashes of light and pellets of flaming energy and an amplified voice:

"The defense of these shores is our responsibility, Americommando! Not yours!"

A trio of paratroopers covered in body suits—one scarlet, one silver, one sapphire—dropped their hokey selves toward the island. They moved stiffly, like automatons, loosing the report of shoulder arms at a rapid clip to intercept and vaporize the fire of the Americommando and his Minutemen.

Nobody on the ground caught any fire at that moment, but the panic into which the crowd flew was vicious. For the most part, I had left off complaining to my companion about the excesses of these problem children or his inaction with regard to them. This example, however, was too appalling.

"They're tearing through a crowd of humanity competing for the privilege of wiping them out," I insisted.

"Yes," the Spectre bothered to say, as impassive as the battered Statue who stood above it all.

"These aren't heroes," I croaked. "They're madmen."

My ghostly companion had responded already to my previous obvious assertion. It seemed he would rather be silent than redundant.

"Look at this. They battle over territory and presumed authority without any care for who gets caught between them."

Nothing came from the Spectre as, with uncaring abandon, the forces of chaos put innocents in the path of a riot on this hallowed ground.

Who knew who all these rumblers were or where they'd come from? Who knew how they heard there was a rumble on the wind? Who knew how they ever knew? Nonetheless, they always came out of the ceramics looking for a fight. This time, through whatever means talk of these things circulated within the metahuman community, the word had gotten out to the Old Guard as well.

"Someone should do something!" The words trumpeted from my mouth as from Gabriel's horn.

Quietly the Spectre deigned to answer: "Indeed."

And with a ripple in the space above us and a shudder in the history around us, seven graying titans of old descended from the sky.

Superman floated toward the fray, slowly enough so that even the nearly sightless could discern that unmistakable figure as he flashed beams of heat from his eyes to divert danger from the innocent.

Wonder Woman, ageless for all her years, rode the currents of the air in a decaying orbit to the shoreline.

Green Lantern, in a strapless mask framed by thin white hair, wore armor and a green flapping cape and held a great emerald lance before him like a trapeze artist balancing down the air. It glowed almost golden in the sun.

Hawkman, with his spear and ancient mace, braced against the thermals and crowed his battle cry.

Power Woman, ever imposing and hot of blood, rode feet-first into the chaos.

The Ray traveled beams of light from the sun, gathering energy to himself to expel surgically in imposition of order.

The Flash, the Fastest Man Alive, blinking in and out of temporal perception, navigated simultaneously through multiple planes and dimensions of reality, holding himself in check to coordinate his entrance with those of his colleagues.

Superman was returned, and thus he drew from seclusion the titans of yesteryear, their emerald flashes and scarlet strobes lighting the darkness of the day. The conflict ended before they reached the ground.

Through whatever arcane means, the Spectre opened my perceptions to all the corners of this little island, its skies, its buildings, the intentions of its occupants, its accosters, and its defenders. I felt the minds and souls of those on and above the island. And the mind and soul that overburned all the others belonged to Superman. He arced through the sky in a sharp descending curve directly to intersect the Americommando. The Man of Steel extended both arms as he approached . . .

. . . and whisked by him—never even touching him—with such speed and mass that the sweep of air and its friction tore off the maniac's breastplate and mask and twisted his face into paroxysms of pain like the face of a pilot-in-training spinning in a runaway centrifuge. Americommando's weapon fell in shattered pieces of metal to the ground and his armor clattered about him.

Green Lantern and Power Woman went after the innocent victims of the fear that these invaders had engendered. The seven thundering angels arrived before there was any inflicted bloodshed but there were dozens of people in the harbor, fighting to keep afloat in waters as wild as the open sea. The Lantern flew with a green glowing lance in his hands, and I saw then that it was a perpetual manifestation of his power. It was not so much a weapon as a symbol, like the emblem on his chest of the battery—the lantern—from which he derived his power. As he held out his right hand the lance became an extension of his arm, its hilt extended straight and its tip a lengthening beam of light. The beam came down, a green cascade, and widened into the shape of a shovel that scooped up a dozen or more frightened innocents out of the breakwater. If anything, they were more frightened at rising through the air on a platform whose floor now dropped into the shape of a bowl and in which there appeared little holes like those of a colander, draining water. They were scared, but safe.

Power Woman, more direct by nature, blew along the coast, snatching up panicky prospective immigrants three or four at a time by the collars or the waist or whatever dangling article of clothing was handy, and depositing them a few yards back inland as softly as practical—which did not turn out to be very softly at all.

Still up in the sky the Flash, or rather the approximation of the Flash whose scant remaining three-dimensional image flickered in and out of phase, waved his arms and legs in concentric circles as he descended. This sent violent eddies of air outward in the direction of the three hokey scarlet-, silver-, and sapphire-jumpsuited hang gliders. Their weapons spun out of their grasp. Their trajectories spun out of control. Their artificial perceptions spun into the world of dreams, where the authorities would be kinder to them than they would be in the real world.

Wonder Woman's eyes lit with the glow of a predator's as she unloaded her Amazon fury on the Minutemen. A bullet flew and a silver bracelet diverted it up at the sky and into the water. And the shooter felt her fist across his cracking jaw before the lovely image of the savage warrior could register on his eyes. Beside him, a cohort in a helmet and coverall and white stars like those of a flag hiding his eyes had a gas mask attachment over his mouth. The mask was color-coordinated, to match the silver-gray of the rest of his costume. These fellows all were inordinately conscious of fashion, it seemed to me. The one in silver-gray turned toward his fallen friend to see, instead, the Amazon still dropping the last few inches from the sky. He raised a long-snouted weapon that was connected to a small gas tank—silver-gray color-coordinated— slung over his shoulder. Before he could raise the snout, before Wonder Woman was even flat-footed on the ground, the gas mask was embedded in his mouth, and he was rolling on the trampled grass before he realized he had four incisors to replace.

Hawkman came screaming, screeching from the clouds with wings spread just enough to catch some of the air and cushion his dive. He held a spear in one hand and waved an ancient mace in the other. I had no idea where he got these weapons, but whenever I saw him he held something that seemed centuries old. But almost on the ground, he flung his spear out to the right to catch one of the Americommando's Minutemen and send him headfirst into a piling at the Statue's pedestal. He hurled the mace out to the left, its chain pulling it up in a parabola on the air. The weight wove among several unwary innocents. It caught another of the henchmen on the underside of an arm. Now the beam of a ray weapon diverted from the crowd to the already cracked right arm of the Statue herself. He lowered his wings hard as he approached the ground and brought himself to a soft landing. And the wind from the rush of wings bowled over dozens of bystanders, whose tumbling chain reaction threw the last of the

Minutemen off his feet and under a pileup of the members of a family of Persian refugees.

The Ray batted cleanup. He simply flew over the crowd taking out insurgents. He wafted back and forth over the island in his jagged golden suit, and when he saw a threatening-looking crackpot in a costume—or in something that used to be a costume—beginning to stir on the ground, he extended his fisted hands downward, and what looked to be a deadly bolt of golden power shot down at the suddenly hapless villain's head. The first time he did it I thought it must be with murderous force. But in each case, the would-be aggressor simply let his head tumble back and lay down gently to surrender his consciousness for the foreseeable future.

Then there were others, like the "Braintrust" that the Americommando had cited as he hollered his way down the Statue. Did they have the metahuman gene or not? I do not know, but they were a pair of little cyberheads hiding out in the crown of the Statue. I found them in my mind's eye as the Spectre expanded it, moments before their defeat. They looked to be an identical pair of developmentally retarded physical specimens, living in elaborate exoskeletons. Their oversized brains were wired to special communications equipment inside the metallic suits to which they were connected like turtles to their shells. It was they who'd coordinated the attack of the Americommando and the Minutemen, and they might have succeeded if they had managed to develop their heightened mental powers to a mature level. They had not seen the need. When the sky began to fall on the Minutemen and their rivals, the Braintrust went into a panic. When I came upon them they were fussing with one button and dial after another on the little consoles built into their arms, and on the internal controls of their exoskeletons, all to no avail. They were still fussing when a man in a black hood with an acrobat's build poked his way through the stairs and into their secret room in the Statue's crown. He wore an old red jerkin on his chest, boots, and tights, and sported a beltful of little chemical gadgets for which he had no need at the moment. It was Robin, the boy who'd once tumbled through the sky over Gotham City at the side of the Batman. He called himself Red Robin now, and wore what he fancied to be the true mantle of the Batman. I knew that. I have no idea how I knew that, but I did. Maybe the Spectre let me know it. Maybe it was the taste of angelic powers that I perceived only later that told me. But I knew this man, if only by reputation.

He emerged in the room holding a small radiation detector with which he'd found these two intrusive little overminds of the Braintrust. He came in the door, looked up at the two of them with their enlarged, hairless skulls and their soft bones. Red Robin looked partly revolted and partly sad at what he had to do. Then a blue flurry of static charges passed sound-lessly between the two creatures' skulls, and Red Robin moved quickly, going backward to the ground on both arms. He caught on the floor, kicking up both feet. One connected with the gut of the first, and the other with the metal-encased receding chin of the second. Both of his enemies dropped.

The acrobat stood over the suddenly vanquished pair and mused. He looked at these aberrations and grew sick to his stomach, then bit the feeling back. Where had this man come from, I wondered, and then somehow I knew. He had been here already, among the immigrants. He'd had a tip from a source that something would happen on the island today, and he'd contacted three friends to help him put down the crime. Of the four who'd waited here for the Americommando to make his move, only Red Robin had moved quickly enough to contribute to the effort. The other three were there on the ground below, as dazzled and inspired as I and everyone else. Suddenly, up in the sky, seven angels were sounding their trumpets, and the music was sweet.

Already, Superman's reemergence was prompting the ini-tiative of those who once had contended at his side or in his shadow.

As the flurry of activity ended—even before some here

knew that anyone had averted disaster—a great chunk of copper slag rose past Red Robin's line of vision. It was the shattered arm of the Statue, now caught in the loop of a golden lasso and climbing. Holding the lasso, hoisting it far in the sky, was Wonder Woman. Below her flew a red-and-blue figure, to fix it in place.

"Hi, Kal," Red Robin said through the thick glass of the crown's windows, in a tone as though the hero were standing next to him.

Superman looked in Robin's direction, and finally a smile lit his face as he nodded and continued to rise in the sky.

With the heat of his eyes and the pressure of his hands he welded and molded the arm and the torch back in place, in better shape now than they'd been earlier in the day. The Statue was still badly disfigured, though. Diana looked up, smiling, as the Kryptonian finished the job, and wondered how she could make sure someone completed the overhaul of Freedom's Lady. I got the impression she was wondering whether she could get Kal-El to help her do it later on. Little bolts of intuition were beginning to drop into my mind—vivid and clear as the visions that had assaulted me in weeks past. It was a good thought, I told Wonder Woman in my mind.

$$\Omega \quad \Omega \quad \Omega$$

"That was very good, Kal," the Princess whispered at the air so only he could hear.

He lowered himself to join the others, puzzled as his eyes draped over Wonder Woman and moved on. He would not realize until she told him some time later that she was referring to the housekeeping he'd done with the Lady's torch.

"Great to see you again, Dick," Superman said, and for a moment he grasped Red Robin's hand. "Can you join us uptown?"

"Seem to have a hole in my schedule," the man in the black hood and red jerkin said, smiling.

I found something in this exchange among old colleagues unsettling, as though these were matters reserved for the very great, among whom I was eavesdropping.

"Mary." Superman allowed a wide grin at the approach of Lady Marvel from the sky. They hugged warmly when she landed. "Can you join us?"

"Of course."

He clapped the Golden Guardian on an armored shoulder. "You too?"

Only a nod from the Guardian, but a certain one.

Superman turned from his splendid company to face the gathering cloud of grateful immigrants, law enforcement professionals, federal officials, the odd journalist or two. Helicopters, more journalists inside, began to breast the horizon to the east and west.

Crowd sounds punctuated the air:

". . . haven't seen them in years . . ."

". . . looks older . . ."

". . . looks great . . ."

". . . really them . . . ?"

". . . really him . . . ?"

". . . story of the century . . ."

"I wonder," Superman began. No one else said anything. What would he say? Why did they all return now? "I wonder," he said, "if all of you would pass the word that we'll be at the New United Nations in—what?"

He turned to the other costumed folks behind him. Wonder Woman shrugged.

"Ollie Queen, is that you?" He pointed at a tall, white-bearded bald figure among the crowd.

The Kryptonian hopped down in front of the man, seemed about to give him a bear hug, but the tall man put up two hands to ward him off.

"Coming with us?" Superman wanted to know. "Can we give you a lift?"

"I think I'll beg off this ride, Supes," Queen said to a perplexed Superman. "Just here to enjoy the Statue," and he receded among the onlookers.

This man in the simple costume of blue and red wore his leadership and greatness as easily as he wore his hair. If the hundreds of onlookers had not been so flabbergasted to be in his presence, some of them might have noticed the comparable helping of love and awe that the colleagues who stood at his side measured out for him as well. He was beyond shrugging off such a phenomenon; he no longer noticed it.

To the bedazzled crowd again: "We'll all be at the United Nations in a few minutes."

Then Superman lifted slowly off the ground. Nine more took to the air behind him, in formation like birds heading home.

Sitting with his legs crossed among a group of Indonesian immigrants craning their necks and pressing against each other for a view, Oliver Queen tapped a flesh-colored collar strap under his shirt and said, "You hear me?"

"The question is, does he hear you?" came a voice from the tiny plug in his ear.

"I'm shielded by a wall of huddled masses. If he wants to hear me, though, I suppose he hears me."

"How does it look?" the voice asked Queen.

"Like a blasted coronation. Turn on your tube and watch. We're going to have to step up our schedule."

"We can do that," the voice in Ollie Queen's ear said, and went dead.

As Superman and his growing company of thundering angels passed overhead, at least a hundred earthbound folks in lower Metropolis called: "Look! Up in the sky!"

Ω   Ω   Ω

The New United Nations fortress stood aside the river, fifteen minutes' walking distance downtown of the Outerborough Bridge where—was it a moment or was it a thousand years ago?—I had begged off the Spectre's mission. The New United Nations complex was a lot like the old destroyed one except for the original's architectural grace. The replacement made up for that with exterior walls reinforced like those of the containment dome of a nuclear power plant, and with pass-and-checkpoint armed security that made the Pentagon look like a tourist trap.

Already, the original company of seven angels was growing.

As they approached from the sky, one nervous guard on the roof of the General Assembly building raised his weapon. Then it grew red and heated up in his hands, so he dropped it from his white-hot padded gauntlets. Furiously he blew on his suddenly blistered palms. The weapon melted into a pile of slag on the roof. The other guards did not raise their weapons as they saw who led the approach.

"Holy crap," one of them said, and dropped his weapon, too, though its temperature was unchanged.

The crowd that milled along the river drive outside the fortress barricades was already large. Sound trucks parked and hovered in the air along the street. Journalists from all over the city asked everyone they could stop—mostly one another, as it turned out—what to make of the second coming of Superman.

". . . making a statement . . ."

". . . think they'll take questions . . ."

". . . got any ideas? . . ."

". . . shh!"

And then they landed.

It was on the city side of the big Secretariat Building, where a six-foot-high retaining wall served as no-man's-land between the delegates' working campus and the security arrangements that protected them from the world they represented. Superman, Wonder Woman, and their colleagues assembled on the wall so the world could see them. The Kryptonian would wait a minute or two before he looked at the sky, impatient over the time it was taking the security guards to open the gates to allow the reporters onto the grounds. With a few seconds' exposure to intense thin beams of heat, the slats that held the locks began to fall off the gates and the metal doors swung open of their own accord.

Wonder Woman glared.

"They'll just need new locks," he told her. "It's in their budget."

She would have to talk with him about that.

"Good afternoon," he said.

Suddenly even traffic seemed to stop.

"Many of you may remember us," he said. "We have been away for a while. That was our mistake."

There was pain in those great glowing eyes. He was unused to this, I realized. In years past, Superman's occasional impromptu news conferences had conveyed the ease of a seasoned politician, of the biggest star on the street, of a confidence that only your best friend could offer. In those days he'd been one of them, I now knew, a journalist in his mortal guise. No wonder he always had been so at ease with words, with appearances in public.

For so long had he kept his own counsel that now he was restive sharing it with others. He paused a lot. He seemed conscious of the need to make eye contact with the cameras, to keep his pupils visible to these witnesses. His body language was no longer that of a capable journalist, no longer that even of one who has had extensive commerce with humans. I remembered his quiet rebuke, back in his Antarctic wheatfield, of the notion that he belonged anywhere else. "Here things grow," he'd said to Wonder Woman then. Had he seen how, surrounded by growth, he so contracted in on himself in that place?

"In our absence," he continued after a pause that lasted just a moment too long, "a new breed of metahumans has arisen, effectively a separate nation without borders or laws. They have grown into a vast phalanx of self-styled 'heroes,' unwilling to preserve life or to defend the defenseless. Among you . . ."

Another uncomfortable pause, but he regathered it.

"Among us now live a legion of vigilantes who have perverted their great powers, who have forsworn the responsibilities that such power entails. We have returned to . . ."

How to word this, he seemed to wonder.

". . . to teach them the meaning of truth, justice, and the American way. Together we will guide this new breed—our children, our grandchildren, our heirs and successors—with wisdom. And if necessary, we will guide them with force, as a good parent must occasionally force truth or discipline on a child. To this end, we are reconstituting the Justice League and, owing to our burgeoning numbers, applying to this body—to the New United Nations—for recognition as a duly constituted state. We will restore order. Above all . . ."

He looked around as if to make sure everyone was paying attention. There was, however, no question of this.

"Above all," he concluded, "we will make things right again."

He did not move or change the resolute expression he had grown during the past few minutes, but he paused long enough to signal the reporters that he would entertain questions.

"Will there be others?" the Cable News guy called out.

"There already are others," Superman motioned in the direction of Red Robin, Lady Marvel, and the Golden Guardian. "Certainly there will be more."

"Are you prepared to shut down those who don't honor these principles and cooperate?" a man shouted. His microphone had the old *Daily Planet* logo on it.

"We don't anticipate anyone acting without our sanction," Superman answered.

Someone had claimed the *Daily Planet* trademark not long after it had expired a few years before, with no one left to challenge the claim. It was little more than a network of web stations claiming to be a wire service on which the venerable old label now sat, but it was nonetheless particularly jarring to Superman that it was the guy from something that called itself the *Daily Planet* who followed up with: "What about Magog?"

No one said anything. Superman only glared.

The kid found either the nerve or the stupidity to continue, casually, "Superman, are you truly prepared to confront Magog, in light of what has gone before?"

Finally Wonder Woman answered: "Magog is a wanted felon. He will be dealt with."

Somebody said, maybe louder than he meant to say, "Yeah, that's happened before," and certainly Superman heard it. If Wonder Woman caught it, she did not let on.

"We doubt that he will surface of his own accord," she continued. "Given the consequences of his actions in Kansas, that seems unlikely. If he does, we will certainly do what needs to be done."

Then the company of journalists and diplomats and on-lookers erupted in a rude confusion of questions and implied doubts. Who would call Magog to account? Who would be responsible for the destruction? Would there be a solution to the impending famine? Was there anyone not afraid of Magog? What about the growing social problem?

Wonder Woman took the flurry of questions, Superman's reticence, and her other colleagues' silence as a fine opportunity to say, "Thank you. That will be all."

"That's enough," a woman from Netservice News said, turning to her hovercam and its remote operator.

And it was.

Ω   Ω   Ω

Upstairs, in a secluded private study of the Secretariat Building, several senior delegates of an ad hoc committee representing nations on six continents sat while an assistant paged Secretary-General Leonard Wyrmwood.

CHAPTER 11

The Rave

N̲o jolly smiling faces—why am I not surprised?"
Wyrmwood asked. It was a rhetorical question.

Since the reconstitution of the United Nations decades
before, the Secretary-General always had been, by tacit understanding, an American. Wyrmwood was the longest tenured
of these so far, having served during the administrations of two
American Presidents. Eight years before, President King had
appointed him the United States' ambassador-level chief delegate. The rest of the world immediately had taken this as a
signal that he would succeed the old Secretary-General, close
to retiring from a long and distinguished career. Before coming
to the Secretariat, Wyrmwood's predecessor had been
Director-General of the World Health Organization, a professor
of International Relations at Metropolis University, chief of the
American delegations at different times to both the old and New
United Nations, the United States' Secretary of State, best
friend and antiquing buddy of a First Lady, childhood refugee
from both Hitlerian fascism and Stalinist communism, and an
accomplished great-grandmother. Leonard Wyrmwood, by
contrast, had been the junior senator from Montana and spent
four years on the Senate Agriculture Committee. He was a self-

made nursing home mogul who had a growing family far more photogenic than he. Wyrmwood had no idea what he was doing here and, as it happened, a profound and immediate understanding of the worldwide implications of the demise of Kansas. He was also, for better or worse, a canny natural politician.

"There's a fear in this room," I told the Spectre.

We were in the expansive conference room of Secretary-General Wyrmwood, in the Secretariat Building in the complex that composed the New United Nations fortress. The meeting room had leather chairs facing the mahogany table that Wyrmwood had inherited from his predecessor. There was even a view of the river if you got up on a chair close to the vertical-slit windows on the outside wall and managed to look at a downward angle through the six-foot-thick concrete and quadruple-reinforced glass that separated you from it. The previous Secretary-General had decorated one of the walls between the window slits with a full-sized copy of the famous portrait of Wonder Woman by Andy Warhol. Wyrmwood filled the space with a display of testimonial plaques from his career in the Senate and some pictures of Montana.

A dozen or more delegates sat around the room. Some faced the Secretary-General somberly. Others fiddled with their glasses or their clothes. A few stroked their foreheads or their hair or pulled at their ears nervously. No one said very much. They waited for him.

"So Superman's back," Wyrmwood allowed with a smile as he clapped a fist repeatedly on the mahogany to the silent rhythm in his head. "Who here is delighted?"

One white-bearded man from Senegal began to ask, "What do we do when he—"

"Applies for nation status?" Wyrmwood finished the delegate's question. He threw his hands up in the air and laughed. And as far as I know, he never answered.

"Not just fear," my spectral companion said to me, "but a validation of fear."

"You mean they've been afraid all along."

"Would you not be, in their position? Humans have long suspected that they are no longer the captains of human destiny."

"And that is now confirmed," I noted.

The Spectre nodded, and as though he were reading my thoughts—I supposed he was, actually—he perceived that I felt we had no more to learn from these scared, tired people in their bomb shelter on the riverbank.

Ω Ω Ω

The room shimmered away, and now the night sky blanketed another city. From the neo-Gothic architecture and the profusion of ornate ledges and gargoyles, I recognized it as Gotham. High above the city, our forms still as big as the largest buildings below, I heard voices. I did not listen to the words, only their timbre, as we drifted downward to a place far below the ground. The voices were happy, a touch wanton, a little of the whisper in their tone if not in their volume. They were voices that did not want to be heard. I knew somehow that it was from the Batman, the presumptive keeper of this place, that the owners of these voices meant to keep their presence secret. I would know, before I saw the Batman again—and I would see him again—whether the voices had succeeded in their secrecy.

Beneath Gotham was a thick layer of solid bedrock. In the bedrock was a second city, a latticework of bubbly caverns already old when the last march of glaciers had laid down the surface above. A collection of bubbles of gas from when the Earth was young had jammed up together and gotten caught in the formation of the bedrock. Millennia later those gases leached out or combined with other elements and left behind, under the suburbs of Gotham, the endlessly rambling cave that became the home first of the flying mammals who inspired the Batman's standard, and then of the Batman himself.

Another mass of gaseous bubbles had collected and congealed and found a sinecure for some hundreds of thousands of years under the land that became Gotham's Midtown. Eventually the gas had leached out of here as well and left behind a cavern and a narrow passageway to it. It was in a corner of this cavern that the Spectre and I found our noncorporeal selves.

It was a party, of sorts.

It was loud here. There were hundreds of them, maybe a thousand, in one room after another. The place was lousy with bizarrely costumed, multicolored, oddly shaped superhuman types, all showing off their particular talents or enjoying the showing-off of others. A slim young woman with gossamer wings growing from her shoulder blades pranced from ridgeline to stalactite along the distant ceiling, snatching up little bats and swallowing them down. A bartender with a glowing fringe of hair along the back of his head and a T-shirt that said EARTH PRIME SUCKS—whatever that meant—leaned across the bar to a patron in what looked to be a French military coat circa the Napoléonic era. Napoléon flicked a thumb out from his fist like a wick off a flint and lit the cigarette with his thumbtip. A face-masked fellow with long orange Day-Glo hair slid his drink down the bar, complaining that it was watered. The bartender wiggled his fingers until a triangular chemical analysis meter appeared in the glass to show that hydroxide levels were below the redline level. The masked man approached the bartender, waved both hands over the glass angrily, and turned away to vanish into the thumping crowd as the drink, glass, and chemical meter vanished. I was grateful that, in my spirit state, my sense of smell did not register the trace elements of the air.

"Oh, jeez, I'm gonna blow," the muffled voice of a man said. It was a fellow wearing what appeared to be a radiation suit. I heard the phrase "Human Bomb" in my head when I looked at him. "Hold me down! Hold me down!" he said as he leaned toward a young masked man in a leather jacket. He extended a forefinger the way a nasty uncle used to do just before he imposed the vaporous waste of Thanksgiving dinner on the dining room air. Gamely, the kid yanked on the extended finger . . .

. . . and a burst of flame and smoke exploded in his face.

These people did not even like each other much.

Good Lord, I thought, this was a den of iniquity where no minister of the Word belonged. A watering hellhole for the scum of the Earth. The gathering sink of the übermenschen of the pit.

I heard a cackle and finally saw somebody whom I recognized: a skinny, yellow old man with a little sprig of green hair on his head and red furry boas flung over his shoulders. It was the Creeper, that wild-eyed misanthropic wacko from the supervillain-spattered tabloid pages of my youth. Evidently he found the entire scene amusing. It seemed the misanthrope had finally found a home.

"These kids," I told the Spectre, "they're a bunch of little monsters. Beasts. They—" I was about to say that they ought to be wiped off the face of the Earth, and then I remembered my designated job here and worried that he might take me literally.

I hesitated long enough for him to answer: "They will be tamed."

Music blasted from all corners. There was nothing soft or evocative of a ballad, but I appreciated that the tastes of the creatures of this place were a bit retrograde. People accosted each other for personal perks and favors as though it were the Nineteen-Seventies. They danced and moved and wailed as though certainly the world could end at any moment. There was an abandon here I had not seen since working in that street mission in the waning days of the Cold War. Then a cool breeze sliced through this killing heat.

A succession of whispered messages began to replace the cacophonous din. The quiet emanated from a corner and grew through the collective sensibility of these rooms like a rolling wave. These were strange sensations I had, standing with the Spectre in this ghostly form. I could hear and see but could not smell or touch. I could not taste even the tongue in my mouth, but I could sense the swells and contractions of emotion around me as if they were liquids mingling in a great shifting sea. And then as the wave of whispers reached us, I felt a lift of awe and surprise. One by one these revelers witnessed him, each after the other: Superman was walking through the room.

By the time he stood at the bar, only the speaker system made a sound. "Would you turn down the music, please?" he asked the plump man in bow tie and mask behind the bar.

"Excuse me?"

"The music. Please." Superman pointedly indicated the tuner on a shelf high above the man.

As the bartender slowly raised his eyes toward where Superman pointed, he snapped out of his daze, said, "No, I'll do it," and leapt the fifteen or twenty feet up to flick a switch, and then landed lightly behind the bar again, smiling sheepishly. Those were old recordings and hard to find.

"I appreciate that," Superman said, and added, "but the refreshments don't help."

A searing beam of heat sliced from those eyes across the shelves of alcohol and other chemical elixirs behind the bar. Bottles burst. Powders fused. Liquids spilled and boiled away. The old Creeper, grinning nearby, inhaled a big breath from a cloud of something or other that rose from the ruin. The Kryptonian gave him a look through cooling eyes, and the old man lowered his head and exhaled slowly through his mouth.

"Party's over," Superman said softly, and it was. "I've come here with an invitation for you," he continued, "to join the—"

"Oooo! I'm a-scared!" a raspy voice said from behind a chair.

"Shaddup," someone else said, more in the sense of a plea than an order.

"Ain't it past yer bedtime, Gramps?" the first voice said, and its source stood and stepped forward from behind a gathering of large bags of muscle.

"What's the S stand for? Senile?" the loudmouth wanted to know.

"We're try'na hear somethin' here." One of the muscle bags shoved the young man, who shoved back.

"Dincha see the NO SOLICITING sign up the top of the ramp, old man?" The loud fellow was barely if at all out of his teens, unshirted and with a lion-tattooed chest, his head shaved except for a tuft sculpted into letters to read KILLER #1.

"We were having a party here before you dragged that big hokey cape in. Y'know capes're over. History," said the self-proclaimed killer, "like you."

"Will you shut up?"

Exasperated, a muscle bag turned and smashed the offender's face in. The loud young man spent the remainder of the evening draped over the bar.

"Thank you." Superman continued as though uninterrupted. "I am here to extend an invitation to join the Justice League. Willingly. I am, as you know, a founding member of that dormant organization. Its history is vivid and honorable. We are, all of us here, colorful people. Vividness and honor are two qualities that I admire and would suppose all of you do as well." He allowed a slight smile, and many here returned it.

He looked around. Silence. Attentiveness.

"There are nine hundred and seventeen people in this establishment tonight within the sound of my voice. I can identify all of you—nearly all by name and all of you by appearance. Eight hundred and ninety-six of you are in a state of consciousness, capable of listening to and understanding what I say. I suggest you convey this message to your unconscious or otherwise indisposed friends. You may consider this, then, a formal invitation.

"The world—as you may have noticed and as your generally wanton behavior proves—is in bad shape. We have a great deal to do and not a lot of time in which to do it. So be advised: We have rules.

"Heroes behave in a certain way. This isn't it. Those of you who choose of your own volition to join us will be as responsible as you are powerful. You will be as effective as you are capable of being. We are people who do not stand by the blood of a neighbor. We are people who never let a friend go into battle alone.

"The League has no formal roster anymore, no dues, no little membership card. To respond positively to this invitation you need only behave in the prescribed manner. You need only use your initiative and talents for the preservation and quality of life. You need only do what you are able to do, to make a dying world live again. You may join my company or the company of those with whom we work. You may urge others to join and to combat the excesses of our time. You may work to undermine destruction, injury, and death and those who bring these things about. If you want to let us know in a formal sense of your positive response, then find me or other members, and tell us so.

"Those of you who do not join us or who respond negatively will be dealt with.

"Our job is thankless, but we do what needs to be done. Right now, we are humanity's only hope.

"Be heroes."

And he left.

Ω   Ω   Ω

It took them a while to catch their breath.

"Do you think it was really him?" someone said.

"What do you mean, do I think?" someone answered. "Look at all these people. Don't you think if it wasn't really him, somebody in this crowd would've noticed?"

"Yeah. Somebody would've." A pause. "So you think it was really him. Right?"

"Are you in?" someone else asked.

"I feel like I was just asked to be the thirteenth disciple," was the answer. "What do you think?"

"See how he looked?" from someone else.

"Good skin," in answer, "for an old man."

"Sure he has good skin. Look who we're talking about."

"So where'd the lines come from? The little wrinkles."

"From inside."

"Oh. Right."

It went like that. Soon the rooms were abuzz again, though with talk now. They saw the light peer down over their shoulders and they were, most of them, good again.

Ω   Ω   Ω

There was a young woman I had seen before. She was quite beautiful, and once I saw her, so help me, I could not stop staring at her. She was the one with the violet chrome star tiara and bright green eyes. Nightstar was her name, I remembered. Then, for staring at her, it seemed, I suddenly knew things about her I could not have known. Nightstar was her real name, her given name. Nightstar Grayson. I saw the name as if I was reading it. She was, like many of the people here, of partly extraterrestrial stock, but her father was an Earthman. Then I realized he was the one called Red Robin, who'd joined Superman and Wonder Woman's company in the course of the incident at the Statue. Suddenly she had a history and a life, and I knew it. I looked around to see whether I could do this generally or whether it applied only to beautiful exotic young women.

I looked at a terribly unattractive young man with tattoos of the Sign of the Beast—the three 6s of Saint John's *Revelation*—over his body. He had a big black 6 making a loop around each pierced and exposed nipple, and a third over his face with its loop ending on his philtrum. He wore a spiked collar and something that might have been a black leather jacket were it to come around and cover his adorned chest, which it did not, and a little bat-gargoyle epaulet. He had no hair. A single small horn pointed from his skull. His left arm was a cyborg attachment of jointed steel. Though he affected the body language of a rumbler, I wondered how he proposed to keep all of his display hardware in place in a fight. I stared for a moment at him nonetheless, and learned something of him.

He called himself 666, aptly enough, and I realized that I had seen him before. It was on the street during the rumble when I had found the little girl and then her mother and brother in the destroyed bus. He'd laughed that day, I remembered. Now I knew he rarely experienced mirth and certainly had not then. He was an unwanted son born to a then-sixteen-year-old cheerleader and a father whose identity neither the mother nor the son had known. But I now was aware that the father previously had been a nuclear plant employee who'd found himself trapped in a containment chamber during a meltdown simulation exercise, and he'd vaporized without a trace. His consciousness and invisible and incorporeal parts had begun over the following months to reassemble themselves spontaneously in the cooling tower of the plant. Only when his consciousness returned to this nonbody did the poor being go mad. He had evolved into a kind of chaotic incubus and happened one day upon the unfortunate cheerleader in her sleep. The girl never could get anyone to believe she had no idea how she'd come by this child, and even the child never had accorded her much credence about anything after that. This 666 had grown up with the capacity to shield his body and its accoutrements in a thin, virtually impenetrable shield—which accounted, in answer to my curiosity, for why the bizarre costuming never got rattled in a fight. The boy was most troubled, and I did not care to spend any more time in his history or his mind.

I looked around the room to see where my apparently expanded perceptions would take me. I found a tall bald man named Oliver with arms like steel cables and a dense white goatee that pronged off in two directions. I realized after a moment that this was Oliver Queen, the man from the Statue. Oliver was behind a wall, listening in on others' conversations. I saw him nonetheless. My new talent was like a superpower, this proximity sense I seemed to have here in this state, and it was intoxicating. No secrets hid from me. These were angelic powers, I realized, not superhuman ones as the children who surrounded me wielded. Angelic powers come with restrictions; superhuman powers do not. I was beginning to understand the problem better.

I turned my attention back to Nightstar and the conversation she was having with another young woman. Her friend was also quite beautiful, though not like Nightstar. Her name was Avia. She had yellow-green flesh—it was a tattoo—and bright red lipstick and makeup. She wore a green headdress and a brightly colored costume whose bizarre design, I came to understand, served to camouflage the many extraworldly mechanical devices she and her parents built into it.

She was the daughter of Scott Free, the escape artist, and his wife, a very imposing woman named Barda who had migrated here from some place whose nature I could not at first understand. Then I saw. Avia was descended from people of another dimension, native to twin worlds. In English they called the world of her parents New Genesis, and Avia's birthright included not only their natural abilities but their technologies as well. This young woman was a person who could only grow in power as her self-awareness gathered within her. Her consciousness, what I could glean from it, seemed almost divine itself. She would be a valuable asset to anyone with whom she aligned.

"Lord, I'd follow that man to Apokolips," I heard Avia say.

"Who? The big guy?" Nightstar wanted to know.

"Who? Listen to you. You ask me who? Yeah. The big guy. Oh my, oh my."

"How do you think he found this place?"

"How? Well, if he didn't just kind of know, I suppose somebody invited him, just like us."

"Jeez."

"Am I crazy," Avia wanted to know, "or are you all blown away, too?"

"I'm pretty blown," Nightstar said. "I mean, I thought my dad was full of crap for being drafted by that guy, but now . . ."

"I'm all butterflies inside. I met Superman once when I was a little girl, did I ever tell you?"

"About four hundred times."

"He's right, you know."

"Do I know? Right about what?"

"The League," Avia decided. "The right way is the League's way."

And a hardwood shaft came shooting through space to plunge solidly in a decorative slat between Nightstar and Avia. Green feathers—ballast—dangled off its tail, and Oliver Queen, in leather chaps, and with studded belts across his chest and holding a longbow, stepped out from behind the wall.

"Is it really?" Oliver, the former Green Arrow, said.

Again the room quieted. This Green Arrow, the archer, the legendary urban warrior, was a man whose shadow passed through endless rumor and swashbuckle. I'd heard he was dead. I'd heard he lived on a South Pacific island with an old high school flame and a Tibetan guru. I'd heard he lost a limb, though he seemed intact. Maybe it was in the tabloids I'd read that he was on his way to Mars to found a colony somewhere in its equatorial regions. Evidently not. He was here.

"So you've heard Big Blue's pitch," he barked gamely at the chastened crowd. "Now for the democratic response."

$$\Omega \quad \Omega \quad \Omega$$

Green Arrow walked out into the middle of the floor. Superman had gathered their attention through the force of his presence, but the archer exacted their attention by demanding it. As still as Superman had stood and as softly as he'd spoken, so was the Arrow bombastic and histrionic, a showman who stomped around the room like a tornado looking for an unsuspecting chicken coop upon which to touch down.

"First of all, let me relieve you of one major preconception," Oliver thundered. "This place is no secret. Several hundred kids and arrested-development cases a night don't show up anywhere without everyone concerned knowing all about it. Supes didn't care until he busted out of the woodwork and decided he needed you all. The Mayor and the police didn't care because, well, they don't care about much these days besides sucking up to old Bats. And Bats still doesn't care—and he sure does know you're here because guess who sent me?—he doesn't care because he knows this place keeps you off the streets and out of his way. What Bats does care about is that you don't go off half-cocked after that red-caped sugar daddy."

Oliver looked up toward the ceiling and hollered: "Hear that, Big Blue?" and looked back into the eyes of his audience and said, "You can bet he heard it. Just like Santa."

He got a laugh with that one.

"We have reason to believe that Superman has stumbled upon a path that will lead to disaster for most of you and for most everyone you care about. If what you want for the future is a fascist garrison state where every one of you is part of a rigid hierarchy of jackbooted enforcement, then fly after the man who just left this room. He's well meaning, but he's wrong wrong wrong. His future is a future of laws without principles, discipline without reason, and oversight without direction. Do you hear me? Is that what you believe in? Superhuman dictatorship? You might have powers and abilities far beyond those of mortal men. You might just have talent—like me."

That brought another laugh. They all knew that there were

few people in this room who could stand up to this mortal bowman in a free-for-all.

"But in a world ruled by the one who has the strongest arm or the farthest sight, the future belongs only to Superman."

He paused on that one a moment, and it sunk in. By the time he finished speaking, the crowd was as animated as he was.

"We too," Oliver concluded, "know pretty much who all of you are. Let the word out that you're with us, and we'll find you." And he worked his way around the room shaking hands like a candidate for Congress.

Avia turned away when Oliver offered her a hand. Nightstar, however, was the daughter of Richard Grayson, the original Robin, who'd grown up in the old Wayne Manor. She always wondered what the Batcave looked like. She snatched up Oliver's mitt and pumped it as though she had been waiting all her life to meet him.

Ω Ω Ω

I stretched my newfound abilities and, without the Spectre's help, found Superman in the sky. He flew high above the clouds, idly circling the city for a time, thinking. Then his image changed to a red-and-blue streak flashing toward the ground and vanished. But before that happened, glory of glories, I found his thoughts.

He was resolving something. Something about another man—an important figure, from the feel of him. Superman was actually organizing his ideas, and I was listening. I could not understand the thoughts themselves, but I felt the march of them. He was lining them up, putting them in place. It was as though he were preparing for a job interview. With his speech before the underground gathering of his errant children and successors, he felt, he was finally able to articulate these ideas. He had a clear sense of his purpose, and he was ready to bring this before—whom? His thoughts were a puzzle, like a passage from the *I Ching*. He was crossing the water to see the great man. Who in Creation could Superman be thinking of?

I should have guessed.

Ω Ω Ω

Bruce Wayne had grown pleased with himself. He had no more secrets, plenty of money, and lots of work to do. His decaying spine held on tight to four inoperable slipped discs. Six years ago his doctor had performed an experimental procedure worked out by Wayne himself, to fuse a titanium framework to his shoulders and backbone and keep the spine from pinching and ripping at its nerve cord in a manner that threatened to make him a quadriplegic. Another set of external bones ran along his arms and another along his legs, fused to his joints, keeping Wayne's muscles intact. A pump arrangement in the framework itself fed a steady stream of fluid into his cartilage to keep it from slipping.

For a long time after the series of operations, he could do nothing but lie forward at an angle on a chiropractor-style platform, manipulating the machinery in the Cave as he watched his monitors through a hole for his face in the platform. When he could move again, he spent most of several months building up his shoulder muscles, torn open in the course of the corrective back operation, to the strength they had before. Today those muscles squeezed at the roots of the framework planted in his bones the way the impenetrable dirt of the desert clutched at the roots of an ancient saguaro. When his back and shoulders hurt the most, he knew he was working as hard as he could and it felt good. He sat in a chair on the flat of his giant truncated stalagmite in the enormous cavern beneath the neglected ruin of his manor house, and kept his city clean.

"It's my job," he said to himself maybe a hundred times a day.

The house that one day would be Wayne Manor had risen from the tough soil of this township in 1779 when Increase Hopkins, Bruce Wayne's ancestor, had judged his family too big to live in their roadside inn. Increase and his wife, Rebecca, had been the owners and managers of the Gothamborough Inn since the week after their marriage, when a buggy had rolled over to crush Increase's parents, Elijah and Chastity Hopkins; Increase had been seventeen at the time, Rebecca fifteen. In thirteen years, they had brought ten children into the world and made their family the most prosperous in the township. As each son or daughter had become old enough to walk on his or her own—"totin' age," Increase had called it—the child had acquired a specialty. One would pile or carry in firewood. Another would monitor the supply of water from the well. Yet another would set and clear the table in the big boardinghouse dining room, the same one where Bruce Wayne had eaten breakfast every morning of every day while his parents were alive. In time Increase and Rebecca's children would take on progressively more difficult and complex responsibilities as younger siblings took over their elders' jobs—all duties that, without the children, Increase and Rebecca would have been doing themselves. By the time Increase had turned thirty years old, his ten offspring—aged two to twelve—were competently managing his family inn; his neighbors had labeled him the laziest man in the township.

A joke, of course.

In fact, Increase Hopkins never had found a moment he could not figure out how to fill. With the first baby old enough to walk, Increase no longer had carried silverware from the kitchen to the dining room; Rebecca, nursing their second child, would count out spoons, hand them to the toddler, and in the dining room Increase would arrange them on the table. He'd spent his newly freed-up odd moments designing a dumbwaiter system to accommodate the new formal dining hall being built upstairs. With the oldest able to carry water from the well, Increase had spent his spare time engineering and digging the piping for an indoor plumbing system. With the oldest, ten, keeping books and welcoming and checking in guests himself, Increase had carried twenty-pound property markers for the town surveyor until he learned how to survey land and draft property maps for himself. By the time of America's Declaration of Independence, the Gothamborough Inn, with its fine dining hall and indoor plumbing, had become the most widely renowned lodging place in the north. The night George Washington slept there, Increase Hopkins was out subdividing the southwest sixty of the four thousand forested acres left to him and his wife after the untimely departure of Elijah and Chastity Hopkins.

During the summer of 1780 the Hopkins family moved into the large annex that Increase had attached to the inn. The family annex soon grew appreciably larger than the inn, and, by the time Increase turned thirty-five, his children were contracting out the management of the inn and had opened a tavern on the far side of the Gotham-Barrington Road. Rebecca and her husband had been pioneers in the field of municipality management, with Increase surveying and subdividing several dozen small lots on and around the outermost reaches of their property. The outskirts of Gotham now were home to a thriving chicken and dairy industry, at whose heart was the cooperative of families who had leased or bought— against a promise of future productivity—small pieces of the Hopkins family homestead.

Gotham had not turned into a metropolis overnight, but through the work of Increase and Rebecca Hopkins and the habits they'd impressed upon their children and descendants, Gotham had become, by the end of the Nineteenth Century, a great palace city of the Northeast. By the time Judge Solomon Wayne of Boston settled there, married a Hopkins girl, and gave the family and manor its name, the scions of this industrious homesteader family were this city's most brightly shining light. And in the dreams of Bruce Wayne, the last scion of that breed, people walked Gotham's boulevards and browsed its shopping centers with a pride and a bearing as though each were the lord or lady of this manor, and in Bruce Wayne's Gotham each of them was in fact. In his dreams, this palace had no King or Queen, but every citizen who strode these avenues and enjoyed these pavilions was responsible to every other. No child was in danger on these street corners, and all could trade in confidence that it was his work and his product and his honor that every merchant offered, not his artifice. And out beyond the edge of the city proper, on a windswept granite cliff, the patron family entertained and romanced Presidents and paupers alike, with a characteristically American sense of how things are, how things work, and how things can be. All the good things of the Earth flowed to Gotham because of the city's greatness.

But always, in the great city's soft underbelly lurked the cancer of corruption, the impurity of greed, the ravening demon of its sin-infested heritage. Sometimes the demon contracted on itself. Sometimes, as in the days when Bruce Wayne had first donned the cowl, it had reached its tendrils into every corner of the city's corpus, requiring a Dark Knight to beat it back. Deep in his soul, in the places where even this bravest of men forbore to look, Bruce Wayne knew that Gotham never was or would be the paradise to whose ideal he dedicated his life.

All of this I learned when I looked down over the titanium-reinforced shoulders of the good and great man who sat in the chair before me studying his monitors. On a little bronze plaque bolted to the mainframe facing him was a family shield that bore a legend in classical Greek: *APHAYNAI MATAION*—"SURRENDER IS FUTILE."

An UNAUTHORIZED ENTRY legend began to flash on all the operating monitors, several seconds before a warning light and beeper indicated a fast-moving object approaching the property from the air. Only one thing ever moved fast enough to trip off the entry signal even before its approach registered. There was no danger here.

Upstairs, Superman walked through the wreckage of the once-stately Wayne Manor for the first time. He was familiar enough with this enormous place to know where everything belonged. Here the fourth-floor roof lay on the open-air second-floor formal dining hall. Down that corridor the bed of the maid's suite still had crumpled, soiled sheets stuffed into chipped Ming-era vases and flapping with the chill wind. In this short passageway off the dining hall was a winding tunnel that used to be the hidden circular stairway leading down to the kitchen cupboard. The knives and other hardware that once hung from magnetized hooks along the kitchen wall now lay scattered, and he found around the living quarters some of the cutlery still in the plush furniture whose stuffing now gathered in corners. In the foyer was the ruin of the old custom-width Harvard grandfather clock that still pressed against the wall. The glass of its cabinet lay shattered, sharp blades and pointy crumbs of glass still arrayed on the floor. The pendulum had not swung for years.

Superman tapped it, and it caught a rhythm. It was not the rhythm of time; on the leftward swing, it hit a skewed slat of cabinet, and the beat was not regular. Nonetheless, it was not the clock of a dead man. On the third swing Superman moved the hands of the clock to 10:47 as the pendulum continued to rock. A lock came undone, and the entire frame of the clock swung forward to reveal a passageway not found by the vandals who'd attacked this place. As he had before, in the days when the Earth had sung the names and praises of the Last Son of Krypton and the Dark Knight of Gotham, Superman walked down the hidden stairs to the Batcave.

$$\Omega \quad \Omega \quad \Omega$$

"Bruce?" he called when he reached the bottom of the stairs.

No answer.

He walked in the direction from which he heard the slow thumping of an athlete's heart, then stopped. Wrong direction. That was a woman's heart. The beat was not as strong or quite as regular as Bruce's, and there was another one nearby. Neither belonged to Bruce. Bruce's heartsong came from down the cavern, mingled with the creaking of a pivoting chair and the occasional tapping of keys. "Bruce?" he asked again, in the new direction.

More tapping. Another heartbeat. The telltale whirring of a video camera turning on an automated fixture.

Halfway across the open area between himself and the dimly lit humongous sliced-off limestone stalagmite, Superman realized he was walking on water. Trophies and mementos lay in puddles: a huge Joker playing card with dog-eared corners. A giant Lincoln penny. A life-sized tyrannosaurus with its fiberglass frame poking out the tips of its claws. This place had gone to seed. "Bruce, you know you can't hide from me."

"I bow to your superior wisdom," came the answer.

Superman rose as if riding an invisible flying carpet to the rock platform where Bruce Wayne sat. A tight white T-shirt hugged a cable-hard chest under the exoskeletal frame that held together his insulated back and shoulders and limbs.

"After all, you're the world's ranking authority on hiding—" Wayne swung his chair around to face his old colleague and smiled sardonically. "Aren't you, Clark?" Bruce's renown as a fighter grew from an uncanny ability to press on an opponent's weakest point.

"Don't call me Clark," Superman could not keep himself from saying. "What happened to stately Wayne Manor?"

"Bane and Two-Face happened to it. My identity got exposed. Doesn't matter." Bruce Wayne turned back to his monitors and console. "I've got everything I need down here. Besides, it's not as if anyone intrudes on me. That hardly ever happens. Clark."

"I saw your granddaughter tonight, Bruce."

"My what?"

"She's quite beautiful. A young lady."

"Dick's girl?"

"She has a name. She's—"

"Nightstar. Yes, I know. I saw her once. Stared shamelessly through the skylight at the preschool. Felt like a pervert. That doesn't matter, either."

"You're not in touch?"

"I never adopted Dick. He's only fourteen years younger than I am. He never asked for anything."

"He has to ask?"

"Who do you think you are? You walk around with your own damn gravitational pull until you check out on everyone who ever cared about you. And now you come back here to dispute my parenting skills?"

"Just wondering."

"No, he didn't have to ask. In fact, when Starfire was dying—and I didn't even know her well—there wasn't a specialist on circulatory problems or a theorist on alien anatomy in the world who didn't find a helicopter sitting on his favorite golf course and a pilot with a satchel full of hundred-dollar bills to coax him into a consulting trip to Mass General. We could've used your help back then too."

"Does Dick know you were behind that?"

"He didn't ask."

Superman paused. Bruce took a breath and returned to his monitors and keyboard. There was a purse-snatching on Broad Street. At Bruce's command a robot Bat-Monitor lowered a hook from the sky in front of the fleeing perpetrator. The snatcher gently draped the purse strap over the hook and lay down on the street, shaking, his hands over his head.

"Yeah, I'd heard your nights became free once Genosyde blew up Arkham Asylum."

"Not to mention Belle Rêve Prison and Blackgate. Not an action I'd condone. I wonder, though, if I'd prosecute as rabidly as some others might. Clark."

Now it was Superman who stood on silence.

"I mean"—the Batman turned again to his sometime ally—"tell me the thought of it doesn't give even your superhide a little tingle."

"I don't have that dark a side."

"Tell that to your tailor," and Wayne pointed a thumb at the new S emblem on Superman's chest, red on a field of black. "A new look for you?"

"It's for Kansas."

"Oh my." Wayne laughed. "Is there anything you can't justify?"

"I can't justify our being a couple of grotesquely sad old men who should've become friends a long time ago instead of having this same sniping conversation every time we run into each other."

"Uh-huh."

"Bruce," Superman said, "the League needs you."

"I'm busy."

"Too busy to help save the world?"

"The crisis at hand isn't new. Where have you been? Oh, I'm sorry. Perhaps I should ask Magog?"

Superman seemed taken aback—even hurt—by the venom and the spin of his colleague's big chair. For a moment the Man of Steel stood silent, crossing his arms, trying to find an opening, and in that moment Bruce Wayne's objection grew into a rant.

"Frictions have built to a head for years, Clark. The metahuman population boomed while you were gone. Ordinary folks decided you and I were too gentle and old-fashioned to face the challenges of the Twenty-First Century. They wanted their heroes strong and ruthless. Be careful what you wish for. Now it's the metahumans who have the keys to Earth's kingdom. Wresting control is a delicate matter. It requires finesse. It requires meticulous planning against more hidden enemies. It can be done. But it needs to be done without Superman and the Justice League booming into town, punching now and asking questions later."

There was a moment for a breath and Superman filled it. "Dick doesn't see it that way," he said.

"You got him to reclaim the Robin mantle. Is that supposed to sway me? Try harder. Did Dick and I ever see eye-to-eye? I have my own controls in place, thank you. They may be more methodical than yours but they get results. My affairs and my city are more important than your sudden interest in empire-building."

"Your city is a police state," Superman snapped. "No, excuse me. I mean a vigilante state. Does the Mayor have to clear his choice for police commissioner with you now, too?"

"Generally does, though I've never asked him to." Wayne turned back to his battery of monitors, where one showed two gangs of teenagers congregating on opposite sides of a downtown church. He pressed a button that brought the scene on the main large screen and he spoke into a microphone: "Units eighteen and forty-four. Maneuver sixteen." Then he flipped off the microphone and said, "In fact, no one's been elected Mayor without my explicit endorsement in twenty years."

"And you think that's a good thing?"

"You used to brag about Metropolis, Clark. You used to tell me how hard you had to work to find anyone there doing anything remotely illicit. You thought you lived in some kind of Earthly paradise." He flipped on the microphone and said, "Variation E," and flipped it off again. "Whose city is a paradise now?"

On the screen, a pair of flying twelve-foot Bat-Monitors touched down back-to-back between the two collections of kids. The gangs scattered by the time the robots took three steps.

"Lovely," Superman said. He was facetious.

"I know." Bruce Wayne smiled. He was not.

"Your whole act has always been based on fear, Bruce."

"Did you come here to debate philosophy?"

"You've turned a whole city into a superstitious and cowardly lot. Haven't you ever read Machiavelli?"

"My favorite philosopher. Next to you, of course." Now Wayne was being facetious. Partly.

"You can rule through fear and superstition or through love and trust, Bruce. You've chosen fear. You've proved you're the aristocrat you always claimed not to be."

"They'll fear me more than they'll trust you. Even *I* don't trust you. After all, you left. I stayed. Love's a two-way street; fear's straight down the line."

Superman knew there were others among the Batman's allies. He even knew there were others here in the cave, but who they were was none of his business. They were none of his business unless the Batman again became his ally.

"We're warriors, Bruce. We have an obligation to wage combat when combat is appropriate."

"We have an obligation, Clark, to create the conditions wherein combat becomes unnecessary."

A pause. Both tried to grasp the precise little philosophical difference keeping them apart.

"Then you're sure you won't join us?" the Kryptonian asked.

"For a man who can hear clouds scrape together," Wayne observed, "you don't listen very well."

Finally, Superman unfolded his arms.

"The only thing I wonder about your totalitarian solutions," Wayne concluded, "is whether I'd be the first to be 're-formed' by your new world order. Goodbye, Clark."

$$\Omega \quad \Omega \quad \Omega$$

Like shadows coming out of the shadows, three figures emerged to Bruce Wayne's side in the seconds after Superman vanished.

"Were you here for all that?" Bruce asked.

"Ollie just came back in," the woman said, "but Ted and I monitored it from the time he came down the stairs."

"I recognize Oliver Queen, the Green Arrow," I said to the Spectre. "Who are these other two?"

"Dinah Lance, once called the Black Canary"—the Spectre was unusually responsive and forthcoming—"and Ted Kord, once known as the Blue Beetle. Urban warriors."

"He knew we were here," Oliver Queen grumbled. "I could feel his X rays. Hell, I'm probably sterile now."

"Let it go, love," Dinah Lance said, taking him by the hand.

"Actually, Ollie," Ted Kord said, "given the low level of roentgens involved, I'd calculate nothing intrinsically harmful about—"

"Stop making the world safe for science, Beetle," Oliver snapped. "Let an old man be paranoid. Of course, if they're after you, it ain't paranoia, is it, Bats?"

"If the League are allowed into our arena, the world is doomed. Superman has no idea what he's really up against, but we have our own team to call into play."

"You sound as if you have a plan," Dinah said.

Ollie, her husband, smiled. "How soon they forget."

"Does the Batman ever not have a plan?" Kord added.

"We have contacts across the world," Bruce Wayne said, punching a flurry of keys and looking over the images they brought up on a battery of screens. "It's time we drew that web tight."

They went on like that, joking and talking and saying not much of anything. I could gather very little of their intentions or their thoughts, and I asked the Spectre why.

"They are strong-willed," the Spectre said, "especially here in this context."

"In the Batcave, you mean?"

"They are at home, and their will is, to us, a solid thing. If they view their concerns as theirs alone, then you can no more read them than you can, in your corporeal state, walk through a wall."

The physics of the Spectre's existence, it seemed to me, were more confusing than quantum mechanics. Nevertheless, I watched the Batman and his allies, and I learned very little. There were more than these four, it seemed. They secretly had been recruiting among the superhumans for months, and with some success.

For what purpose? They had no intention of allowing me to know.

PART II

... To Make
Our World ...

CHAPTER 12

Mr. Mind

~~~

Her best friend had been missing for weeks, and she was worried. The guy who was supposed to take her bungee jumping at Mount Saint Helens last night had stood her up. But this morning all was right with the world. Today Avia flew with Superman.

I had been a widower too long. This long-legged flying creature with the golden body tattoo yanked at my aging cleric's soul. I knew it was my soul and not my flesh; the Spectre's imposed condition had relieved me for the moment of human physical urges. Those remaining were the passions that rose from my character rather than from my hibernating chemistry.

There was something hormonal, something aggressive in the very makeup of the metahuman—as opposed to the traditional human—that Avia seemed to recognize as a spirit akin to her own. While she had been born here and lived here, she was not of this Earth. Neither of her parents, Scott and Barda Free, was even remotely related to an Earth person. While like many other alien races they were clearly human, or at least humanoid, there was not yet any evidence that they could reproduce with human partners. DNA of many alien races, however, proved surprisingly adaptable to the protocols of the building blocks of Earthly human life—of which Avia's friend Nightstar was an obvious case in point.

"Do you think there's some aspect of the metahuman gene that makes individuals more belligerent or aggressive?" Avia flew up beside Superman somewhere in the sky over the outskirts of South Coast City.

"Pardon?" he asked.

"Do you think there's something inherently different about the metagene?" she asked. "I mean as opposed to conventional human DNA?"

"I'm not sure," he said. "Let me think."

It had been a month since Superman had walked alone into the party cavern under the outskirts of Gotham and first asked the children, grandchildren, and successors of many of his old colleagues and foes to join his cause. It was the same cause he had always championed: Be a hero and save the world. At the time, though, it felt so promising and new. Certainly Superman was fresh and tireless every day, even if he was a little morose sometimes. And Avia herself could not be more thrilled to get up in the morning and pursue this quest with the great man. To some of the others, though, it seemed to be getting old.

They traveled in a company of nine Justice Leaguers, moments from flying into a high-risk situation. With Superman and Avia were Wonder Woman, Whiz, who was one of the new generation of Marvels, Golden Guardian, Green Lantern, Hawkman, Red Robin, and Flash.

Cathedral—he of the involved jagged costume reminiscent of Gothic architecture—Phoebus, the new Red Tornado, and Tyra, who was the human "daughter" of the supercomputer Brainiac, rumbled in a residential district of South Coast. This conversation in the sky would not cause what happened next to miss a beat.

"I think it's a kind of stand-and-fight survival response you're noticing," Superman said as the angle of his approach dropped toward the position of a power dive. "Not aggression per se."

"Really?" Avia followed suit and headed precipitously toward the ground. So did everyone else. "Then how would you explain the metahuman tendency to respond violently to stimuli that normal humans would treat logically instead?"

"Dominance," Superman said, pointing his fisted hands downward and diving among the glistening towers of South Coast City. "Not on our part, but on that of conventional humans," he called back as he left Avia and everyone else far above.

On the roof of a four-story apartment building, Cathedral heard a loud male voice come from somewhere unexpected: above. Was somebody calling down to him from a higher building? Cathedral had his hands fisted together and was about to bring them down on the roof to rattle the stance of the oncoming Tyra and—nominally—shatter this multiple-family home into a zillion pieces. Superman went after Tyra first.

The girl had a fingertip fireball launcher. She was shooting little licks of flame in a wide pattern in Cathedral's general direction, smiling, enjoying this. Superman always thought of her as such a contemplative, intellectual girl; a good girl. Then he remembered that throughout history there were good people, thoughtful people, who—in keeping with the force of their times—owned slaves, or followed unjust orders, or advocated the rule of racists and tyrants because they were in power, or waged war. Like them Tyra was a product of her time and her generation's rage, and only by comparison was she a "good girl."

"What do you think you're doing, young lady?" Superman demanded as he clapped down hard on the roof, blowing cold air over the fireball launcher until condensation froze it unworkable, dripping icicles.

"I don't know," she stammered. "Hi, Superman, I—"

"Don't you know better than to be rumbling where people live? What's gotten into you? All of you?"

Behind him, Red Tornado and Phoebus flew out from behind nearby buildings, forgetting their fight to gape in wonder at the celebrity they seemed to have attracted. Then Wonder Woman, Avia, and the others landed, and clicks and whirring gathered from all directions. Local news hovercams rose in the sky around them. The chattering of reporters' narration punctuated the air. Clicks came from nearby buildings. People who moments ago had run for cover now poked cameras out windows, looking for a visual souvenir. Cathedral was gone, but nobody seemed to notice.

"Catch!" came that raucous voice from down on the street—

—and an old rattletrap 2014 Chevy came tumbling fore-over-aft up through the air, fell just short of the roof, and smashed into the side of the building.

"Son of a sire!" Wonder Woman spat. She dove off the roof headlong at Cathedral's throat, slamming him back-first into the piling of an old center-city oil pump that gathered rust on the wide traffic island dividing the street. She slid him hard against the fossil ruin down to the ground.

Wonder Woman was sick and tired of the effort they all were putting into this project over these weeks, growing into months. She was sick of the upstarts a fraction her age who thought they could make a name for themselves by poking their betters in the eye. She was tired of all the energy she had to put out just getting her leader to budge a little. "This is the way we do things," he insisted, "this isn't the way we do things," and "that is the way things are done." Ends justify only ends, and means don't get justified by anything, he was always telling her. He had to be true to underlying principles; it was like a religion to him. She needed only to get each job done, one at a time. "Consider the implications of our tactics," he would tell her. "Consider the implications if we fail," would be her retort—angrier and more snappish every time she snapped it out. Perhaps there was some vindication for Diana in the fact that, over these past weeks, as their efforts had become more tedious and martial in nature, Superman had begun to refer to her openly as his second-in-command—always smiling that thin smile while saying it. But the others took the title seriously, and she became his first officer in fact. Then again, sometimes it seemed that all this exalted position afforded her was the need to be the one to argue with him. Today she could not be bothered. The Amazon's fist smashed into the delinquent's face.

"Think that's funny, boy?" she demanded of the bizarrely costumed Cathedral and hit him again.

"Unghh," he said.

"You like throwing heavy machinery at your betters, do you?"

"Unghh," he said again.

"Diana!" Superman looked at the sudden damage his first officer rained down on the mildly deluded boy. But he also saw the old woman with the camera, rushing over the ground at the mess of the facade of her home.

"Want to play rough, kid?" Diana wanted to know. "Let me know when you want that to start."

"Unghh."

"Robin, Avia, stop Diana," Superman said.

Before Avia could say, "Who? Me?" Superman was gone to peel the woman with the camera away from danger and shield her from the explosion that ripped the already restive air of this corner of town.

"Diana." Red Robin was there first, lightly taking hold of the wrist that Wonder Woman had hauled back to pummel the shattered face of the rogue metahuman Cathedral.

"Don't you ever dare touch my—" Diana spun to unload her wrath on a man she had known since he was a boy.

Dick Grayson never had felt quite comfortable around the Amazon Princess. Few women and almost no men ever do. But he never before had felt the sensation of the daggers of those ancient eyes in that perfect unlined face. It was unsettling, even for this man who was trained to react to the uncanny and unbelievable before the wonder of it could register.

She was about to pound him, to redirect her anger with the delinquent against the man arrogant enough to question her. And Red Robin could no more stop her than a bird could stop a snake who held it hypnotized by its gaze.

"Princess. Please—" Avia quickly reached the scene but could not think of what to do or say to calm this rage. "Remember your station." She'd have to settle for that.

Avia had no idea whether it was what she said or the fact that it was a woman's voice saying it, but Wonder Woman relented. Diana looked surprised, looked at Avia, looked at Red Robin, and—with some horror—at her fist.

"It's all right, Diana," Red Robin said.

"No, Richard, it's not." Diana swept a hand over Red Robin's hood to pull it back and kiss his forehead. "But thank you for saying it is. And thank you, Avia." Contrite and ashamed. It was a sight to behold.

Wonder Woman caught an air current back across the street to the building where Superman stood with the old woman and her camera, shielding her from the fire and shrapnel.

Avia said, "Uhh."

Red Robin did not do much better. He said, "Wow," touching a hand to his forehead. Avia thought to pull the hood back down over his face.

Diana was still breathing hard when the explosions of the car stopped. Still shielding the woman with his body, Superman extinguished the flames in an exhalation. The woman just clutched at the heavy red cape and shivered despite the waves of heat from the quenched fire.

"Calm down, Diana," he told his friend. "Take a breath. They're not evil. They're kids. Not warriors."

"They want to act like warriors, do they?" she said. "I'll show them war."

"You're right," Superman said, solicitously pulling away

the woman from his cape and checking her physiology. Just a touch of nervousness, he thought; her blood pressure would go back down when he left. It always did. Maybe Kryptonians had some sort of pheromone, an idle corner of his cerebrum suggested, that stimulated humans' nervous systems. Then again, maybe there was an easier explanation than that.

"Avia, would you stay with this woman a little while?" Wonder Woman suggested as Superman stood back.

"They seem to have learned little regard for human life," Superman said to her.

"No they haven't learned it," she agreed. "They haven't learned anything worth knowing. You weren't here to teach them."

She lifted up into the sky, and he did not see her for the rest of the day.

As for the four young rogues whose rumble had brought this contingent of the Justice League, it was a split decision: Tyra, Red Tornado, and Phoebus took the tacit pledge and joined the League; Cathedral came awake with a start, began healing as these children did rather quickly, snarled something, and went on his way.

"You will be dealt with," Superman called after him.

"You really think it's not catching on?" Avia asked Superman in flight later on, trying to rev up their conversation from earlier in the day. "Our quest, I mean?"

"I don't know what to think," he said. "I've never been much on this active-leader-type stuff. I've always worked alone, really, even with the Batman or . . ." He trailed off.

"You don't even know what you've accomplished already," she said, but neither she nor Superman quite understood to what she was referring.

Unfortunately, averting Armageddon was certainly not among those accomplishments.

Ω Ω Ω

"We've had the inquiry we've been waiting for," Bruce Wayne said into the local-address microphone.

Dinah Lance, in the gymnasium, pointed at Nightstar and asked her to take over the aerobics session. Here the gym consisted of a sixty-foot-high cavern outfitted with trapezes, trampolines, rings, parallel and uneven bars, and inch-thick tumbling mats over an uneven limestone floor. The dominant feature of this landscape was a crevasse across the center of the gym, eighteen feet at its widest point. A dozen colorfully costumed folks—those who had manifested special powers or had undergone genetic tests were metahumans, as Ollie Queen had said, whereas the others were just talented—did aerobics and calisthenics around, over, and inside the great gap in the Earth.

While Superman and Wonder Woman were abroad across the globe with their merry band of world-savers, the Batman's absence was something no thoughtful observer could miss. That was what Bruce Wayne had counted on. He could be as quiet as he liked as he gathered and trained his alternative force. Those he really wanted to find would inevitably come looking for him as long as he stayed patient. But, with this message from Ibn al Xu'ffasch, Bruce Wayne's patience was paying off.

Jennie-Lynn Hayden—Jade—the delicately featured lime-skinned daughter of Alan Scott—the Green Lantern—and Harlequin, worked out tumbling and running in place on a flying carpet treadmill generated by her power. The treadmill hovered twelve feet over the crevasse. Obsidian, her brother, solemnly did jumping jacks barefoot on the cavern floor aside the mats, nonstop for a solid three hours. Olivia Queen—Ollie Queen and Dinah Lance's daughter, who now called herself Black Canary, the name her mother and grandmother both used—maneuvered hoverpads on her feet up among the stalactites and deep into the pit simply by shifting her body weight like a unicycle rider. Wildcat rode the trampolines, occasionally hanging, for however long he could, on extended claws from the cavern roof and then tumbling to catch a wobbly trapeze far below. The teenage girl who called herself Flash—she assumed she was the daughter of the noncommunicative dimension-spanning Wallace West, and so did everyone else—ran laps of the cavern, twelve of them in the last second, and she was slowing down. Darkstar, the son of Donna Troy, the middle-aged woman who once called herself Wonder Girl, tumbled from parallel bars to trampolines over and around the big room, at one point making a tumbling leap over the cleft in the ground and landing on his feet well clear of it. A tall, uncertain-looking man in a trench coat—I could not see into him, but Bruce Wayne called him J'onn—stood in a corner, watching and flickering in and out of phase, as if unsure in what world he belonged. And there were more, a legion of them here in a Batcave better used to solitude.

When Dinah and Ollie Queen arrived, with Ted Kord, on the platform where the Batman kept his elaborate workstation, they found him virtually catatonic.

"Snap out of it, Bruce," the Green Arrow demanded. "You scare the crap out of me when you do that."

There was an image on the main computer screen and Bruce was staring at it, analyzing it, trying to see in it something more than there was.

"Who's that?" Dinah asked. It was the image of a strikingly handsome young man in a business suit, sitting in a big chair among what looked to be a family of ancient European nobles done up in medieval splendor.

"That?"

"Yes, Bruce. What's wrong?"

"That's Xu'ffasch," Wayne said. "His name is Ibn al Xu'ffasch. He runs an international cartel. Makes King Farouk look like a pauper."

"He's so young," Dinah said. "I've never heard of him."

"You will," Bruce Wayne said, and studied the picture some more, as if trying to find imperfections among the pixels. "He's the one who contacted me about a meeting at Luthor's place. We're going."

"The inner circle?" Ted Kord said with some wonder. "Think he'll let me look at his lab?"

"Oh, for jumping hunchbacks' sake, Ted, get off it." Queen blew air. "What's spooking you about this kid, Bats? Jealous of the bankroll?"

"No," Wayne said, and tore his gaze from the screen, flipping off the monitor. "No, nothing. Come, we've got to study the files on who we're meeting."

Ω Ω Ω

"I said 'two sugars,' you ignorant cow," were the last words Theresa Freed heard before Vandal Savage snapped her neck and left her draped over the back of her desk chair.

I felt a chill wave across the ether as the Spectre bristled, even before I realized that the brute had murdered the girl. My companion had a particular aversion, it seemed, to the black-bearded immortal with the big hands. The frustration was born of his being somehow beyond the Spectre's reach.

"What is this?" Lex Luthor demanded as he stepped out the door into his reception area.

Luthor found three people in the room, including one deceased: Vandal Savage, King of Spades, and his late receptionist.

"I'm sorry," King said, taking his cigarette from his mouth and looking around for an ashtray. He reflexively flipped through a deck of cards he kept in a pocket and he dropped his ash into a fruit bowl. "Would you prefer I didn't smoke? It's so out of fashion these days."

The phone rang. Luthor stomped over to the desk and picked up the receiver as he felt Theresa's carotid for a pulse. "Executive suite. Hello." There was no pulse. Luthor realized he had not answered a phone in years unless he'd known already who was on the line. For a moment, in his anger with Savage and King, he forgot the necessary vocabulary. "No, excuse me, we're not taking calls," and he hung up.

"I just had her trained," Luthor said, turning to his guests. "Did you do this, King?"

"No, I did," Savage said, stirring his coffee with a spoon and mingling a sip of it with the bite of strawberry in his mouth. "Why?"

"Do you know how hard it is to find someone who can handle—" and the phone rang again. Luthor picked up the receiver, looked around, and hung it up again. "Savage, my employees represent me. When you assault or abuse—or kill—them, that is a direct challenge to my personal integrity. Do you understand that?"

For a moment Vandal Savage appeared amused, then covered it up. "I'm sure I can replace the employee. I didn't think."

"I assume one could interpret that as an apology," Luthor said. "Come on in. Everyone else is here. Good thing too," he muttered, "or there'd be no one to open the door."

King of Spades, with his cigarette and his deck of cards, and Vandal Savage, with his sweetened coffee and a handful of strawberries, followed Luthor through the hallway door and into the conference room at the corner of the building. Savage was, by his own reckoning, roughly fifty thousand years old. He had to be: He was Cro-Magnon, not Homo sapiens. He was of a relatively successful race of early humans who had lived in southeastern Europe, Asia Minor, and north Africa in the dark times when most of that land was covered still with sheets of permafrost.

The chieftain of a Cro-Magnon tribe calling themselves the Blood People, living on what became the Balkan Peninsula, Vandar Adg had been a bully and a ruffian fifty thousand years in the past. One day a fireball had fallen from the sky, bathing him in a gene-altering collection of chemicals and stimuli and sending him into a coma. In the course of his elaborate tribal funeral, Vandar had sat up and resumed his duties as chief. Despite the death of his people, he continued to live, growing in strength until superhuman and growing in knowledge until brilliant. The only area where he'd not grown was in character. Once, in Rome, he'd assumed the name Julius Caesar, risen to rule, and, having grown bored, contrived his own death. Once, in Mongolia, he'd become a man named Genghis Khan and laid down an empire across the steppes of Asia and Europe. He'd founded the Bavarian Illuminati and the Sumerian Empire. He'd ruled Egypt in the fourth dynasty as the Pharaoh Khafre. As the Nazi Chief of Field Counter-intelligence in the Second World War, he'd nearly insinuated himself into the position of American Secretary of War until Alan Scott, the first Earth-based Green Lantern, upended his plan. Through the centuries he'd stood on the backs of the conquered and at the side of the conquerors. And now he'd slaughtered an innocent woman not because she made a minor error, but because her employer had stocked the small cube-shaped pellets of sugar in his coffee room instead of the larger rectangular ones.

"One would suppose that in all those years of life," the Spectre said, "this creature would have grown a hope of Heaven."

My wraith companion was growing a sense of philosophy. Encouraging.

The King of Spades was better than Vandal Savage only because he was younger, but he was immortal as well, as he'd learned scant decades ago. He'd had time to grow his new mentor's savagery—or outgrow it. King of Spades—Starly King, actually—was the surviving member of the Royal Flush Gang whose rank as second-in-command came as a result of his name. They were a group of teenagers who'd banded together to take over their neighborhood. Years later all five members had been incarcerated at Belle Rêve Prison when Magog and the Justice Battalion vaporized it and everything within a mile of it. Only King had survived: He had been on a work leave that day, raking leaves in the big playground of a public school on President's Day weekend. King had thanked Lady Luck that Magog did not take off on public school holidays and, after a suitable period in hiding, had retrieved the gang's considerable stash of gems, precious metals, and bearer bonds from the hollow cornerstone of the southernmost piling of the Long Island Sound Bridge in Orient Point.

Lex Luthor was not a prejudiced man, he fancied. If you controlled assets in excess of fifty million dollars and you did not make yourself an enemy, he considered you his equal. That was why Vandal Savage and the King of Spades were here. In the conference room were the others: Lord Naga, the leader of India's Cobra Cult; Ibn al Xu'ffasch, the young hegemon of the shadow empire consolidated by his grandfather Rā's al Ghūl, who once was the Batman's greatest enemy; Selina Kyle, once the Catwoman; and Selina's companion, a small but unsettlingly cute little old man named Edward Nigma, who'd spent most of his years serving time for crimes committed in the identity of the Riddler. He looked unrelentingly dignified, yet smiled constantly for no apparent reason. Nigma was the odd duck here. Luthor needed Ms. Kyle, whose immense cosmetics firm was not only a gold mine but a valuable avenue to billions of devoted consumers all over the world, and she'd come on the condition Nigma came with her. Nigma was merely an accessory, a fashion declaration like armor or tattoos.

"We call ourselves the 'Mankind Liberation Front,'" Luthor said, introducing King and Savage around. "Our newest members."

"As is Eddie," Selina Kyle said.

"Who, I remind everyone," Luthor said, "is here solely as a courtesy to Ms. Kyle."

"And isn't it a very gracious one, Lex?" added the smiling Nigma.

"Simmer down, Eddie," Selina whispered to her companion, and everyone else pretended they did not hear it.

"Gentlemen," Luthor began, "status reports. Xu'ffasch,

how stand medical attention and disaster relief for the refugees from Kansas?"

"Delayed," the crisp young man responded. "According to my monitoring operations they're backed up for weeks."

"Splendid," Luthor said.

"Why is that splendid?" Nigma interjected, and looked around at the silence. "If I may ask?"

Luthor exhaled.

"Because, dear Edward," Selina said, "the metahuman community have made a tacit declaration of their primary commitment to the reclamation of the survivors and the salvaging of the real estate. To the degree that they fail, it is to our advantage."

"Ah, isn't that perceptive?"

Selina leaned over to Nigma, and everyone supposed it was to tighten his tether. Rather, it was to point surreptitiously at Xu'ffasch and tell Nigma, "He's the one. The son." Nigma's response was to put a hand to his chest and catch his breath. For a moment he could do nothing but stare at Xu'ffasch.

"Lord Naga," Luthor continued, "what resources do we have to allocate to ordnance dispersal this quarter?"

"We have recruited another sixscore vigilantes since our initiation of counterpropaganda to the Justice League campaign," the cult leader offered. "With the Arkham Asylum and Belle Rêve Prison survivors, along with ourselves and our various hangers-on and affinity groups, we are now responsible for eight percent of the identified superhuman population. There's an updated spreadsheet in your database."

"Excellent," Luthor said as he slid back a panel at his end of the big table, punched a few buttons, and studied what he saw. He slid back the panel and again he said, "Excellent. Selina, what are your projections of—"

"I wonder—" Nigma interrupted again, pausing for the requisite indulgent silence. "If you'll pardon the question, why your esteemed selves find it necessary not only to impede the reestablishment of public services for the suffering, but to arm metahumans as well? Where exactly does the 'Mankind Liberation' part of this concern come in? Did I miss something?"

"Selina," Luthor suggested, getting down to the ring of his cigar, "for your own good, keep a tighter leash on your guest."

Selina Kyle put a hand on Nigma's thigh and glared at Luthor, but it was the King of Spades who answered.

"I had a similar concern," King said. "Am I correct in assuming that our little MLF has embraced the tactic of raising the stakes rather than relaxing them?"

"A good-enough way of putting it." Luthor was a bit mollified. "Our objective is to heighten the tension between humans and metahumans—for the ultimate benefit of humanity in general."

"So you want us to throw in with a political pressure group," Savage suggested.

"In a manner of speaking," was Luthor's wary answer.

"What manner would that be?" Savage wanted to know. "Of speaking, that is."

"Look, Savage, I'm not sure we have time for semantics."

"I don't get tired of pointing out, Luthor, that I for one have all the time in the world." Savage smiled, and the Spectre bristled some more.

"Quite right," Luthor said. "Yes, Vandal, we are essentially a political pressure group whose eventual aim is to direct the inevitable bloodshed and war to which this world is undeniably headed. In the end, humankind will once again rule the Earth."

"That I understand," Savage said, satisfied.

But Nigma was not. "Humankind. So would a rough working translation of 'humankind' in that context be, 'you guys'?"

There was no answer for Nigma, so he posed another riddle.

"When is a villain not a villain?"

"When he labors for a greater good," Luthor said, the last bolt of his cigar's fumes shooting from his nostrils.

Luthor stubbed out his cigar and went on. "We have another problem. As you all know, since last we met, the gods have stepped down from Olympus. We have to adjust our long-term plan to accommodate the sudden resurfacing of the so-called Justice League. Their advent has contracted our ten-year agenda into a ten-day stratagem."

"I didn't think they'd return in a million years," said Savage.

"But we have now formulated a plan to neutralize them and their influence, turning their arrival to our advantage."

"Neutralize?" Naga asked. "By that, do you mean eliminate them?"

"Hold them to a stalemate," Luthor said, "until they are no longer players."

"How?" Savage pressed.

"I would rather reserve that information," Luthor said, continually punching buttons on the keyboard and small monitor built into the hidden recess at the head of the conference table. "I'd like our new alliance to gel a little bit first, but you can all thank young Xu'ffasch here for reestablishing some old family ties."

No one but the tall patrician Ibn al Xu'ffasch knew what Luthor meant by the remark, and that was the way Luthor liked it. The inveterate boss snapped a finger, and the door near him swung open so that Luthor's valet could stroll in with a fresh cigar and lighter.

"And Superman?" Nigma asked, smiling still.

The ice of Luthor's breath did not even melt against the flame that the young valet in the red suit held up to him as the boss sputtered and the unlit stogie flew out of his mouth with a spray of spittle.

"Superman will not lay a hand on—will not—he cannot—" and he stopped himself. He realized he was screaming.

"Are you all right, Lex?" Selina wondered. The question gave him a moment to draw himself back into himself.

Lex Luthor collected his composure and said, quietly,

" 'Superman,' as they still insist on calling him, will not touch us." Luthor drew the flame through a fresh cigar. Then he took a long puff that he expelled through his nostrils. "He certainly won't touch me."

"And have we heard this before?" Nigma smiled still.

The fumes seemed to be irritating Luthor's nasal passage, but just for a moment. "I have the most marvelous anti-Superman option ever devised." He looked up at the tall red-suited valet who now stood by his side at parade rest. "Haven't I, boy?"

"You do indeed, sir," the valet said.

That valet looked somehow familiar, Nigma thought. The stance nearly six and a half feet high, the yeasty handsome face, the wide grin, the narrow laugh-lined eyes; this was not the sort of mien you normally found on those anonymous functionaries who stand at the side of greater men. Then Edward Nigma solved the riddle before it finished forming in his own mind. He knew who this tall young valet was, and his smile dropped to a gaping stare.

If anyone noticed the change in Nigma's demeanor, no one let on. Like the man in the red suit, Nigma was the waiter here, the pet dog, the person whose face they would all forget as they left the room. Pity.

"I'm sure you enjoy a good cigar, don't you, Savage?" Luthor asked the aristocratic Cro-Magnon to his right.

"I do."

"Excellent. These are Churchills by Paul Garmirian. Who else would like to try one of these little masterpieces? Son, go get my humidor, would you? Here, Selina"—Luthor handed her his cigar and offered to light it for her when the valet went for the humidor— "accessorize away."

And as the tall man in red vanished into the next room to fetch the little cedar box for the master, Nigma found his voice again to whisper only: "Shazam."

Luthor glared at him, and both were relieved that nothing happened.

CHAPTER 13
New Oa

T o the Fortress?" he asked her.

"No, I don't want to go back there. Besides, they wouldn't know where to find us," she said.

"Is it private enough here?"

"They're our friends."

"Is it safe?"

"The gyroscopes are good enough for Green Lantern."

Superman and Wonder Woman had spent the past week adding eighty-four souls to the informal roster of the Justice League and making a note of only nineteen among those with whom they'd met who needed further persuasion.

"I just really need a break," she said.

There would be no break.

Ω   Ω   Ω

The satellite New Oa was named for Oa, the lost world at the geographic center of the Milky Way where the Guardians of the Universe had made their home and headquarters for eight billion years. If the glow of the original Oa's nameless star had been much brighter, it would still be visible to astronomers on Earth, who looked back over forty million years of time to see it. We knew that Oa and the Guardians themselves were lost, their star gone nova and planet vaporous. We knew this because the interstellar paramilitary force the Guardians once founded and directed, the Green Lantern Corps, now drifted on of its own weight like the movements of the stars themselves. A handful of individual Green Lanterns had thought to bring some order to the force over the years and tried to take command. Because of the nature of the far-flung Corps, however, no one could find an effective way to keep track of all three-thousand-odd holders of the power battery, each of whom had a sector of the Galaxy in which to keep order. Like many Green Lanterns, Alan Scott had spent most of his career unaware of the true source of his Lantern-energy, ascribing it to magic until an extraterrestrial colleague came across him and explained it all. Scott never either aspired to command or thought it was necessary. When they retired or before they died, Green Lanterns generally managed through some means to pass on the accoutrements of their power to someone worthy—or at least potentially worthy.

Astronomers on Earth did not have to look as far to see New Oa, the name that Alan Scott, the longest-surviving Green Lantern of Earth, had given to the city-sized green-glowing satellite he'd built to patrol the skies. It completed an orbit of the Earth tracing the ninetieth longitude line in precisely one sidereal day: twenty-three hours, fifty-six minutes, four and one-tenth seconds. People with good eyesight could see it unaided, a dim green star crossing the faces of the countries of the Earth. The day Alan Scott had begun construction on it—the assembly taking only six days—the hushed word in aerospace circles was that it was some sort of reconnaissance craft of an alien civilization. With word of this suspicion quickly becoming worldwide news, Magog had taken it upon himself to check the place out.

Magog had encased himself in the protection of his confederate, Alloy, the malleable metal-fleshed android, then propelled both of them up to find the enormous satellite nearly built. Green Lantern, tired and weighed down with work yet to come, had been in no mood for little leaguers or their games. With the pair close enough to see, Green Lantern had stood on an emerald wing of the most extended platform and waved Alloy and Magog away.

But they had kept coming.

Green Lantern had resumed work on an engineering problem, chalking up calculations on a big ray-energy blackboard hanging in front of him in space. Slowly Magog and Alloy sidled up beside him and circled once, as if trying to figure out his actions. They looked over the satellite, as if by looking at it they could see whether it was something to which they could reasonably object. Then, with Alloy's protection, Magog drifted over toward Green Lantern, struggling with a three-headed monster of a math problem, and tapped him hard on the shoulder.

Absently, Green Lantern loosed a curved shoot of energy from his power-charged suit of green armor. It widened to form a man-sized funnel. In the time between Magog's first tap on Lantern's shoulder and his attempt at a second one, the funnel enveloped both Magog and his android friend, sealing them with a dense cushion forming inside, and sucking them back Earthward just fast enough for the G-force to knock Magog unconscious.

At the nearest point on Earth's surface—a small island off the southern coast of Alaska—a great green trumpet like that of a cornucopia touched down within sight of Sanaz Tunari's bait-and-tackle shop. Sanaz snatched up a little disposable camera from his counter and ran down the icy path to the phenomenon. The funnel had burst open on the beach, depositing Magog and Alloy ungracefully on a blanket of fresh snow. Shaking his head awake, Magog got his footing with the help of the android's shoulder, and said, "Well, I don't think that'll be a problem for us, do you?"

Alloy shook his head, and neither bothered Green Lantern

again. Sanaz' pictures had made it into every sleazy tabloid on the Pacific Rim, and with that found money he built a new house behind the bait shop. And up in space, tracing the path around the globe of the ninetieth meridian, Green Lantern sat watching out for alien invasions until the day Superman and Wonder Woman asked to use New Oa as the Justice League's new headquarters.

Ω   Ω   Ω

Donna Troy and Roy Harper had once been Wonder Girl and Speedy. A generation ago—a few dozen self-important costumed villains ago, a couple of failed marriages, and a few more destructive relationships ago, triumphs and crises and a character change in the world ago—Donna and Roy's history had begun. Once upon a time they'd been a pair of extraordinarily talented and lucky innocent kids who liked to dress up and planned to make the world better together. And with the games of childhood evolving into the complications of adulthood and the preoccupations of middle age, these two had leaned on one another for support when they needed, for the sake of their own sanity, to be selfish and immature for a little while. They were good friends. They had a kind of shorthand language together.

"They were staring out the window on the observation deck," Donna told Roy. "I thought I heard her say she needs a break."

"About time," Roy said. "They haven't let up since the Statue."

"Who else is aboard?" Donna asked him.

"Just Lantern and the sleep shift. Everyone else is out. Somewhere."

"Should we cover them? Cut them a break?"

"Can we?" he wanted to know.

"We can try."

Ω   Ω   Ω

There is no such thing, I had learned from my late friend Wesley, as elephant privacy. Wesley was always a compendium of generally useless but always interesting information. I once had tried to put his observations on elephant privacy to use in a sermon, but there was no avoiding the essential frivolity of the analogy in order to make my way around it to the point—whatever that might be. But here is the basic idea:

Elephants are extremely intelligent animals. They are also undeniably huge. When two elephants are moved to develop a personal relationship, there is no place they can go to find privacy: no tree wide enough, no rock big enough, no corner isolated enough. So elephant friendships have evolved into a function of the herd at large. What substitutes for elephant intimacy generally involves the entire circle of family and friends in mass rituals of bellowing and pounding down the bush out of boundless joy over the value of such fellowship to the community.

Stomping and trumpeting. Stomping and trumpeting.

That, according to my friend Wesley, is what elephants do.

Ω   Ω   Ω

"What do we do about this topographical data?" Roy Harper asked Green Lantern.

"What you usually do. Get it to Superman," Alan Scott told his navigator-in-training.

Years ago, the least favorite way Roy's mentor had spent his time was marking it in the Justice League satellite. Green Arrow—Ollie Queen, who'd raised Roy Harper and trained him in archery and derring-do—had groaned whenever it was his turn to warm the helm of the old Justice League satellite. Now, grown into the hi-tech archer Red Arrow, Roy found something very elemental about space flight, something that fed his soul. He was suited to it as a baseball is suited to the air. Green Lantern rode the rhythms of space as well as any man alive, and Roy could have no better teacher.

The latest topographical profile of a random sector of the Earth below showed a number of anomalies. There was land where there should have been none; water where there'd been none the day before. The survey was over only three or four hundred square miles of sparsely inhabited ground—but still.

"Where is the survey?" Red Arrow asked Green Lantern.

"Rain forest," the old ring-wielder said, and adjusted a stabilizer. "Southern Amazon basin."

"I'll get Donna," Roy said.

"What can she do?" Lantern asked him.

"I guess," Roy supposed, "she might know what to do."

"Some reason you can't ask Superman if he'd check it out?"

Roy hesitated. "No reason," he said.

Lantern moved so he was between Roy and the control console and spun a dial about twenty degrees to the left. Roy grabbed a handhold on the wall and steadied himself as the ship lurched. Green Lantern looked around innocently at the younger man.

"What was that?" Red Arrow wanted to know.

"What was what?" the old man snapped back. "You green under the gills, or is that just a reflection from the walls? Look, son, we've got Magog on the loose, and this could just be him. You telling Supes about this anomaly or what?"

"Sure." Roy excused himself and stepped out into a long emerald tube that led from the navigation deck to the complex of passenger pods.

And the orientation of the satellite itself shifted so that the Earth below jumped from a little crescent of ocean at the translucent green walkway below Roy—to fill his frame of vision. In a moment he felt sick.

Red Arrow tried to rush down the corridor to a water closet, as crazy old Alan Scott dubbed the suction waste disposal units with which he peppered the satellite. Roy could not make it before he ran into Donna Troy coming around a corner.

She looked at him questioningly for a moment as he careened past her into the small chamber off the corridor tube, then poked her head into Green Lantern's navigation bridge.

"Alan?" she asked the big man. "Is there something wrong?"

"Wrong?" Lantern asked. "What could be wrong?"

There was a lurch of the craft. Lantern's hands were off the controls, and Donna could see the image of Earth rattling in the window, then shifting back.

"That," she said.

"Turbulence," Alan Scott deadpanned.

"We're in space, Alan."

"Then we know it isn't air turbulence, I guess."

"Well, what is it?"

The big man shrugged.

"Where's it coming from?" as the rattling of the satellite became markedly pronounced, like the slow and steady rocking of an oceangoing vessel. "Can't you figure out where it's coming from? You've got a power battery, for Heaven's sake."

"All right, all right!" Green Lantern huffed as Red Arrow stumbled back into the room. "Hey, Roy, is that why they used to call you 'Speedy'?"

"Amusing." The former Speedy wiped his lower lip.

"All right, kids," Lantern said, "there's a yaw on Inspiration Point."

"Inspiration Point?" the former Wonder Girl asked.

"The observation deck," Roy answered. "The old man's having second-childhood fantasies. Calls this navigation bridge the Playroom."

"Fourth, fifth, maybe eighth childhood," Lantern said as he reached behind himself to spin a pair of switches like the dials on an Etch-a-Sketch. "Lost count."

The craft took a sudden dip.

The colossal satellite tumbled end over end in space, and it was all Donna and Roy could do to keep their stomachs intact.

"They make pills for that now, kids," Green Lantern said as he continued playfully to violate the stability of the craft. Both of these "kids" were well into their forties. The older man was immensely amused that the pair still did not realize it was he who was making the giant craft lurch. They must have thought he was crazy as Captain Queeg pretending not to notice it. "Hey, go check out Inspiration Point for pressure leaks if you think it's important."

And Roy and Donna giggled and held their stomachs like kids going up and down in a moon bounce as they crashed and shoved their way along the corridors and convection chambers of New Oa.

Ω Ω Ω

"He has been scrupulously secretive about his personal life since he was a very young man," the Spectre said to me, "yet you knew that these two were not life companions. You knew right away that there had been someone else. How?"

"I told you. I'm a minister. Men and women. Life and love. Relationships. It's my stock in trade."

"I do not understand it," the Spectre admitted. "Any of it. It has been so long since I was incarnate, and I have so filled the time with deeds and experiences. That was why I asked to impose upon your wisdom for this mission."

"What don't you understand? Relationships?"

"Among humans. They are so complicated. I am sure that I never experienced one of the magnitude that these two have, yet you imply that this pales against the experiences of their youth."

"Its magnitude is no less, perhaps," I said. "Youthful loves are different, is all. There is less of the intellectual sharing than these two have, but more of the emotional and physical sharing."

"When first I introduced you to Kal-El and Diana," the Spectre observed, "you said that women scare men. I do not remember this from life."

"Perhaps I was saying," I observed, trying not to smile, "that such a woman as this would scare me. Superman seems not to be scared. Certainly, though, he was scared of Lois. Did you know her?"

"I did. I even met her once, shortly before she left mortal life."

"What was she like?"

"Like this one," the Spectre said, indicating Wonder Woman. "Unafraid. Unpredictable. Not like the mortal women I remember."

"Would you say that Lois might have been a woman suited only for life with a very strong and sure man?"

"I do not know."

"This woman Diana," I said to the Spectre, "is very much unlike the public persona of the Wonder Woman I remember."

"How is that?"

"The Wonder Woman of my youth was an icon. She appeared from nowhere to solve problems. Her tools were persuasion and intimidation, as much as her sword or her magic lasso. This woman is not so monolithic. She is complex. Certainly she is intimidating, but she's thoughtful and intellectually honest. And she is unpredictable. The things she does, things she says, genuinely surprise Kal-El sometimes. He is exasperated and delighted by that, I am sure. I just don't think a young man—even a young Superman—could be wise or brave enough to enter her intimate world. This is a relationship of maturity."

The Spectre looked impassive. He always looked impassive, but I went on anyway.

"These are people who come together only after doing a lot of living," I explained. "Only after being vulnerable and disappointed a lot. After loving and being loved a lot. Both of them. A woman this formidable needs a man who's weathered, sanded down around the edges—or she needs to be with no one at all. And a man this weathered needs someone capable of making him forget the ghosts of his own sad stories—or he needs to be with no one at all."

The Spectre looked at them some more, with clinical interest.

"Then again," I said, "I may be wrong."

"You may be wrong? You have been correct consistently. I have learned much from your insight," the ghost said.

"Thank you."

"But you are telling me that in the realm of human relationships there are no definable rules. Is that possible, Norman, in the context of God's Creation?"

"I'm not saying anything of the sort. Certainly there are rules. We are just not smart enough to know what they are."

Ω Ω Ω

Looking for the source of the strange instability of the New Oa satellite, and fighting the gyrations in space caused by Green Lantern, Roy and Donna reached the door of the observation deck. Donna was about to press the panel to slide it open when Roy stayed her hand.

"Shouldn't we knock?" he asked her.

"If they're in there, they already know we're here." The satellite spun a bit again. It lurched. On the ground a tremor like that might measure close to six on the Richter scale.

"Okay, then let's open the door."

They did . . .

. . . and found the observation deck dead as a ghost town. The globe of the Earth hung big and blue, 22,300 miles out the window. Then the floor shifted, and when the satellite stopped moving, the planet was only a crescent along the

emerald pane and the constellation Orion hung where the
Earth had been.

Donna leaned back against a wall and put a hand over her
mouth. She was the spacesick one now.

It was a long shaky walk back to the navigation deck to
find Green Lantern and tell him that Superman and Wonder
Woman were nowhere to be found. Probably, Roy and Donna
thought, the two of them went off somewhere for a deserved
respite. That was not the case.

"All right, give the kids a break, Alan," was what the two
former Titans heard when they stepped, queasy and uncertain,
back onto the navigation deck. It was Wonder Woman's voice.
As she said it, Lantern smiled, and the rocking and rolling of
the satellite suddenly came stable.

Superman stood next to Green Lantern studying the topographical printout, and peered with telescopic vision out the
bay window at the Amazon River on the planet out there. The
Kryptonian looked down at the unrolled printout in his hands,
then up at the Earth; down again, up again, comparing.

"Just natural annual river runoff," Superman said. "No environmental dislocation as far as I can tell. The Amazon is
pretty wild this time of year. The Earth will shift beneath your
feet on a moment's notice."

Wonder Woman smiled at that and motioned for their two
younger friends to come on in.

"No Magog?" Donna asked.

"No, haven't found him yet," Superman said as he put
down the printout and clapped Alan Scott on the shoulder. "I
hear you've caused these two a rough night."

"You were doing that on purpose, Alan?" Red Arrow
asked. "Making the whole satellite bump and grind like that?
I thought—"

"You thought a spacecraft I built with my own hands
would pitch like a rowboat just because we've got a crew
who've been known to play a little rough once in a while?"

"No," Donna said, "but we just thought—"

"Never mind what you thought," the Green Lantern barked. "You two'll learn to be competent space engineers before this thing is over, or you won't keep down another meal."

"Are competent space engineers required to work for days without letup and contend with their commander's penchant for riding the bridge like the Bizarro Captain Ahab?" Roy wanted to know.

"Occasionally," Alan Scott said, and as he reached for the stabilizer panel again, Wonder Woman grabbed at the nearest handhold. "We've got more work to do. What's everybody say to some java?"

"I'll get it," Superman said. "I can brew it up in about a tenth of a second."

The Man of Steel, unbound by inertia or the wages of fatigue, would have no trouble negotiating the gyrating corridor to the galley and back. Donna, Roy, and Diana laughed like kids at a carnival, clutching the green wall bars and hanging on to the magnetized floors of this emerald space palace. And Alan Scott, custodian of the power battery of the Guardians of the Universe, spun his stabilizer dials around and around, and the satellite pitched and yawed and spun and spun and spun, stomping and trumpeting: the Elephants' Dance.

CHAPTER 14

Atlantis

Those who dwelled in the kingdom of the oceans were never as preoccupied as their surface-dwelling cousins with filling slots. Perhaps the casual attitude down here was based in metaphor: Water is more visible in filling a vacuum than air is, if not as eager as air is. The office of the President of the United States had never been unoccupied for more than a few hours at a time in its two and a half centuries. Asian, European, and African nations were, over the dynasties, inclined to put children on their parents' unoccupied thrones and wrap those tiny fingers around the scepters of power, if only to keep authority away from eager and plentiful usurpers. Napoléon Bonaparte once declared his yet-unborn son King of Rome. When Rā's al Ghūl's spent and ancient body finally had crumbled seven years before, the forces of the shadow empire upended cities and rattled sedate civilizations in a frenzy to recover the Demon's callow designated successor and explain to him the responsibilities that the rest of his unnaturally long life would involve.

By contrast, when Atlantis' last ruler had expired, its civilization patiently waited. The new King completed his education and played out the extended drama of his youth before finally assuming the burden of the people's crown. In Atlantis—even as a violent young culture sitting high on a volcanic rock in the sunshine millennia ago—a King did not have subjects so much as a nation had its King.

Now he was wise and grizzled beyond his early middle age. He'd grown up believing he was only Arthur Curry, dreamy son of a lighthouse keeper. He thought every kid could swim to Cape Horn and back in an afternoon and talk to the fishes on the way. Now he sat on the ancient Abalone Throne, and here he would stay for the foreseeable centuries.

"She remembers Aquaman," Arthur told his Queen, "though I can barely recall the young fellow myself."

"There was talk of a royal alliance in those days," Delphia said.

"Really? Between whom?"

"Atlantis and the isle of the Amazons."

"Through me?" The King had never heard of such a thing before and found the suggestion startling.

"Your exploits among the superhumans were fodder for popular entertainment throughout your youth, Arthur. Every rotation new odds were cast in the grottoes concerning whether and when you would marry her."

"But we never even—"

"Never?" she asked.

"She's an Amazon, for Neptune's sake, Delphia."

"Oh yes. I forgot about the surface men's elaborate legends surrounding such women's proclivities. They are a defensive mechanism, you know."

"Pardon?"

"The prejudices and peccadilloes of a youth mostly spent on land." The clear-skinned Queen smiled at him. "You still have traces of it, don't you, my King?"

"I certainly do not," he said.

The Queen smiled and expelled a trail of water bubbles as the Princess floated—struggling to appear to walk—into the throne room with her imposing consort behind her. The surface dwellers would not recognize the Queen's trail of bubbles as an expression of mirth, and she could continue to poke at her husband's spiny hide even in their presence.

Wonder Woman wore a pressure helmet and speaker; Superman did not require the undiluted oxygen and could communicate as the Atlanteans did through deciphering throat exhalations, much in the manner of speech.

Diana went down to one knee, floating upward from the sea floor as she lowered her head, and said, "Offering Your Majesty thanks for his gracious grant of an audience."

"Diana, you look wonderful," the King said. "The tides of time have been kind to you, Princess. Please speak freely. You know Delphia."

"Of course," she said. "This is a beautiful kingdom, an architecture worthy of Paradise Island."

Superman started to extend his right hand to his former colleague and thought better of it. He simply said, "Hello, Arthur."

"Good to see you, Kal." The King turned back to Diana: "You have not aged a day since we met."

"Thank you," she said, observing the elaborate protocols necessary to ease the social encounter into a discussion of substance. "Would that the outside world had fared so well, but times above have grown hard and harsh."

"The surface world is in a crisis, surely you know," Superman jumped in to explain.

"Ah yes." The crowned head nodded. "I see that the ocean trenches in which your cities dump your garbage are beginning to overflow. Is that the crisis you mean?"

"No, Arthur," Superman said. "Certainly you're aware of the—"

"The extinction of entire races of sea life upon whom surface industries have made themselves dependent? Is it that crisis?"

"Arthur, I'm sure you've—"

"Or perhaps you refer to the crisis of identity of the surface race. To their assumption that they are the rulers of the Universe, the assumption that obtains in their tiny little minds until they realize what a small part of a tiny speck in a vast cosmos among an enormous expanse of Creation they really occupy. And then when they realize that they don't even really hold sway over their own minute fraction of a speck, they have—what did we used to call it?—an identity crisis. That crisis?"

Unlike Superman, Wonder Woman realized that a King's suggestion to speak freely comes, like any other free lunch, with hidden costs. This is true even when—or perhaps especially when—the King is an old friend whose youthful exuberances peck at his memory. Or perhaps Superman was simply unused to paying such costs. Diana stood quietly—as protocol determined she ought to do—until she could stand the wait no longer. Then she interrupted.

"Your M-m-majesty." She stammered a little.

The King cut himself off, smiled at her, and said, despite his Queen's obvious amusement, "Please. Call me Arthur."

"Arthur." She tripped over the name as though it were uncomfortable for her to say. It was not uncomfortable, of course, but rather the name by which she had addressed him for years. Unlike her companion, however, the Amazon Princess knew that there were appearances one had to perpetuate. "Arthur, please excuse our presumption."

"Nothing new," he said. "I've been excusing it for years."

"A new generation of metahumans has made the surface world harsh. The environment is becoming unlivable from a sociological standpoint as well as a physical one."

"And this is a surprise to you?"

"Arthur," she said, "surely you remember the virtue of many of the surface dwellers among whom you lived for so long."

"What exactly do you feel you need from us, Diana?"

"Your political skill, Arthur, and your diplomatic—" Superman began, but she put a hand on his arm and interrupted again.

"We need something quite substantial. We need the seas to provide a buffer between the rebellious metahumans and the land-dwelling society. We need your permission to build an underwater penal colony for the rebels."

"Excuse me?" This time Superman interrupted, surprised.

"Don't insult me by acting disingenuous, Kal-El," tossed off the King. "You're Superman, for Neptune's sake. Don't pretend the Princess is making a request of which you were unaware."

"I really didn't know that—"

"He didn't." The Princess bowed her head with some contrition. "He has not yet agreed that such a facility is necessary. I just thought that it was unlikely that Your Majesty would want to leave his kingdom to undertake a dangerous and unlikely enterprise, but that you certainly would see the necessity of detaining and reeducating miscreants."

"I do see the necessity, Diana," Arthur said, "but our kingdom has grown too used to being burdened with the surface world's refuse. Request denied."

Superman realized that a few years ago he would have been better at this sort of thing—dealing on a personal level with a chief of state. In ten years of self-imposed exile, however, his interpersonal skills had eroded somewhat and his sense of protocol had virtually vanished. He determined at least to make the request he'd come here to make.

"Arthur, if only you could see the trouble we're in up there," Superman said to his curiously imperious old friend. "Stand at our side as you did in your youth. You have no idea how valuable just your presence would be. Please join us."

Neither the Amazon Princess nor the Atlantean Queen had any idea what effect the frank plea of this one extraordinarily powerful man might have on this other extraordinarily powerful man. For a moment even King Arthur paused. Then he said, "Oh, Clark."

Superman tilted his head.

"You are still Clark, aren't you?"

"No, Arthur. I'm afraid not. Clark died some time ago."

"Oh, I'm sorry," the King said. "I liked him."

"I did, too," Superman said, "but now he's gone."

"I miss the camaraderie of those days, too, though I was never comfortable being your 'Aquaman.' I've left that name and role to Garth, my protégé."

"He's joined us, you know," Superman said. "Perhaps if he were to come and explain to you—"

"No, Cl— No, Kal. That would not work, either. Garth knows better."

"I'm sure he does," Wonder Woman added.

Finally Arthur softened to Superman, though his point of view did not. Perhaps it was the memory of the role the Man of Steel played as the ordinary but stolid newspaperman that woke the heart of the King. I wondered what Clark Kent had been like, wished I could have met him. I was sure I would have liked him, too.

"My subjects need me," the King told the Princess. "You have hundreds of champions to defend a few paltry land masses. I protect the other seventy percent of the world. You could have no idea of the responsibilities I bear to my people here. Certainly you, Princess, are aware of the moral weight of a royal crown."

"I no longer have my royal station, Arthur."

"No?" The Atlantean was genuinely surprised. So was Superman, I knew, but he did not dare allow Arthur to see that. "What happened?"

"Recently my Amazon sisters who chose me as their ambassador to the outside world determined that my mission was a failure."

"How so?"

"They were right. I failed to make the outside world a better place than it was when I left Paradise Island. Still, I insisted for one reason or another that I needed to continue. So they relieved me of my royalty and my heritage. I am no longer welcome on Paradise Island."

"I am sorry," the man who once had been Aquaman said. He paused and took a long gillful of the water around him. "I only wish that could have some bearing on my decision. But it cannot."

The meeting had been over minutes before. It was only now that they were willing to recognize it.

Ω   Ω   Ω

"How long were you planning on keeping that from me?" he wanted to know. He would like to have known this the moment she'd suggested building a prison installation, and from the moment she'd mentioned the loss of her crown. Here in the open air, rising through the clear sky, was his first opportunity to bring it up.

"Which time?"

"Both times. You made me look like a fool in front of the King. He didn't even believe it was news to me."

"I probably should have brought it up before."

"Probably? Diana, you're suggesting a fundamental tactical and philosophical shift about which I have grave concerns."

"We've got rogue metahumans scattered in prisons and makeshift facilities all over the world. Most of them, though, are running around loose with your unspecified threats still ringing in their ears. More captives than converts."

"And you suggest that we arrogate to ourselves the position of judge, jury, and Grand Inquisitor." They flew fairly slowly. Only now were they reaching the edge of the atmosphere, where even these two could no longer hear one another speak until they reached the satellite.

"Kal, I'm tired," Diana said as her musculature flexed and pulsed around itself in that impossible way it has to do in order for a person to fly. "You don't know about being tired, and it's a stretch for me, but the pace of this thing is horrendous. So sometimes I just want to get things done and I leave things out. I'm just used up sometimes. I'm sorry, all right?"

For years, this man had lived with a human wife whom he'd loved and regarded as his partner and equal. He'd grown up in the home of two normal parents, fine people with no powers or abilities beyond those of mortal men. Now he was pressing this Amazon prodigy to the walls of her own strength. He should have known better, he knew. "I'm sorry," he said. "All right?"

And for a while it was all right.

Ω   Ω   Ω

"And there was a rainbow round about the throne," came the echo in my memory of old Saint John through the voice of Wesley Dodds, "in sight like unto an emerald."

Everything aboard New Oa was as green as Atlantis, and glowed as well. Against the backdrop of space, it made for a surrounding that seemed far more verdant and vital even than the teeming sea floor. The big satellite spun above the Indian Ocean and moved due north.

"We've done pretty well at attracting large numbers of our colleagues and successors," Superman began. He stood at a seat around a large round green table. He paused and continued, "but we struck out on two big ones. Most of you know by now that Bruce Wayne—the Batman—and the former Aquaman, King Arthur Curry, have declined to join us."

There were creased foreheads and murmurings around the table. Evidently everyone here did not already know this. For many, both the Dark Knight and the King of the Seven Seas were nearly the role models that Superman himself had been. Garth, the new Aquaman, whom Arthur once had considered his son, was especially disappointed but not surprised.

"He told me to play out the extended drama of my youth," Garth said.

"Guess what, Garth?" whispered his old friend Red Arrow.

"What?"

"You're graying around the gills, pallie. It may be too late for that drama."

"We've all got that problem"—Superman smiled for the first time today—"except maybe Diana."

The Man of Steel chaired the meeting quite informally. More than two dozen powerful and accomplished women and men sat at this table or stood in the room, but rather than trying to impose parliamentary procedure to keep order, Superman simply approached it as though he were having a conversation with his friends. If someone interrupted him, he supposed that person had something important to say. As it happened, no one—not even among this collection of colorful types—interrupted him lightly.

Around the table in the Earthrise room of the New Oa satellite sat the members of the Justice League who had made themselves the most active in the past weeks. Among the older ones were the "Seven Angels" who'd stormed the Statue the day of the New United Nations news conference, as well as Captain Comet, Tornado, Donna Troy, and others. The younger ones—Avia, Starman VIII, Bulletgirl, Tyra, and the others—wondered how they'd ever made it here.

Superman looked across the room at Garth again and mused: "It would be like Arthur to call the cratering of Kansas a 'learning experience' for the people who died there."

Garth took it as a rebuke but he need not have. Diana saw him trying to blend into the curved green wall, grinned at him, leaned in, and shoved his shoulder with her own. Certainly the friendly shove would have knocked me to the ground, and it nearly did that to the new Aquaman, but he smiled back.

"Any other new business?" Superman asked.

Nothing.

"All right," he said. "Back to work. Diana and I are off to eastern Europe today to do some recruiting. Anyone without a specific assignment is welcome to come along. We're adjourned."

As Superman left the room with Wonder Woman behind him, Captain Comet got up from his chair and smiled at the quizzical Avia. She whispered to the older man, "He's so casual, and somehow unattainable at the same time."

Captain Comet nodded.

"He has no idea what he's accomplished here already," Avia put forth, and the Captain shrugged.

Avia talked and the Captain gestured toward the door. Both of them knew that Superman could well be listening.

CHAPTER 15

Citizen Wayne

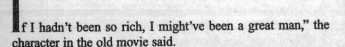

I f I hadn't been so rich, I might've been a great man," the character in the old movie said.

As he always did, Bruce Wayne doubled over on his seat and rolled to the left. He used his titanium framing as a rocking pontoon on the couch, and he laughed. Slowly, in what spare time he afforded himself, he was restoring parts of the old manor house with his own hands. The living room with his beloved grandfather clock where his mom once had read to him from Dr. Seuss and from Hans and Margaret Rey, where his dad used to smoke his pipe until dawn, sometimes over a mystery novel, was nearly done. It was done enough to be watertight, done enough for a couch and a monitor. Wayne had not laughed so hard and so long from the age of eight to age fifty. Then the line about being a great man had begun to strike him funny.

He laughed so loudly that he missed the next line. It had been so long since he had not laughed that Bruce Wayne forgot what the line was.

In the years after Superman dropped from the world's stage, especially once knowledge of the Batman's identity had entered the collective consciousness, with some of his surviving enemies trashing the most visible trappings of his enormous wealth, something strange had happened to Bruce Wayne. Gradually, without reason or explanation, he'd become happy. There was no denying it, and it had puzzled him at first.

Ω   Ω   Ω

There were two things in this life with which Bruce Wayne had to come to terms: First, his parents were not coming back; and second, no matter how much and how painfully he taught himself to be better at sharing his soul and his life, there would never be a woman able to handle him properly. Even setting aside his incalculable wealth, Bruce Wayne was undeniably a high-maintenance guy.

His parents had been taken from him when he was eight. Dr. Thomas and Martha Wayne had died at the hands of a petty thief. It'd happened when social taboos against killing a child obtained even among the dregs of the community, probably the last time such a gunman would leave behind even an innocent-eyed witness to robbery and murder.

If the gunman had simply asked for the necklace, if he had not resolved even before he met them to kill his victims, then Thomas and Martha probably would have found a way to break the natural laws of engagement and solve the problem. Martha might have looked at the robber—a boy himself, really—with that tilted head and that piercing temperament and the can-do attitude that had brought her through four years of Army intelligence work. He would have relented—just enough—when she asked him what the problem was, or what drove him to thievery, or how she might make it all better with a few phone calls and a chance for honest work. Even if he was not interested in honest work, she had that way of convincing folks that they wanted what she thought they ought to want.

And when the young man did not lower the gun, Thomas

would have evened the sides by offering to buy the pistol from him. What is that thing, he would have asked, a little Raven? What'd you pay for that on the street, about forty-five bucks? Will you take a hundred for it? Give it here before you hurt yourself and I have to take you to the emergency room. Come on, come on, he would have said as he threw open his jacket and casually revealed the location of the secret cash pouch in his belt and peeled off a pair of hundred-dollar bills for the guy and offered to buy him a bite with the family, too. We just saw *The Mark of Zorro,* he would have told the former gunman as Dr. Wayne tucked the little pistol into the lining of his tailored jacket. They re-released it, you know. Don't hardly make movies like that anymore, he would have said . . . introducing his little son—This is my boy, Brucie—to the man who might have changed the child's life, and they would have shaken hands.

Never happened. It took Bruce Wayne most of a lifetime to get over the fact that it never happened. In the course of that most-of-a-lifetime he chased after the ghost of the man who had murdered Thomas and Martha Wayne in the street and made even more miserable the lives of hundreds, maybe thousands, of people who thought they might get a leg up by stepping on the backs of others. In the course of that most-of-a-lifetime he spent several fortunes on computer hardware and paramilitary vehicles and travel and research and relief funds and cavern renovation and a big spotlight with a special lens that cast a signal on the sky and what-all. And in the course of spending all that money, the family fortune under his stewardship only grew to monstrous proportions. Bruce Wayne—with the collusion of Alfred Pennyworth, whom Martha and Thomas had given a home after the death of his father, their servant—had taken charge of his own life at the age of eight. No one but Pennyworth ever caught on to the little mogul's innate genius, a secret both of them guarded gleefully. Technological and industrial breakthroughs that the Batman had made in the course of his ongoing war on the denizens of the Gotham underbelly formed the basis of the reinvention of Wayne Industries.

Bruce Wayne believed in the supernatural, and he believed that the energy that drives the Universe is an intelligent force. Like his Puritan forebears, he took his success as an indication that he was doing what he was properly meant to do. Then one day he realized that his hoary old city, his family heirloom Gotham, was finally the palace of his dreams. Even in these restive times, every citizen who walked these avenues and enjoyed these pavilions was responsible to every other, and no child was in danger on these streets. It was still a garrison state where his great mechanical bats patrolled the skies, but he was close enough finally to know that his efforts were working, and Bruce Wayne was happy.

He was happy.

There were no parents, and they would have made great old folks too if they had ever had the chance, but they did not. There was no one with whom to share all this, not even Talia, who would have made a great partner if she and Bruce had ever had the chance, but they did not. Hell, any of a hundred strong women would have made a great partner, but Talia would have made the best one. Bruce Wayne was doomed, he'd decided long before, to share his life only with his male friends: with Alfred, who was dead, and Dick, who was estranged, and Clark, who was on his own mad crusade these days. So now there were Ted and Ollie. Sure, there was Dinah, who belonged with someone else, so she may as well have been a man for all he cared. But Bruce Wayne was doing his job.

He had many luxuries, but the greatest of them was knowing where he belonged in the world, and knowing that was where he was. He thought about Talia often: Talia, the daughter of perhaps the greatest of his enemies—Rā's al Ghūl; beautiful, exotic, brave Talia; a memory of love swallowed up by circumstance.

This afternoon, in the few hours a week he gave himself

for leisure—and he did give himself a few hours a week for leisure now—he punched up a disk of *Citizen Kane*. It was a comedy. At least it was for Bruce Wayne. He laughed raucously all the way through it and could not for the life of him remember how somebody could be that rich and still be that miserable. And he thanked God and went back to work.

CHAPTER 16

Magog

"**Y**ou know I've never been comfortable with forcing others to follow my lead, Diana." They were in the twilight room of the emerald satellite. Earthrise filled the lower right-hand corner of the dome window, and soon the big blue marble with its shifting white patterns would fill their line of vision. "Now we're about to imprison those who won't."

"That seems to be the prescription, Kal."

Superman was not in the habit of pacing, of forcing his mind to percolate an idea, but in the face of this woman's prodding, even his mind could not work fast enough to bubble up an alternative. So he paced.

"What's the problem, Kal?"

"You want us—me, really—to be judge, jury, and jailer. I am simply not comfortable with—"

"Since when did you require comfort?"

"You're talking like a fascist, Diana."

"Well, I can admit to being a monarchist, but that's not something I've ever imposed on anyone, and I don't advocate doing it now." She allowed a deep breath and turned away from the looming globe of the Earth to face him. "In a war you don't stop to consider secondary principles. And that's what this is. A war."

"So we're forced to crack heads among our own kind."

"Will you stop that 'our own kind' garbage, Kal? We're all stake-holders in that planet out there. No more, no less. It's our role to be protectors of humanity. And these people we're talking about are barely human. Get some perspective, will you?"

"Is that you, Diana?"

"Is that you, Kal?"

"You seem so angry."

"Not angry. Passionate."

"Oh. That."

Somehow there was suddenly no space between them, and the satellite and the planet and the sun beyond faded from their perception.

And someone coughed.

"'Scuse us?" Red Arrow said.

"What?" Superman wanted to know.

"It's Magog, Superman. We found him."

$$\Omega \quad \Omega \quad \Omega$$

I thought for a while that I was a dupe of the prophets of old, that my burden of tongues and visions was a curse foretold and required by our holier ancestors, who'd walked through life having conversations with their Creator the way we might talk back and forth with a friend. Magog was the real dupe.

Somewhere toward the end of the book of *The Revelation of Saint John the Divine,* the book from whose account of an apocalyptic future I found myself quoting against my will in languages in which I have never been fluent, the mad old visionary mentions something called Magog. It is refreshing, as I tell this story, to have to look up the exact line; refreshing not to have it blossom unbidden like the weed of my cerebellum. Saint John gave to us a narrative prophecy of what would happen when the Beast—man and God's implacable ancient enemy—takes over the world. John wrote:

> And when the thousand years are expired, Satan shall be loosed out of his prison, And shall go out to deceive the nations which are in the four quarters of the earth, Gog and Magog, to gather them together to battle: the number of whom is as the sand of the sea. And they went up on the breadth of the earth, and compassed the camp of the saints about, and the beloved city: and fire came down from God out of heaven, and devoured them. And the devil that deceived them was cast into the lake of fire and brimstone, where the beast and the false prophet are, and shall be tormented day and night for ever and ever.

So what was this Magog? *Our* Magog? Was he a player in this ancient dance between God and Satan? Between Man and Beast? Whom did he fancy himself to be in this fossil of a morality play?

I was feeling strong. I was growing into the eternal age-lessness of this spirit state in which I had already "lived," it seemed, for so long. I touched the soul of Superman himself and of uncounted others whom the casual observer would surely judge far greater than I am. When the Spectre and I found Magog—moments before Superman and his company did, in fact, on the barren floor of what once was Kansas, trying to reassemble the broken pottery of his crime brick by shattered brick and bone by ashen bone—I felt through the ether and the souls around me as I learned to do, and sought out the story of this most tortured of God's creatures.

Ω Ω Ω

Magog had been, for a short time, a particular target of the investigative journalist Lois Lane. His path to acceptance among the general public in Metropolis had eased with Ms. Lane's demise. By the time of my arrival with Ellen in Metropolis, Lois Lane was already very renowned and accomplished, with half a dozen Pulitzers and even more Peabodys, a perennial presence on the best-seller lists, once winning a Grammy for a video edition of a book on the Mount Pisgah conspiracy—the attempted coordinated terrorist attack on several heavily populated areas of the Middle East that her investigation had helped to avert. For some time the tabloids and the personality magazines routinely had referred to Lois Lane as "Superman's Girl Friend," always in capital letters as though an official title. An obvious match: the hero of the planet with the woman seeming to exemplify initiative and courage and all those qualities that we like to think are the best in the human community. Ms. Lane and Superman had been friends, certainly, but Superman had a lot of friends in those days. The loose talk of "Superman's Girl Friend" stopped abruptly with Lois Lane's marriage to Clark Kent, a reporter on his way to becoming the last editor-in-chief of their newspaper, the *Daily Planet*. From then on—in public as well as in private—every utterance from this most liberated of women seemed to be punctuated with "Clark says," or "Clark thinks," or "Clark always insists," or simply "my Clark." So she had not been "Superman's Girl Friend," despite her adoring public's wishes. The title that never evaporated from Lois Lane was "America's Sweetheart." That one stuck.

Many of the people who'd admired Lois Lane found it ironic that Magog finally had avenged her death. A world that had begun to collect superpowered champions of principle and justice like barnacles had accumulated villains and menaces of comparable potency: a sociological trend of the late Twentieth Century that—as we should have realized then—would presage the conflagration to come as the line between hero and villain fuzzed and finally faded away. Probably the most bizarre of these criminals was a homicidal madman who called himself "the Joker."

The Joker had blamed his criminal obsessions on his deformities, in turn blaming those deformities on the Batman. In the course of an attempted robbery at an industrial plant, the criminal who would become the Joker and a group of his colleagues had encountered the Batman. During the consequent mêlée the criminal fell off a catwalk into a vat of chemicals; his skin was bleached white and the musculature of his face cauterized against the bones of his jaw so that the tightened white flesh of his visage resembled a death mask. The hair all over his body turned a sickly green. Rather than being repulsed by the misfortune of surviving in that state, he embraced it, painting his lips red, affecting bizarre colorful costuming, giving himself a fanciful name. And he laughed—loudly and publicly—and the angrier his crimes, the more raucous his laughter. At first, the sole object of his rage had been the Batman, but later it included anyone or anything about which the Batman seemed to care. Then anyone who assumed a position of authority. Then, finally, anyone or anything within his reach that seemed more fortunate than he. He became fortune's hostage-taker. The Joker eventually was responsible for the *Daily Planet*'s demise as one of the country's last remaining great newspapers.

The banner headline on the *Planet* that last day of operation had heralded another in Lois Lane's ongoing series of exposés about the socially objectionable activities of the superpowered, self-proclaimed hero Magog. Apparently Magog had been confiscating radioactive materials from environmental terrorist groups and dumping the materials indiscriminately into the ocean off the coast of Metropolis. No one seemed to care very much. The more famous Lois Lane had become, the less important was what she had to say. This was an ancient tautology, going back at least as far as Cassandra in Greece and King David in ancient Jerusalem, with Ms.

Lane only its latest celebrity victim. Many of those who claimed to love her most had listened to her least.

The Joker was always a Priest of Chaos who delighted in the absence of any pattern or predictability in his public activities. This warped logic—such as it was—remained internal, like the self-indulgent poesy of obscure prophecy forever whispering in his ear. The reason behind the Joker's last escape from Arkham Asylum in Gotham City—his home away from home, where he spent more of his life's time than anywhere else—was an aging, chronic recidivist from Metropolis, who had tried unsuccessfully to bust out.

This little old man known as the Prankster had failed a psychiatric examination, probably due more to age than to inclination, and found himself interned at the Arkham Asylum for the Criminally Insane. One day he'd tinkered around with a few of the battery-operated children's toys that Arkham's small clinical staff kept in a "playroom," where they observed some of the inmates who they thought might respond well to such manipulables. The Prankster had turned a little radio-controlled toy car into an explosive device, programming it to roll down the hall late at night, befuddle several electronic checkpoints along the way, and explode outside his cell door. That was evidently the idea. Instead, after the Prankster's exploding toy had signaled the cell door to open, the groggy old man did not manage to get out of the way before the consequent blast sent him, fragmented, to whatever reward awaited him. The Joker had resided in the contiguous cell, and, upon awakening at the sound of the explosion, he'd found a crack blown in his own outermost wall wide enough to wriggle through. In the ensuing horror he did precisely that, dropped thirty feet in the dark into a drainage canal, and waded through his fellow inmates' effluvium to freedom: a suitable exit.

As a tribute to his deceased unwitting liberator, the Joker targeted the most visible public symbol of the Prankster's primary opponent. For years, the *Daily Planet* and Superman had been identified together in the public consciousness. Many of the Man of Steel's friends worked there: Clark Kent, the editor-in-chief; Lois Lane, its most visible reporter; James Olsen, the chief of its foreign desk. The *Planet* was where Superman went to make his pronouncements and to express an opinion when he felt the public ought to know what he thought about something. Generally, even the nets and wire services had to quote the *Planet* when a big Superman story broke.

Lois Lane had been in the old Cray room when she heard the laughter. Years before, when he'd been involved in a dispute with the administrator of the reference library that his staff normally used, Clark Kent's predecessor—the late Perry White—got it into his head to outfit the newspaper with the most powerful mainframe computer in existence. Bruce Wayne owned a Cray; so did the Pentagon; the European Union had pooled its dozen governments' resources to buy one. Perry White had wanted a room in his own office where every news story and photograph, and every network news feature in the history of American journalism, was available to any of his reporters on a moment's notice. Mr. White had had an old storage room outfitted to be airtight and vapor-proof, keeping it at a constant sixty-eight degrees Fahrenheit. When he'd realized that programming all the desired information into his new Cray would cost about thirty times as much as the computer itself and take six years to accomplish, Perry White had aborted the project. The Cray room never had been home to a Cray, but it'd become a fine repository for Mr. White's admirable stash of cigars and, unknown to anyone else at the *Daily Planet,* Clark Kent's wardrobe room of choice. The only visual access to the room had been a peephole in the door, and Clark had not needed even that degree of visibility. Lois Lane also had spent quite a bit of time in that quiet place amid the tumult of the news office, working out the structure of her big Sunday magazine pieces, probably what she'd been doing in there when the Joker had arrived, although a fortunate soul who left the building about ten minutes earlier swore that she'd seen Lois ducking into the Cray room with her husband, Clark. (Later, investigators dismissed that as unlikely.)

"Good afternoon, ladies and gentlemen," the Joker proclaimed from the landing that overlooked the City Room, "and welcome to today's gruesome tragedy."

No one had seen his arrival, whether he'd stepped off the elevator behind him, now locked up tight, or out of one of the stairway entrances to either end of the landing, likewise locked. We know now that he had come into the building via the roof, where police later found a small hovercraft and two armed confederates still waiting for their boss. People had looked up from their business, maybe some trying to resist or object, but no one died of bullet wounds from either of the pair of uzis in the hands of his two gunmen escorts. No one is sure exactly how it took place; no one survived.

All we do know is that the last survivor was Lois Lane, who could have laid low in the safety of the airtight Cray room, could have walked out of there eventually, but chose not to.

Late midsummer, a damp stifling day. The new air-conditioning system had been installed right around the time that Clark had the old crank-opening windows sealed. And by the time the Joker appeared on the landing, all the exits had been locked, their edges caulked from the outside.

There was a clear ceramic globe that the Joker probably had carried in under his voluminous frock coat. He made his little announcement, then dropped his globe into the middle of the room. And out came green death.

Laughing death.

All three men, the Joker and his two armed confederates, had to have stood there sucking on their oxygen filters in the City Room, watching as ninety-odd people died. Perhaps the Joker had looked around in vain for Editor-in-Chief Kent, knowing him to be in one of the inner offices somewhere, dying.

He may as well have been. It was a curious, painful death, the gas from the shattered globe simultaneously tickling and irritating the back of the throat and lodging below the diaphragm, forcing the victim to expel air with a repetitive spasm resembling laughter. With no air left, the diaphragm would still pump. In the weakest victims, the diaphragm or a rib or two would rupture, puncturing the lungs and flooding them with fluid, drowning the afflicted. In the strongest, the diaphragm would create a vacuum in the chest cavity, with the implosion of one vital organ or other the eventual result. Most just suffocated. When the laughing and heaving ended, Lois strained to look out the peephole, seeing only prone bodies, faces frozen in a ghastly death rictus. Then she heard the shattering crash of a window.

Probably she'd called "Superman!" at the top of her lungs while piling out of the Cray room, across the field of death, toward the perpetrator, standing at the shattered window, reaching for the nylon cord and pulley rig hanging out there.

On her way across the room Lois had swiped a keyboard off a desk, and the startled Joker spun around to see the crazy screaming woman swimming through the clearing air. If the Joker's own later account was to be believed, she'd faked out the faker—possible only because she had no intention of surviving. He'd assumed she'd been trying to get by him. He spread his legs and arms to stop her, and she flew right at his midsection, sweeping the keyboard across the madman's face and shoving him off balance. He barely missed the shattered window.

He'd gotten hold of her belt, not letting go. Again she surprised him. Instead of struggling, she reached out the broken window and yanked on the loop of the nylon cord hanging there. Two stories above, a man yelled in surprise and grabbed the eave of the building as a loosened pulley snaked by him and carried the cord down the side of the building to the ground. The Joker would fail to escape, and so would Lois.

"This is most indelicate," the madman said, according to his own account. "Miss Lane, isn't it?"

Maybe she nodded at him or glowered the way she did. Then the Joker reached across a nearby desk, snatching up a big brass paperweight in the shape of the ringed *Daily Planet* logo and bashed in her skull with it.

Whenever Superman thought of Magog after that, the scene of his Lois sacrificing her life so the criminal would be apprehended smashed through his great tortured mind. One of the disadvantages of the kind of flawless total recall that Superman possesses is that no matter how much time goes by, memories never soften. They only become more vivid.

He'd been the first one on the scene; that was how Clark Kent died.

Clark had in fact ducked into the Cray room with his wife, but it had been Superman who left the room a moment later—before the Joker's arrival—faster than any human eye could see, in response to a distress message coming into Mission Control from a space station about to collide with a freight module. He'd heard it interrupting a police band monitor in a nearby building, and was off in space averting the imminent disaster before the astronauts aboard the station finished communicating the details of their problem. He always had liked being in space, the absence of air giving him a respite from the cacophony that he continually had to decode in the sound bath of the Earth's atmosphere. He'd taken a few minutes to secure the rogue pod and steady the space station, smiling and waving through a porthole at the astronauts who scrambled like excited tourists to take snapshots of their visitor.

When Superman reentered the Earth's atmosphere, the first thing he heard was the insistent ultrasonic whine of a signal inside the wristwatch of an old friend. He turned his trajectory steeper into a power dive, burning the air around him during descent, and for hundreds of miles people wondered and shielded their vision and prayed as the pillar of flame drew itself down the sky. He'd been too late anyway.

"You did this," Superman thundered uselessly, stepping

through the wall into the City Room of the newspaper that would never again go to press.

"Yes," the Joker said, laughing momentarily as the steel fingers that could change the course of mighty rivers closed around his profane windpipe.

There had been ninety-two dead. Superman had reported ninety-three casualties—almost as an afterthought—while delivering his insane captive to the nearest police lockup. There seemed no more point to continuing as Clark Kent; his last close link to conventional humanity had been severed. Superman removed all the bodies from the editorial offices of the *Daily Planet,* along with a realistic dummy of a tall dark-haired man on which he'd planted Clark's wallet. He'd identified each of the victims by name. Not even the commission the Governor later named to investigate the affair had thought to question those identifications, which had been supplied, after all, by Superman.

Clark and Lois Kent had made quite a bit of money in their careers, but never had found much use for it. She required few creature comforts beyond his ability to provide, and he needed only her. The funds left in their bank accounts barely covered their outstanding credit card bills, because most of what they earned had gone directly into the Jonathan and Martha Kent Foundation, which they formed shortly after their marriage. Their wills left their Midtown condominium and the old Kent property in Kansas to the foundation, which invested aggressively and provided university scholarships to needy Kansas high school seniors. Mainly as a result of the Kent Foundation, Kansas was the fourth-best-educated state in the nation by the time it became a crater.

For a few days after the Joker's crime, Superman had wandered through the paces of his life, drifting among the clouds over Metropolis, occasionally dropping from the sky to avert a car accident or to return the contents of a picked pocket to the rightful owner. He'd slept for minutes at a time floating on the thermals. Once he'd woken several feet under the Earth, realizing after a moment that he had sleepflown over two hundred miles from the city and collided with a peak just above the treeline. After Lois's death, the ache in the man's soul got a little worse every day for about a week or two, then stayed about the same. It never got better.

During the time following the death of Lois Lane, the police had moved the Joker from midtown lockup to a federal detention center upriver at Pocantico. Probably Superman made a point of avoiding the scene, which would explain why, when the extensively manacled Joker got out of the police van and Magog appeared suddenly, Superman had been nowhere in sight.

"Sic semper criminalis!" Magog howled into the sky, lowering his spiked golden sceptre in the direction of the Joker's gut. For an unjustly brief moment, the Joker had looked into the face of the true wages of madness. Then a pulse of golden energy flew from Magog's sceptre and dissolved his stomach, liver, four ribs, and parts of two others, a lung, both ventricles of his heart, and all the surrounding muscle tissue.

The howls and scrambling of the police officers on the scene summoned Superman, who arrived in time to see the remains of the Joker hitting the ground.

Superman had sputtered, opening his mouth to say something he could not say, then snatched back his composure. Finally, he demanded of the police captain on the scene, "Arrest this man for murder."

"You've got to be kidding," Magog said without leaving.

Gingerly, the police captain snapped handcuffs around Magog's wrists, the Man of Gold snickering and Superman saying nothing.

"How many murderers?" Magog shouted. "How many goons and thugs? How many crime lords? How many more misanthropes like this pile of sludge on the ground will go unpunished while we play out the charade of my incarceration?"

Still, nothing from Superman.

"How many more?" Magog impatiently tore the cuffs off his wrists but carried them in his fist, sliding into the front passenger seat of the police captain's car. "How many more," Magog wanted to know, "because Superman doesn't have the stones to mete out justice?"

No reply.

"You can't judge me," Magog said in a calm, clear voice while riding away; Superman, who certainly could still hear him, was already miles in the sky.

Superman would say not another word in public until he testified, eloquent and persuasive, against Magog at trial a month later. Virtually everyone could hear him; virtually no one listened. The jury of twelve Metropolitans unanimously cleared Magog of all charges, and some enterprising fellow printed a mock-up of the old *Daily Planet*'s front page with a picture on it of Superman's face, snapped as he had come out of the courthouse—the last clear photograph of Superman anyone would take for ten years.

Magog had become the new hero of Metropolis. And Superman then deserted the city that had endorsed the denial of justice to the man who killed the woman he loved.

$$\Omega \quad \Omega \quad \Omega$$

For all this time since the fall of the Heartland, Magog had wandered the floor of the desert he'd created, looking futilely for things to rebuild. A stick here. A bone there. The intact wall of an old post-and-beam house lying on an evaporated riverbed.

We'd gone through a similar epiphany, Magog and I. Both of us had sought solace at some time in madness, and for both of us—for me because the Spectre had chosen to rescue me, and for him because his sheer power had prevented his mind from perceiving reality in a faulty light—this solace was elusive. My sympathies went with him: We were both humans who had made fallible choices, his, by chance, wrong.

So there he stood, scrupulously sane and still beset by poor judgment, gathering up a farmhouse from the splinters of his Holocaust. He had unmade them, and now he sought to make something again. He gathered up fiber and chips of wood, and, with the heat of that pointed rod he used to focus his power, fused the pieces in boards. Most of it would burn away, but he would use what was left to construct a house. It was mostly built now, and he carried the completed shell of the building to a flat piece of land. Maybe he intended to live there.

Having seen the Ray less than an hour before, Magog reckoned Superman was coming. The Ray traveled to and fro across the irradiated land fusing rogue ions together and clearing the earth of nuclear contamination. It was a long, slow process, akin to drawing a pencil line up and down the state until the whole expanse is covered with graphite; a job that only the Ray did well. When the land reclaimer's thin line hit Magog, quietly rustling up a farmhouse for himself, the Ray had taken only enough time to blink and draw up into the sky, startled—long enough for Magog to see him there, but not long enough for him to care.

Magog did not know much about building things. He put together the shell of a house without any crossbeams and tried to set it down on a flat strip of soft earth without any foundation. First the lower strips of outer wall began to give way under the pressure of the upper beams. Then the building's center of gravity began to shift with its weight on the unstable ground beneath. Angrily, Magog brought up his rod and blew the shell apart like the big bad wolf. If he'd known for sure that Superman was watching him, he might have tried harder to fix it.

"What are you doing here, Magog?"

"Well, as I live and breathe"—Magog turned around to the left so his working eye could hit his antagonist first—"if it isn't the Abominable Plowman. Still grow the best icicles south of the Equator, Supes?"

"If you can't make it work, then destroy it, eh, Magog?" the Kryptonian asked, evaluating his opponent's building skills.

Behind Superman, every flying being who'd been in the New Oa satellite at the time of Ray's call—he'd gotten them the news of his discovery from a pay phone in a suburb of Denver—touched down on the desert floor.

Green Lantern, Red Tornado, Aleea Strange, Hourman, and others kicked up the worthless dust that a few months ago had been the most productive farmland on Earth. Superman had told them all to stay at the satellite while he dealt with Magog, but only Wonder Woman had even considered staying behind, though ultimately she did not.

"I never left," Magog said, ignoring the others, "unlike your eminent self."

"I didn't come here for a verbal joust, kid. I saw the satellite footage of your last big mission, and believe me, it will be your last."

"Hey, you're not the same, Supes. No summons? No jury trial this time? No due process? Not even a bill of bloody attainder?"

"Consider it an act of martial law, Magog. You brought six powerhouses out here to gang up on one deluded little Parasite. Not only did you blow apart your own ill-served allies, but in the first minute after the clash you killed one million people. Who knows how many have died since?"

"Oh get out of town," Magog said, and laughed. "Oh, I'm sorry. You already did that."

"You'll be confined for an indeterminate period, during which time you will undertake a much-needed educational schedule."

"What are you talking about?"

"We're less interested that you pay for your crime than in assuring that it never takes—"

"Crime?" Magog thundered. "My crime? You've got a lot of nerve."

Superman stood silently, containing.

"This was all your fault," Magog said. "Don't you see it?"

It was Green Lantern who took a step forward from behind Superman first. "Kal, you don't need to—" and it was Diana who yanked the big man back by the armor of his wrist and shushed him.

"My fault?" Superman whispered to Magog, astonished.

"Sure," Magog said. "Just ask any of your buddies over there to explain it to you."

Now Superman put up a hand to wave back his colleagues. "Maybe you should explain it to me, Magog."

"See, you were supposed to be the mentor figure," Magog said, "but instead you were the shadow wizard. Don't you get it?"

Superman just stared at him, shaking his head almost imperceptibly.

"Haven't you read the literature? They wrote about you. About me. Even about them, your golden horde."

Superman steamed. Surely with whatever powers he had, Magog could see the fumes coming from the Kryptonian's ears, from his nostrils, the heat waves trickling up from his scalp. But this was Superman. He did not lose his temper. Instead, he actually sat down on a big rock. The rock was hot, throwing off radioactivity as Superman's own torrents of fury shadowed it.

"When I was a kid, you know," Magog went on, talking faster, nearly manic now, "you were everybody's mentor figure. You were the elder. The great gray god. Everyone you inspired—including me—had to be the hero of his own story, right?"

Magog waited for a nod, for a raised eyebrow, for some confirmation of concurrence or at least understanding. Getting none, he continued, faster now.

"But you didn't want to give up the throne. Didn't want to pass the torch to your natural successor. Couldn't bear to recede from the light. So you had to be overcome. I had to overcome you, and it was your manipulation that made me do it. You know that, right? You must know it, or you wouldn't have skipped out on everyone when I finally beat you. When you finally made believe I won. Right?"

Magog stopped even looking up for reassurance now. He just explained away, faster and faster, staring at the ground; at the horizon; at his rod; at anything but Superman's corybantic eyes.

"You bought into the will of the people. The American thing. The American Way, you always called it, right? Well, anyhow, I knew by the time I was an adult that was just a selling point. I thought I understood the day-to-day marketing of superheroism too. It was easy to figure out. I thought when I got the powers myself, using them would be just as easy. That's where you tricked me."

"I tricked you?"

"You admit it, see?"

Superman took a deep breath and silently counted to a billion.

"You tricked me into killing the Joker so you didn't have to. The Joker wiped out ninety-two men at the *Daily Planet* that day—"

"—and one woman."

"Whatever. Over ninety guys, and you didn't know how to deal with him. I knew how to deal with him. I was the one who finally blew his innards into the next county when the police were transferring him. And what do you do? You get me arrested for murder.

"For murder. For killing the Joker. That was the joke. The killing joke. You called me a criminal. In public. And then you testified against me. You didn't care about any of the hundreds of people the Joker had killed. Humans are like pets to you."

Superman wheeled to his feet, his eyes glowing red and then white with anger, for just a moment, and then he cooled. He stood there, staring at Magog in fury and wonder.

For his part, Magog was so lost in his take on history that

he seemed not even to notice the Man of Steel now on his feet.

"They let me off, of course. The people of the city did. That was who they were. They wanted the guy who'd be tough. Who'd protect them. Who wouldn't be afraid to kill. But even when I won the judgment, you deprived me of my triumph. You turned tail. You rose into the air and headed south and never came back. That's when I realized who you were. You were the Destiny that blew Odysseus' ship all over the Mediterranean. The Wicked Witch of the West. You would be secretly controlling my life until the day I defeated you. And until I could defeat you, overcome you, transcend you—until I gained the boon that the hero gets when he vanquishes the dragon—until that day I could only work to prove myself over and over again, make myself stronger and stronger, until this day—" Finally Magog slowed down the manic pace of his speech to some arguably rational rate and looked up at Superman, who stood just steps away from him. "This day, today, when I've got you where I want you."

Reflexively, many of the men and women among the dozens of costumed folks still trickling down from the satellite to the desert floor took a step forward. Their leader needed defending. But Diana put up her arms in front of them like the schoolyard monitor, and, so help me, they all stood their ground.

"Your heritage is fear, Superman," Magog accused, "the fear of a child huddled under his covers that the boogie man will get him before Superman arrives. Fear that a rumble will come down on your house and nuke you and your whole state. Fear that the real Man of Tomorrow is me. That's your heritage, Superman, Man of Steel, Last Son of Krypton, Defender of the Defenseless, Keeper of the Faith, King of the Universe, and this out here—"

He gestured grandly at the busted shell of a house, at the evaporated lake bed beyond, at the barren desert that once was Kansas.

"—this is my heritage," and Magog fell silent.

Said Superman, dripping sarcasm: "You must be proud."

"Proud?" Magog whispered. Then, "Proud?" he screamed as loudly as stepped-up lungs could scream, and because he could scream no louder he spun the hollow golden spear in his hand in Superman's direction and loosed its chilling cry at Superman's midsection, and the desert floor went thunderous and white.

His cape burned away under the power of Magog, but when the light settled and the echoing flew too far away to hear, there still stood a Man of Unbending Steel.

It was the moment Magog had awaited from the time a god or a demon gave him power. It was the power Magog had focused through the rod he'd clutched like a talisman through all these empty years. It just rolled over Superman like light over his face, as Magog always knew it would. Superman took not so much as a step toward Magog, nor did he toss him a glance of those radiant eyes.

Still, Magog went down.

He went down to both knees, and his golden-antlered helmet tumbled off to reveal the tendrils of the biomechanical suit wrapping up from his spine to hold the seams of his body together. His patchwork body was strong and firm as ever, but his hair was gone. His scalp peeking up among the strands was the only indication of the battering of radiation that Magog had withstood during these past months.

"Proud?" Magog said. Truly there was little left in either the body or soul of the human he once seemed to have been, but Magog himself remembered the notion of contrition from the shadows of those ancient days of his life. "You think I'm proud to be the Man of Tomorrow? The world took a jag off the straight and narrow, and you claimed too much dignity to follow. So they chose the man who would kill over the man who wouldn't, and now they're dead. Yeah, a million of them in the first minute and who knows how many more in the days after. Dead, at the hands of their own anointed."

Wonder Woman took a step forward, and Green Lantern followed. Then so did the others. They came as close as their own powers would allow them to come to the still-steaming hot figure of Superman, who forbore to put a hand on Magog's heaving shoulders because no one knew how much heat the Man of Gold could take.

"Proud of being the Man of Tomorrow? It's your fault, you self-important bastard," Magog said.

Magog looked up, and around him the figures of the great and the powerful gathered. But he saw only the countless figures that danced in his mind. "A million ghosts," he said. "Punish me. Lock me away. Kill me. Just make the ghosts go away."

Diana knew that Superman needed to feel a comrade's hand as surely as Magog needed an undeserved comforting one. She put a hand on that enormous shoulder, touched the scalding blue shirt that felt like a gossamer pulled tight over a slab of hot-tempered steel. They would leave this tarnished Man of Gold here for the moment, here in the desert of his own making. No harm from him would come to anyone; there was nowhere else for him to go.

Superman looked down at Magog, at the crumbled wreckage of the torrent of demon energy that ten years ago had ended his career, and he said, "We are at war."

CHAPTER 17

Apokolips

War is something you know about," I heard Superman say. "I need to learn."

"Where are we?" I asked my Spectral companion.

"Somewhere new," he said cryptically.

Cryptic was one of his less endearing moods.

We were listening to a labored conversation between Superman and someone with a deep rumbling voice. That voice answered Superman's request, "I am not a teacher."

I saw a vast rocky world. There was no Aurora, no azure hue to the sky, no sun; there were no clouds. We approached the surface of the land, and the rocks grew to mountains, and the pebbles grew to buildings and linked to form a great city of pipes and bridges and tunnels among the structures. The buildings or their adjuncts and connectors covered every visible iota of surface. Steam belched from smokestacks, and heat erupted in patterns that seemed at first random, but then grew rhythmic.

The prepossessing blankness—the sunlessness—of the sky loomed only larger as we dropped toward ground that seemed to get larger and more distant as it grew discernible. After what felt like a hundred years of approach and the coming-together of a vast planetwide latticework, we touched down finally on what seemed to be the city floor. The orange star burned cold across the black and sooty sky. I looked down at what ought to have been the ground, but suffered a sudden attack of vertigo. I was not on the ground, but on a wide elevated course of foot and vehicular traffic. Dark hooded creatures and smoke-belching craft rumbled by on all sides. The city descended farther below us—for miles, it seemed—to vanish finally in a cloud of surface gas that obscured the depth of the buildings.

"This time it is really not Earth," I told the Spectre.

"No," the Spectre said. "Not Earth. Another world in another vibratory phase of Creation. The people of this place call it Apokolips."

"It's real?"

"Quite real, but not the fairy tale of a final judgment that many of your colleagues have told to countless children. It is a world like your own. Its history is all that makes it different."

Moments after I had looked down and felt like falling, after my dour spirit had told me that there but for fortune went my own tortured Earth, a flash of color punctuated this drab sky. He touched down within our sight. He stood now, that great red cape hanging flat in the breezeless dawn, on the peak of a building maybe a quarter-mile from our vantage point.

The dark voice, coarse as fresh ground ice, was behind me now. It continued, "These days I have only my own realm on whom to make war."

The figure on the rooftop vanished from his perch and lifted into the sky, to reappear at the side of the Spectre. Certainly Superman did not know that he was there—or that I was, for that matter. I was still uncomfortable with the notion of people walking through me, so I stepped back to look at the source of the rumbling voice. It was an enormously thickset fellow in a regal tunic that looked like it would better fit another man. The hooded company of passersby parted for his every step. He moved, as unmindful of his subjects as of the Spectre whom he walked through, to grasp Superman by the forearm.

"Kal-El," the ruler said.

"Orion," the Kryptonian answered. "The place looks . . . the same, actually."

"That it does."

The big man in armor, Orion, was the ruler of this land, but he seemed somehow ill suited to the role, uncomfortable. He walked the roads and platforms of the realm as a common man, but the commoners sliced him a path through their commerce as though his very being were a knife slicing away their lives. Superman was uncomfortable as well. Me too. What kind of a place was this?

"He is the son of the one known as Darkseid," the Spectre told me, uncharacteristically unsolicited.

"They are helpless," Orion said.

"They have you now," Superman offered.

Orion looked around at his subjects. They cowered in frank fear as they noticed him standing in this public spot. They went about their business, looked away or smiled expectantly. Expectantly. Perhaps what they expected was a lightning bolt in the small of the back.

"They elected me, you know," Orion said.

"Excuse me?"

"They did. It was quite fair."

"Orion," Superman said, "I find myself a little disoriented here. Do you suppose we could talk in some more private place?"

Orion looked around at his faceless minions, evidently wondering why it made a difference, then shrugged in acquiescence. They both took to the air, Orion with the help of a jet mechanism built into his sleeves and boots and Superman under his own power. The Spectre propelled us effortlessly in their wake. I closed my eyes and had no sense of movement.

I am sure that what disoriented Superman—that most interplanetary of Earthmen—was the tendency of Orion's subjects to accord him the deference a dog accords its abusive master. Yet he stood among them, walked among them, conducted business and conversation among them as though he were one of them. It perplexed me.

Now we stood in a big room of a dark palace, open to the world like an elaborate balcony. Beyond and below was the endless expanse of Apokolips. I could not imagine who would want to live in such a place, let alone rule it. I wanted to reach into Orion's mind, but he seemed so powerful and forbidding.

"Can I do this?" I asked the Spectre.

"You are immune," my companion said. "Any notion of physical restraint or pain, any corporeal sensation at all, is but a remnant of your Earthbound consciousness. A conditioned reflex. Reach out and understand Orion, if you like."

So I dove in. I reached out a hand, passed it inside the ruler's head as the Spectre had done to me when first we'd met, and suddenly I was sucked in. It was like diving feet-first with my arms extended upward into a churning whirlpool. The sensation was not pleasant, but I stayed until my consciousness began to decode the signals swirling about me. He was not happy, this Orion, and he was not certain why.

"They really did elect me," he said to Superman as they stood looking out upon the vastness of this tiny fraction of Orion's realm. "We had no heritage of free choice, so I even retained the oversight of some of the election experts of your Earth."

"Really? Anyone I know?"

"You know all of them, I think. A former American President, a former Russian President, the South African Archbishop, a few others."

"Impressive. It should have worked."

"I suppose it did. It did not seem to matter, though. When I overthrew my father and declared the ruling councils null, no one had any idea how to govern his own actions, let alone a planet. They looked to me for leadership. I won by what you and yours might call an obscene plurality."

"Congratulations," Superman said, and smiled a rueful smile. "Given the nature of my own struggle, I had hoped that Orion, the Dog of War, could lend some wisdom. I was mistaken. I can learn nothing from you."

I got nothing from Orion so much as the idea that I was communing here with a modern-age Moses, though without the street smarts. When Moses upended the despotic intentions of the Pharaoh who'd raised him, he found himself traversing a desert with a nation of slaves. Though it should have taken only a few weeks to shepherd these people to their Promised Land—even on foot—he'd walked them around in circles until the generation of slaves was replaced by a generation of free men and women. Smart. Orion was an intelligent man and full of fine intentions, but he was not a smart leader.

"You have conditions here," Superman observed, "that are much like those I would have expected on Earth if I had followed the easier course of my life."

"Eh?" This was something of which Orion had not thought before.

"I was equipped to rule," the Kryptonian said, "as surely as you were."

"You were," Orion agreed. "I often wondered why you never took the strands of power from those less worthy than you."

"I could find none less worthy than I was," Superman said quietly.

Both of them stood looking across Apokolips for some moments. Within their far-reaching sight they could see all manner of illicit and depraved goings-on. There, on a platform of public space between two factory structures, not ten minutes' walk from Orion's palace, a man stood distributing harmful comestibles to young people in return for small economic markers. In a public square a crowd placed wagers on the outcome of a tearing fight to the death between two animals that, on Earth, might have been house pets. There were temptations for the taking, people for sale, confidences up for grabs. And over all this ruled one whom these people considered a living god.

In the days when God talked to the people of the Earth, when His Light peered visibly over our shoulders, people sinned. One day on Earth, we had come to sin so little that evidently God changed the rules, giving us all a measure of home rule and making it just that little bit more difficult for us to be good.

Here, however, the new god of these people—so long under the crushing thumb of Orion's evil but nearly omnipotent father, Darkseid—had given them their free will perhaps a generation too soon. Maybe in the future when the children of this casually corrupt nation take control of their lives—even as Orion had taken the wheels of empire from that despot—they will begin to find a role model suitable for a free people to emulate. Freed slaves worship at the feet of those they perceive as gods; left alone, they would not emulate one such as Orion.

"Most of these souls I once thought to save are irredeemable," the emperor told the super hero.

"Then what do you plan to do now?" The hot breeze from the open portico rustled in Superman's cape.

"Often have I considered uprooting the more aberrant lowlies," Orion said, "exiling them to some distant world." He paused, pulled back his head as if annoyed with my silent monitor of his sensibilities. "It seems unconscionable, though, to inflict such grievous wounds on another planet. I am sure you agree."

"Far be it from me to argue with the Lord of Apokolips," Superman said, quite nearly amused at the legendary prince's dilemma. Certainly he found Orion far more flummoxed and stiff even than Aquaman, but the mitigating sympathy born of long years of friendship did not apply here. "You seem, finally, your father's son, Orion."

"So it was prophesied. I am sorry I do not have more to contribute, Kal-El. Our story has forever been a generational one. Many men eventually become their fathers."

"I wouldn't know," he said, and looked down at his feet for a moment. "I was pleased to learn that you finally had usurped your father's throne. I looked forward to seeing what you had accomplished. Frankly, Orion, of all the old allies I have encountered, you disappoint me the most. You have absolute power here. You can change your world."

"Or destroy it," Orion said. "You would be surprised, I fear, at how easily one can lead to the other."

"I am looking for answers to my own world's ills, Orion. I have miscreants enough to deal with."

"What you need, Superman, is a deportation center." Orion looked up, suddenly aware that there was a way that he could help this Man of Vaunted Steel. "Bring your rebellious and uncontrollable elements to my realm. Certainly they would be no more challenging to me than my own subjects. They may even infuse a needed dose of initiative and inspiration to this wanton race."

"Orion, I have no desire to uproot even the most troublesome of beings from their homeworld. Deportation is not a punishment I feel comfortable imposing."

"Perhaps you should be more eager to play the judge, Kal-El."

"An Earthly political theorist wrote that a ruler makes a choice of whether to rule from love or from fear."

"My father made that choice for me."

"I find here, Orion, a nightmare of what my own Earth could become—or could have become. Is there no one here who can help me to turn a world from rabid self-destruction born of fear to . . . to . . ."

"To some alternative?" Orion wanted to know.

I withdrew from Orion's sensibilities—with significant relief—as he told Superman that, yes, there were two people here who believed there was an alternative to fear and insisted on imposing it. A dogged pair.

Ω Ω Ω

Barda and Scott Free had spent a lot of time on Earth in their youth, on an altruistic mission of cross-pollination; maybe a good example could be set in the process of mixing up the local technology with some of their own. It did not work out that way. His talent made Scott Free, effectively, the greatest escape artist of any world. As Mr. Miracle and Big Barda, the Frees made a lot of noise and a fine living with their stage act, and did some impressive superheroics along the way. Scott and Barda learned far more from Earth than Earth learned from them. They put on a few good light shows, participated in one of an endless succession of reformations of the Justice League, fell in love, settled in New Hampshire, and had a daughter—Avia. By the time Orion got around to summoning them home to be lieutenants in his revolution, neither of them any longer had a taste for battle.

With Orion safely machined into the palace and into the reflexes of the underclass, Barda and Scott had stripped away the fears and superstitions of the next generation of Apokolips denizens—and continued to do so.

"We're bringing them culture," Barda said to Superman. Surrounded by students, she was sitting with a mound of clay between her spread legs on the floor in the middle of a classroom. She molded, and the clay grew to a widening obelisk. When she ran out of mass she bored into the top of the mound, gradually hollowing it into the shape of a rather lopsided vase. The eyes of her two dozen or so students, young children to apparently middle-aged adults, were variously wide with wonder to narrowed with cynicism.

"Culture," Superman repeated, watching the vase take form.

Barda was a big woman, the more so for the loose smock she wore and the clots of clay hanging from both her and the smock. "Free their bodies by freeing their minds," Barda told Superman, boring into the mouth of her creation.

"Well, from the sound of him," Superman said, "I'm sure Orion applauds your efforts."

"Orion is a superannuated schoolroom bully with delusions of purpose," came a voice from behind Superman, and every face in the room but Barda's suddenly twisted into a mask of abject terror. Then the voice laughed as Scott Free, Barda's diminutive husband and co-instructor, strutted into the room.

"There you are," Superman said. "I was afraid I'd miss you."

Gradually people began to realize that no lightning bolt fried the room. No flood washed through the valley. No masked horsemen swept down from the hills to sack and pillage and burn. Then the timid souls born under the weight of a tyrant's imperative looked up and began to suppose that, even in the presence of their presumptuous teacher, they would probably live through the day.

"Here I am." Scott clapped Superman over the back of the steely shoulder like the adrenaline junkie he was. "You've been out of circulation, I hear. 'Smatter, no more challenges? You can always move in here, you know."

Superman smiled, about to answer with something mildly clever, but lost the chance.

"So how many sculptors-in-the-making've we got here, Barda?"

"Don't know yet, Scott."

"You know what you do when you make art, gang?" Scott asked, and he answered himself, "You do the same thing you do when you make philosophy, or song . . . or rebellion. You do something Orion himself can't do. You create something that was never there before. Get it?"

Scott Free was not good at waiting for answers to his own questions.

"Of course you do," he said. "And you're beginning to get it that a slaughterhouse is not a home and a ruler is not a leader. Nice work, Barda."

"Thank you, Scott. Anyone else ready to try?"

Nobody volunteered. Nobody ever did.

"You. You. You. You," Big Barda pointed out a sociological cross-section of their seminar. They understood and obeyed orders; she and Scott meant to fix that. "Grab an armload of clay and start molding."

She got up from her floor, clapped the clay off her hands and arms, went to where Superman and her husband talked, and gave the big man an enormous hug.

"Better reception than I got from Orion," he said.

"Orion?" Scott repeated loud enough for the class to hear. "That fatted boorish bore who wouldn't recognize a new idea if it cornered him in a Boom Tube and bit his head off? That Orion?"

The class cowered, but worked on, intent on their clay sculpture.

"That Orion." Superman smiled. "A little confused just now. Like me."

"Orion is a pretty well-meaning guy," Scott said, hollering only the first word of the phrase, then adding in an even louder voice: "for a flat-willed, concave-minded intellectual microbe who hasn't got the intelligence to get in the shower when civilization's burning down, Orion is."

Barda clapped and whooped, the students shuddered and grimaced, and, despite his mission and the mood of his aging soul, Superman laughed. But when he told this pair the saga of the lost prairie and the lost generation of metahumans, even they regained sobriety. He told them of the tricky business of containing that which was born never to be contained.

"We've been having the time of our lives here," Barda said. "I mean, look at us. We're home again, but no one here knows quite what to make of us."

"We owe Earth a lot," Scott said. "We plan to owe her lots more, if what we're doing here bears any fruit at all."

"So where does that leave us?" Superman wanted to know. "Are you two in?"

Barda began, "You'll need a facility with a solid security force. Scott and I can put together the best—" but the rest of what she meant to say got cut off by a . . .

BOOOM!

A wave of air swept over the little campus and through the room. Eight students leapt for cover. A pillar of smoke arose from nowhere and vanished; in its place, there appeared a long tunnel snaking off into the infinite like mirrors reflecting in mirrors. And out of the tunnel stepped Avia.

"There you are, Superman," the girl said. "I came to retrieve you from Orion's lair but you were gone."

"Nice to see you again, too, dear," Barda said to the daughter who had gotten a tattoo and done about four hundred other things over the past few years against her parents' expressed wishes.

"No time for that now, Mother," Avia answered, more nervous than hostile. "Hurry. I cannot keep this Boom Tube open much longer."

The Boom Tube was a link between dimensions, a wormhole through the stuff of Creation. I found it encouraging—a nice reflection on Him whose cause I'd made my own throughout my career—to find that the Spectre and I needed no such device to find our way home.

"You were counting on us to work alongside Avia?" Scott shoved Superman, who, to no one's surprise, did not budge.

"The League is large," Superman said. "Besides, I was told that your history has always been a generational one. You're family. You are doomed to be together. Coming?"

They were.

CHAPTER 18

A Mountain Moves

~~~~~

I wondered about the chronic sinners, those who called themselves the Mankind Liberation Front, just wondered about them. From the Aurora I saw the face of my guide, the Spectre, grimacing and throwing aside the curtain, and we were in the dark lair again, with the sun streaming in the big picture windows high above Metropolis, the sun itself unable to shed light here.

Again, the evil company sat around the long conference table with Lex Luthor at its head. Nigma, the smiling pet dog who once had called himself the Riddler, was still here at Miss Kyle's protective side. The tall valet also smiled, wider now, standing against the wall behind Luthor, his arms crossed over his chest like a genie eager to grant his master's next behest. The young one, Ibn al Xu'ffasch, slim and crisp and moving with the fluid grace of European aristocracy, sat at Luthor's left hand.

"Congratulations to our friend Xu'ffasch," Luthor said, "for negotiating the one union that may yet make the world safe for mankind."

Luthor looked around the table. Kobra, Savage, King, Naga, and the others stared expectantly at Luthor. Behind him, the tall genie still smiled.

"Friends," Luthor said, "I present our newest ally in the war against the gods"—Luthor snapped, and the genie flung open the door—"the Batman."

Through the door, smiling as if for all the world they belonged here, walked Bruce Wayne in his titanium bonehangers, Oliver Queen the Green Arrow, Dinah Lance the Black Canary, and Theodore Kord the Blue Beetle. If I had been conscious in a conventional sense, I think even I would have fainted. As it was, my perceptions went blank for a moment. I could not see into these people's intentions or their pasts or their souls anymore. They were a puzzle to me.

Handshakes all around. Smiles and winks. Batman whispered something embarrassing—I have no idea and did not think to listen—to Selina Kyle. The room settled.

"They've begun to build a Gulag, you know," Wayne told Luthor.

"I know," Luthor said, "that I don't want to spend my remaining days there. I can hardly believe you're here."

As they all took their seats, Bruce Wayne smiled that smile that I'd hardly seen leave his face in all the time I'd observed him—a smile unlike any expression one would expect to find on the Batman.

To his found ally, Luthor said, "This must be killing you, Wayne. If I had known a common enemy could bring us together, I would have invented one years ago."

"Given the circumstances, what choice do I have but to throw in with Lex Luthor?"

"Alone, neither you nor I can expect victory," the ancient enemy of the Man of Steel said, "but together we can curtail the Justice League once and for all."

"Strange times," the Batman said, squeezing the villain's hand. And he looked at his friends—at wary Oliver, at inscrutable half-smiling Dinah, at contemplative Ted—and said again, "Strange times."

CHAPTER 19

Gulag

Scott Free never had met Captain Comet before their collaboration on the Gulag. They got along so poorly that later on, after Comet had become the first casualty of the war that finally did happen, Scott felt enormously guilty every chance he got.

"You better move, Comet," Scott said, "or that structural beam's going to Rube Goldberg you out of there."

"What are you talking about?" Comet the engineer, the Merlin, the genius, asked him, not really wanting to know.

"You're in a trap," Scott Free replied. He spoke into a microphone from the hovercraft observation platform in the sky above the city-sized building that rose from the desert floor.

"Uh-huh," Comet said, sitting high on a gigantic cherry-picker, tapping away at his keyboard, barking orders into a datamike, trying to say as little as possible in answer to Scott so his construction programs did not get confused.

Scott Free, the escape artist, designed the Gulag as a maze within a labyrinth within a web, an escape-proof prison the size of a city. It took Captain Comet—Adam Blake, the ageless son of midwestern farmers born back in the days when more people lived on farms than in cities—to figure out a way to fit it all together. They were a team, doomed to collaborate whether they wanted to or not, like Superman and Batman.

$$\Omega \quad \Omega \quad \Omega$$

In years to come, history might call Adam Blake the first modern man, just as, in other times, similar titles had gone to Socrates or Copernicus or Franklin. Blake was probably the first man whose worldview included an intuitive under-standing of the Einsteinian model of the Universe. That is, he understood relativity better than Einstein himself; to the physicist it was a way of looking at the Universe, while to Adam it was an everyday fact. Of course light bent a little as it flew by a star; so did everything else. Of course your physical dimensions changed and your mass approached in-finite as you approached the speed of the energy you used; or else how could you tell the difference between energy and yourself?

"Of course everything is relative," young Adam Blake had told the kindly but personally disengaged physics professor with the thick German accent who'd taken an interest in the boy's case.

"I thought I said that," the professor had wondered.

"Did you really?" the child asked. "And you thought it was your idea?"

At the University of Southern California, in the dark years before the Second World War, Adam, five, aging very slowly, had not yet grown the last of his baby teeth. Until he was fully ten years old, he would still have a soft palate and speak with the damp lisp of a toddler. Some of the things he said as a boy, however, had no business coming from the mouth of so young a child, let alone in a toddler's voice.

"If fusion takes place readily at elevated temperatures," the five-year-old had asked the professor, "wouldn't it be easier to vary other conditions like pressure and mass to induce fusion in the laboratory, rather than try to reproduce an arbitrary level of heat?"

"Pardon?" The professor had thrown back his random shock of white hair and asked the boy to elaborate on his question.

"If everything is, in fact, relative," the child had said, talking slowly so that the alleged greatest scientist in the world might not fail to understand him, "then is temperature not a variable like everything else?"

The professor had sucked on his cherrywood pipe for quite some time before realizing it had burnt out. He had seemed perplexed by this realization, seemed to have forgotten what to do with an unlit pipe. Then he'd remembered and lit it and thought some more, puffing. Through this, little Adam Blake had sat patiently on the chair in the professor's office.

For amusement, Adam had looked out the window, counting the striations in the big frond of a nearby palm tree, and calculated its approximate surface area and how long he supposed it would take for a single inchworm to consume the whole leaf. Six years, four months, and two days, he'd concluded. Now considering the gestation period of an inchworm, supposing you had a fertile female inchworm, assuming moderate year-round California weather, the absence of inchworm predators, and around-the-clock munching, how long would it take the inchworm and all her progeny to consume the frond? About sixteen hours, little Adam had estimated, just as it looked like the professor was about to say something.

He'd pulled the pipe from his mouth, looked at Adam, walked from one end of the room to the other, stopped by a rollaway blackboard, and said, "Cold fusion, eh?"

"Yes sir," Adam had said.

"Interesting," and the professor had wandered out of the room, never to remember to return that day.

It is possible that if the professor's attention had not wandered from Adam's ideas to wherever they wandered that day, the whole world could have averted half a century of fossil fuel consumption and moved into the relatively clean energy generation we enjoy today. Maybe not.

Adam's mother, Martha Blake, eventually found her five-year-old son in the chemistry lab next door to the professor's office, burning dismembered strips of palm fronds in a meeker burner and timing the combustion.

Mom and Dad Blake had been rather appalled to find their boy alone, and relieved that in the near future the professor would have to return to Germany to retrieve his family and re-settle on the American East Coast. "Perhaps you could rec-ommend a mentor for our son," John Blake suggested the following afternoon.

"You mean someone who might be not only familiar with child prodigies, but more accustomed to the needs of five-year-olds?" The professor smiled, then introduced the Blakes to Emery Zackro, another physicist, teaching at the University of Michigan—one exhibiting the twin virtues of a relative dearth of absentminded quirks and physical closeness to the Blakes' home. Emery thereafter became Adam's teacher and collaborator. Perhaps Emery, like the older professor, might have won the Nobel Prize and been a renowned world figure one day, but Adam's initiatives sideswiped any ambitions of Emery's own.

"He's a mutant," Emery told the Blakes, who first were horrified and then rather delighted, "an accident of genetic matching. He has the intellect and physical capabilities of a person on the next quantum level of development." Human DNA—deoxyribonucleic acid, the encoding material of all Earthly life forms—effectively had remained unchanged for the past hundred thousand years, and showed no signs of evolving soon. To say that Adam was the posthuman pro-totype of, say, one hundred thousand years in the future would be only the most approximate of guesses.

Adam's curiosity and capacities had given both Zackro and the boy himself an entire constellation of knowledge simply beyond the reach of contemporary human capacity. A cold-fusion, antimatter, multi-lightspeed spacecraft of his own design eventually brought the teenage Adam Blake to the richest sources of information in this arm of the Milky Way Galaxy. By the time he uncovered an alien plan to invade Earth and strip it of its mineral and labor resources, Adam could speak uncounted dialects of hundreds of languages of sixty extraplanetary communications forms—if one could count Betelgeuseian aerial architectural signage and Rigellian facial tics, for example, as language arts—by the time, in the Nineteen-Fifties, that Captain Comet made his public début and upended the threatened invasion.

He never had felt quite at home among "the ancestors"—his private term for normal Earth people. With the coming of Superman and that generation of colorful heroes, the metagenetic phenomenon asserted itself, and he began to spend more time here. He'd been devastated when, after an extraplanetary absence of a few years, he returned to find Superman retired and the world in the thrall of a wanton club of metahuman juvenile delinquents. Captain Comet was among the first to rally to his side when Superman declared the reformation of the Justice League.

Ω   Ω   Ω

Despite their clash of personal styles, the cerebral Captain Comet worked dutifully and carefully with Scott Free—the erstwhile showman, Mr. Miracle—to fit together the intricate pieces of the city-sized prison that would be the Justice League's Gulag. Nonetheless, when Scott told him he was in the pod of a trap, Captain Comet was too engrossed to take the warning seriously.

Then came a sequence of events that even Adam Blake's remarkable mind could not have predicted. Comet sat in his booth on top of the big cherry-picker with three keyboards, two small lapel microphones—one for communication with Scott and the other connected to the central server for verbal orders to the automated assembly system that he'd designed to put to-gether the Gulag—and four monitors connected to four little hovercams that Comet directed by microphone to various sec-tions of the construction site. A quarter-mile away, a gust of wind scattered the ash of what was left of a nuked-out tree trunk into the desert sky and eventually landed, draping a thin blanket of dust over the lens of Captain Comet's hovercam number three. At that moment, hovercam three was trained on a section of one of the Gulag airlocks that Scott called the "tiger trap." The tiger trap was a nifty piece of New Genesis technology for stopping anyone trying to leave the compound in an unauthorized manner; it encased the person in a globe of energy that first enveloped and eventually contracted around the quarry until he or she pulled all his or her limbs together at the midsection and twisted into roughly the position of a roped pig. One of the nifty little qualities of the trap was that it con-sisted of a membrane capable of discriminating between bio-logical and inorganic material. It could actually snatch a person out of an escape vehicle, or a suit of armor, or his clothes, and render the escapee helpless and motionless on the ground.

Ambient radiation from deep below the ground regularly blacked out one or another of the hovercams for short periods of time. Comet ignored the problem. On his observation platform Scott became more and more uncomfortable—unac-countably so. He mentioned the "trap" about to spring on Captain Comet once more, and listened to the old man snort at him over the voice mike. Then Scott looked down to see that the arm of Comet's cherry-picker was snapped off at the shaft, and Comet and his engineering booth were nowhere to be seen.

Comet had ignored Scott's warning, usually dismissing as baseless anything that was a result of inexplicable intuition. In fact, Comet believed, intuition is not always baseless, but to the extent that it is inexplicable it is generally more trouble than it is worth. So was Scott.

"Down," he said into the central server microphone at his

throat. The booth lowered into the rising structure of the Gulag. "Bearing eighteen vertical seventy." Comet estimated his position and then ordered, "Angle thirty-five deep, angle eight long, angle zero high," to effect the three-dimensional direction in which he moved to be able to see in the construction site what he could not see on his monitors.

Comet tapped the one blank monitor in his booth, hoping that it was perhaps a localized problem. It was not. He tapped it again, illogically he supposed, to make sure, and the next thing he knew he was in a very small, dark place. And it was getting smaller.

"This is going to take a while," Scott Free's muffled voice said.

"Well, I haven't got a while," Captain Comet said, prone on the ground with the membrane of the tiger trap contracting around him. His clothing—it was most of his Captain Comet suit, absent only the helmet—already lay on the ground in shreds, among the shattered remains of the booth and all the monitors and data processing equipment that were inside it.

"Just hold still and keep your mouth shut, or it'll immobilize you with your mouth open," Scott said, stepping off his lowered hover platform and yanking a tool chest, full of hardware rarely seen on Earth, along with him.

"You're an escape artist, aren't you, Free?" the trapped Comet bellowed from inside the membrane. "Escape me, will you?"

"Calm down. Calm down," Scott said to the man who soon would have little alternative to calm. "You tripped a random entry port and activated the tiger trap."

"I already know that."

"Figured that out with that amazing famous stepped-up intellect of yours, did you, Comet?"

Comet did not reply. Scott was not sure whether that was because the trap was not letting him, or because his dignity was forfeit.

"I'm usually inside the trap when I do my escaping, after

all," Scott said, working on getting Captain Comet disassembled from the multidimensional maze of this deceptively complex membrane. "Told you I felt a trap springing, didn't I?"

Grumbling and muffled expressions of disapproval came from inside the decreasingly writhing mass that slowly contracted on the desert floor.

"It's a gift," Scott said.

Ω Ω Ω

The Gulag rose. The residents came. Some of them came kicking and screaming. Some of them came cooperatively. A few here and there came voluntarily. Mostly, they came unconscious.

For example: About twenty miles east of Odessa, in a little town called Krivotzer, Green Lantern, Hourman, and Avia quashed a rumble and failed at first to recruit a young four-armed man named Shiva who'd fashioned his persona after that of the Hindu god of destruction. Whether this Shiva actually believed he was a Hindu deity, I did not care to determine. With Ibis the Invincible from North Africa and a Red Brigadier—he'd called himself by the anachronistic name "Iron Curtain" so long, he virtually forgot what his mother called him—from among the loons training for a restoration of communism on the Russian steppes, Shiva terrorized the skies over Krivotzer. Avia tackled Shiva in the sky, and Green Lantern clapped a cage of energy around the other two. Hourman made the pitch for the Justice League—in Russian, as it happened—and the three of them dismissed out of hand the notion of changing their ways. Shiva, Iron Curtain, and Ibis spent the following week in a state of suspended animation induced by a little chiropractic maneuver Avia had learned from her mom, until these three became the first inmates at the Gulag.

Ω   Ω   Ω

It did not take long for Von Bach, the would-be dictator of a reunited Yugoslavia, to join them. Von Bach was another strong-armed metahuman whose most visible "super-power"—other than strength that rivaled that of Wonder Woman—was his sociopathy. His whole body was tattooed—again with that same slate-blue fashion statement—except for the image remaining in flesh-tone of the martial cross on his chest and the two words in German on his right and left forearms, respectively: LIEBE and HASS—"LOVE" and "HATE." When Superman and Wonder Woman came upon Von Bach, he was whipping up a barroom crowd in Montenegro to go down the road to visit a family of Serbian Muslims who were building a new house on the edge of a small town. The idea was to burn these people out of the trailer they were using as temporary housing.

"There'll be no burning today," Superman said in a perfect High German accent as he stepped out the kitchen door of the beer hall and faced Von Bach from across the room.

"Übermensch." Von Bach smiled, as though honored to have the celebrity visit his little gathering. It was the last word he spoke in German. With Von Bach stood a few allies, all distinctively costumed: Germ-Man, in an armored trench coat and a shoulder tank containing enough of some nightmare venom to start a pandemic, and three other young heavily armed fellows with the rudiments of cockamamie tattoos of their own. In English as good as Superman's German, Von Bach said, "You have no place here, Superman. This is an internal matter."

"Internal to what?" Superman answered, continuing in German so the afternoon beer crowd would understand as Wonder Woman stepped out the same door to stand beside him. "You dwell on externals and exploit the most marginal of differences among people in order to turn them against each other. Like every racist propagandist."

The men in the hall looked around uncomfortably, perhaps out of fear of the seemingly inevitable battle brewing among the titans or perhaps with trepidation at the presence of the outlandishly fierce-looking Amazon warrior, the only woman in the room. The afternoon revelers suddenly sought a means of graceful escape, but of course there was none.

"This is a Yugoslavian matter," Von Bach insisted, "for Yugoslavians pure of ancestry. Not displaced offworlders or pagan throwbacks."

"Really?" Superman insisted on continuing in German, playing to the crowd as well as his quarry. "Is that what the last leader to unite the Balkans would have said? Your hero, Tito?"

Marshal Tito was indeed Von Bach's acknowledged hero, though the only thing they really had in common was a belief in absolutist rule. Tito had supplanted the German fascists here at the end of their occupation of Europe, first aligning with the Russian communists of the Soviet ruler Stalin. But when Stalin's security had proved more costly to the chronically conflicted people of the Balkan Peninsula than his animosity could ever be, Tito had promptly banished the Soviets from his newly liberated country, becoming a leader among nonaligned heads of state and spending most of the remainder of his life—about thirty years, as it turned out—keeping the Serbs and Muslims and Croatians and other trace ethnic groups from burning out one another's homes and families. He succeeded in this until his death, at which time Yugoslavia began to break down into ethnic conflict, and within ten years the nation built by Tito had become a land without a country.

For all his repression and absolutism, Tito was still revered as a hero in these parts. For decades, every would-be dictator who sought to reunite Yugoslavia—tinhorns all, from the murdering crew who carved out spheres of influence in the Nineties to this super-strong tattooed Von Bach—first had invoked the spirit of Tito and then had flown in the face of all his accomplishments. I had to have at least a little sympathy for Von Bach and his henchmen trying to go chin to chin with the Last Son of Krypton and the Princess of the Amazons. They had such a lousy heritage of role models to emulate.

"Do you think Tito would have begun a revolution by turning his own people against one another as you have?" Superman asked Von Bach across the sea of sinking heads of afternoon beer swillers. "Come with us, Von Bach. Join the Justice League and you will have the world as your stage, and even your own country will be the better for it."

And this time Von Bach answered in Elizabethan English: "Better to reign in Hell than serve in Heaven."

Superman and Wonder Woman looked at each other, weary of the diminishing returns they were experiencing. There should be more joining us, he'd insisted to Diana. When they had started out on this quest, most of the superfolks they'd encountered were excited to join them, to mend their ways if appropriate. Now with the public's identification of the Justice League and Superman as champions of the American Way, whatever that really meant, there was more resistance to it every day. Superman was no longer used to the indefatigable drive he had brought, in his youth, to his never-ending battle. He was showing his strain, but it was only his adversaries themselves who resisted, he realized, not the people over whom they sought to lord.

"He is right, the American," Superman heard a patron at a nearby table whisper in German to a friend, and the friend nodded.

"The Justice League is the way," the friend said.

Von Bach heard it, too, and he turned from his verbal joust with the Man of Steel, directing his rage and, heaven forbid, his strength on this poor brew-logged pair with the loose lips.

Von Bach raced as fast as a glance across the beer hall, and an enormous fist whistled through the air on a dead course intersecting the mere mortals' midsections. And before the two men realized what danger they were in, Von Bach's fist landed with a thunderclap in Superman's extended palm. The men

felt a gust of wind, saw the hammer of a fist for a moment in
the hand at the end of the blue sleeve, and that was all . . .

. . . before Von Bach left the ground and arced, with his
captive hand at the center of the circle, out across the room
and through a wall, through a kitchen, through another wall,
to land on a cobblestone street outside.

Superman clapped his hands together lightly, walking after
Von Bach through the holes he'd left in the shattered walls and
kitchen equipment. The four confederates—Germ-Man and
the others, whom I still did not recognize—launched themselves after Superman with a clatter and a pounce, but
Superman did not seem to notice. Wonder Woman caught all
four of them, one at a time, with the speed of Hermes, and
yanked them—out of the sky—off a table top—out of mid-
lunge—down from swinging from one ceiling beam to another—until they realized that surrender was their only
option.

With some weariness at the inevitability of it all,
Superman loaded Von Bach, clearly flabbergasted by the ease
with which the Kryptonian dominated him, over his shoulder
and took off with him into the sky in the direction of the
Gulag half a world away.

Ω   Ω   Ω

Then there came the others: Tokyo Rose, the Japanese
martial artist. Mr. Terrific and the Joker's Daughter from my
experience on the Outerborough Bridge in Metropolis. In
Tokyo, Power Woman took down the Kabuki Kommando in
mid-bladeswing, and Red Arrow blinded the Jade Fox just as
Superman arrived.

Stars and Stripes, youngsters who took their models from
the Star-Spangled Kid and Stripesy of a couple of generations
back, got caught smuggling Stealth and the new Catwoman
into a neutral, left-leaning country in Central Africa in an attempt to destabilize the government there. Wonder Woman

flew headlong with her arms outstretched upward across the windshield of Stars and Stripes' camouflaged and converted DC-3. When they swerved in surprise, creating a moment of zero-gravity inside the plane, the craft's engines cut out. To the horror of all four people aboard, the craft was out of control. To their subsequent consternation, it did not crash, but rather turned in the sky and headed west. They knew where they were going and who was in charge—carrying the plane through the air under its bulging belly—long before they arrived in Kansas.

Then to the Gulag came the Braintrust, whom I had seen at the Statue, and with them came the still-recalcitrant Americommando with his Minutemen, and two of those three hang-gliders who had tried to ambush them. The three turned out to be metal alloy androids named "Red," "White," and "Blue," and there was no telling who controlled them—but for whatever it was worth, Red was still at large.

Then Pinwheel with his spinning blades, Black Mongul with his dozens of followers from the hills north of the Great Wall, and Cathedral with his elaborate costume weaponry.

Then Demon Damsel and the Insect Queen. Then Shade and the Manotaur waving his horns.

Stealth. Blue Devil. Buddha. The Icicle.

Thunder. Fantom of the Fair. Black Manta. Lightning.

Bizarre names. Grotesque colors and costumes. Outlandish powers. They were as different from each other as a peach is from a prickly pear. If they had one thing in common—and this too is a subjective judgment—it was that none of them had an accurate sense of self. None of them was capable of significant analytical thinking. Not a single one had a discernible unit of intellectual or emotional values.

Those who had these qualities but who still would not join with Superman and his new Justice League, it seemed, found their way to Batman's group—or to Luthor's Mankind Liberation Front.

Captain Comet and Scott Free, the wardens, along with

Superman and Wonder Woman, the icon and the teacher, put together elaborate reeducation programs. Scott saw little need for them, but he too felt that it was important to articulate values even to the amoral and valueless. Students have to want to learn, Scott cautioned Wonder Woman over and again, and she shrugged. The Amazon solution to an opponent's recalcitrance, she told Scott repeatedly, was force—and they had plenty of that. Superman holograms were all over the city, spouting aphorisms and extended verbal treatises wherever the rogue metahumans turned. In the middle of an ill-founded escape attempt, there would loom the unsettling figure of Superman talking about the value of humility in the context of the historical development of empirical knowledge, or some such thing. Comet began to think that just the repeated shock of Superman's holographic presence inside the Gulag did more to quash compound-breaks than all of Scott's elaborate traps and illusions.

$$\Omega \quad \Omega \quad \Omega$$

And one day, from out of the desert wandered Magog, helmet in hand. He knocked politely on a pillar of the enormous Gulag structure. No one heard him knock, but he stood there quietly and decorously until a monitor alarmed Captain Comet to his presence.

Comet knew immediately that Magog was there, but, so help him, he hesitated to go down to greet the felon. "Where's he been?" Comet barked into his Justice League communication link.

"Colorado," said the Living Doll, from the New Oa satellite. She scanned through a file and found the reference. "A previously abandoned federal prison in Golden, Colorado."

"Well, he's not there now," Comet said. "He's here. He escaped. Isn't Superman monitoring him?"

"I'm sure he is."

"Was," Comet said.

"Is," the Living Doll repeated.

And from the doorway of Captain Comet's command center Superman's voice said, "I saw him leave. I knew he was coming here. Let him in."

Eventually Comet walked up behind Magog in the shadow of the Gulag. Magog turned and smiled lightly, putting his helmet and energy spear on the ground as the older man approached.

"We've not met," Comet said. "I'm Adam Blake," and he extended a hand.

"I'm Magog," the caller said. He extended his own hand to take Comet's, the first time someone had shaken his hand in years, he thought. "I need a place to think. I need a place out of the sun. I understand that this is the village of the damned. I understand that this is a place where I might be welcome."

"Yes," Comet said. "Come in. We'll find you a room."

Ω   Ω   Ω

There was a right and a wrong in the Universe, and that distinction was not very difficult to make.

CHAPTER 20

The Quintessence

I told my congregation my favorite story about Heaven and
Hell about once a year—giving them just enough of a break
between tellings that I could be reasonably sure they'd forgotten the story from the last time. It goes like this:

A man dies and he meets Saint Peter at some gate or other.
Peter takes him on a tour. They walk through fluffy fields of
clouds and down a long corridor. Along the corridor are two
banks of windows: one on the right and one on the left. What's
all this, the man wants to know. You're walking the thin line
between Heaven and Hell, Peter says. Through the windows to
your left is Heaven, and through the windows to your right is
Hell.

So the man looks as he walks along. Through the windows
to his right, on the Hell side, is an endless banquet table.
There are all sorts of luscious foods distributed all along the
table and people seated for miles and miles, all in on the feast.
The only problem is, their arms are all frozen stiff and
straight. Anyone can pick anything up, but there is no way to
get your hand to your mouth. Hellish, the man thinks.

Then he looks at the Heaven side. And there too is an
endless banquet table with a marvelous and varied repast.

And there too everyone's arms are fused straight, and no one can bend an elbow to feed him- or herself. These places are identical. Identical setup. Identical food. Identical hardships. Why is one Heaven and the other Hell, the man asks Saint Peter.

And Peter answers: In Heaven, the people have learned to feed each other.

Ω   Ω   Ω

The Gulag was that kind of Hell.

Everywhere this place was magnificent. Pillars graced the facades of buildings as in ancient Greece. A soft pink light suffused the air the way it did in Jerusalem. Boulevards were as wide and as airy as they were in Salt Lake City. Beautiful sculpture and art, as one might find in the streets of Paris or Rome, punctuated the scenery wherever the eye could rest. It was only the people here who were a reminder that this was a prison.

To tell the truth, even the people—crazed or misguided or just plain nasty—were beautiful too. Their skin and clothes were every color under the sun. Everyone was buff, even the older folks. Their bearing was regal. Their confidence level was high. They contended for their viewpoints. If only they could learn to contend intellectually more often, and physically—dangerously—more seldom. Magog, his hair beginning to return, spent virtually all of his time cooped up in a single room. It was a nice room, with books and with commlinks that had only minimal firewalls. They all had nice rooms, and no one had an unwanted roommate. In almost all cases, inmates here were living in better conditions than they'd left, which was not saying much when one considered the average metahuman's scant affinity for creature comforts. All the Justice League—and its agents Scott Free and Captain Comet—required was that they listen to reason and that the sky have a ceiling through which they could not pass.

Listening to reason, after all, included listening to Superman—or rather his omnipresent holograms. Big messages, little messages, the occasional aphorism would materialize and disappear randomly around the city. Everyone, depending on the individual case, had to appear for occasional "classes," which Superman had prerecorded holographically. "Students" could submit questions by commlink, and Superman or another member of the education committee—Wonder Woman was in charge of that, as it happened—could answer them. Mostly, classes were on ethics and values. Questions from the participants ran like this:

Who the hell do you guys think you are?
Who the hell do you guys think we are?
How many different ways can you spew that Pollyanna
    crap?
Who do you think toasted Rā's al Ghūl, and hey, how
    many lives do you think guys like you saved anyway?
and so forth.

This reeducation thing would take a while, Diana realized whenever she reviewed the previous day's "classroom" inquiries.

Ω Ω Ω

The confused young man called 666 sat reading a mildly censored bondage magazine in a gazebo on one of the small pedestrian squares that peppered the city—pretty little greenways like those that punctuate Savannah—when the image of Superman bubbled up from nowhere to say, "Please understand that you are not here for punishment, but for education."

"Oh, I'm sick of this crap!" the troubled 666 howled, and stomped along the grass leaving exaggerated footprints behind.

The holographic image followed the trail of his body heat and said, "With the powers we have, we need to inspire ordinary citizens, not terrify them."

"Yeah? You ever fight the Slaughter Brigade, sport? Inspire this!" 666 said and walked a little farther onto a wide mall where scores of people could see him being trailed by the heat-seeking hologram.

"Above all, we must adhere to a moral code that places the preservation of life first among our concerns," Superman's voice said.

"Man of Tomorrow! Hmmph!" the fellow said as colorful passersby on all sides stopped to watch his frustration and disgust. "Man of the Twentieth Century is more like it. Where's that projector, dammit?" and he found it. A hovering multilens sat high above 666, camouflaged against the pale violet surface of the dome that kept him and his neighbors from the outside world. There had to be a very slight electrical arc between the projection and the projector, he reasoned.

"I'm sick and tired of the old man's medieval thinking"— 666 dumped whatever there was of his composure all over the mall, swept his artificial robot arm through the hologram to watch its light scatter, and unloaded a static charge through his main nervous circuit—"and tired of his moral code that's as empty as this hologram!"

The static charge shattered the image of Superman into so many points of color, spraying and fading like shoots of a Fourth of July sparkler around the square. A bolt fired upward to shatter the multilens high overhead. The image that Captain Comet beamed in from the Operations Center half a mile from this mall sent a feedback signal. It knocked 666 to the ground, and a few onlookers laughed, but he got up and brushed himself off before he heard:

"I'm sorry to hear you feel that way," Captain Comet said, hovering in the air above. Behind him, flying in from the Operations Center, was Big Barda, Scott's wife, whom Comet had asked—partly to deflect his personality conflicts with her husband—to be his deputy operations chief.

"Are you a hologram, or can I kick your ass?" 666 asked his warden.

"Neither of the above," Comet said as he came down slowly to try to help the young man to his feet.

666 refused, of course, and got up by himself.

"Leave alone the boy," Von Bach demanded, striding through the gathering crowd and across the mall like Caesar himself.

"Trying to build an empire here too, Von Bach?" Barda asked him.

"This is my fight." The young man waved off the Yugoslavian.

"This isn't a fight," Comet said. "It's a clarification."

"Fine," 666 said. "It's my clarification. Lay off, Von Bach."

"I'll where I please go and when I please go," the pretender to a Balkan throne told his fellow inmates as well as his keepers in that pronounced street German accent, "and no else will this *schweinehund* tell me."

"The specific reason you are here, Von Bach, is that you killed opponents who already had surrendered. Not only are you a corrupting influence on these potentially good people, but you take your signals on how to speak and act from old World War Two movies."

"Vas?"

"The colloquialism you're probably looking for, Von Bach, is *schwein*," Captain Comet said, and with just that one word every multilingual person within earshot knew that his accent was impeccable High German. "*Schweinehund* is a term properly found only in old war movies with scripts written by people from Los Angeles and New York."

Von Bach steamed. Even Captain Comet's pronunciation of Von Bach's name was more precise than the man's own.

Through clenched teeth Von Bach said, *"Ich bin der rechtmäßige Herrscher im Königreich des Balkans."*—"I am the rightful ruler of the Balkan Kingdom." Then in English: "I am to your rule and regulation not subject."

Comet walked up to Von Bach. Both appeared to have forgotten 666. In a gesture Comet meant to be charitable—to avoid having the others hear his warning—but which Von Bach took to be an expression of dominance, Comet whispered, in perfect German: "This is not a prison. It is a detention center. If, in order to make other residents' stays shorter, I have to embarrass you in front of them, I will do so. Please make it easier, if not on yourself, then on them," and Comet turned, about to fly away—

—as the livid Von Bach snaked an arm around Comet's throat—

—Barda yanked a pellet launcher from her belt and said, "Adam—"

—and without looking, Comet loosed a telekinetic blast behind him that tore Von Bach off the ground, threw him into the walkway, scraped him along the ground, and slammed him into the concrete base of a delicately pillared structure that looked like a Greco-Roman town hall, where six married metahuman couples made their temporary homes. Barda looked over this scene for just a moment, shrugged, and flew off after Captain Comet.

"Keine Drohungen, Raumfahrer!" Von Bach said as the Kabuki Kommando dragged him to his feet: "I'll not be intimidated by some spaceman!" And he muttered, *"Ich werde diesen Kerl töten!"*—"I'll kill that guy!"—as the big Asian led him stumbling away.

Ω Ω Ω

There were another two prisoners I recognized from earlier: the Blue and White hang-gliders from among the trio who'd tried to break up the Americommando's attempt at xenocide at the Statue. Curious, I reached into what ought to have been White's mind, but there was nothing there. This automaton was following not its own initiative but an elaborate program. I looked closely at this creature, if creature it was, and saw that its single eye was a convex reflector. In it was a fisheye view of everything to which it pointed its "face."

"Its companion has a similar function," the Spectre said, floating up beside me.

"Similar to what?"

He gestured for me to look at both White and Blue. Rather than eyes—where White had the curious reflector—Blue had vertical slits, arranged on its forehead in a similar convex pattern. Looking closer, I saw that the slits were sound equipment, a battery of microphones. I looked back at White, who stood as still as a cameraman, looking deeply at the reflection in the android's "eye." Then I got a sudden attack of something that felt like vertigo: I was falling into the image on White's reflector.

The Spectre drew me outward, through the scene that White reflected. Then we were out farther—but not outside the Gulag. We flew outward amid the continuum itself—the image we witnessed contracting inward as we receded.

The fisheye view of the wide mall at the heart of the Gulag's city became again the fisheye view of the lens. It contracted smaller, and it became a globe, a crystal ball hanging in the air. Further, and the crystal hovered over the extended hand of the third of White and Blue's company: the Red android. Red was somewhere far away, watching. And standing beside the android Red, looking deeply at the images and listening to the sounds from within the Gulag, was Lex Luthor, his arm slung over the shoulder of his tall young valet who had so startled the Riddler back at the Mankind Liberation Front meeting.

Luthor was the controller of the three androids Red, White, and Blue, and two of them were inside the Gulag sending him the sounds and sights from there as instantaneously as Scott Free and Captain Comet themselves got them. Luthor was the black widow at the center of this web. And the valet?

"Who is he?" I asked the Spectre. "I tried exploring his mind, but it's scattered."

"You know him too."

I was afraid of that. "Captain Marvel?" I asked.

Spectre pulled us back farther and the scene of the three—Luthor, the android, and the Captain—became yet another of the scenes we watched, as if we were theatergoers, taking place behind the astral curtain of the Aurora. I had no sensation of movement through all of this, only witness: cacophonous, furious witness. We hung in a space that was beyond space and watched whatever scene transpired at this time as the Spectre held back the Aurora that formed a multidimensional borderline among defined spaces on the world it enveloped.

"What is Captain Marvel's role?"

"He is another of Luthor's ciphers," my companion replied, "another once-powerful soul meticulously enslaved to the will of an evil man. What Luthor may cause him to do, or what he may choose on his own to do, are mysteries to me as they are to you, as they are . . ."

Suddenly I found that we were not alone. There were others here, and they were aware of our presence. There were five of them.

" . . . even to the old wizard who first called down the thunder to him."

They were enormous, each one big as a planet, hanging there at an angle to us in the firmament. As I looked at these looming figures the Spectre put a hand on my arm and changed our angle toward them. And as our angle changed, so did we become so much bigger—or they smaller; the notion of perspective is a meaningless physical concept in the spirit realms—that we momentarily stood aside them, and our scale was as massive as their own. Now they were just five curious, deep-visaged men who, as the Spectre joined them, discussed the doings of one of their little pet planets, this Earth.

"Who?" I asked him. "Who are these people?" The one speaking, the one with the long white beard to his waist, seemed the most passionate.

"Please," said the long-bearded one—the one to whom the Spectre referred as an old wizard. "Please, I could love him no more if he were my own son. And he is lost. We must show him the way. We must take a hand, for the sake of all of them."

"All of them, Brother?" said a thickset old man whose bush of a white beard hung in ringlets. "All seven billion of them?"

"Seven billion. Seven billion," the first one said. "Perhaps only the ones we love."

"And how do you propose to quantify love?" the smallest of them asked. He was a blue-skinned man with the emblem of the Green Lantern glowing on the red robe that draped him.

"Who are these people?" again I asked the Spectre, who seemed curiously distracted from me, rather than detached, as was his habit.

When I asked, they all turned to look at me.

"Are we a part of the grand tour, Spectre?" a taller one in a trench coat who looked younger—though there was not much of his face I could see, for the shadow of his hat—asked idly.

"This is my circle, Norman McCay," the Spectre told me. "The Quintessence, we have been called by some who have sought us. The group does change somewhat with the centuries. These are Highfather, the progenitor of the worlds of New Genesis and Apokolips"—a wild-haired old man with a shepherd's staff nodded to me—"and the Phantom Stranger." The trench-coated one grunted my way. "This is Ganthet, survivor of the Guardians of the Universe"—the little one with the Green Lantern emblem smiled a kindly smile and nodded—"and Zeus, of whom you have no doubt heard."

"The real Zeus?" I asked. "Lightning bolts and Mount

Olympus Zeus?" So far, this trip was only a confirmation of the dearest of my beliefs. Was I now to go through some sort of painstaking reevaluation? Was there something to paganism?

"Well, of course there was something to paganism," the thunderer thundered, certainly hearing my thoughts as clearly as my outward wonder. "Why would that involve reevaluating your beliefs? You mortals still have such narrow intellectual passageways. Do you still feel the need to dismiss an old notion every time you consider a new one?"

"Well, I—"

"And this is the wizard Shazam," my host said huffily of Captain Marvel's emotional advocate.

"Do not engage this child to his disadvantage," Shazam scolded Zeus. "Have we not already enough senseless conflict?"

"I am sure they all know you, Norman McCay," the Spectre assured me. I found this unsettling.

"Know me? How?"

"They watch," the Spectre said.

Shazam the wizard was the one, I learned, who had given Captain Marvel his power. The age-old wizard was the synthesis of the particular talents of many of the greatest of Earth's sentient creatures—physical and supernatural alike. Shazam took the power to import Solomon's wisdom, Hercules' strength, Atlas' stamina, Zeus' power, Achilles' courage, and Mercury's speed. A generation ago, Shazam found a boy pure of heart and bestowed all these magic powers on the child, making him Captain Marvel. Now that purity was twisted and perverted by Luthor, another human of great power, so that these eternals themselves—this Quintessence who watched over us all like paintings on an ancient wall—shuddered at the implications.

I had visions of trudging normally through life, slipping on banana peels, flunking French tests, giving bad advice, taking bad advice, picking my nose, so help me, with a small fraternity of godlike figures watching me do it all. This was far more disturbing than monotheism. I did not even know these guys.

They all laughed at me. Even Ganthet the Guardian. Even gloomy Shazam.

"Through the millennia," the Guardian said, "we have often lent our wisdom to the Earthlings, only to watch them march proudly to disaster."

"Ganthet is not wrong," the one named Highfather responded. "The humans are not our responsibility. They are but motes in the cosmos. An insignificant factor in the grand life equation."

The Spectre bristled. "How interesting that you insist upon this. You are all so concerned with how unconcerned you should act. Do you dwell on the Earth's problems because you are cosmically bored? Or do you congregate in order to prevent each other from interfering?"

I felt this conversation was not for my ears. I turned away, embarrassed, I suppose, with the assault on my mortal senses.

"Hiya. Have a little faith, Padre," a voice from behind me said, and I turned around to see the face of a dead man. Smiling. Through a skull.

I think I said something like, "Yow!"

"Boston Brand's the name," was what came from the flapping lower jaw of the skeleton in the tattered red flying suit. "I'm a ghost. Nice to meet you."

I guess then I said, "Excuse me?" which was better, but I was not being very coherent. It seemed the Quintessence had matters of Earthly influence to discuss, and the subtlety of what they were talking about, along with the bizarre environment of this outer-space netherworld, was too much for me to integrate all at once. I found my sensibilities welcoming this obstreperous new being.

"They're talking about the pros and cons of intervening. It's actually pretty boring," Boston Brand said. "Cosmically boring," and he laughed. "These guys just hang out here with one another so each can keep the others from doing anything."

"Why?" I asked him as the Spectre joined in a heated discussion among his peers.

"I don't get it myself. Guess I haven't gotten used to being a former self yet after all these years. I used to be a daredevil in the circus. Now I'm an agent of a higher power. Can you imagine?" and he laughed some more. "Oh, of course you can. I forgot who I was talking to."

I had no idea how he could "see" me with no eyes or "talk" to me with no voicebox or "laugh" with no air pumping through no lungs.

"You've got to stop trying to think with your brain, Pastor," he told me. "Your body's just there to slow you down. You can see only when you get beyond—what did you guys call it?—optics. Determining reality by telling the difference between lights and shadows—that's like drawing a stick figure and thinking you've created life. It's ludicrous."

I was not following this. "To tell you the truth, Boston, I can't imagine any of this. I have yet to understand why I'm here."

"To add to the greater glory of the Creator of the Universe. It's why any of us are here, natch."

"Is the Spectre really an angel?"

"I suppose," Boston said. "An angel of death is more his speed. Used to be a regular guy. A cop detective if I remember right."

"Corrigan," I said. "Yes, Jim Corrigan. He told me that."

"Well, then he got tapped by You-Know-Who for this special detail—which goes to show you it could happen to anyone. He started getting detached, like. Out of touch with whatever in him used to be human. That's why he needs you, at least that's what the others figure."

"Can he use his power to stop this coming disaster?"

"Disaster? Oh, you mean the one on the critical path down back with the physicals. Yeah, sure. But he can't avert it altogether. And if he stops it for now, he could change its eventual outcome, almost certainly for the worse. That's why Zeus stopped playing that game after Troy fell. Ever get the itch to be a god, Pastor?"

"Oh, for Heaven's sake."

"I don't mean God," he said, and I actually saw the capitalization of the word in his voice. Was I hearing without my ears now? "I mean like these guys. Look at the Phantom Stranger. Heck, look at Zeus. Story is he was just a guy who found some kind of magic rock from near the beginning of Creation, and he right away started in waging wars and founding nations and things. Freaky."

"People become . . . become what you call 'gods' by chance, you say?"

"No, not by chance. But not on purpose either. What turns a cop into an avenging spirit? Probably the same thing that turns a nose-picking kid into a minister."

"It must take a lot of courage," it occurred to me.

"Not that much. No more'n you've got, Padre. No more'n he ever had, either." Boston Brand gestured in the direction of the Spectre, who was leaving the conference of the Quintessence to rejoin me. "Hey, you get to the other side sometime—don't hurry it along or anything—but look me up, will you? Like to see what you think of it after you've been through all this."

"I'll try to keep that in mind," I told the ghost as he faded off at ninety degrees to perception.

"Are you rested, Norman McCay?" the Spectre asked me.

"Was that what I was supposed to do here?"

"Mortals rest when they have the time, I have observed," he said.

"I suppose I'm rested," I said. "Why?"

CHAPTER 21

Stone-Skipping

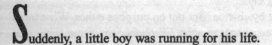

Suddenly, a little boy was running for his life.

I was this boy, and I could see this boy, too. And my belly roiled.

He was a beautiful boy, no more than eight or nine, in a red-and-yellow sweater and jeans and eyes like Michelangelo's David. Like David of the sculpture, his face was frozen in a mask of terror, and no one of his world was here to set a table for him in the presence of his enemies.

A giant robot with a pointy skull and a single cyclopean window where an eye belonged, stomping over the landscape, rained searing licks of flaming light. They made steamy black footprints in the dirt around him, in front of him, in the very steps through which he ran.

Others ran. Other children, big people, regular folks, people the boy would have thought could stand up to anything. Lions and tigers and bears would have run.

Tentacled monsters dropped from the sky without warning, planting themselves—*splat!*—in the ground and snaking in all directions. One grabbed a big man and made him scream. One grabbed a kid, and there was no sound.

Flying people—in armor and helmets and in just plain

muscles that would ping when you flicked them—collided in the sky. They threw each other through the air and at the ground to make long irregular ditches, and they'd get up and rise in the sky like vampires and slam each other again. One of them smashed down in front of the boy and made the ground rattle, and the boy fell over him and he got flipped up in the air and fell on his face when the flier lifted back up in the sky, ignoring him.

The boy got up and tried to remember how to make it stop. There was something he had to say.

A laughing little man with a hooked nose and no hair hung out on the horizon. Out where everyone was headed—being herded—he cackled like an evil hen. What was his name? The boy knew it: Sivana. He was an enemy from another life.

And what was the word? The magic word?

The boy opened his mouth to scream. Spits of hot light kicked up divots of the Earth. What was the word? Monsters snatched up running kids as if they were hunks of meat and squeezed them until they popped. The word. The scream. The horrors chewed up the Earth. Rolled over the ground like they had to lay new carpet.

He knew the word. He opened his mouth to say it. It was: "Shaz—"

—and a bolt of heat pierced his chest.

—and a blinding light appeared in his path and faded to leave a blackened hole.

—and the boy could not reach even the darkness in front of him because there was another hole where his heart and his lungs used to be.

—and he knew the word and he could not summon the air to scream it.

—and he went down.

—and the world continued to howl all around him.

Ω   Ω   Ω

"That's what it's like out there, Billy," Luthor told the boy when he was a man again.

"That didn't really happen," Luthor's valet—his name was Billy—told him with a pout.

"Oh, it happens every day, Billy. It's happening now."

"Every day," Billy said, more quietly now.

"It's what the superhumans do all the time. To all of us. But you don't have to participate, do you, Billy?"

"No."

"No, you don't. Not if you do just as I tell you. Isn't that right, Billy?"

"But there's something I want to know, Mr. Luthor. How come if I've got all these—" but he did not finish because of the pain at the center of his head, and he wanted to scream again but he could not finish a word. Certainly not the magic word.

"There there, Billy," Luthor said. "Let me help you with that." And Luthor snapped on surgical gloves from his pocket and whipped a long pointy pair of tweezers from his lapel pocket and stroked Billy's hair to stop his shaking.

Then Luthor pulled open the drawer of a small toolchest by the side of his film projector and lifted out a petri dish full of what looked like inchworms.

"He was a genius, wasn't he, that Sivana?"

And Billy quaked at the sound of the name and tried to say, "Shuh—shuzzuh—"

"No no no," Luthor said quietly, like Father Abraham gently tying his son to the altar. "We'll get that all settled down now, won't we? It was the left one last time, wasn't it?" And Luthor took a lively wriggling worm from the petri dish and dropped it into Billy's right ear. "Now turn around, Billy," he said.

This Billy did, and Luthor put on a little pair of glasses with a tiny halogen light on its bridge and carefully tweezed another inchworm—this one was sluggish and fat with fluid, hardly moving at all—out of Billy's left ear.

"Oh Mr. Mind," Billy called in a squeaky voice. "It hurts."

"Mr. Pain will be gone, Billy, in just a moment." Luthor cradled the perfect head of this massive, perplexed, magical being in his arms. "We have a special job to do, don't we?"

"Shuh . . . shuh . . . zazzash," the imposing six-foot, five-inch boy-man whispered, and then he was quiet.

"Yes, we do."

Up in a dark corner of the lab ceiling, a tiny Robobat hung upside down taking it all in. Elsewhere, on a catwalk, a man in titanium framing watched and listened to the monitoring device on his wrist.

Ω   Ω   Ω

The first time ever in his life that Superman had tried to skip a flat stone over water was after he was already grown. It's a kids' thing, no doubt, and as a result there's a terrible shortage of flat stones on the land surface of the Earth. Ever since the invention of kids, after all, kids have skipped flat stones over the water and lost them in the drink. Stone-skipping is a discipline far older than geology, for example, and surface-dwelling geologists have a skewed view of the percentage of flat stones on Earth, because the stones kids find in the pursuit of the diminishing flat type are over-whelmingly rounded. This is not true for Atlantean kids, and Atlantean geologists have a much more accurate perspective on the flat-to-round stone ratio. So Superman's forbearance, as a boy, from skipping stones was probably an ecological decision after a fashion. The first time he'd tried it, sitting with Lois by the reservoir in Centennial Park, he'd gotten the thing to skip thirty-seven times. His skill level increased significantly afterward.

Today, on a ledge in airless space outside the navigation deck of Alan Scott's satellite, Superman flicked fingernail-sized meteoroids across the void to see how many space rocks he could hit before sending his stone careening into space.

This required skills that were a combination of those that one needed for stone-skipping and for billiards. The satellite was passing through a thin cloud of space rocks caught over the centuries, orbiting Earth for maybe a hundred thousand years. Superman wore a radio headset built into an oxygen feed so Diana could hear what he said. She sat next to him wearing only a pressure helmet and radio in addition to her royal Amazonian costume and tiara, trying to figure out the rules of his game.

"... so then I flew him up to about, oh, here, and I said, 'Do you see that beautiful blue marble, Brainiac? That's my world. Return it. Now.'" These were the stories he used to tell Lois. They accounted for at least one of the Peabody Awards in the Kent condominium.

"Did he hear you?" Diana wanted to know.

"Actually, not in airless space, no. But he got the message. NORAD was back online within five minutes."

"Where is he now?"

"I buried some of the circuitry on Saturn, some on Argo. The motherboard is in the back of the frame of one of Clark's Pulitzers."

"Oh that's funny. You never told me that story before. Gods, those were better days."

"Easier anyway. Diana, what's this about being ousted by your own people? How did you let that happen?"

"My Amazon sisters, my own mother herself came to suggest that I had perhaps failed," she said into the speaker.

"What's that like?"

"Having your mother bring you the negative judgment of the nation you always had hoped to serve? What do you think it's like? You had a mother."

"Well, my mother was just a mother. She taught me how to ride a bike and fly, but being judgmental was something she tried to avoid."

"Must have broken a lot of bikes."

"Yeah. After a while my father started bringing home bike

frames whenever he went to the dump. So what's it like having a mother who's a Queen?"

"Mostly it's just like having a mother. She spent afternoons with me. She worked at home. She taught me to shoot arrows. She interviewed my teachers. She was never much like a Queen is supposed to be, except when all the women were around or when there was a crisis. You're much more like a King than she ever seemed."

"Really? Me?"

"Well, sure, Cla— Kal. Hey, let me try that. Can you get that big rock over here? That one, the one about the size of a fist."

"This one?"

"Thanks. Now what do you do, give it a little topspin?"

"All in the wrist. I'm not like a King. At least not on purpose, I'm not."

"You don't have to do anything on purpose, Kal. You were born to it. When I first met you, and there were all these articles everywhere about you, somebody wrote that if Krypton never had blown up, you might have grown up to be a plumber or a schoolteacher."

"I wrote that. Clark did, the first time I 'interviewed' myself. What's wrong with plumbers and schoolteachers?"

"Nothing. But they're a metaphor for ordinary people, and I don't think even you believe there's a circumstance wherein you ever would have grown up to be ordinary. Not on Earth or on Krypton or even on Apokolips if it came to that."

"That's good."

"You think so?"

"I mean the spin you put on that toss. Your meteor hit sixteen rocks in the swarm before it cracked apart and spun out. Ever play baseball?"

"No. Never. Kal, I was talking about something."

"I know. It makes me uncomfortable, Diana."

"And since when was your own comfort of any consequence to you?"

"I was just talking about your island and your mom. How did it get around to me?"

"Because what my sisters judged I failed to do is something you succeed in doing without even trying."

"What's that?"

"Get people to change their behavior for the better, just by being better than they are."

"Oh, come on, Diana."

"I mean it. If you were really uncomfortable with this role, you never would have put on the costume."

"It was my mother's idea."

"I figured as much. But look, couldn't you plug as many volcanoes and stop as many floods and fight as much crime and save the world just as often without anyone ever knowing you were there? A gust of superbreath? A bolt of heat vision? An invisible superspeed intervention, and nobody's the wiser? I know you do things like that all the time—or did, anyway—but still you wore the costume and let people see you floating through the sky on patrol like Apollo riding his chariot."

"An ounce of prevention, I thought."

"And you were right, Kal. You were always right. And it worked for you. Always. Then when you left and I stayed and the world tumbled into the sink, my sisters put me on trial. I pled my case, but they decreed that I had not changed Man's World. It had changed me. They saw—they saw quite correctly, I expect—that my version of the woman on horseback out to save civilization wasn't working."

"You believe that?"

"How could I disagree? The Amazons believe in peace through strength. Too often I relied on an olive branch and not a cestus."

"I always admired your gentility."

"It didn't get the job done. The world isn't any better. Everybody put on a costume, but it was all a reflection of your glory. Nobody really caught on but you."

"I'm sorry. You all must have hated me for it."

"We loved you for it. How could we do otherwise?"

"I'm just uncomfortable with the—"

"We hated you for leaving us. That's what we hated you for. And nobody ever gave any more of a damn about your comfort than you did."

He let that sink in. He pitched more stones. Then he grew impatient with waiting for them to float by, so he reached over and unrolled the golden lasso at her waist and she did not stop him. He wondered later whether she would trust anyone else—her sisters, her mother, anyone—with that lasso. She must have been startled, just a little, that he would take it. He was, too. It was magical after all. Superman objected to the supernatural as a concept in virtually any form; he denied the unknown when its reality presented itself, even in the form of a tool in the hands of a dear friend. The lasso reputedly made liars speak the truth. It would bring no conflict to Superman.

But he tossed the noose around six big chunks of busted rock in space and yanked back on it with just the right twist. He must have done the math in his head as absently as a first baseman does it when in a split instant he figures out the vector of a coming baseball and where to stand to catch it. A beam of ultraviolet heat pulsed from his eyes to fuse the rocks back together into one.

It was better to build than to destroy, his action told whoever might have been watching. He thought only Diana was watching, but the Spectre and I and who-knows-who else watched his absentminded lesson in physics and morality. Certainly all of us watchers caught the point.

Diana got the message, too, and perhaps she was a little annoyed by it. She reached for her lasso, and he pretended for a moment not to notice, not to let go.

"How can I do it, too?"

"Do what?" he asked.

"Whatever it is you do. Whatever magic you work."

"No magic. Just principles. Magic makes me crazy."

"What principles, Kal? I've got principles. I've got a

hundred thousand years of heritage and philosophy. For Olympus' sake, Kal, my people invented philosophy. Did you know an ancestor of mine was Socrates' teacher? And another was the mistress to Alexander the Great?"

"His mistress? An Amazon?"

"You do what you've got to do. Amazon philosophy. Go with what you've got. You're so invested in American culture, you think that's Jeffersonian pragmatism. He got it from us, and so did you. We invented civilization, and now our failure to get the message across—my failure to impose order and grace—presides over civilization's end."

"And your solution to civilization's imminent demise is the Gulag?"

"You bought in, Kal. Gentility on the left hand and a sword in the right. Look at the Great Seal of the United States. The eagle has an olive branch in the left talon and arrows in the right."

"It's the other way around."

"What way?"

"Arrows in the left talon and the olive branch in the right, actually."

"Whatever. We gave America its symbol."

"Don't tell me: Ben Franklin had an Amazon mistress, too."

"A teacher, not a mistress, believe it or not. I'll introduce you to her someday. You know something, Kal? Your adopted country has always been a special project of the Amazons— the way Greece was when it first got started. That's why they sent me."

"Really."

"And you know what else, Kal?"

"What, Diana?"

"It's why They sent you."

"Who? The Amazons from Krypton?"

"No, Kal. I mean it. We all have a mission, and yours and mine are the same one."

"No, it's not, Diana, because I don't buy the baggage that comes along with it."

"Not baggage. Philosophy."

"Right. Philosophy. First try to teach them, and then if they don't learn it, ram it down their throats."

"That's not— You said it yourself, Kal: 'We are warriors. We have an obligation to wage combat.'"

"Yes, I've said that and I'll stand by it. But here's another thing you might take to heart: If what you want to be is a role model, then you're going to have to learn that it's your gentility that people will respond to, not your force of arms."

Finally, she yanked away the rope from his loosening hand.

But it was he who kept talking: "Given who we are, Diana, given the power we possess, our obligation to keep the peace is greater than our obligation to wage war. War—particularly the war we wage today—is not some glorious struggle. It is a failure of negotiation."

She looked at him with her head atilt, wondering whether she wanted to disagree with him, not even considering how she might if she chose to do so. Then it was too late.

"Only the weak succumb to brutality," he said, and flew Earthward.

Ω Ω Ω

They—that amorphous "they" who sent out the signals for the weekly news magazines and wrote the billboards for the local newscasts—used to call Captain Marvel "the World's Mightiest Mortal," and he may well have been. All the super hero celebrities had catchy nicknames in those days. Batman was "the Caped Crusader" in the supermarket rags, "the Dark Knight" in the tabloids, and "the Batman" in the *Times,* with a lower-case *t* on the omnipresent article before his moniker, as if to highlight the editorial contention on the part of "*The* Paper of Record" that he was just another costumed vigilante whose real name no one knew. Superman, of course, was "the Man of Steel" everywhere except in his biographies, where he was "the Last Son of Krypton." We had an "Amazon Princess," a "Scarlet Speedster," an "Emerald Warrior," and a "Battling Bowman." Now I fancied that I knew all these people I followed around in this spirit state. But this Captain Marvel—this man who, as a boy, had derived his powers through the machinations of the ancient wizard Shazam, one of the Quintessence—was someone nobody seemed to know very well.

Certainly he did not know himself very well.

"Our other guests are beginning to arrive, Billy," Luthor said firmly as he walked through the door to the factory catwalk, where he found the Captain and the Bat. "Why don't you see to their entertainment while I talk with Mr. Wayne?"

"Yes, Mr. Luthor," and Billy scurried off the catwalk.

"You didn't tell me that you'd initiated triple-shifts," Wayne asked as Luthor joined him overlooking the robot production facility.

"It's not as though we have to worry about union rules," Luthor said.

"As a matter of fact, Luthor," prominent technocrat Bruce Wayne offered, "I have found in those few enterprises where I have had to hire nonunion tradespeople, that productivity actually increases when I invest in the sorts of humane working conditions that unions mandate."

"Yes," Luthor said, "I read about the eight-hour workday you strapped on that factory in Phnom Penh. Positively antisocial."

"Along with the day-care center, the alcoholism and depression clinic, the annual two weeks' paid vacations, and time and a half for overtime, and people all over Cambodia are beating down the doors to come work for me. It's become the most productive ceramics plant in all of Southeast Asia."

"LexCorp has a similar plant in Singapore that's a third as productive and has a tenth the labor costs."

"Maybe that's why you've never gotten as rich as I have, Lex."

"Oh, Brucie Brucie Brucie. You did have a head start. Eight or ten generations' worth, by my count. And it's taken you this long to learn that there's strength in numbers. Just look at this production facility."

It was impressive. It was a secret loft in the middle of Metropolis, three stories high and the area of two city blocks. From the catwalk, Bruce Wayne and Lex Luthor could watch the entire assembly line as it produced three complete flying Bat-Monitors a day.

"Magnificent, aren't they? Between your design and my production," Luthor said, "the Justice League doesn't stand a prayer of survival. Soon we'll crush them with a flotilla of un-yielding steel soldiers."

"I can feel your pulse throb from here, Luthor," Wayne said with a snort. "Don't double-cross me. Our objective is world order, not world domination. Don't forget the agenda."

"Wouldn't dream of it."

"Ridding the world of the League is a necessary evil. Humankind was never meant to bow before a Kryptonian and his ilk."

"My thoughts exactly."

Wayne sniffed condescendingly. Condescending sniffing was a genetically communicable talent that I have seen before in people in Bruce Wayne's class.

"Well, you arrived early, my dear Batman." Luthor ignored his ally's mild slight. "I do believe we have a meeting."

And the catwalk faded from my sight as another room came up around my taciturn spirit guide and me.

CHAPTER 22

Summit Meeting

Once Superman and his toadies are out of the way," Luthor said, his grin involuntarily getting bigger as he said it, "the Mankind Liberation Front can seize power. And with your little Bat-Knights keeping peace, we will return the reins of civilization to the humans."

"Sounds like a plan. Then again, couldn't we just drop a K-bomb on Big Blue's spit curl?" Oliver Queen asked between sips of herbal tea.

"All right, Ollie, a little decorum," Bruce Wayne snapped. "He was a friend of yours."

"Sorry, Bats," Queen said after a pause.

"Strife, my old friend," Luthor said. "Heartwarming."

It was Luthor's war room, and Bruce Wayne was curiously at home here. The conference table was smaller than the one upstairs, but the space was bigger. Electronic displays of maps, grids, and constantly changing graphs girdled the room.

Around the table were the principals of the Mankind Liberation Front and Bruce Wayne's three closest friends: Oliver and Dinah Lance Queen, and Ted Kord, who hovered around the walls clucking over the enormous sophistication of the information-gathering systems here.

"Sadly, Mr. Queen, the problem with kryptonite is that it no longer packs the punch it did in the good old days—as I learned the hard way." Luthor went on, "Chalk it up to the solar radiation Superman's cells have been guzzling all these years. He has never been more powerful. Gentlemen, ladies, we would not be competent if we allowed the strain of our association to affect the work that we have come together to accomplish."

"Oh, Ollie's been jealous of that spit curl since he had hair of his own." Dinah Lance rubbed a hand up and down her husband's arm, and Bruce Wayne smiled.

Ted Kord, the Blue Beetle, took his seat as the others of Bruce Wayne's team began to arrive.

"Once war begins, Batman," Luthor wanted to know, "can your players advance to the front lines if necessary?"

"We will be in place, Luthor. Obviously we cannot match the raw might of Superman's army," the Batman said as Jade, Nightstar, Tula, Obsidian, young Black Canary, and the others began to move into the room and assemble behind him, "but we have the fire of youth on our side. Among our partisans are the sons and daughters of many of the Justice League."

"And these people," Xu'ffasch said, not a little bit astonished, "are prepared to fight tooth and nail with the generation who sired them?"

"Aren't all young people? I believe I'm speaking for all of those who have come to our side," Bruce Wayne told the heir to the greatest of his enemies, "that it is their world and their century that we are here to build. Not Superman's. We are all prepared to fight when I give the signal."

Xu'ffasch raised an eyebrow. Then he saw Nightstar.

"Mr. Luthor," Bruce Wayne said, "here in this room and in the production facility above us are our force of arms. I expect you have devised a collection of strategies that somehow involves the Gulag? Are you prepared to share them with us now?"

"Why . . . why, yes," Luthor said. "Yes of course."

"Details?"

"Soon enough." Luthor vamped. "In fact, I'm awaiting word on a few details myself. Now if you'll excuse me, I need to step out for a moment, and you all need to meet one another." And Luthor was gone.

Bruce Wayne walked by Oliver Queen, squeezing his shoulder and saying, "Well done," on his way to speak with a tall weathered man who'd come in with the young people and now stood in a dark corner of the room. "Hi, J'onn," Bruce Wayne said to the man, "how're you feeling?"

J'onn nodded, but did not smile.

Xu'ffasch stood and introduced himself to Nightstar. Ollie and Dinah both put an arm around young Black Canary, their daughter, and asked what she had been up to. Billy, grinning, walked around the room passing out hors d'œuvres and asking if everyone was all right. No one answered him, and he did not seem to notice. A few people pointed at him and nudged one another as he went by, but no one spoke to him. They knew.

"I know what you're thinking. I do," J'onn, in his corner, told Bruce Wayne.

"Of course you do," Wayne said, "and because you do, you know how we all feel about you, old friend."

"Yes," J'onn said, "but I know what else you're thinking."

"Am I wrong?"

"I'm not sure."

"Help me."

"You're thinking maybe I can't."

J'onn's hands shook just a little bit. He was suffering, but for all I tried I could not figure out from what.

"I'm thinking maybe you can," Bruce Wayne corrected. "But let's not do this telepathically. You won't stay focused."

"May I have that?"

Wayne handed J'onn his cup of black coffee but was careful not to let go of it, and for good reason. J'onn's unsteady fingers passed through the cup like those of a ghost.

Like those of my own. But J'onn could touch it if he concentrated, and he did. He needed the coffee.

"Talk to me. Just relax and talk," Wayne told him. "Here, let me take that for you," and Wayne caught the cup that fell from his friend's lips and through his fingers just in time.

"Who is he?" I asked the Spectre.

"He was once a Martian champion. Now he is not much of anything," the Spectre said, but I knew the answer was more complicated than that. The Spectre explained that this everyman was of a race of people who once had colonized our neighboring planet, who'd become of that planet as easily as a key fits in a lock. I saw briefly what he really looked like: seven feet tall, green skinned, powerful. When his race had scattered, and J'onn found himself among the Earth humans, he'd tried to fit in as well here, using his abilities of telepathy and illusion on this world of scattered emotions and chaotic thoughts to such an expanse of effort that he shattered his own emotional infrastructure.

"I have seen this before," I told the Spectre.

"Where?"

"Most recently? In my congregation," I said, "the Sunday morning after Kansas."

"What can you tell me?" Bruce Wayne asked the Martian disguised as a man.

J'onn raised a hand and lifted his eyes in the direction of the big man who smiled and circulated his tray of hors d'oeuvres among the crowd through a path that cleared for a yard or two on all sides of him. "I will attempt . . ."

The tall man wore an eerie grin. He seemed a shark, trawling the room for prawn. "May I see that, please?" Billy said as he put down the tray and reached for Black Canary's crossbow.

The girl and both her parents looked up at him, each succeeding to a varying extent at masking his or her alarm. "Oh! I mean . . . sure. Help . . . help yourself." Reluctantly, she handed the big man her weapon.

He looked it over, sighted along its trajectory path, and handed it back to her.

"Cool," he said, and walked on with his hors d'œuvres.

"I can't," J'onn told Bruce Wayne.

"Okay, okay, that's fine."

"No, I can help you. I can tell you something you can use. What can I tell you?"

"You can tell me you'll go home and rest, J'onn."

"Too much noise. Too much. I can't take the noise."

"Go home and rest. Dream of red sands and silent stars."

J'onn touched a hand to the Batman's head, then withdrew it. "Yes," he said, and when no one but the Spectre, the Batman, and I were watching, he walked through a wall and was gone.

Ω Ω Ω

Superman stood at the window of the big satellite, perusing the Earth from another room crowded with talented people in costume.

"Germany is all clear," he said.

On his shoulder, a tiny woman—the Living Doll—with a tinier clipboard said, "Check."

"Italy, Austria, both okay," Superman said. "Yugoslavia and the Balkan states are a little chaotic, but if there's any activity, it's scattered and ineffective."

"Let's count on it," Living Doll said. "So that covers metahuman activity in Europe. How about Africa?"

Five old friends stood whispering across the room, on the far side of a navigational device.

"He can hear you," said Donna Troy, who once upon a time had fought at the side of these four men as Wonder Girl of the Teen Titans.

"Listen," Red Robin insisted. "I was all for the Gulag. But throwing Von Bach into that cauldron with those other jokers is like poking a hydrogen balloon with a match. Superman's prison is a pressure cooker enough as it is. He thinks he can get everyone to behave like they did when times were brighter, but even he can't turn back the clock."

"So tell him," Garth the water-breather suggested.

"Me? You tell him!" Red Robin said. "Look at him. Can't a man with telescopic vision see the world around him?"

"Shh! He can hear you!" Donna warned again.

The Flash was almost standing still. The brief conversation must have seemed to him to take forever, but he liked these people. He could hear what they were saying, I understood, but given his speed, no one other than Superman himself could understand a word he said.

"What do you think, Wally?" Red Arrow asked the red blur among them. "Is he listening?"

They heard a high-pitched hum from their speedy friend's direction, and the word "Yes" from that of Superman. He might have been talking to the Living Doll, but it still made Donna nervous.

When earlier we'd left Luthor's nerve center, it seemed to me that Zatara, the young man with the magical powers and the trademark top hat, had looked startled, just for a moment, as he gazed in my direction. Then I thought no more of it, but I should have. These are very perceptive people; they even occasionally perceive what to others may seem not to be there. The Flash—Wallace West—was a man too fast to be contained in one dimension of time or space. Apparently, entire strata of reality are open to him. I had grown so used to my role of silent, unseen observer that I did not realize what was happening when I poked my face into the conversation with his former Titan colleagues. What happened next was, for the first time, my own fault. Before I realized what was happening, the Flash threw his arms around me and tore me out of my own comfortable neoreality into his own.

Suddenly I felt pinpricks all over my body, the way a foot feels when it is waking from sleep. I took several heavy breaths of filtered air and felt them in my lungs; felt my heart jump-start my blood again. An alarm sounded. A recorded voice said, UNAUTHORIZED ENTRY. Dozens of people, maybe a hundred or more, as colorful and vivid as ever, appeared in the room like a swarm of giant bumblebees. Wonder Woman vaulted over a balcony rail to stand by Superman's side. Avia rushed toward me, but a blur of white beat her to me. Power Woman grabbed me by the shirtfront and demanded to know who I was and where I'd come from.

"I . . . I . . ." Usually I am more articulate.

"Answer me, dammit!" this extraordinarily powerful woman in white demanded. "What are you doing here?"

She pulled back a blue-gloved fist. I had no idea that a woman's fisted hand could look that huge. Superman took her by the wrist and gently led her away from me. I must have been a sight.

"Well?" he asked.

"I'm," I said, then I did not say anything. Neither did anyone else, so I said, "My name is Norman McCay and I've been . . . I'm supposed to tell someone who is . . ." I paused.

Certainly I could tell these people nothing that would surprise them. They reinvented surprise, each of them in turn. "This isn't going to make any . . ." Then I remembered my prayer and lifted my eyes.

"I need to warn you," I finally said to Superman.

"Warn me."

"Please understand. A catastrophe comes! I see armies. I see them. Armies raised against you and an eternal night and rising storms of dust and shards of metal and treachery."

His was somehow the only face before me.

"I see this as clearly as I see you. A golden eagle contending with a flying bat in the sky, and a flag in the shape of a man pounding at the wretched ground in sorrow and despair until the very Earth shatters under his blows." I could think of no more to say, so help me.

He stared at me with X-ray eyes that, for the life of me, began to glow, then faded, looking for meaning to my babble.

My mouth dry, I could find no words save those I myself have heard before: "And the third angel sounded," I said, "and there fell a great star from heaven, burning as it were a lamp, and it fell upon the third part of the rivers, and upon the fountains of waters. And the name of the star—"

" 'Is called Wormwood,' yes, I've read the book, too," he interrupted me.

He spoke to me indulgently, as if I were some crank who'd tripped into a space warp. And I had to continue, though for all the world and all the firmament, I knew in my soul that all I could do by continuing would be to look like a fool in front of the people I admired most. "And the sun and the air were darkened," I said. "Fear God and give glory to Him," and I whispered because I had no more breath to speak but had to, "for the hour of His judgment is come."

We both were silent for a moment before Superman said, "Listen to me."

Like an idiot I nodded.

"I don't know who you are or where you came from, but your words are meaningless. Armageddon is hardly on our calendar. Let me assure you, sir, that while these are dark days, we have matters fully under control. Can we talk about how you—"

"Holy God!" Red Robin called from across the deck, and I was sure he was calling, in fact, to God, but everyone here looked in his direction nonetheless.

"Word just came in from Scott at the Gulag!" he said. "There's a riot going on! The prisoners have gone berserk!"

Wonder Woman took a step back from Superman—a signal to the others that the commander was in the room.

"Any more information?" Superman's was the only collection of neck muscles that did not snap to attention and contract for battle.

"No," the man in the black hooded cloak said. "Superman! What do we do?"

PART III

~~~~

...A Fit Place
for Heroes

CHAPTER 23

Martial Law

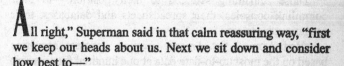

"All right," Superman said in that calm reassuring way, "first we keep our heads about us. Next we sit down and consider how best to—"

"Flash! Green Lantern! Power Woman!" Wonder Woman interrupted in a steely bark. "To the Gulag. Now. Take control. Report directly back here at your first opportunity."

They all looked away from me, unaware that I was still there. And sometime in the course of the exchange I no longer was there. The Spectre spirited me back and I was just a watcher again. "You are finished here."

"No, not quite," I pleaded, but his hand settled me.

The person to whom the others looked was Superman.

He thought a second. A full second. A second of indecision. They—even I—could feel him considering how or whether to countermand Wonder Woman's sudden seizure of control. Certainly no one here would stand for a mutiny against Superman's will, but there was that second of indecision and everyone saw it. And at the end of it he said, "Through peaceful means, of course," and effectively confirmed Wonder Woman's order.

"By any means necessary," she said to the three order-takers who bolted out to the airlock. She would just keep shoving at him—at Superman. She was the only one who would ever do that. He could counter her at any time, but on some level he knew she was right.

She was the one who gave the orders that he could not bring himself to give.

"Ray!" she called across the big satellite conference room. "Phoebus! Stand by to join them if called. Everyone, monitor your individual responsibilities. Wherever possible, stay within eyeshot of your backup monitor. You've all got your assignments. As those assignments change for emergency duty, you must see that your stations are covered. Be aware of and advise me immediately of any potential communications gaps."

Those remaining scurried to their positions—to their commlink consoles, their spreadsheets and databases, their scenario generators.

"Red Arrow," the Amazon barked, "project scenarios based on the most up-to-date data at one hundred four percent of capacity. Robin, strip archived memory and divert it to the operating system. Now. No resources for nonessentials."

"Umm," Superman interrupted, finally, "we need the archives for a history file. If there's an inquiry later on into our actions, we'll need documentation."

"Documentation's for historians to write when we're all dead. Strip the archives, Robin."

Red Robin looked at Red Arrow. It was the archer who said, "We can run scenarios at a hundred percent without diverting the archives. The disparity would be negligible."

Wonder Woman glared darts at Superman, who was never intimidated by a threatening look. He was impassive. It was she who blinked, as she had to do.

"Fine. A hundred percent. No maintenance goes into archive documentation. Let it run on automatic. Robin, prepare the launches for the nonflying members."

That was the only audible strife that scraped through New Oa as the vanguard of the Justice League joined Captain

Comet and Scott and Barda Free to lock down the Gulag on the planet far below.

The inaudible strife, however, was thick as a dwarf star's core.

"The old man," she said. "Where did he go? Who was he?"

I stood just inches—and a dimension of reality—away from her.

"I don't know and I don't care," he said, and he took her arm and turned her around and demanded, "Why did you undermine my authority?"

Through clenched teeth: "Why did I? When—

"—did—

"—you—

"—exercise—

"—it? I saw a crisis. I reacted in a confident and unqualified manner. The others need to see that sort of authority—" She paused. "From someone."

"All right, calm down," he told her when he realized she needed it said to her more than he needed it said to him. "We're juggling enormous forces here. If we have a difference of opinion over tactics—even over the appropriate use of our own power—we discuss it first. We work it out. All right?"

She let out a breath. This was what passed, for him, as a concession, and she knew it. "All right," she said. "But you have to take firm positions and issue decisive directives. Can you agree to that?"

"Yes, I can. You and I work together. But you let me know what's on your mind before you impose presumptive authority. Agreed?"

"I don't need to agree to it," she said. "It's an order. I can take orders."

"Good."

Ω   Ω   Ω

The satellite was a beehive of activity. Everyone covered his or her station, monitored, fed information, or processed data. There were thirty-one people aboard New Oa when the news of trouble at the Gulag arrived, and someone here was in touch with another hundred fifty members of the Justice League before Superman initiated his dispute with his first officer. The roster of Justice League members, as the organization's concerns grew more specific, was growing more formalized every day. Members were putting their lives on hold all over the world and arriving both here and at the Gulag even as the two to whom they looked for leadership debated the issue.

"Pull yourself together. We are overdue for a meeting with the Secretary-General," Wonder Woman told Superman. "We can be sure the United Nations is aware by now that we've built and populated the Gulag."

"Then I guarantee they're going to be wondering on what authority we have begun to decree and enforce our own laws within the borders of the United States," Superman said.

Wonder Woman started to leave. "Come, we have to convince them that we are the good guys."

CHAPTER 24

The White House

~~~

American politics, at the dawn of the Millennium, became world politics. Like Superman, its longtime symbol and standard-bearer, the United States had shied away from its inevitable role on the world stage every chance it got. Yet time and again, crisis and necessity pushed leadership upon the nation.

A major point of contention among foreign nationals was the fact that only Americans got to choose the President of the United States, who was effectively the emperor of the rest of the world. If this President was to be a democratically elected leader, should not all the people governed by the President have a voice in the choice of that President? some reasoned.

"Just now it's a moot point, Ambassador Jiang," Jennifer Capper told the Consul-General from China who brought it up again at a meeting under a tent on the White House lawn. "Notwithstanding that, however, the next time your government directs you to inquire after a voice in internal American elections, you might ask them when the people of China will finally begin to have a vote regarding their own leaders."

"I protest, Madame President." Ambassador Jiang rose

from the chair to her full six feet one inch, towering over all of the men in the tent with the exception of five of the six Secret Service agents who hovered around the meeting. "I protest most resolutely. The reforms in my country have given such a voice to a wide range of persons."

"As long as they own businesses or have a family history of correct political activity," the President debated gamely.

"The agenda for today, however"—Leonard Wyrmwood rose, smiling for the guests whom he'd brought to lunch today—"does not include that. The President's time is at as much of a premium as our own, so we need to get back to the matter of international foodstuffs redistribution."

The White House was more than two hundred years old now and was in constant use, not only as a family home but as a large office building, every moment of every day. It had not seen a structural overhaul since Bess Truman had insisted on one at the midpoint of the last century. Last year, when a large gray rat had tumbled through an upstairs kitchen air vent while President Capper's teenage son, Bryan, was rooting through the refrigerator on the fourth floor of the White House, the President had decided that it was time to get Congress to gut and rebuild the old mansion again from the inside out.

Artwork went to storage and information went to archive. Walls and fixtures were carefully tucked away around the city. Today the entire stripped-to-the-rafters White House was under a fumigation tent, and the President's meeting with the Secretary-General and the delegates to the United Nations Security Council was under another tent on the rambling South Lawn. Also under this tent was a gourmet meal from the temporary White House kitchen in the partitioned-off lobby of the Old Executive Office Building across the street. A four-piece orchestra played Bach fugues as the diplomats ate and talked.

"General Wyrmwood," the President said, "thank you. In the next two months, ladies and gentlemen, I will be traveling with the chief executive officers of the three major agricultural corporations who still have extensive land holdings outside the irradiated areas. Also traveling with me will be Dr. Nevin Scrimshaw of MIT, the nutritionist. My office will make a public announcement of the trip next Monday. Any countries whose governments want them on my itinerary, let me know by then."

"Excuse me, Madame President," the Englishman Lord Wainwright said, "but are you interested only in countries with historic malnutrition problems? We in Britain are heavily dependent on American produce and already feel the pinch. And I'm sure Their Majesties would love to see you again."

"I'll pencil you in. Get confirmation, please," the President said.

"We would hope," the Israeli delegate said, "that this trip is not just a—what do the schoolchildren call it?—a booster club for American produce and processed foods. Does it truly have a substantive purpose?"

There was a tapping outside the tent. One of the Secret Service men poked his head out in the direction from which the tapping came. A flustered-looking young man came bounding into the meeting tent, past the musicians and directly behind the President as she said, "Of course it has a purpose, Ambassador Rifkin," and he handed the President a folded slip of paper.

President Capper opened the note as she said, "High-level, high-visibility goodwill tours such as this focus the energies of local agencies on the immediate problems." She looked the note over. "They allow heads of state and heads of departments and ministries to coordinate signals to mid-level operatives about priorities," and then she stopped. "You all will have to excuse me a moment," she said, and turned and left the tent.

She walked less than fifty yards toward her temporary office quarters in the Old EOB, turned, and came back. When she returned, the delegates were murmuring, puzzled.

"Perhaps, ladies and gentlemen," the President said as she strode toward her seat at a large round table among the company, "it would be more appropriate to share this information with all of you before I act on it through my own resources. We've all heard the intelligence reports about the construction of some sort of structure the size of a small city at Ground Zero in the former American Commonwealth of Kansas."

Already, the delegates were impressed. For one thing, it was the first time any of them ever had heard her allude to the notion that her country now had one fewer state. She had their attention.

"A brief report now confirms for me that the so-called Justice League has in fact constructed a detention center—a prison, a Gulag—on that site. It further informs me that the walls of this containment facility are no longer secure."

A general hubbub erupted among the delegates. Forks clattered. Pill cases opened and closed. Water pitchers poured, and one fell and broke in a million pieces. Voices murmured. Matters did not calm down that moment when the Secret Service agents, as one, murmured something inaudible. Four agents scrambled out of the tent, and the remaining two gathered warily to either side of the President.

"What?" she said, and one of them shrugged and the other tilted a head at the tent exit. She stuck her head out of the tent, then stepped out, motioning dismissively in the air. "Superman, Diana, hello," was what most of the delegates heard her say.

"Madame President," Superman said.

"President Capper," stated Wonder Woman as they followed her back into the tent.

Now the delegates were quiet again.

"We went to United Nations headquarters and found that the Security Council was meeting with you," Superman said—President Capper could not tell whether that was by way of apology or just explanation.

"My agenda's shot to hell," the President said as she plopped in her seat. "The floor's yours."

"We thought"—Superman turned to the assembled delegates—"that we ought to report to you on our current activities in the irradiated areas of the American Midwest."

"We beat you," Wyrmwood said, sitting at the President's table. "The President's just told us about your concentration camp. We're flattered that the mighty Justice League has finally deemed the human race worthy of conversation."

"There's no need for sarcasm, Secretary-General," Wonder Woman snapped.

"Sarcasm?" The Secretary-General laughed. "Forgive me. We're simply no longer accustomed to being advised or consulted. Forgive me, delegates, if I speak as an American for a moment. And forgive me as well, oh great and mighty ones, but imagine our surprise and apprehensiveness to learn of the presence of a metahuman prison in the very center of United States national territory."

"We have taken every possible step to secure it," Superman said. He was falling back into the familiar patterns of the skilled public figure by now. "We have taken redundant steps, in fact. The Gulag's labyrinthine layout is familiar only to its designer, Mr. Scott Free, who is also its codirector."

"With you?" the President asked.

"With Dr. Adam Blake," Superman answered. "Captain Comet."

For a moment, the President was impressed again. Dr. Blake had declined her offer of a cabinet post a few years ago, but had not turned down a job with the Justice League.

"All right, Superman," the Secretary-General continued. "Are you here to report that your detainees are fully docile and eager to acclimate?"

"Eager? No. We're working on that. Docile? No, that's why we built the facility. Again, however, we have taken this step to secure the world's safety, not—"

"Then you're telling us, hard as this is to believe," the

Secretary-General interrupted—and the President gave no indication that she thought he should not interrupt—"that with the unauthorized and unlicensed use of American territory and private property for a government-controlled function, you have diminished the prevailing danger of the metahuman presence to nil?"

Superman did not answer. Wonder Woman wanted him to say something. So did the delegates, but he did not.

"Aren't you telling us even that the end justifies these grossly irregular means? Is that true, Superman?"

"Not entirely," Superman said. "The Gulag is a work in progress. It is our duty—the League's duty and the duty of those responsible people whose gifts involve extrahuman abilities—to guide those of us who insist upon working against the common good. I admit there is some danger, still. There is less danger than there was without the Gulag. I chose to put the renegades together where we can monitor and teach them."

"Inside an enormous powder keg," the Secretary-General said. "Superman, Wonder Woman, we have lots of prisons in Montana. Federal prisons. State prisons. Local jails. Detention centers. People—normal, nonsuperpowered people—find a way to get out of them all the time. But we've learned something about prisons where I come from. One of the most important, basic things we've learned is that you don't put the slyest, craftiest, most escape-prone people you've got all together in one place. Because if one of them gets out—and one of them will, somehow, get out, that's pretty much the rule—then in that case the rest of them are always going to follow. Why didn't you maybe pick up a phone and ask us about that? Are metahumans—are you, Superman—the only source of information and wisdom worth consulting now?"

"We're consulting you now," Superman said. "Up until now we've been kind of busy."

"Oh, and you come today because you've got time on your hands? You've got an insurrection in progress and you're just trying to soften the spin," the Secretary-General said with some restraint. "Superman, the confidence and hope your reemergence engendered is fast eroding."

"Perhaps," came a low-pitched rumble voice from the far end of the tent. Lord Wainwright supposed, because of his own near-deafness, that nobody heard him when in fact everybody did, so again he said, "Perhaps."

The President urged everyone else to quiet down as the ancient Englishman rose slowly on the hand-carved cane that Churchill himself had once cracked over the head of an annoying Labourite.

"Global economy is still catastrophic," said the senior member of the Security Council. "Worldwide trauma is staggering. Confidence in institutions is at a historic nadir. Neither this body nor any government on Earth can afford another Kansas, I promise you that."

Superman prodded, "You're saying, Lord Wainwright . . ."

The ancient diplomat did his best to strip away decades of tact and forbearance and managed this much: "Perhaps it is time that we began to decide some things for ourselves. Good day."

Ω   Ω   Ω

"Stop it," Diana said to him as the White House and Foggy Bottom receded behind them and became a dot on the face of the blue globe beneath them.

"Stop what?" He pretended he wanted to know.

"Stop looking so stunned. Did you seriously think they'd want us to sit there and reason this out with them at our leisure?"

"Well, that is their purpose, right? They're the United Nations, after all."

"They're scared, Kal. And their fears may soon outweigh our solutions. We have to act."

"I don't have the luxury of fear."

"Nice turn of phrase, my old journalist, but it doesn't dismiss the problem. Whether you like it or not, you're a world leader now, and even the League members are getting tired of waiting for you to adjust to that role."

"I'm an old guy. I adjust slowly."

"Well, guess what, Kal? I'm older. And as far as I'm concerned, if the situation with the Gulag prisoners—"

"Residents. Students. Detainees maybe. Not prisoners."

"—if it gets one micron worse, then the League will be forced to take final, decisive action."

This time she flew off ahead of him, and he let her.

CHAPTER 25

Pandora

Bruce Wayne and Ibn al Xu'ffasch had to be amused that they were wearing the same suit, but neither appeared to notice.

Lex Luthor had left the room a few minutes before in the middle of a conversation with Zatara. They were talking about the relative merits of a mechanical army versus one that Zatara conjured through an elaborate supernatural process. Then Luthor had left that discussion in a hurry, and Zatara had finished the conversation by himself. Now Luthor burst back into the room—filled to the discomfort point with all manner of bizarre creatures from Catwoman's pet Riddler, Eddie Nigma, to that ineffably beautiful hybrid creature Nightstar, who doted on Bruce Wayne as if he were the grandfather he would have wanted to be.

"Good news!" Luthor bellowed. "The moment has come to begin our final strike! The Gulag is in turmoil! The inmates are—dare I say it?—revolting!"

The most significant malefactors of his lifetime and a couple dozen costumed do-gooders were assembled in his conference room, and Luthor was about to throw down his trump. This was the tastiest moment of his life.

Around the table were the Mankind Liberation Front. Against the walls and windows were the last of the living, free metahumans who'd rejected Superman's Justice League: the second Zatara, grandson of the first, whose family heirloom is knowledge of the arcane constellation of forces that the fearful still call "magic"; Oliver Queen, the Green Arrow, tough as nails and still stinging like a bee at sixty-something; Dinah Lance Queen, his wife, as deadly a martial artist as there was on Earth; Darkstar, the son of Donna Troy of the Justice League and her estranged husband; Nightstar, who gave Bruce Wayne constant back rubs and called him "Gramps"; the Huntress, an archer in jungle camouflage; Red Hood, the relentlessly agile daughter of Roy Harper of the Justice League and the late villainess Cheshire; Fate, sorcerer of the gold face helmet and one of the dozen or so most powerful people on the planet; Jade, the green-skinned ring-wielding daughter of the Green Lantern who'd built New Oa; her brother, the dark and brooding Obsidian; the fourth Flash, who fancied herself the daughter—after some fashion—of Wally West, who now fixed the wind-retardant goggles to her eyes; Wildcat, the human/feline hybrid who was attracting the fascination of Selina Kyle; Tula, the scantily clad Atlantean merwoman; and more. Not even Luthor knew all of their names. The ripest presence here, though, was the ever-loyal valet standing by his side.

"Superman's prison has become a cauldron of hate and chaos. That's our cue to deploy our steel legion," Luthor said, "but not before someone tips that scalding cauldron right onto the Justice League! Someone I've been saving for just such a task. Isn't that right?" he said, turning toward the imposing figure of his assistant.

"Me? But all our talks?"

"Ladies and gentlemen, by now you all no doubt have figured out that my assistant is not simply a manservant. Many of you who know him haven't seen him since he was much younger. Introduce yourself, son."

"Mr. Luthor, I thought—"

"Introduce yourself to our friends."

"Nice to meet you all. I'm . . . I'm . . ."

"It's as I've always said, young man," Luthor went on in that telltale teacher-to-slow-pupil tone, "the superhumans are evil. You can't argue with that."

"Yes, but I—"

"Only you can ensure their destruction, isn't that right?"

"That's what you told me, Mr. Luthor."

"And that makes it true, right?"

"Yes."

"I'm ordering you to demolish the Gulag so that its prisoners roam free. Free and angry. And easily eradicated in a war that no one can win . . . save us. So tumble down the walls of Jericho, boy. You remember that story, right?"

"Yes, Mr. Luthor."

Bruce Wayne stood slowly from his seat, spirited his way around the room through the crowd of colorful colleagues, edging silently, invisibly in plain sight, toward Luthor. Nightstar leaned over to whisper something to her friend Xu'ffasch, who looked back at her in silent alarm as she squeezed his upper arm. Everyone else was transfixed by this scene.

Luthor reached up to press on the lobe of his servant's vulnerable ear and said, "Do it and worry no more about losing control. You won't. I've seen to that. Go ahead," and he paused. "I insist."

Suddenly the piledriver fist of the Batman slammed against the jaw of the bigger, younger man as he folded over the floor. Before the big child-man could gather a thought, Bruce Wayne crouched on his rib cage and held tightly to his throat.

"Sorry, Billy," Bruce Wayne said as his charge tried to expel a word. One word would have been too much.

"He—he's not—?" Oliver Queen was indignant. "You're kidding me! All this time we've been in mortal fear of Billy Batson, not Captain Marvel?"

"I'd suspected it for a while," Bruce Wayne explained, "and J'onn's telepathic probe confirmed it. It seems Marvel's dual identities are in quite a bit of mental conflict. All these years as Batson grew to manhood, Luthor kept him in check by turning him into a stew of schizophrenic psychoses."

Luthor swarmed over the Batman's back, pounded at his

shoulders and neck, yanked at his cyborg framing, all to no effect. It may as well have been Superman Luthor was trying to fight hand to hand.

Ted Kord, the nerdy hack who used to put on the Blue Beetle outfit just so he could be someone else, grabbed Luthor by the scruff of the neck and threw him against a wall and enjoyed doing it.

"But our goals?" Luthor said through his aching face.

"My only goal in allying with you," the Batman snapped, "was to unravel your connection with Captain Marvel and undo it. In this entire global conflict, he was the wild card. And I hate wild cards."

"You—you double-crossed me!" Luthor shouted. "You double-crossed me first."

"An amusing notion." The Batman smiled. "I learned from you." Then he looked around the room—at everyone frozen in place. He held tight the larynx of the man who was Captain Marvel.

"Then may we assume you've given the signal?" Darkstar asked.

"Absolutely. Strike."

And the room exploded in combat.

Selina Kyle rose to elbow Tula in the chest and bolt for the door. Jade caught her in a will-induced green bolo.

The Riddler tried to duck under the table, but before he could, his chair spun around fourscore and seven times. When the Flash finally stopped it, she thought she might have to give the little guy a heart massage.

The Wildcat dove across the table onto the immortal Vandal Savage.

Nightstar spirited Xu'ffasch off into an adjoining room.

Obsidian enveloped the King of Spades in his cloak, and the evil one emerged unconscious on the floor and still quivering.

Lord Naga tried to rise from his seat and found himself with his own clothes tacked to a wall by half a dozen arrows from the bows of Red Hood and the Huntress.

Luthor jammed out the door, distracting the Batman

enough for Billy to grab at his foot and topple him off his chest.

"Ted!" Bruce Wayne called. "Follow Luthor. Don't let him get to the Bat-Knights!"

Luthor huffed and puffed his way down the hall toward his production loft.

"That's where I want him, Bruce," Ted called back from halfway down the hall, yanking something from out of an inside pocket. "You worry about Marvel."

And the Batman did. Billy Batson, scared as a rat in a cathouse, barreled into a stairwell in the direction of the spare little bedroom off Luthor's biology lab.

Luthor himself lumbered onto the open elevator platform to the floor of the bat-robot production facility. Standing on the catwalk above him, Ted Kord, the mechanical genius, smiled.

In his hand, Kord held a remote control the shape of a big blue bug. He pressed a button, and Luthor's platform stopped halfway between the catwalk and the floor.

"What?" Luthor said. "What the— Who's here?"

Not that it would have mattered, but Kord did not answer. Instead, he pressed another key.

Around the room, thirty-four completed Bat-Knights flashed on their pairs of eyes and advanced at Luthor.

Luthor, high of cholesterol and ample of girth, climbed off his platform and tried to get down its superstructure. He caught a trouser leg on the elevator gate and lost his footing. A twelve-foot-tall robot caught him halfway down, and the others congregated around. "No!" Luthor screamed.

On the catwalk above, Ted Kord grinned and played with his toys some more.

Ω Ω Ω

"Billy, stop! Please!" Bruce Wayne called after him.

Billy ran on without a word. Then he got caught in a dead end in the lab, and Batman was in the door holding a tranquilizer pistol in his hand, and both of them stopped. The safe thing to do would be to put a dart in Billy's neck and ask questions later, but there was too much Wayne needed to know immediately—and Billy had enough poking and prodding and things sticking out of him to suit an Abkhasian's lifetime.

Keep him silent, Bruce Wayne told himself. Lower the tone here. He spoke softly: "Billy, you don't have to run anymore. I figured out what Luthor did to you. Captain Marvel retired early, didn't he, Billy?"

Billy said, "Captain Marvel."

He could as easily have said something else. Careful, Bruce. Edge into the room. "Of all of us, he had the hardest time adapting to the grim new world around him. One sad day he spoke his magic word for the last time and vanished inside a scared little boy. Maybe it was because Superman left. Or maybe because things just changed too much and it was too crazy. Maybe . . ."

"Too crazy, yuh," Billy said.

". . . maybe you thought all these bad things these young guys, guys like you, were doing, made you a bad person, too, but they didn't, Billy. Luthor took you under his wing and told you so, but Luthor lies. He lies, Billy."

"Mr. Luthor."

"He's a criminal, Billy. Always has been. And he never let you forget that deep down you were something big and hard and super. He told you the same thing the world was telling you. That super heroes were monsters. Terrible, repulsive beasts. Don't think like that, Billy. He's twisted your brain around that insanity. The worms. He found a way to engineer those worms to secrete certain chemicals into your mind, right?"

"Mr. Mind."

"Well, they're eating away at your brain—driving you mad. Breaking the synapses, I'll bet. But they can't beat you, Billy, because of what's deeper inside you. Billy or Marvel, either one. The world depends on you. You can fight—"

"No, he's bad. He's bad!" Billy hollered and bolted out of his corner.

Bruce Wayne stood his ground in the doorway, and Billy did not want to slam by him. He took a step backward. He turned, flailing. Billy remembered a key to the far door in a drawer somewhere and bolted to the right, toward a cabinet.

"Billy, look out!"

The big glass-encased electrostatic generator whose inner walls crawled with inchworms was in his way, but he did not see it until he shattered it.

Batman lit into the room just as Billy tumbled on the floor in a pile of glass and worms. Now Bruce Wayne could not trank him; if a worm got into Billy's ear, there was no telling what effect the mix of chemistry would have on his body.

The worms were all over him: on his clothes; on his hands; on his hair and face; crawling toward his eyes and ears. He was terrified. Pain and suffering, to what remained of this big boy of a man, took the form of a worm.

"Billy, stay calm. I can help. Stay calm. It's all—"

There was only one way to protect himself from the pain and the fear of the pain:

Billy Batson said, "Shazam!"

And the genie was loose.

A thunderous clap of cold light shattered the Batman's ears, and he fell backward onto the floor. By the time he rolled up again on his titanium framing, he was alone in the room and there was a new man-sized hole in the far wall.

"Damn it," Batman said.

Zatara was the first in the room. Then came Nightstar dragging Xu'ffasch by the hand. Then Ollie Queen and his daughter.

"Batman, are you all right?" Zatara wanted to know.

"For the moment," Bruce Wayne said, brushing himself off and gathering his thoughts. "What about Luthor and his men?"

"In custody, every one," Zatara said. "What about Marvel?"

"No longer a wild card, unfortunately. He's under orders from Lex Luthor. There's no telling what the specifics of those orders are, God help us."

More of them came in. Batman did not need to explain. His face had grown more scrutable over the years.

"To the cave," he said to Zatara, "take me to the cave. Now."

"Enoyreve ot eht evac," Zatara said, *"won!"*

And they were gone.

CHAPTER 26

The Sword of Hephæstus

Superman found the first report from Green Lantern discouraging. He found Wonder Woman's reaction to it more so. With the insurrection almost a day old, Comet, Barda, and Scott were putting out fires and loosing their limited supply of containment bubbles from their floating command stations in elaborate hovercraft outside the Gulag structure. These they reserved for people who actually made it out through the gaps in the walls. Green Lantern, the Flash, and Power Woman were inside, everywhere at once. They needed to be. Captain Comet ran out of containment bubbles and used this as an excuse to indulge his impatience at being detached from the action itself. He anchored his floating command station to a point in space and jettisoned out. As, on the New Oa satellite above, Wonder Woman took her red-white-blue-and-gold shield from its cabinet in her temporary quarters, Captain Comet negotiated his way through the jagged hole in the artificial sky of the Gulag.

"Watching you dress for battle is almost indecent," Superman said to Diana as she affixed the golden eagle wings to her back. "Yet another side of you I'm not comfortable with."

"Get used to this one," she snapped. "A soldier unprepared has no business calling herself a soldier."

He walked into the room and idly lifted the sword from the sofa and ran his hand down its length. Its blade, on its point, would reach from the floor to her shoulders. "Where'd this come from?" he began to ask her before he said, "Ow!" and looked with great surprise at where he'd caught his thumb and found the tiniest droplet of blood.

"You always were a bit vulnerable to magic. Be careful," she said, taking the sword from him by the hilt. "Hephæstus made this as a gift for my mother. It's thirty-five hundred years old if it's a day."

"I hope she was impressed." He went to press his thumb to his teeth but found it was already healed.

"She was. It can carve the electrons off an atom."

"Amazons invented atoms, I've heard," he said facetiously.

"Only atomic theory." She was not facetious.

"You don't expect to use that thing, do you?"

"I expect to be a soldier. And a soldier unprepared has no business on the battlefield."

"More Amazonian wisdom. Isn't it possible that we've already won the big fight? Once the rioters are calmed, we can instill—"

"What makes you think they'll get calmed? And what makes you think once they're calmed they'll want to listen to us? Have you seen the receptivity graph in the study the Education Committee did last week?"

"Well, of course I saw it. It's not a significant sampling, and—"

"And you'd be crowing from here to Thanagar about it if it'd come out the way you wanted. Right?"

"I will not sanction lethal force against rioters. I'm uneasy with the blade," he said.

"Not all of us have heat vision," she shot back, and walked away.

Superman followed her into the conference room, where

Earth hung through the window and eighty-five Justice Leaguers in full battle array stood awaiting an order.

"There are lines we do not cross," Superman said to this woman who, so help him, had not looked better than she did in this moment since the day he met her and promised always to be her friend. "We have rules."

"Show me the line."

"We don't murder."

"You're the writer, Kal. Know the difference between murder and killing?"

Eighty-five Justice Leaguers who fairly worshipped the ground Superman flew over heard it all, and more were swarming in, both from below and from other points on the satellite.

"Our prisoners don't see that line, Kal. That's why they're prisoners. And if they don't remain our prisoners, your world is going to look a lot different tomorrow from the way it looks today. You made the decision to put them away—for the good of humankind, remember?"

"And maybe that was my mistake. I won't make this one. Maybe we should have let the human community decide how to deal with them."

"You and I joined the 'human community' for lunch at the White House yesterday, Kal. How equipped did they seem then to deal with our problems?"

"—for the love of God, can you hear me?" a voice thundered through the room louder than anyone's inclination to outyell it.

"Lantern? Alan!" Superman answered. "Is that you?"

"Hello? Somebody answer!" and a face like the great and powerful Oz appeared against the big window and rolled and bubbled like the image on a dying television. It was Green Lantern's face, spattered with blood.

"Alan! It's Kal. Can you receive?"

"Hello? Send help. I can only assume you may be getting this message," Alan Scott said. "We're . . . we're in trouble.

The fight at the Gulag goes worse than we expected. The prisoners have already begun to breach the walls. They can't hold much longer, nor can we. There have been casualties."

For all Green Lantern knew, even the power of the battery encased in the body of his armor was unable to transmit through the waves of the conflict that gathered around him. Nevertheless, every face in this conference hall was fixed on him.

"It is my duty to report that Captain Comet has been killed."

"Excuse me?" somebody said.

"Dr. Adam Blake was murdered by Von Bach, his neck snapped, in full sight of a hundred or more people." Green Lantern's face flicked to the right, as if something out of our sight assaulted him, but he turned back to face us. "Please send help if you can hear me," he said. "I have to go."

And he faded away.

"No!" Wonder Woman bellowed and slammed down her fist, shattering the big green table.

"Gone?" Superman said, his hand out and his face blank as all of his followers looked for a sign.

"What?" she took the moment to ask him. "Captain Comet? Or your preconceptions? So your world's finally turned completely topsy-turvy. How do you want to handle this, Commander?"

"I . . . don't know," he said.

"Then, I do," she answered.

The others did not look to him for even tacit assent.

CHAPTER 27

China Syndrome

A warrior," Wonder Woman told him as she stepped into the airlock, "is someone who never lets a friend go into battle alone."

"Diana. Wait." Superman reached out.

"What?"

"What will you do?"

"Give them an ultimatum. They must surrender."

"And if they refuse?"

"Then, it's war."

"But you can't have a war without people dying."

Wonder Woman knew that. So did everyone else in the room. In his desperation, Superman hoped this was news.

But she did wait. She stepped out of the airlock and kissed his mouth. Marble scraped steel, and she was gone. It was a kiss completely devoid of passion. It was a farewell.

Superman stood watching his former supporters follow her out the airlock. He looked at each of them in turn, without a word to any of them. Most of them looked back.

Ω Ω Ω

Superman stood alone. Then, alone, he left.

He smashed through the wall of New Oa in the direction of the Earth, and to hell with the internal life support systems. Below him was India, and to the east he could see his destination through the bending mantle of the Earth.

And he made a smear of space.

Smash! Into the ground at an acute angle beside a Southeast Asian formal garden.

Through the crust of the planet.

Through the bedrock of its mantle.

Through the molten, heated core.

Back through mantle.

Crust.

Limestone.

Up through the floor of the cave and into the face of a man who ought to have known better.

There were others here, also preparing for battle, preparing transportation as well.

He did not bother to avoid noticing who they all were. He was not surprised by any of them. He was through being surprised.

Ω   Ω   Ω

"I need your help," Superman told Batman.

Bruce Wayne stood, his back to Superman. The crash of molten matter against limestone notwithstanding, Wayne rhythmically leaned back and forward, exercising the artificial spinal column that held up his shoulders, looking for comfort.

"We've been through this already," the Batman said, not turning around.

"Shut up," Superman said, and spun him around bodily. "I don't have time for your holier-than-thou cracks. There's a war on and this time you're not above all this, not now, not with the stakes this high."

"War," he said. "Your Gulag, you mean?"

"Yes. *My* Gulag. We're racing the end of the world here, Bruce, and you can sit around with your buddies assigning blame to me or anyone else you care to if you live long enough. Meanwhile I've got a half-a-second lead on Armageddon, but by all the stars in Heaven that's not nearly long enough. Even as we speak, Wonder Woman and the League are headed for the Gulag, and they're past taking orders."

"You mean to tell me you never imagined it might come to this?" the Batman declaimed.

"I need you. No matter what you or I have done, that's the way it is right now."

"Did you ever consider that a war might be for the best? That perhaps humanity's only chance is to shake loose of this hell your issue—our imitators—have wrought and let the superhumans swallow each other?"

"Don't give me that. The deliberate taking of human, even superhuman, life goes against every belief I have—and you have. That's the one thing we've always had in common. It's what made us who we are. More than anyone in the world, when you scratch everything else away from Batman, you're left with someone who doesn't want to see anybody die. We can still intercede. Gather your forces. Together we can be the world's finest team again."

Bruce was silent. Then: "Do you have any idea how badly you've screwed up this—"

"Save it for later! Tell me you'll help me."

"I will tell you this one thing."

"What?" Superman grabbed the front of the vest and pulled Bruce Wayne forward so hard it ripped; the move would have cracked the rib of a lesser man.

"There's another player you haven't counted on. Captain Marvel."

"Marvel?"

"He's been brainwashed severely. Luthor did it. Once, there was a good kid inside him, but he's been driven out, and I don't know how you'd ever find him again. Marvel's headed for the Gulag, and he's going to break it wide open onto the Justice League. What do you expect me to do against—"

And as Bruce Wayne ambled at only human speed toward the end of a sentence, the skin on Superman's face transformed into an expression of surprise—and maybe a little touch of fear—and when Bruce Wayne looked down for a moment at his control panel and then back in effectively no time at all, Superman had vanished from the space he had occupied an instant before.

No sound.

No rippling breeze.

No trace.

"So that's what that feels like," Bruce said to himself through that sardonic smile.

Then, at only human speed, Bruce Wayne took action.

$$\Omega \quad \Omega \quad \Omega$$

Without a word, my spectral guide opens all horizons to me at once.

I am in the Batcave, where Bruce Wayne marshals his forces and dons a suit of armor with jets, wings, and bat-ears. The suit is itself a jet plane, most of whose weight is that of its protected pilot.

I am at the Gulag, outside whose crumbling walls the dawning horror in the face of the battle-arrayed Wonder Woman looks suspiciously like a fear that this gallant soul has never known.

I am within the walls. A flying, marching, screaming array of malefactors whose limitations all their lives have been bound solely by their imaginations are now confined there. They thunder against the very notion of incarceration and will not countenance such a thing for a moment more.

I am by the side of the Man of Steel, racing through the sky along the skin of the countryside, faster than thought itself. I see the air scorch in his wake.

Etched over Superman's face are the most desperate of hopes. He has known enormous loss, and contradiction, and defeat. He has never known failure of the magnitude that he contemplates, a failure that his hope denies.

In the Batcave, a gifted mage named Zatara appears in response to the Batman's electronic summons. Another mystic, Dr. Fate, appears a moment afterward. In Fate's wake, dozens of allies pop into existence at Fate's summons of their spirits. Where the soul goes, I learn from such as these wielders of magic, the body cannot help but follow. Some of the Batman's allies are disoriented for a moment, some resigned, some grim and ready for business.

At the Gulag walls, amid great rumbling, the Amazon Warrior directs her troops to take assigned positions on and above the ground. I see the dawning horror in Wonder Woman's eyes.

Inside the Gulag, the flashpoint far behind them, super-beings direct their energies against the immovable object that contains them, and they make it budge just enough.

I see twilight at last unfold.

Approaching the face of the borning battle, the Last Son of Krypton speeds within sight of those who have made themselves his allies and—by the souls of the billions of lost ancestors who made a barren planet live and then died with it—he vows to deliver this world.

And he stops.

Short.

On his back.

I was there to see all these things. All at once. And then I could focus my mind and gaze on nothing but the Last Son of Krypton.

Superman smashes into the desert soil that once was rich

enough to feed a world. He crumbles like a beetle under a giant's thumb. The desperate hopes of one man turn to ash and cinders by a single bolt of lightning.

Groggy, Superman turns his head upward to face the red-and-gold streak that has intercepted his stride. He looks into the smiling face of the World's Mightiest Mortal.

"Captain Marvel," he whispers to the man who once was his friend. "Let's stop this thing. Together."

But the Captain can hear only the thunder that assaults his mind and chews away chunks of his great soul.

Armageddon has arrived.

CHAPTER 28

The Physics of Magic

Shazam," the Captain whispered, and the thunder sounded and lightning flashed. But Billy Batson did not appear where Marvel stood; Marvel suddenly stepped aside, and the lightning struck the furious hero in red and blue. Superman went down with the force of the magic lightning's blow.

Superman rose. Slowly. Reached for Marvel. And as the Kryptonian's hand brushed the Captain's sleeve, Marvel said again, "Shazam!" and vanished from the space he'd occupied, so the blow from the sky came down squarely on the Man of Steel. And Superman melted for a moment as Marvel appeared just a few feet away even before the image faded from where he'd stood a moment before.

"Shazam!" Again the Captain declaimed the word and moved with the speed of Mercury before the blow transformed him. And the engine of his diverted transformation pummeled the Man of Steel again.

Captain Marvel leaned in close to the rattled hero. Superman again pressed his knees and chest into the ground.

"Shazam," Marvel said again without malice or love, and battered the Man of Tempered Steel.

"Shazam," the boy-man said again. Lightning dropped from the sky and jangled Superman's vision.

And again, "Shazam." And Superman's body burned and his mind rattled.

The Last Son of Krypton loosed the fetters of gravity to pull himself again to his feet. He put the pieces of himself together.

"Shazam!" and the moment was gone again. The Kryptonian went down.

There had never been a time in his vigor-bedecked life when Superman was more powerful than he was today. Even kryptonite, the rare remnant of his native world whose specific radioactivity often sapped his life force, was no longer a threat. He was a man of this place and time, growing in strength with every photon he drank in from the brilliant golden star that had been his most constant partner since his infancy. But there was something about whatever it was that people called "magic." It was not one thing, magic, but a constellation of unknowns. It was almost as though by failing to understand the nature of a thing, that gave the thing a power over Superman. It was the unpredictability, like physics' exclusion principle: by understanding something you subvert its nature. Superman could never understand Captain Marvel or believe in the gods that had given Marvel a power to rival his own.

Superman had a thought.

Then the lightning struck him again and it slipped away.

He snatched back the thought: If he simply dismissed logic and tried to understand some aspect of this mysterious concept of "magic," then to that extent it was possible that the power of the illogical could not hurt him.

That was the thought, but every time he tried to grab at it—or at his adversary—the universe lit up to blind him, and the energy of the light swatted him down like a horsefly. Wait, he demanded of himself, this is important; this may be the solution to a weakness that has dogged me all my life. Got to think this out. And he would get up again, and go for his opponent again, and grab for that thought again.

And he would drop again.

Superman wondered: How many would die before he logicked out the illogical?

The most stolid and clearly reasoning among them, this Superman who shrunk from the leadership that embraced him nonetheless, arrived a moment too late. Greeted on his arrival by the repeated unreasoning force of a brainwashed former ally slinging bolts of magic lightning, battered and bloodied, Superman saw his efforts gone to neutral.

Ω   Ω   Ω

I glared at the Spectre now. "It's happening. Just as the visions foretold. Superman came too late. War has begun. Do something! For the love of God—make it stop!"

"I cannot. I can take no action. Not yet," my guide said.

"Why not? What in God's name has to happen? How much time must pass?"

"There will be a reckoning, Norman McCay. Be prepared." Now it was the Spectre who suddenly spouted from Scripture at me rather than the reverse: "Fear God and give glory to Him," I heard him say as though he were whispering it into my ear, as though it were news to me as the battle raged around us, hand to hand, power to power, "for the hour of His judgment is come."

"Is that the only reason I am here? To watch some hideous judgment?" I demanded.

He had no answer; strangely, I was not surprised.

Ω   Ω   Ω

Through the dust of the kicked-up ground, Superman snatched at the shadow of a waving limb as . . .

"Shazam!"

. . . he heard the word, and it was not soft flesh below cloth but the impossibly dense cabled arm of Captain Marvel wrapped in its gold cuff that he grasped. He squeezed tightly, not very effectively, but squeezed nonetheless. A Cheshire-cat smile under squinting eyes poked out at him through the roiling air. And every time he said it . . .

"Shazam!"

. . . the mad grin vanished and appeared somewhere else, and Superman was down and trying to struggle to right himself.

"Damn it, Marvel!" Lungs of Reproved Steel expelled in pain. "Snap out of it. You can't do this!"

"Shazam!" A bolt blew Superman backward—

—and Marvel said "Shazam!" and threw him down to his back.

"Too much is happening too fast," Superman gasped. "We have to work togeth—"

Marvel delivered not a bolt from the sky but a blow of his foot to his adversary's rising chin and, with energy born of the same mystical source as the lightning, tossed him flat against a growing sand dune where once wheat had waved and perhaps tomorrow a slaughtered hero would lie dead.

Marvel tumbled after Superman again, and the Kryptonian heard "Shazam!" and "Shazam!" again and felt his tortured mind skitter to the outer edges of temporal reality.

Ω Ω Ω

On all sides and to an expanding perimeter the battle raced over this barren wilderness. As in the rumbles back in the city, heroes and villains were hard pressed to tell one another apart. On and around and through the borders of this ill-contrived walled city, across a plain once verdant and lately gone to fire and dust, the greatest of the Earth came like locusts to a patch of grass—to annihilate one another.

Red Robin, cowled and intent, spun to catch the fashionably tattooed Swastika square and hard on the chin. Swastika came up from it; he had to be slowed. Tokyo Rose bounced end over end to the scene. Through the smoke she recognized a Batman-like figure. Her enemy was a known quantity, but a formidable one. Martial skills, to this thickly muscled man, were second nature, a lifestyle. He did not so much acquire them as the skills acquired him. As a child he'd swung from trapezes without a net and flown through empty space to grasp the limbs of loved ones as often and as easily as drinking milk. As a youth he'd bounded among the rooftops of Gotham at the side of the Batman, startling and flattening men and forces of nature multiples of his size. As a man he was a brick wall. There was no surprising him. Tokyo Rose knew that to overwhelm Red Robin was the only option. Calculating her speed and force, she leapt through the air over the head of her ally Swastika, the balls of her feet propelling through the air at Robin's barrel chest.

I have no time for this, Red Robin snarled to his inner self, banishing the laughing demon-child he'd played as a youth and summoning the spirit of that old craggy bat.

Red Robin shoved his hand up underneath Swastika's rib cage, lifted the man, and tossed him to the left. Then he had just enough time to thrust upward with both feet . . .

. . . to catch Tokyo Rose coming at him in midflight, squarely in the belly.

I turned and saw the armored Wonder Woman, a javelin in her fist, the Sword of Hephæstus at her hip, and a war cry discharging from her throat. Half a mile away, Mr. Terrific stood on the head of a statue of Hestia, the fair-minded sister of Zeus. It used to be the mall where Captain Comet had confronted 666. Mr. Terrific unloaded a loud whistle.

The whistle was the activator for a program deep in archived memory of the robot N-I-L-8. Dormant in a depression in the back wall of a building that bordered the mall, the eyes of the big automaton came alive with flashing red lights. It peeled itself out of the wall, then took to the sky above. It flew through the spreading storm directly over the heads of both Mr. Terrific and the family anomaly Hestia. And as it flew over the man who'd summoned it, the robot's enormous mechanical arm—the arm outfitted with a gun the size of a cannon, whose firing mechanism Scott Free carefully had disassembled upon Hawkman's delivery of the machine a few weeks before—fell off into Terrific's outstretched arms. The robot continued flying slowly out to nowhere until, eventually, a shock wave caught it.

Mr. Terrific kicked off a boot. From a pocket in a thick callus that started at the back of his heel and stretched halfway up his Achilles tendon, he pulled a narrow tool that he fit into a slot in the doomed robot's dismembered arm. He twisted it a certain way and yanked the tool out again like the pin of a grenade. The costumed fellow slung the refitted weapon up to his shoulder as he listened for the distinctive click of a secondary ammunition clip tumbling into place. His shoulders dropped as he sighted the big weapon—somewhere on the little strip of ground between Power Woman and the Ray who fought back to back, flinging an unending succession of the temporary residents of this place into walls, into the ground, into each other—

—and from out of the sky, Wonder Woman's javelin pounded into the hull of Mr. Terrific's big gun to shove it from his thick hands. As it fell he reached for it, forgetting himself for a moment, and he tumbled to the ground. He landed at the base of the statue of the peacemaker of Mount Olympus, out cold. Even when Wonder Woman retrieved her javelin to puncture the shoulder of the flying insurgent, she would not notice Mr. Terrific behind Hestia's pedestal. He would lie there, unconscious and unnoticed, for the remainder of his life.

Everywhere, the conflict grew. Emotion gave way to action. I had seen this before, all of it. There were voices, and thunderings, and lightnings, and an earthquake. It was my own fever dream no longer. It unfolded here.

Ω Ω Ω

Through the flashing images of his haze-encumbered fight with the World's Mightiest Mortal, and the dreamy unconscious flashbacks from his own colorful past, Superman could only wonder how it had come to this. I shared the terror. Whatever Solomonic wisdom once suffused the mind of his adversary lay dissolved or befogged by the artifice of the megalomaniac Lex Luthor. The Captain, who had once been among Superman's most valued allies, was now an agent of chaos. This was the one warrior who could counter Superman's every move.

Superman held the power to contain this battle and, because of his hesitation, had fumbled it. Now he believed he could stop it all were it not for the obstruction before him repeatedly coaxing magic down over his head. About this, Superman was right.

Superman believed as well that he was the only one who held power sufficient to avert the gathering war. About this, he was wrong.

CHAPTER 29

The Security Council

At the New United Nations fortress, in a conference room on the fourth floor of the Secretariat Building, the Secretary-General dismissed his senior staff and asked his assistant to send in the ranking representatives of the Security Council states. Secretary-General Wyrmwood's advisors left through a hallway door as the Council delegates came in from the outer office. Only young Chief Jean-Paul Kasavubu of the Congo River Federation was fleet enough on his feet to make it in the room in time to see any of the staff leave.

"Apparently the news is bad," the young Chief said in his Chestnut Hill Boston accent to the Secretary-General as the far door shut and his colleagues filed in behind him. Then he repeated to the nine other Council delegates in general, "The news is bad."

"There's no news yet," Wyrmwood snapped, "not until this Council makes its decision."

"I saw the look on your military attaché's face as he ducked out," the young Chief from Brazzaville and Brandeis University insisted to the rest of the Security Council. "He was as white as I'm black."

"Don't infer," Wyrmwood insisted.

"Cut the crap, Leonard," the British ambassador Lord Wainwright told Wyrmwood through wattles of flesh, as with great pain he lowered himself into a seat at the conference table.

Now the youngest and the eldest of the Security Council delegates had weighed in with their first impressions. Wyrmwood was a good politician who recognized consensus when he saw it. He would feed them no crap today.

"There's a rumble in the Gulag," Wyrmwood said. "The walls are breached. It's going on now."

"*Oh mon Dieu,*" Consul-General Diefenbaker, the French delegate, said.

Chief Kasavubu sat back in his seat, chastened.

"When? How long?" U Chua, the no-nonsense retired Prime Minister of Myanmar who now served as his country's United Nations ambassador, wanted to know.

"Minutes ago, as far as we can tell," Wyrmwood said. "We intercepted an emergency flight path clearance from Gotham that could only have been Bruce Wayne. The seismic data began a minute or two before that."

"What was the flight signature?" Ambassador Yevgeny Posner, the former cosmonaut from Kiev, wanted to know.

"Unknown. Faster than anything we've got. Or than we're able to track, for that matter. Practically instantaneous. The only way we know it moved was that the same signature appeared both over Gotham and above the Gulag."

"A prototype from Wayne's flight shop, no doubt," said Shanna bat-Yitzchak, who had been chief of the Israeli Mossad before coming here. "If it is a plane at all."

"Do your people know anything about it, Shanna?" young Kasavubu wanted to know.

"Heavens, no," the Israeli protested. "When we get a mole into the Batcave, we'll send out a news release."

There might have been a few smiles or chuckles, but they seemed out of place.

"Is this 'rumble' expanding, Leonard?" the Chief asked.

"We have no data on that," the Secretary-General said, "but we can only assume it is. Simulation models suggest that such a conflagration could cross state lines in less time than this meeting has already taken."

"What has the President said?" the Englishman wanted to know.

"I haven't said anything yet," came the voice of Jennifer Capper. The sound from the small speaker built into the center of the conference table surprised everyone other than Wyrmwood. "But I plan to say lots."

"Madame President." Lord Wainwright began trying to gather himself to his feet, but he was the only one who did, and Wyrmwood motioned for him to settle himself.

"Morning, ladies and gentlemen," the President said, and most of them answered politely.

"Do you have any further information, Madame President?" Diefenbaker of France asked.

"No, Monsieur le Général," the voice from two hundred miles away answered, "just options. I'm loaded with options."

"Options," Ambassador Jiang Jiang of China asked, "such as?"

"We've run every endgame scenario that the Pentagon's substantial data projection systems can generate," Jennifer Capper said over the secure line. "They've run over ten thousand variations in the past few minutes, and I've told them to rerun all of them as data continues to come in, but the end result is always the same: destruction of the biosphere. The only variation is that of time. Without direct intervention on our part, our analysis gives us maybe hours, at best a month or two. My latest report shows that only eight possible scenarios out of—what is it here?—eleven thousand four hundred fifty-seven variations gives the human race as much as a year to survive after this day."

She paused. Every delegate around the table knew that these contemplative moments were expensive.

"We all have seen their rumbles in the cities." Jiang, to everyone's surprise, was the impatient one who broke the calculated silence. "We do not need empirical projections to know that this is not a conflagration that is destined to die out of its own weight. This is wildfire. You have a proposal, Madame President?"

"Well, to start with," she said from her office in Washington, "we must seriously consider launching Abraham, Martin, and John."

Again, the costly silence.

Then Jean-Paul Kasavubu leaned to the right and whispered to Posner, "Abraham, Martin, and John?"

"Operation Holy Martyrs," the former cosmonaut answered.

The Frenchman crossed himself. The others reacted similarly, each after his or her own fashion.

Ω   Ω   Ω

"Hold it right here," I told the Spectre.

Suddenly the Secretary-General and the delegates of the Security Council froze in whatever awkward positions they occupied at the moment. Dust stopped flowing through the air. Light in fixed shoots of photons hovered like long fingers lancing through the windows and from the lamp behind Wyrmwood. Limp objects like electrical wires and the delegates' clothing seemed fixed in place like papier-mâché.

"Why did you do that?"

"It appeared to be an order," the Spectre said. "Time continues as it ever did, but our own rates of consideration have become relatively faster."

This must have been how Flash viewed eternity, in a series of little disasters about to happen. I realized for the first time what a lonely hopeless time he must be having, as he watched distant Armageddon creeping inexorably closer with the expanse of every moment. "What are you, the genie in the lamp?" I demanded.

"I have far more power than that, and far less opportunity for initiative."

"Are they talking about some sort of preemptive strike?"

"Yes."

"Do you take orders from me now?"

"When it is consistent with my mission."

"What does that mean?"

"You guide my path, Norman McCay."

"I what?"

"Your human sensibilities provide the metaphorical signposts of my course. You are humanity's witness. I need you, or I will fail."

"Fail to do what?"

"To judge properly."

"Oh, for Heaven's sake. I'll just order you to stop time when the world's about to end, so it'll never happen."

"You can do that, but it would make no difference. It would be akin to watching a very slow-motion projection, prolonging the period of greatest pain."

"Stop it now. Get us out of this lousy moment. I don't like it here."

And time resumed again, though I was not sure that was what I wanted.

Ω   Ω   Ω

I was certainly sure that this was a pile of steaming karma in which I did not want to step.

Ω   Ω   Ω

In Kansas, the Gulag was no longer recognizable as an object that once had walls. Superhuman blood flowed over the desert the way water once flowed over the prairie. Captain Marvel said "Shazam!" and blurred out of the way and said it again. From a thousand miles and a moment to the northeast, the Batman approached by air with reinforcements representing three generations, and only God knew on whose behalf they would join the battle.

CHAPTER 30

Faster than a Speeding Bullet

~~~~~~

Leonard Wyrmwood had the charge of the President of the United States, the consent of the United Nations Security Council, and the conviction that this was as proper a thing to do as anything anyone could think of. He needed two more things: (1) to inform the United Nations General Assembly, who did not have to consent; and (2) to convince three of the most courageous, best trained, and least contemplative fighter pilots on the planet to carry it out. These pilots did have to consent, and he believed he had a solution to that problem: Colonel Nelson M. Chan, the commander of the Blackhawk Squadron.

The Blackhawks were an elite international corps of fliers whose ties with this body went back to the old League of Nations and the days before the Second World War. Nelson Chan represented its third generation of leaders and commanded fliers of the fourth and fifth. If there were airmen on Earth as skilled or single-minded as Howard Hughes or Chuck Yeager, they flew with the Blackhawks.

Once upon a time, when his grandfather had been chief of the Blackhawk Squadron, nineteen-year-old Nelson had wanted to show the old man that he was good enough. He'd copped a Flying Wing and taken it on a joyride along the East Coast, not harming a fly. Unfortunately he'd logged an Air Force transportation bill—airline charter fare, field use permits, restricted airspace fees billed at the commercial rate, custom fuel, interference with air traffic control at an inflated hourly rate per inconvenienced controller, that sort of thing. Paying off the bill for his joyride had occupied his career for years thereafter. Nelson had to become a Blackhawk, become more valuable to the Squadron than the amount of his outstanding fees with interest, or else he never would have gotten out of the hole.

With his grandfather's retirement a few years before, Nelson was the obvious successor, and a good thing too. The United States government had wiped clean his debt and added a sizable termination bonus. He went to work for the New United Nations commanding a collection of fliers who were unsettlingly similar in temperament to himself. Nelson Chan was perhaps a week from becoming a grandfather himself, and, finally, he felt, there was something to this life in which he had a stake. When the red phone rang, it could only be bad news.

"Mr. Secretary?"

"Yes, Colonel Chan."

"Something to do with the Kansas crisis, no doubt."

"Yes, Colonel, and unfortunately it's gotten bigger than that. I need you to scramble yourself and for your other two best pilots to pick up three packages at the General Assembly chamber immediately."

"And the delivery?"

"You'll know when you get the packages," Wyrmwood said, and hung up.

$$\Omega \quad \Omega \quad \Omega$$

"You're kidding," Nelson Chan told the helicopter pilot who escorted him from the pontoon carrier off the southern

tip of Metropolis to the United Nations heliport on the roof of
the Secretariat Building. "Right here on the roof?"

"Where else would the United Nations keep its nukes?"
the 'copter pilot asked, rhetorically. "It's not like the UN's got
large tracts of national territory to pepper with silos like we
used to do."

It took Chan and the pilot—a colonel as well, retired from
the United States Marines and with extraordinary security
clearance—less than a minute to load the three unarmed nuclear warheads from their storage into the belly of the helicopter. It was a matter of entering their respective security
codes onto a punch-pad, waiting for a ramp to assemble itself
from the innocuous-looking rooftop shed, and watching the
three blunt-faced bombs—code-named "Abraham," "Martin,"
and "John"—deposit themselves where they belonged.

The Marine stood guard while Nelson Chan ran down to
confirm to the Secretary-General in person that he was on the
case.

$$\Omega \quad \Omega \quad \Omega$$

The Secretary-General was in the General Assembly
chamber, rubbing his forehead and listening to one national delegate after another. There were more than four hundred constituent states of the United Nations, now that membership was
open to artificial island free ports and independent indigenous
tribes within the borders of larger countries. There were three
fewer members, however, because of the events of recent
months. Three Native American reservations had been destroyed in the Kansas crisis, and their remaining unlucky delegates were now nonvoting members. Here stood Leonard
Wyrmwood, explaining why it was necessary to drop UN tactical nuclear weapons on American territory.

There was nothing any one of these constituent states or its
representatives could do, no vote to bring to the question, no
parliamentary or political maneuver that could reverse the de-

cision. It was made. It was final. All they could do was hold the Secretary-General in this room and make him account for himself.

"This is not a rational argument," Wyrmwood exclaimed, "but these are not rational times. We are at the flashpoint of human existence. My God, you can hear the battle even here. At any moment, it threatens to engulf the world."

Few noticed the tall Asian man in uniform as he walked up to the exhausted Leonard Wyrmwood and saluted. Everyone did notice as he took a sealed envelope from the Secretary's hand. Then Chan opened the envelope, blanched when he read his assignment, tucked the orders into his flight jacket, and left.

Meanwhile, the ambassador from Baja California continued to try to convince the General Assembly to revise the New United Nations Charter on the spot, allowing the General Assembly to overrule the Security Council. If he could do it—which he could not—it would make no difference. Operation Holy Martyrs was under way.

The members of the General Assembly were still arguing over it as Chan arrived by helicopter at Fort Dix a few minutes later. Shortly afterward, he and his two handpicked Blackhawks rolled a trio of Boeing-McDonnell Birds-of-Prey onto the tarmac.

"Courage, men," he told his Blackhawks. Then they lifted the bombers into the air to carry their deadly cargo, several times faster than a speeding bullet, in the direction of Kansas. Most of the way, Nelson Chan thought about his unborn first grandchild.

Ω Ω Ω

The Secretary-General begged off the General Assembly session for a few minutes, pretending to need a trip to the men's room. Instead, he went into the next building and up the elevator to his study. He could always think and decompress there. It was like home.

On Leonard Wyrmwood's desk in his small private office off the big reinforced conference hall was a picture of the beautiful wife he still felt he did not deserve, their two sons, and their baby girl. Next to it was a white coffee mug, a third filled with coffee the temperature of a comfortable day, with a legend in red across the front: WORLD'S BEST DAD. He was not decompressing here. His unaccustomed anxiety was getting worse. He wondered what going home would be like from then on.

CHAPTER 31

Hephæstus' Children

~~~

The defrocked Amazon Princess wondered what she was doing, trying to back her enemies into a structure whose walls could not now secure a mouse. This was not a fight that would eventually die down. Was this the way the world would end?

Out of the sky tumbled the Batman, on wings and jets. There was no longer any demarcation between Bruce Wayne the boy who'd seen his parents crumble and the Batman the terror born of that tragedy. No more than the difference between the man of flesh and the hardware that gave him his locomotion and his physical power. The titanium strapping that held together his shoulders and limbs, now clamped onto the streamlined flying battle suit. He was a jet, propelled and steering from the corners of his mortal joints. He was a tank. He was a Dark Knight dropping out of the clouds. He was a man and bat and the ghost of the dread Gotham night. And others came from behind:

Phantom Lady and Fate floated on the ether. Two Black Canaries rode the bouncing sound waves that the younger of the two generated down to the ground. Steel snatched Wildcat out of the air, and both rode under the power of the armored one's costume. Zatara caused himself and Green Arrow, dangling from a rope, to waft Earthward. Tula and Samurai flew on the Condor's wings. A Bat-Monitor, one of the robot urban patrollers, carried Obsidian, Red Hood, and the Creeper, who joined in for his own mad logic. Nightstar, Jade, and the Blue Beetle—getting the first use out of his new battle suit—dropped down and caught themselves under their own power. And there were more: eighty or ninety of them who were there with the purpose of stopping the slaughter.

Their mission was to stem the conflict, and for a moment—when the coherent among the battlers realized that the Batman was there—it might have worked.

"If you get in a fight that lasts more than five seconds," Wesley once told me, "you've lost."

It took far more than five seconds for the Batman's troops to land. By the time they all did, their presence was just another element of the chaos. Ultimately, the difference it would make was that there would be more here to die.

Ω   Ω   Ω

There were casualties. Zatara fell on the ground in the darkness of a cloud of dust. He looked around him and up just in time to see Von Bach, holding the shattered torso of Blue, one of Luthor's trio of android moles, over his head, and about to bring it down.

His throat—that magical instrument that could make dreams come real—was frozen by the moment. The moment was too long. Zatara knew before he could gather his speech that it was too long. But Wonder Woman was already in motion.

"Du wirst wie eine Wanze zerquetscht!"

As Von Bach was about to bring down the android carcass and smash Zatara's skull, he felt a prick in his back—

—and saw the bloody point of the ancient sword that could

carve the electrons off an atom pierce his chest from behind and hang there for a moment like an orphan limb.

Wonder Woman withdrew the weapon, and the would-be murderer went down backward in a pile of tattooed slag.

"Diana?" the Batman said in awe and horror. The dust cleared for just the moment it took for the battle-armored Bruce Wayne to see his old friend save the life of his ally—to see her kill a man who had killed before in order to do it.

"He left me no choice. They began this war. I will finish it."

"She killed him!" 666 whispered, then found the breath to yell, "She killed Von Bach! Did you see that? Get her!"

And a dozen, two dozen more of the malefactors who'd tumbled these walls collected into a living ring of fire around Wonder Woman.

Zatara rose and tossed spells of force shields, sweeping many away as they came.

The Batman leapt to the Amazon's side, back to back with her to protect her from the ravening horde, yet appalled at what she had done.

She swatted them to the ground with the flat of her sword. She tossed them hither and yon with a yank on her golden rope.

Batman used his winged armor to slice through their ranks, to make them retreat. He exploded pellets from his belt in their faces, and when they continued to advance, he cracked the mallets of his fists into their faces.

But he would not kill.

"Who do you think you are, Diana, taking life like that?" he demanded of the woman he defended. "Some helpless victim on a dark street who has to fear from her assaulter for her own life?"

"I'm a warrior and an Amazon, Bruce," she said. "I will finish this without you. Your people are out of their league here. Take them home."

"And let you 'force peace' at the point of a sword? We're here to save lives rather than take them. I came to stop you more than I came to help you."

"We're left with no choice. If you stand in my way, Bruce—I will remove you too!"

"Spread love and understanding"—Bruce said through a cloud of dust and a haze of bloodied knuckles; he wondered what they now looked like under the gauntlets—"but don't be afraid to bust a few heads to do it. You still subscribe to that bleeding Amazon paradox?"

He fought. She gritted her teeth and fought as well. Steam rose from the body of Von Bach. Opponents went down but no more died on this spot.

"I've heard rumors that the Amazons relieved you of your duties and heritage for not being strident enough," he bellowed over the din. "Face the truth, Diana. You won't win back your royal station by overcompensating."

"You aristocratic bastard!" she spat.

"The Princess accuses me of being a patrician. I'm cut"—he slashed at a low-life called B'wana Beast, who went down—"to the quick."

She spun and faced Bruce and smashed the flat of her bloodied sword against his armor. She dented the framework, but he did not go down.

"How dare you condemn me?" she demanded, and could have been demanding it of her sisters as well. "You will not judge me."

And in the instant he needed to regain his footing, she snatched him by the armor's chest and put handholds in it with her slicing fingers. She lifted him up, up, up, hollering into his aghast face: "Do you hear me? Do you understand, you son of a sire?"

Flashes of magic lightning swarmed by them as they rose in the sky, hitting the same spot on the floor of the desert beside the raging battlefield. Neither noticed it. Neither knew that Superman was here.

"After all these years, you have the nerve to swagger out of your cave," she cried in his face, "and expect us all to bow before your precious wisdom? Before your divine right? Well it's too late for that, Bruce."

If they had looked down, they would have seen what I saw: The smoke rose from the battle and fell across the expanse of the land. The fighting receded into the dark smear on the sands of two ant colonies vying for territory. The rumbling gathered. The lightning fell and crashed and fell again.

And they rose over the level of the highest clouds, armlocked in the frozen grimace of philosophical subtlety.

"We tried to hold order—but it's too far gone! Our only option now is war! Our only answer is—" and Wonder Woman stopped shouting.

In the distance, three specks moving across the bending skies of the continent slowed in lockstep formation.

He knew what they were before she did. She knew only when he went limp with certainty that, finally, the frightened world at large was coming from out of the distance with something bigger than they.

Ω Ω Ω

"Marvel! In the name of heaven, wipe that empty smile off your face," Superman pleaded. "You were a friend once. How can you do this? How? Look at the horror you've let loose! Damn it—say something for yourself."

"Shazam!" the boy-man said, and the big man went down.

And the Kryptonian rose with eyes flashing heat.

"Shazam!" and Superman went down again.

Ω Ω Ω

On the ground where once the Gulag had stood, the race of metahumans threatened itself with extinction.

Ω Ω Ω

"Shazam!"

Ω Ω Ω

Diana's fist tightened around the bending plate metal of Bruce Wayne's armor.

He said, "Open your eyes, Diana. Your answer flies on metal wings. Those are nuclear carriers. The ultimate war-bringers."

She looked with understanding and growing horror at the approach of Abraham, Martin, and John.

"Our war is not one act of violence at the cost of some lives. Our war ends in extinction," Bruce Wayne said. "All the lives below. And all life."

Wonder Woman loosened her grip on him, finally let go, and they both hovered, facing each other, looking at the winged bullets approaching in the distance.

"The fearful sent the brave to stamp us out," he said. "Only Blackhawks can fly a mission like this. They're just like us, those pilots, and they'll probably die today, too, if their mission succeeds.

"If you're that devoted to your Amazon honor that you're willing to die and kill and your soul genuinely longs for atonement according to your own narrow cultural definition, then keep fighting, and let the planes do their work."

She fell away from in front of him, facing the oncoming bombers.

"Me? I've got a killer to stop," was the last thing he said to her until it was all over.

Ω   Ω   Ω

At precisely the right moment—there were no other moments—a pair of close-contact lasers from the Batman's Utility Belt sliced through the clamp carrying the bomb under the sweeping plane. The minion of death tumbled away, impotent, a moment before the pilot sent the signal to arm the weapon and let it go.

The bomb tumbled to the desert floor, where it kicked up only its mass in dust. There it sat, its deadly critical mass of radiation inside, still locked under its shield and unarmed, until weeks later when the golden figure of a man came through irradiated air and carried it away.

There were still two more.

Ω   Ω   Ω

The Amazon Princess gathered her speed as she never had before, flying in the same direction as another oncoming bird of prey.

Like a relay racer lunging for a baton, the big bomber caught up to her, caught her by her extended hands, and yanked her along at a slowing pace that was still breakneck speed, even for this warrior.

Both hands held fast to the underbelly of the craft, just above and aside the bomb. It was all she could do to hold this place against the wind and friction. She needed to let go one hand. Needed to go for the sword.

She heard the click. Was it armed, or was it just sending an electronic signal?

It did not matter.

She hung by one hand from the clamp of the bomber construction. Her feet dangled against the ripping wind, feeling like they could yank off at any moment. She sliced the Sword of Hephæstus across the bottom of the plane and dismembered the bomb and the tempered structures that held it fast.

The action tore her loose. She tumbled through the sky, disoriented, clutching the sword by the hilt, its flat against her chest and face, until she gathered her orientation. The bomb, unarmed, fell free of the bomber.

There was still one more, and it was well out of reach of either Batman or Wonder Woman.

Ω   Ω   Ω

The pilot in the remaining bomber armed and loosed the bomb and asked God to have mercy on his soul.

Was it Commander Chan, or one of the others?

No one cared.

Ω   Ω   Ω

"Shazam!"

"Enough . . ."

For one frozen instant, the storm cleared. The Captain stood over the Kryptonian now, and looked up at the little flash of red in the sky.

It was the triggering device that unlocked the end of the world.

In an instant suspended between two eternities, the Last Son of Krypton wiped a steel hand over the features of the World's Mightiest Mortal and held tightly to his mouth.

No words.

No crippling blast of lightning.

There were no vestiges of the wisdom of Solomon in this manchild's shattered mind. But in the recesses there was Billy, who never had the chance to surrender his innocence—as the lucky among us do—of his own accord.

In the hush, ears that can hear even a cell divide pick out with chilling ease the scream of human rage. A wave of X rays confirms the bomb's potency. A telescopic glance calculates the seconds before impact. He must act now.

"Now, listen," Superman began.

Ω   Ω   Ω

"It is time," the Spectre said.

"For what?" I did not want to know.

"Judgment has come, Norman McCay. The hour tolls. Our entire journey has brought us to this moment. It falls on you to tell me the names of the guilty."

"I respectfully decline."

"You will determine the fate of the world. If the bomb falls, then the superhumans will become extinct, but humanity will be spared their violence. If not, they will live on—to fight a battle that will, in time, swallow the Earth and all the lives that dwell therein, including their own. In either case, we face the evil of genocide. And my task is to punish those responsible for evil. But who shall be held accountable? Whose sin is this? The humans' or the superhumans'? Tell me, Norman."

"I respectfully decline."

"Judgment, Norman McCay," the Spectre insisted.

"Take an action," I said.

"Yours is the soul that guides me."

"How can I? There is no 'evil' here. There is tragedy and bedlam and—"

"Judge. Carefully."

Ω   Ω   Ω

There were a few small but crucial gaps in Superman's education. Heroes especially need to understand—and he did not fully understand it yet—the value of the things of a life: its artifacts, its ideas, its loves. It is the markers you leave along that road that define you. It is the trees a man plants, the children he raises, and the stories he tells that signify his life. It is the palaces a people build, the heritage they inspire, the art they create that make their civilization.

All his career he'd recoiled from magic. All his career he'd smashed through things—the things of people's lives—in order to save people's lives. Today, if he thought about it—and yes, later on he would—he would learn, finally, the nature of the artifacts around him. He would learn—at long and painful last—the nature of magic. It was moral force—whether for good or ill. Here in the world of spirits it had a nature; it was describable as surely as the dimensions of a box or the sound of a cry. But in the physical realm where humans and heroes lived, it was just an idea. What Superman realized today was that ideas were real.

When next he touched the Sword of Hephæstus, he would have nothing he needed to heal.

$$\Omega \quad \Omega \quad \Omega$$

"Billy," Superman said, "I don't know what to do. You can see that, can't you?"

All Billy wanted to do was say his magic word, but he could not speak through the grip of a hand dense enough to generate its own gravitation. And perhaps now the magic would not stop even Superman.

"Every choice I've made so far," Superman said, "has brought us here. Has been wrong. I can no longer trust my own judgment. I have to trust yours. So listen to me, Billy. Listen harder than you ever have before."

To their side the battle raged. A few looked up and saw the red burst that turned on the trigger, and fewer knew what it was. Few of them knew that Captain Marvel was here somewhere. Fewer realized that Superman was here. All of them fought. Some of them fought to stop the fighting. Kryptonian ears now bled. Indestructible white antibodies seeped into the biosphere. Thousands of single threads of a red cape lay over the battlefield and wafted through rising air.

Superman's palm spasmed around Batson's jaw, and Batson whimpered. The clock was racing. Only moments remained before the blast.

"Look around us," Superman said. "Look at what we've come to. There's a bomb falling. Either it kills us, or we run rampant across the globe. I can stop the bomb. That much I'm sure of. What I don't know is whether I should be allowed to. Superhumans or humankind. One will pay the ultimate price. And that decision is not for me to make. I'm not a god. I'm not a human. But you, Billy, you're both."

Seconds ticked. Physics continued along its inexorable path: gravity, fission, and soon fusion.

"More than anyone who ever existed, you know what it's like to live in both worlds. Only you can weigh their worth equally. I'm going to let go of you, Billy. I have to save these lives, worthy or unworthy, because they're lives. You can let me go. Or with a word you can stop me. I don't know what you'll do. I want you just to stand here and think, okay? Fight the brainwashing. Do you understand the choice that can be made by you alone?"

Another second.

Soon I would have a judgment to make as well. I had to exact blame. This was most assuredly out of my line. I had no more idea what I would decide than I knew what Billy would do.

Billy's tears answered for him.

"Ready, Billy?" and Superman removed his hand and he said, "Then decide. Decide the world."

Superman lifted himself into the sky and Billy Batson whispered, "Shazam."

CHAPTER 32

Judgment

And when he cried . . .

"Shazam."

. . . seven thunders uttered their voices.

"Shazam," he said. And again, "Shazam." And louder, "Shazam!"

Superman, shaky but sucking in the strength of the sun the way a thirsty root sucks at the dew, was already a mile in the sky and rising. That brain-dead misanthrope said it again, but the Kryptonian blew out of the bolt's way in search of a bigger blast to fry. He gave Marvel the chance to make the decision, but Superman would be damned if it was not the decision he wanted to hear, and what he did not want to hear again was "Shazam."

Concentrate. Concentrate. Gather the speed, he told himself. Millions die by fire if I am weak, he told himself again.

And something tugged at his foot.

With the strength of Zeus and the speed of Mercury, Captain Marvel flung the Kryptonian out of his course. Superman snatched at his opponent's midsection. That was his mistake. All he came back with was the white-and-gold cape from his adversary's back. Superman did not realize how little he held in his hand until his own enormous bulk dumped a crater onto the desert crust. The impact's consequent temblor gave the desperate combatants downwind a taste of the imminent shaker to follow.

Ω Ω Ω

It was not until later that Superman realized that his wresting of the cape from the back of this magical being was a new breakthrough for him. It should never have ripped off in Superman's hand. Superman always had supposed that things like Marvel's cape were protected from the likes of him. Just now, the Man of Steel was preoccupied with the more immediate.

What was Marvel doing? Superman wanted to know. There was no time left. The only remaining card was in the hand of the deluded giant who pressed against the monster from the sky. Marvel had the nose of the bomb in his hands, flying upward, even as Superman from below saw the red flare of the bomb's ignition blast.

Does Billy know anything about nukes? Superman wanted to know. Does he know anything about anything?

The Captain was pushing so hard and traveling so fast that the bomb was several miles higher in the sky—as far off as he could get it when he summoned a magical bolt—

Ω Ω Ω

—and it blew.

Ω Ω Ω

Oliver Queen, the Green Arrow, saw the red flare in the sky, and something in genetic memory told him what it was. He had the time to dive across the injured form of Lady Marvel, to grab his Dinah. Oliver pressed his Pretty Bird—

wounded by a stray round to her waist—close to him. He held her face to his chest and looked up through his final tear as his flesh melted into hers.

Ω   Ω   Ω

The Creeper, his mad heart changing for the third time in the past day, had just decided to switch sides to that of the Justice League when he saw 666, the tattooed man, elbowing aside Tokyo Rose, the martial artist. Rose was already injured with a blow from a heat beam in the side, and 666 wanted to get a clear shot at Robotman, the liquid metal cop he thought was a particular pain. Creeper grabbed 666 by the head from behind when the first shock wave hit. What might have happened next is lost to history.

Ω   Ω   Ω

Hawkman, wielding spear and mace, was offended to be here at all. This was land made profane first by the crippling exploitation of its natural wealth and finally by the mindless expense of destructive power for its own sake. When he looked up at the sudden light—in the second and a half that he saw the growing wave of displaced air bulge down from the sky—his thought was that dying here was, at last, a proper use for this land.

Ω   Ω   Ω

Professional escape artists have a kind of second sight when it comes to traps. That was the reason Superman had asked Scott Free to design and build the Gulag. Scott was never a person that a trap could take by surprise. To his credit, Scott spent the time from the moment he saw the trap springing to the minute before the sky ignited, trying to track down his wife and daughter.

The one-time Mr. Miracle had dodged bullets before they were fired, lightning bolts before they were thought of, slashes of swords and claws and fangs before their wielders appeared out of dust or smoke or shadow.

Avia knew the design of the Gulag as well as anyone alive save her parents. She ran through the tumbling labyrinth of what was once the maximum-security section. She blew missiles and potential opponents out of her way with the protection devices in her bio-armor. She scanned the darkest corners of the lockdown city for those who might be trapped in the dark. She detected a life form behind a hidden panel in a trembling wall. She looked for a latch to open somewhere but could not find one. Avia was about to vaporize the wall panel when it opened from behind and, to her surprise, her father stepped out.

"Do you have Tube access?" he asked without saying hello.

"Yeah, but—"

"Your mother's on her way. Fire it up."

"You can't mean we should desert the fight, Dad."

"Now."

Avia pressed a switch on her lower thigh just above her knee as Barda stormed through a hallway behind Scott.

"I got your homing signal, Scott," Big Barda told her husband over the din of the battle that raged outside and above. "What's this about?"

"He wants us to abandon the battlefield," Avia said as the rising hum of the Boom Tube gathered gradually in this small place.

"Is that true, Scott?"

"We don't have time to discuss this, but it's not going to be a battlefield much longer," Scott snapped, grabbing for the control dial woven into the leg of his daughter's clothing. He turned it to the maximum, far past the safety slot. "Avia, how many more times do I have to say 'now'?"

The tunnel to another dimension of reality rippled into being and snaked its way between two worlds. Scott grabbed the arms of the two most important and assertive people in his life—both physically larger than he. Rustling them into the Boom Tube, he shut down its Earthside egress precisely as the walls of the innermost chambers of the Gulag grew white-hot. Behind Scott, Barda, and Avia was the awful scream of metal and bone twisting and melting into nothingness, but only the sound followed them to the place called New Genesis.

"How did you know?" Avia asked her father as he grabbed his hips and twisted his head down to his knees to catch his tortured breath.

"He always knows," Barda said.

Ω Ω Ω

Early in the battle Red Robin turned in a reflex and flung a leg deep into the midsection of a stealthy figure coming up on his right. If he had known when he telegraphed the kick that it was Tokyo Rose, he probably would have done the same thing.

She was down for the duration, and that was probably what saved her life.

Ω Ω Ω

Wallace West, the Flash, shimmered in and out of dimensional reality, his existence unbound by the norms of Newtonian physics. Newton, however, never accounted for the behavior of lightning bolts. The Flash caught one on the back of his calf, a stray from a flurry emanating from half a mile away. It was Lightning—the jagged-figured woman with the static-electricity aura I'd seen in the rumble on the streets of Metropolis the day of the first Kansas disaster—who tossed off the bolt. Flash was on the ground and barely vibrating among the dimensions, nearly a solid figure.

When the metal started melting, the Flash ordinarily would have been able to save himself—and perhaps a few others. His injury made it possible for his daughter Park—Flash IV, who arrived with the Batman's group—to save him. Park West carried her father on a pillar of air to the edge of the battleground. There, the injured Green Lantern was summoning a shield to protect anyone within the range of his flagging concentration. Lantern had three of Oliver Queen's wooden arrows lodged in the energy armor of his arm and legs. They sapped energy and altogether too much blood from the limbs underneath.

Park West, not nearly as fast or prudent as her father, went into the battle to find more people to save. With her speeded-up perceptions, she saw the shock wave touching down. She turned to outrun it, but it caught her in midturn. It would have been nice to have told her father in words that she loved him, but words were never central to the West family tradition.

Ω Ω Ω

Nightstar was luckier. Her father, Dick Grayson, lay on the ground wounded, as well. She keened over him for only a moment, then flew him away in her arms, leaving a contrail of mist in her wake. They were eight miles west of Ground Zero when the shock wave caught up to them. She tumbled. Lost altitude. For a moment she lost consciousness. But she held on to Red Robin, her father, until they reached the foothills of the Rockies over the Colorado state line, and safety.

There, in the woods off the edge of a highway rest stop, Dick awoke hours later to find his daughter shivering beside him, welts from radiation burns all over her face and legs. Now he carried her, staggering, to flag down a car on the road nearby. He was scarred as well, but with the help of a friend they could deal with that. Dick, however, had sixteen broken bones and two popped tendons, and now he was only making them worse.

Both would suffer the pain of long-term healing, but both would live.

Ω Ω Ω

This company of extraordinary people who contended and defended and tried to wrest redemption and rescue from a killing field had, on the average, quite a greater degree of intuition than the common mortal. Though his thuggish, strong-arm superpowers did not include any form of prescience, a dozen years of fighting in the skies and in the streets had left Magog with as heightened a level of perception as anyone. There was a flickering green hope in the corner of his eye.

Over toward the edge of the battle an old man lay against a radiation-streaked rock slowly growing a green energy field. Magog looked around to see what he could do. Tokyo Rose lay on the ground, doubled up and gripping at her belly. The Manotaur staggered erratically, hit and jangled by something, disoriented. Trix, whose biomechanical abilities formed complex weaponry, leaned against a slowly toppling metal beam. Walking wounded.

Magog put both hands under the prone martial artist, said, "Rosie, hold on to your spandex," and slung her unceremoniously over a shoulder. With his freed hand he grabbed Manotaur by the long horn and directed the muddled bovine in the direction he wanted to take him. "Trix!" Magog ordered. "This way. Help is on the way. Come on. All of you."

Magog, carrying Tokyo Rose, dragged Manotaur by the horn. Behind him trudged Trix. This procession came through the firelights of battle in the direction of the green glow on the periphery.

Ω Ω Ω

Green Lantern himself snatched the Ray from the sky and encased him in his energy field, even as others huddled inside. If any were to survive the aftermath of this day, then Ray Terrill's talent for demystifying radioactive ionization would be too valuable to lose.

Ω Ω Ω

Garth, the new Aquaman, would never see the ocean again. Neither would his daughter, Tula.

Ω Ω Ω

Donna Troy, once Wonder Woman's protégé, and Roy Harper, the Red Arrow whom many considered Oliver Queen's successor, were gone.

Ω Ω Ω

Power Woman. Hawkman. Wildcat. Zatara, tongue-tied by horror. Darkstar. Hourman. Thunder. Bulletgirl. Golden Guardian. All of them vivid and colorful; all of them and more, gone.

Ω Ω Ω

High, very high in the sky, above the reach of the weather, Captain Marvel called upon his strength and the last blast of magic he would ever summon—

"Shazam!" the Captain said to divert, upward and away, much of the terror of the bomb.

"Shazam!" Billy Batson managed to choke, tumbling downward across the bending sky and the superheated air that enveloped him.

"Shazam!" Captain Marvel whispered after he rose again to touch Death on the face so his lightning could push most of what remained of her sting.

—and Billy Batson knew that just once more he needed to fight the fire with his cold heat in order to save the skins of those directly below. He could not gather a gulp beyond his last breath to contain the conflagration any further.

Ω   Ω   Ω

"Judgment," I heard the Spectre say.

In that moment and in that place—the place and moment where the light made the daylight seem as the darkness of the pit—I thought I too was in Heaven.

CHAPTER 33

Sentencing

Perhaps the shock wave was too loud for my ears even to register the sound. Perhaps the explosion was too great for my meager spiritual senses to perceive. I did not hear it. I saw only a color that gradually faded to white. And all I heard when the moment came was the hollow voice of the Spectre. "My mission is complete," he said to me.

Again I saw Superman on his knees and in excruciating moral pain even as the emerging sun restored his starborn strength. Again he threw back his head and again he screamed and again his eyes burned with searing heat. But this time it was not in my mind's eye; it was in the line of sight before which I stood. On Kansas, a ruin laid to ruin.

He howled at the sky.

He pounded the earth with his fists.

He threw his head back and howled that deafening wail.

Down he came again with his fists extended to arm's length to batter the ground beneath him and cause the ashen skeletons, some of them still wearing their armor with colors faded against the heat, to leap from the ground and dance for a moment and drop. They were bones gone shapeless, ground to powder, into the white-hot poison dust.

At a loss to express the degree of my consternation, I could tell the Spectre only, "You cannot possibly be serious."

"I thank you, Norman McCay."

"Oh no, you don't," I told him.

Over and again, Superman repeated his sorrowful regimen, screaming and pounding, screaming and pounding, then he rose to his feet. His cape was gone, but now it was his eyes that glowed red. His hair and face were ashen, gray. His costume hung torn in a dozen places. His own blood clotted over wounds that his singular physiology had already healed. When he rose into the air he did it slowly at first, without thought or direction, in the same posture a man might wear to stand on the ground. Then he brought his fisted hands up above his head and pounded them together with an anger that cast a wave across the air. He straightened his bearing, pointed his toes, and a thunderhead of dirt and dust and debris twisted beyond discernment rose below him as the speed he gathered took him suddenly away from even our perceptions.

His disappearance distracted me from the growing frustration and horror I was building to bestow on this insufferably dispassionate Spectre.

"Where?" I asked him.

"Undoubtedly to confront his human attackers," the Spectre said. "He feels alone. He need not. There were survivors. They are fewer in number, and their pain is great, but their war has ended."

Then I saw them, a handful, huddled together in a cloud of green. I would have looked more closely in that moment to see who they were, try to determine how they had lived, but my anger was gathering steam again.

"Judgment has been passed," the Spectre declared like a segregation-era judge clapping down his gavel to lock tight the vault where he folded away the conventional wisdom. "I am no longer needed. Farewell, Norman McCay."

"Farewell?" I thundered across whatever ether separated figures in this spaceless timeless place. "Farewell?" I bellowed. "You think you brought me all this way just to watch people die? Think again. No, you're not done."

The Spectre stood, unmoving, unfading, unflapping. "Is that your considered judgment?"

"You want to confront evil? That's what you said, isn't it?"

"I do not believe I did, but given the opportunity—"

"Then look in a mirror. You saw Superman. You saw an anger that can twist steel. If what happens next happens the only way it can"—I tried to find some reaction in those shaded eyes and found none—"and if you let it happen, then that is evil."

"What do you propose?"

"Get us the hell to the United Nations. Now!"

CHAPTER 34

The Kingdom

The Spectre and I reached the New United Nations as Superman blew through the outermost wall. A debate droned over the floor concerning whether the Security Council should or should not bomb the American Heartland. It was broadcast live over Netservice News, but then again everything was these days. I wondered, only for the moment I had in which to wonder, whether it would have concerned these petty bureaucrats and narrow-visioned folk to know that the bombing was done; that the war in the Midwest was over. Maybe some of them knew and debated some more anyway. Maybe that was just what they did because they could do nothing else.

Then a screaming came across the sky. And a sound from somewhere outside the big room made heads turn, though the speaker who held the floor continued without missing a beat. Among those in the room only I—and, I presume, my ghostly companion—knew that it was the sound of Superman bursting a hole through the concrete-and-steel exterior wall of the General Assembly building.

Successive bursts of sound grew louder and closer, and soon the cries made even less relevant the debate on the floor that, in the face of this new crisis, dwindled and stopped. Superman came through the wall of the General Assembly chamber. A gaping hole hung high on one wall, and plaster and chips of wood rained down on those below.

The room devolved into confusion, then quickly to panic.

A person's native language is the one in which he or she responds when the telephone rings at four in the morning, or the one in which a person embraces fear:

"Courez pour vos vies!"

"He's mad! Mad!"

"The doors! He's welded shut the doors!"

"Cover your head!"

"Out of my way!"

"Mein Gott!"

"Out of my way!"

"God in Heaven, run! He's gone berserk!"

"Salga del Medío!"

. . . in every language and dialect under this polyglot city's bending sky.

Superman's eyes glowed not with heat but with something akin to madness.

He stood against the high ceiling over the General Assembly chamber, slowly pressing against a central structural beam, watching as capillaries of plaster and concrete formed along the lines of the massive ceiling and chipped down in small pieces to reach the floor and the panicky diplomats below. He watched them running and screaming and praying. He wondered to whom these creations of some god inferior to the One he knew, were moved to pray.

"My God, he's bringing the roof down!" I exclaimed. "He'll kill them all. Somebody's got to do something!"

"After ten years," the Spectre said, "he has finally set free a wrath that would move Satan himself to cower. How can any man possibly calm the fury he feels toward his persecutors?"

"Clark?" I asked him. He did not hear.

He began slowly to press the sides of the steel structural beam in on themselves, apparently to see what would happen.

"Make him see me," I demanded of the Spectre. "Up there"—I indicated the highest observation balcony near him, the one already empty of people and ankle-deep in debris— "make me whole."

I was in that balcony and I felt for the ability to read his soul, to see things that could not be seen, my temporary angelic powers. I felt those powers fade and I felt my physical self become whole again.

And I asked again, "Clark?"

His back was to me, but he did not need to turn to see me. I was reflected in a hundred crinkles of the steel in his hands as he exposed the beam that, before, was wrapped in decorative caulking.

He could not reason through the rage or speak through the sorrow. I waited. He looked at me but faced away, and I was grateful not to have to feel those eyes piercing my being just now. I must have confused him for a moment. Then something inside him reached down and cupped his rage in a compartment, and he allowed himself to say quietly, "You again?"

"Yes. It's Norman. We've met, yes. Listen to me. You blame yourself for Captain Marvel. For Magog and Kansas. For mistakes and misjudgments over ten years that ended today. You're angry at the only one you've ever allowed yourself to be angry at: yourself."

"What are you talking about? How would you know what I feel?"

"I minister. It's my job. I minister to pain and joy and numbness. Today you feel only pain. And you have forgotten what humans feel. What they fear."

He let go the ceiling, and as he did he floated around in place, as if on an axis, to look at me. At first, I did not know whether I could handle that. Then I remembered before

Whom I had stood previously, and I was fine with it. "Who are you? Why are you here?"

"To bear witness. The job imposed itself upon me through circumstance. Much as yours did."

"Don't talk to me in riddles." The anger welled up in him again and I had to press it down, God help me.

"Now listen to me, Clark," I said, with as much authority as I could handle. I said it slowly. Perhaps I struggled to figure out what to say; perhaps I merely wanted to stretch out the time that those on the floor below had to live. "Of all the things you can do, all your powers, the greatest has always been your instinctive knowledge of right and wrong. It was a gift of your own humanity. A gift from Clark. You never had to question your choices. In any situation, in any crisis, you knew what to do. But the minute you made the 'super' more important than the 'man,' the day you decided to turn your back on humankind, that instinct fell away. And it took your judgment away with it. Take it back. You must want redemption, Clark. We all do. For you, it lies in the very next decision you make. Make it as a man. And make it right."

He turned to face me. Did he want me to say more?

To my surprise I found something to say, and I went on: "They won't forgive you for this, Clark. Forgive yourself."

He hovered. So I asked him, "You never had to question anything before, did you?"

"Sometimes."

"The question of right and wrong, I mean. Did you?"

He paused. "No," he said. "No, never."

He was like a child, I realized, a weathered, graying giant of an adolescent eager to learn whatever he could learn. I wondered how long he would live, how he would age, whether he would have a single black strand left in his head when he reached effective maturity. I was in awe of this being whom I had followed invisibly all this time, this modern-day titan, this high-water mark of human capability.

He was nothing but a man. I had to make him understand that.

There was a great hole in the wall high above the reach of the hundreds of mortal women and men—diplomats, ambassadors, observers, reporters, kids on class trips to the United Nations—who stood in the great hall straining but unable to hear words of the conversation we had. Now some of them, terrified at what might happen next, looked toward the sounds they were hearing from that great hole in the wall. But I kept talking. It's my job.

"Once, not long ago—in a cavern deep under the suburbs of Gotham—I watched you walk into a haven for spoiled monstrous superchildren. That day, you made many of them into far more than they had been. You gave a simple, powerful talk and then left them to their own decisions. Do you remember the last thing you said to those people, Clark?"

"Yes. I said, 'Be heroes.'"

"Well, Clark," I said, "be a man."

He looked down to the floor where faces looked up, expecting to die. Others watched the gaping hole in the wall. He looked at the hole, the source of new noises, of whirring and clattering and something approaching. I saw him stare at it pointedly, stare beyond it, and the corners of his mouth twisted upward just a little.

"Survivors?" he whispered. "Norman, were there—"

"What?" I asked him.

"Norman?" he said, looking at me, then looking to either side of me. "Norman?"

"Right here," I said. "What is it?"

"Norman?"

He did not see or hear me. There was more I needed to tell him. I needed to talk to him about the nature of civilization. I needed to explain how a people are defined by what they leave behind. I had to talk about the importance of buildings and icons and art and poetry. I wanted to tell him how the Sword of Hephæstus had been able to cut him not because it was stronger than he was, but because he did not understand its magic. I looked around, and behind me was the tall figure of the Spectre again. He decorporealized me before I could say any of these things. I made a spectacular exit and did not even have the sense of drama to appreciate it.

"I need to tell him—"

"You have told him," the Spectre said.

So that's what it felt like.

"Now we must again let events take their course," the Spectre said. My ghostly companion, on the other hand, had a sense of drama for which I failed to give him credit.

The first one through Superman's makeshift entrance to the General Assembly hall was the Batman; the wings of the remarkable craft that was his battle suit caught the faintest of breezes to lower him gently like a glider to the floor. Wonder Woman, with her golden eagle wings and ancient sword, followed. She was less concerned with a soft landing. Green Lantern flew in with his injured daughter, Jade, in his arms. There, thank Heavens, was the Ray. Once already he'd swept the radioactive contaminants from the sands of Kansas and returned the surface to rich topsoil; he might do it again. There was a blur of red; the Flash. There came the maniac with the black swastika tattooed over his face and torso; I was even glad to see him. Magog, absent his headdress, poked his head over the edge of the opening, wondering whether he was welcome here. He was, finally. The clown lady in the checkerboard trousers, the Joker's Daughter, tumbled down the wall. Red Robin was wounded badly. Yet here he was, on the shoulder of the daughter who yesterday was estranged from him. Together—mostly through her effort—the two rappeled to the floor. Beneath his own mask Bruce Wayne winced at the collective impact that such efforts and bruises and bones broken and healed and broken again were certainly having on the integrity of his sometime ward's physiology. There were a handful of survivors, still coming down the wall. Slowly, Wyrmwood and some of the others collected closer to these objects of their recent fury.

"Is this everyone?" Superman asked.

"With his dying breath, Captain Marvel managed to get the bomb high above Ground Zero before he detonated it," Wonder Woman said. "More survivors huddle in shelters in Kansas still. Most are injured. The Green Lanterns willed up an impenetrable shield. Flash whisked some outside the expanding shock wave. For others the Ray diverted the impact of the energy. But there was so little time to—"

"How many?"

"Enough," Batman offered, "to leave us with the same problems as before. The same impasse. The same dangers. The same distrust. The same everything."

"What now?" Wonder Woman wanted to know.

Superman looked at Wyrmwood, who looked away. Superman kept looking until the Secretary-General who had set free the nightmare looked up again and caught the Kryptonian's eye.

"I'm sorry," Wyrmwood said.

"For what?" Superman asked.

Wyrmwood shrugged.

Superman took his hand. "We need to set things right," Superman said. "Years ago I let those I swore to protect drive me away. We all did. That was where we went wrong."

"We saw you," Wyrmwood said, "as gods."

"And we accepted that illusion. Eventually we began to believe it. We were both wrong. Today I lost many friends, and you surrendered a part of your soul to pursue what you thought was a correct decision. I no longer care about the mistakes of yesterday. I care about riding into tomorrow, together."

"Thank you, Superman," the Secretary-General said.

"We'll talk," Superman told Wyrmwood. "Talking is good."

Magog stood against the wall, wondering why he was still alive. Then Superman told him.

"We have a great deal to learn from one another, Magog, don't we?"

"I have a lot to learn in general," he said, his famous face scarred with the ordeal from which his power grew.

"Together," Superman said to him, and then to the group at large: "The problems before us are problems we all face. Nobody solves them by putting on a costume and flying through the air. We'll solve them all right, but I've learned that the first step to doing that is to approach them together. No longer will we impose our power on humanity. No longer will we arrogate to ourselves the responsibility of ruling over you. We will live among you and thus we will earn your trust."

Wonder Woman smiled as she stepped up to Superman's side, removing the tiara that symbolized her royalty. Batman's armor fitted over his artificial skeletal frame and only suggested now the thermal bat-suit he'd worn in his youth. He lifted off the pointy-eared helmet that covered Bruce Wayne's head. Once, revealing the face of the billionaire industrialist beneath his cowl would have been anathema to the Batman, and the midpoint of waves upon waves of news ripples all over the world. Kal-El had been bringing in the harvest years ago when the news had broken. He wondered what it had felt like for some fortunate reporter to break that particular scoop of the century. He wondered how it had changed his friend's life, and supposed they would talk about it sometime.

Superman realized that a grand gesture was in order here. He wondered, would this be grand enough?

"For a long time I went under another name," he told his colleagues and the General Assembly and the world peeking in via Netservice News. "I was a man named Clark. Clark Kent."

Many of those here recognized the name. By the "end" of his life, Clark Kent had accumulated a worldwide reputation as a fine newsman.

"As Clark I was a rather ordinary man," Superman said, "with a job and responsibilities, living in Metropolis with my wife, Lois . . ."

Ears perked up even more now. The death ten years ago of Lois Lane the journalist had promoted her to legendary status. Now everyone learned that she'd been the wife of Superman himself. Stories and headlines tomorrow, the day after the United Nations nuked the super-humans, would cover this historic revelation here on the General Assembly floor.

Superman could change the course of mighty rivers, and the old newsman in his soul could wrest the public imagination to spin in a new direction. It was, as I had told him, Clark's gift to Kal-El.

"Less than an hour ago," Superman said, "I asked someone to choose between humans and superhumans. But in his wisdom, Captain Marvel knew that was a false division."

Superman stepped over to Jade, who leaned against her father. She had found and now held in her hands an icon of a simpler time, when it had been easier to determine right from wrong. She handed Superman the white-and-gold cape he'd torn off Captain Marvel's back and left to flutter to the floor of the battlefield.

"He chose neither of the options I saw, but made the only choice that ever truly matters. In the hope that your world and our world could be one world again, he chose life. That is his legacy."

Superman walked up an aisle to the main door of the General Assembly hall, the one that led down the stairway that heads of state take when they come here. He ran a fingernail through the melted steel jamb that held the door shut and threw it open.

Wonder Woman took his arm and tilted her head toward the door. Chastened, he stepped back through it and fused the steel and the hardwood that composed it back into the form they'd had before. She was teaching him that there was magic in cleaning up the mess you leave behind you.

Everyone followed them out to the main courtyard of the New United Nations fortress. There, Superman rose along an unused flagpole and lashed the cape of the late Captain Marvel by its decorative golden cords to the top.

Green Lantern walked over to Leonard Wyrmwood and, removing his mask with his left hand, extended his right. "Mr. Secretary-General," Lantern said, "my name is Alan Scott. Pleased to meet you."

Jade took the hand of an officious-looking young man among the crowd. "Jade Scott," she said. "I'm a Green Lantern."

"Jean-Paul Kasavubu from the Congo River," the young man said in an accent that spoke rather of Bunker Hill and Faneuil Hall. "I'm a consul-general and a tribal chief."

The Flash, slipping in and out among the dimensions that surrounded the UN courtyard, extended the multiple-image of his hand to the figure of a man who was tall even though he stooped over a cane.

"Anthony Wainwright," the tall man said, extending his own hand, "Earl of Harlech and representative of His Majesty King William to the United Nations."

The Flash buzzed something that Lord Wainwright could not possibly understand, but encased the old man's hand in a cushion of red handshake that made his limb relax up and down the arm.

"This is my friend, Mr. West, Your Lordship," Wonder Woman leaned over and said. "Wallace West."

Red Robin asked Nightstar to help him in the direction of someone to whom he wanted to speak. He wiped back his hood and extended a hand to the tall white-haired man in the titanium suit of armor. "Richard Grayson, sir," he said. "I understand you're a friend of my daughter's." Robin's daughter, Nightstar, had long since taken to calling the Batman "Gramps."

Bruce Wayne took his onetime protégé's hand and pulled him in to his chest and hugged him tightly. Then both men did something neither had done in a long time, certainly not in one another's presence. They cried.

Ω   Ω   Ω

"Do you want her private line?" Wyrmwood asked. "It's classified, of course, but I'm sure she wouldn't mind in your case."

"Wouldn't want you to breach national security on my account," Superman said, smiling. "Besides, I have ways of getting in touch. Tell the President I'll set something up with her scheduling office this afternoon."

"Can I get a picture of you, sir?" the young man with the digital camera asked. "Maybe with the Batman?"

"Sure," Superman answered, and motioned toward Bruce Wayne.

"Come on, Princess," Wayne said to the Amazon, "you need to be in this one, too."

"Just a second, son." Superman stopped the photographer, his journalistic sense awakening from dormancy. "Over here."

You want us to pose for pictures? the Amazon's face demanded silently. Superman nodded back at her—just as silently but in a manner that spoke volumes. She would drop her objections and argue later. Bruce Wayne turned away when Superman motioned to him. Unaccounted numbers of their friends were gone and now this presumptuous man wanted to pose for the cameras. Though the eyes of the world were on them, no one saw Superman whisper into Wayne's ear: "I know this seems frivolous, but it isn't about us or our fallen friends. The healing starts here. We owe this to the ages."

In the coming weeks and years Superman would begin to grow an awareness he never possessed before of the things of the world and their power: a rhyme, a monument, the relic of a treasured memory; the things that give a human life its demonstrable value. This is where he would start. From the

wreckage of the old United Nations complex someone had
harvested a shattered granite slab, reassembled it, and planted
it here on a pedestal in the New United Nations courtyard.
Superman walked his friends Bruce and Diana over to it. In
front of this legend did the photographer take their picture:

> *They shall beat their swords into plowshares,*
> *And their spears into pruning hooks;*
> *Nation shall not lift up sword against nation,*
> *Neither shall they learn war anymore.*

The photograph served as the following week's cover for
Time magazine. It was the fastest-selling issue of that venerable publication, and in all the magazine's history a most
treasured keepsake in millions of homes.

CHAPTER 35

Novus Ordo Seclorum

T he meeting went relatively well. Superman did not try to out-talk President Capper, and she did not try to overpower the super hero. Both were growing into unaccustomed roles—she, long a gifted administrator of large systems, as the spokesperson of a grander vision; he, a renowned role model, as the manager of a vast complex of independent forces and sources of power. They had a lot to learn from one another.

In the study off the Oval Office, they went over the day's order of business. Bruce Wayne would rebuild Wayne Manor and outfit its non-living spaces as a series of convalescent wards. She offered to recommend a Medicaid subsidy but the big man laughed.

"It's Bruce's house, Madame President," Superman insisted, "and when everyone is better, he gets to live there. He doesn't want any subsidies."

"Well, Congress gave me a hefty subsidy to rebuild my house," she said.

"Tell me that, Madame President, when the White House is as lavish a place to live as Wayne Manor. Besides, I don't think Bruce wants Congress dictating the décor in the Batcave."

"Perhaps we can provide the facility with a security system."

Superman shook his head.

"Maybe not, Superman," she said, "but we need to funnel funds into these projects in order to be a good example to the other industrial states."

"All right, so how about a feed and grain airlift from Antarctica, Madame President? That'll cost you plenty and set a really good example."

"How's that?"

"Well," he explained, "Antarctica's been under ice for fifteen million years. President Capper, I have discovered that under that glacier is probably the most mineral-rich soil on Earth. I've been farming thirty-six hundred acres of wheat and alfalfa there for the past ten years and distributing it anonymously in the drought areas of Sudan and Ethiopia. Interesting thing is that practically nobody in Central Africa who has eaten that grain or fed it to their livestock has died of natural causes in all that time."

"We've been studying that."

"You have?"

"There's a National Science Foundation commission trying to figure out why the life expectancy has gone up in Central Africa by seven years over the past ten years. It's perplexed us."

"Well, there's your answer. Now call back your commission and put the money into reclaiming the glacier and distributing the harvest."

They talked about the reeducation program on Paradise Island, and Diana's return there.

"What about the rule that says no men on Paradise Island?" she wanted to know.

"What's the matter, Madame President," he said, "don't you believe in magic?" Even through lines like that, which made Jennifer Capper grin, he wore a glum face.

They agreed that Alan Scott would serve as the permanent Justice League spokesperson in the United Nations.

"He's been a recluse for as long as you," she noted. "Is his presentation up to the job?"

"He's relatively housebroken," Superman answered.

He said he thought Raymond Terrill, the Ray, and Alan Scott's daughter, Jade, could restore the quality of Kansas' farmland over a short period of time.

"Do they need funding?" she asked.

"Given Jade's effect on men and Ray's arrested development," he suggested, "maybe you could buy them a pair of blinders."

He told her about the property his foundation owned in Kansas, the old Kent family farm. He wanted to turn it into a shrine and cemetery.

"They'll want to bury you there, you know," she told him.

"They'll have a long wait."

And the President looked at Superman and said, "How are you?"

"Excuse me?"

"It wasn't a trick question."

"We're fine," he said, and did not smile.

"We?"

"Me," he said, and wondered whether the President wanted to be nosy or make friends.

"It would be good to see you smile, Superman," she told him. "It's how most of us remember you."

He paused for a moment, thought about it, nearly smiled, and said, "Sorry. Soon." Then he said, "Maybe."

Ω   Ω   Ω

On Paradise Island her sisters subjected Wonder Woman to a community inquiry on her extraterritorial activities—essentially a trial. They asked her why she'd prodded Superman into building a Gulag; why she'd opposed the Batman, her friend, to the point of violent combat; what she thought the martial women's role in the new world ought to be—questions like that. Her answers did not always conform to Amazonian orthodoxy, but they always challenged the intellect and the assumptions of her questioners. At the end of it, Diana's sisters not only returned her previous station, but gave her a crown.

Her answer to the question of the Amazons' role in all of this had to do with her belief that Amazon philosophy had grown stagnant with Paradise Island's isolation from the world. As this very inquiry vividly demonstrated, she said, her sisters needed to become truly an Amazon nation. There was a surfeit of training and philosophy in her people's lives, and a scarcity of actual living.

"For example," Diana told her sister Cressida, whose otherwise impassive face in the course of exhaustive questioning betrayed a growing uncertainty about what answers she wanted to hear, "who among you has actually met a living soul who does not live on this Island?"

A few hands went up among the four- or fivescore assembled sisters. Then even they went down when everyone realized what their former princess meant by "living." Not a single one of the long-lived residents of this Island had had contact with a single outsider in more than seventy years.

"This needs to be fixed," Diana said, "and the way to fix it is by becoming teachers. By turning Paradise Island into a great center of philosophical thought. My sisters, it is time that we all dare to put down our spears and our bows and our physical culture and—through articulating it to others—relearn the ancient principles on which this culture is founded. It is time we applied those principles to the worldwide society of our own times."

"And who would these students be?" Diana's mother, Hippolyta the Queen, asked. It was her first question, and her last.

"Mother," Diana said, "it is time to change the rules."

In the following weeks all manner and conditions of

arcane folk set foot on Paradise Island and proposed to stay. Most of them were men. Most of them, as well, were veterans of the Gulag. Magog would come here and become a kind of dean of students. And also the Manotaur, whose ancestors had so bedeviled Diana's own.

Diana regained her title and resumed her station, but declined her old job as ambassador to the "World of Men." That portfolio went to Cressida.

"And good riddance," Diana said.

Ω   Ω   Ω

The older man noticed himself trading in his black garb for white. In the T-shirt and the titanium shoulder framework he was enormous and imposing. The younger man with the shock of black hair was quite handsome and wore the prepossessing manner of European aristocracy. "I understand," the older man told the younger, "that you are my son."

They were in the part of the once stately manor that Increase Hopkins and his kids had built, the part that had been the Gothamborough Inn. This was the section of the mansion that Dr. Thomas Wayne, Bruce's father, had converted to a recovery ward during the time when the polio epidemic had filled the hospitals of Gotham with suffering children. Now it accommodated patients and guests again, survivors of a nuclear bomb deployed in anger. Tall, recently glazed windows and long recessed ceiling lamps lit the room as brightly as if it were outside. The white walls still needed some cosmetic patching, and the twelve-foot Bat-Knight frames that perched at periodic distances along the wall gave the place the look more of a theme park than of a hospital room. Wayne knew that the best environmental filtration system available anywhere was the one with which he outfitted his flotilla of urban patrollers. He had an oversupply of these robots after shutting down Luthor's production facility, and here was the best use for them.

Everywhere was the red bat: on a ceiling mural, on the converted robots, silk-screened on Wayne's white T-shirt. Once, long ago, Bruce Wayne had sat over a drafting table with protractors, triangles, and an overworked pencil sharpener and spent the better part of a week designing the stylized sign of the bat that had punctuated his career. Once he'd developed the design of which he was proud, he wondered whether he would have been an artist if he had not been born to wealth and married to tragedy. He rarely sat down at the drafting table now. Here in Gotham the Renaissance was not over; certainly not here in what this aging Batman laughingly referred to as Wayne Manor and Supervillain Convalescent Home.

Ibn al Xu'ffasch, heir to and hegemon of the late Rā's al Ghūl's empire, looked up from turning the sheet over the face of Lady Marvel, who had thus come to the end of her radiation-induced coma. For all the aversion training his grandfather had imposed on him in his long exile, the young man had what amounted to a genetic reflex against the concept of death. There would be more deaths in this place during the coming months, all of them more drawn-out and most of them more painful. Perhaps this was therefore not the best place for him to spend these days, but when Diana invited him to Paradise Island to teach with her, he was adamant about coming here instead.

"How long have you known of our relationship?" Xu'ffasch asked Bruce Wayne, who sat down on the bed with a hand on the boy's shoulder.

"Since not long after you called me to come to that first meeting at Luthor's. I had just assumed you were Rā's' son, but I had never heard of you before he died."

"Why didn't you say anything?"

"There didn't seem to be time until now. Welcome to the ancestral home."

Xu'ffasch looked around at the relative paucity of these surroundings compared to what he was used to. "I grew up in Andorra."

"Yes, I know. In the family of Prince Hugo. Did you know of your pedigree?"

"Not a clue. I thought I was some adopted waif someone left on the doorstep. My 'brother' Pietro—Hugo's real son—got an education that centered on manners and business management while I had to study science and history and ancient languages. I was jealous. I didn't know what it was about. Not until the day a skyful of paratroopers came to claim me and hand me a kingdom."

"You'd be just thirty-two now, right? Your family members have always looked younger than their years."

"It's part of the birthright," Xu'ffasch said, referring to the Lazarus Pit, the steaming chamber of chemicals that had sliced decades at a time off Rā's al Ghūl's age and extended his life to several centuries.

"And your mother?"

Bruce Wayne had no idea, until he investigated Xu'ffasch, that he himself could possibly have fathered Talia's child. Rā's had only his daughter and was preoccupied with the idea of the Batman being his successor. For his part, Wayne knew it would never happen.

Rā's al Ghūl's empire was a country without borders. The organization's economic interests centered on mineral cartels and shadow governments that occasionally overthrew legitimate ones and drove ethnic groups to war over natural resources when they thought they were fighting over principles. Nonetheless, Talia was brilliant, brave, and exotic, and she'd stirred Bruce Wayne's heart and soul as no other woman ever had. The last time he'd seen her was during one of his flirtations with her father's ambitions. For his damned principles he'd tricked and betrayed Rā's, much as he used and betrayed Luthor. Talia had taken it personally and disappeared from his life forever.

"She's fine. She follows you in the news," Xu'ffasch said.

"Excuse me?"

"They have a pretty good commlink in Calcutta now, thanks to my new fleet of satellite transponders."

"She's alive?"

"You didn't know?"

"How would I know?"

"You're the Batman."

"I'm not God. Where? Calcutta, you say? What's she doing there?"

"She's Mother Talia. She's the mother superior of Saint Teresa's clinic."

"I didn't even know she was Catholic."

"Well, she wasn't. We're Muslim, I guess, if we're anything, but you know . . ."

The master of this place stalked past beds full of ailing victims and "volunteers" who were here in lieu of long prison terms. He was never very good at bringing conversations to an end, even with a newly discovered son.

He was halfway out of the room when he called back, "How do I get in touch with her?"

"Here," Xu'ffasch said. He jotted an address on the late Lady Marvel's chart and rose to hand it to his father.

Standing by the door of the ward was Lex Luthor, drawing corrections and extrapolation marks on a recently minted computer data chart. He was allowed to do this because all of the bedpans were empty. Like most of the rest of the members of his erstwhile cartel—Catwoman, Vandal Savage, Lord Naga, the Riddler, and the others—Luthor wore an electronic restraining collar that confined him to this wing of the house. It would be an interesting game to anticipate and quash his escape attempts when he made them, but so far he had not. No one made any attempt to force him to tend patients, Heaven forbid. Luthor was never adept at bedside manner. He was, however, making some significant progress working out a cure for Crohn's disease here.

"Shazam," Bruce Wayne gibed through a side of his mouth as he stomped past Luthor.

"Shutup," was the criminal mastermind's clever reply.

Ω Ω Ω

The granite sign at the main roadway leading to the cemetery read HOMESTEAD MEMORIAL PARK, and a stone beyond the sign was engraved with:

For those claimed by the Great Bomb
And for all those who lost their lives to our mistakes:
We wish we had known you better.

Along the road leading into the park a little historical marker told that this property had once been the site of the farm of Jonathan and Martha Kent. There was no mention of all the other people who had ever passed this way or events that had taken place in the area. No one was sure after the Kansas disaster exactly where, for example, the little spaceship from Krypton had touched down all those years ago. The rest of the story would be clear enough in the accounts yet to be written. With all the cataclysms and revelations of the past months, it seemed history was beginning again.

Kal-El returned alone to the land. Not to the Antarctic, but to his boyhood home. He determined above all not to let Kansas go the way of the other lost planet of his past. Of course he was all over the world all the time now. If anything—as for many active men—his retirement promised paradoxically to be more hectic than his career.

I should talk.

The Spectre turned out to be something of a friend. He put me through a kind of rejuvenation process before summarily depositing me back into my life. There is no rigid sense of time in a spirit's existence, but there is a kind of moral fatigue that serves a similar purpose. I spent a period suspended in a kind of bubble of light, growing energy of spirit before I finally picked up the loose ends of the life I'd left behind when I went off to judge the world. I was rejuvenated—no younger than I was before, unfortunately, but stronger, gamer—when I walked the spirit planes with the Spectre for the last time. It was on that farm in Kansas that I witnessed a most affecting tableau.

Clark had an enormous plowshare, bigger by far than the largest farmhouse. Maybe he'd fused it together from the metal of melted swords. Maybe not. It had grooves along its face, and as he pulled it along like Pegasus in a yoke, with each stroke it prepared maybe twenty rows for planting. He wore work clothes, like those of a farmer: jeans and a white tank top. The only thing that distinguished him from a farmer was simply that he did not break a sweat. And of course there was also the flying. Here was what remained of the Kent farm, all loamed and turned over for sowing. And there in the near distance was the memorial park with rows upon rows of headstone markers.

Before the flying woman in the red tunic was even in my sight or the Spectre's, the big man undid his yoke, floated to the ground, and, staring out across the cemetery, said in a terribly loud voice: "The topsoil was down to just an inch or two in some places. Bedrock was poking through the loam here and there. But not anymore."

It would be a few moments before she flew close enough to respond to him. Wafting through the sky she managed to look better in her flowing, shapeless outfit than most people look when they go to their high school proms.

"The Breadbasket was getting thin, eh?" Diana commented as she touched down to join him at the edge of the plowed field and look across the acres of neat white marble monuments.

"When the Native Americans first arrived here—what? about eight or ten thousand years ago?—the rich dark soil reached six, eight, twelve feet down at its thinnest point before you hit even a hint of silt or sand. When the Europeans took the land for farming, it was probably in better shape than when the Indians found it. It's only in the past two hundred years that we've sucked up the minerals out of the Heartland and turned it all into oatmeal and white bread."

Then he was quiet for a few minutes, just looking across the reclaimed land, at the headstones. Diana took his hand and held it lightly.

"Kal?" she said.

"Hmm?"

"They haunt you only when you forget what they had to teach you. Let them rest in peace."

"I'll do my best."

"We've got a world to rebuild."

"We do. I'm starting here."

And they were quiet again for a while until she reached into a pocket of her clothing and took out a small wooden box.

"For you, Kal," she said. "A little something to help you see more clearly."

He opened the box and found a pair of glasses inside.

Clark Kent had worn glasses. He put them on, and kissed her. Then he smiled. More than by the long-gone smile, I was startled by how different he looked with the glasses. I wondered whether he would grow the beard he wore in his seclusion again.

"Take care, Clark," she said.

"Are you rested, Norman McCay?" the Spectre asked me as she took off.

"I feel like I could pull that plow," I told him.

"Time to go home," the Spectre said. Then it occurred to him that I thought by "home" he meant my eternal reward. I thought of the ghost of Boston Brand, the circus acrobat. I thought of Ellen.

"I'm ready for whatever's next," I said. I never seriously thought I would get out of this alive.

Reading my thought, the Spectre said, "Not yet, Norman McCay. Your own mission is not yet complete."

"Spectre," I said, and reached up to stay the magic of his hand, "all the sins have been exposed. Tell me. In the end, whom do you punish? Who is responsible?"

"No one need suffer any further for the tragedies we have witnessed, Norman McCay," my companion answered me. "Do not mock me."

"I don't mean to. I just wonder. When you first appeared before me, you said you needed a human soul to be your anchor. And yet you yourself were once a mortal man. Tell me, what would his perspective have been?"

"Ever the minister," and somehow I felt he was mocking me in the gentlest of ways. Then he took down the hood and revealed his face for the first time. It was a good face, ruddy and angular, with just a patch of white hair in front among a thicket of red. "Be well, Norman McCay. You have watched the titans walk the Earth and you have kept stride. Perhaps you are more like them than you realize. You exist to give hope."

Then the church, my church on Jefferson Avenue, materialized all around me.

My body was heavy again. Suddenly I was bound to the Earth again. It was all right; I could handle it. I was even relieved. According to the calendar, to which I'd paid little attention all this time, I would soon be yet another year older. And considering that among us survivors human life expectancy was about to take a dramatic jump, due to richer soil in the Heartland and a sudden abundance of minerals in the food we ate, I was but a lad.

"Wait!" I told the Spectre before he faded completely from my sight. "Will I see you again?"

"I expect you will see quite a bit of me."

Ω   Ω   Ω

". . . and the Lord God sent His angel to show His servants . . ." I recited now from my head and my heart. No longer did some compulsion press the ancient words out my mouth. The congregation that sat before me finally befitted the fine church where we met. People crowded. They hunted for seats. They had to touch one another to pray here. I liked that.

The first member of my newly minted Confirmation class walked into church holding her mother's hand on a Sunday not long after I left the Spectre's world. She was a pretty little girl named Diana, as it happened. Somehow during the following weeks more and more families with young children appeared and filled up the new Sunday School class. For their benefit I had to enlist some young fathers to help me rake out one of the storerooms off the sanctuary balcony. After a while I began to assume that many of these young families knew each other, had a history together, and that it was word of mouth that gradually brought them to our little church on Jefferson Avenue. Asking around, however, I found that they generally came here through chance: the recommendation of an uncle or aunt, an old article someone saw somewhere about the sounds that once had come from our pipe organ, or their walking down the street and seeing what a beautiful building we were in. A lot of people were beginning to walk down the street again: normal people mostly, without costumes, without the power to fly or to tie their shoes just by thinking about it.

Still, the average age of the congregation, as my friend Wesley used to quip, was now just a bit younger than dead. It did not matter. We were building a little community here in the heart of the once and future City of Dreams. My adopted city again was becoming a city whose people walked its boulevards and browsed its shopping centers with pride and a bearing as though each of them was the lord or lady of this manor, and where each of them was in fact. Once, not long ago, Metropolis was a palace. That is how it would be again. As for myself, I had a new best friend.

Jim Corrigan started showing up occasional Sunday mornings. He was a striking man, tall and beefy, and with a patch of white at the fore of his full head of red hair. I suppose I was the only one in the congregation who realized that he was mostly illusion. Then again, there was a case to make that a creature in such close touch with his higher self was more "real" than either my congregation or myself.

Then there was another who wandered into the sanctuary one Sunday morning. He was nearly as tall as Jim, and even beefier. He wore a flannel shirt and slacks, and glasses that a friend had given him. He found a seat toward the back. In my sermon that morning I was talking about perfectibility.

"Our forebears found comfort in the notion that anything on which God placed his hand was thus the model of absolute perfection. They had no evidence to suggest such a thing of course, but they wanted it to be true, so they said it was. The Earth was at the center of a symmetrical Universe, and anything that went wrong was the result of some evil force or of the shortcomings of frail humans. Well, evidence has shown us—and the recent history of our own lives has brought it home for us—that the Universe, this Creation of God, is an imperfect place, and we are not even at its center."

I talked about what our lives would be like if everything around us were a clockwork of order. I said that God had created an imperfect Universe so that we could have adversity to overcome and so that we could be his partners in the most Godly work of creation.

"Know what this is?" I pulled a visual aid—an orange, actually—from the shelf under my pulpit. It was such a pleasure to have children again in the sanctuary. The youngest sat with her parents and her big brother in the fourth pew near the aisle. "What's this, Sarah?"

"An orange," Sarah said.

"And who made the orange, Jeremy?"

"God did," Jeremy said with some authority.

"He did. But that's only part of the answer. Where did we find the first orange?"

That stumped both of them for a moment, then thoughtful thirteen-year-old Jeremy said, "On the first orange tree. Wait, weren't there plants before there were people?"

"By most accounts," I said, "but not oranges." Then I pulled another, bigger piece of fruit out from behind my pulpit. "Anybody know what this is?"

After a moment, Jim tentatively raised his hand. This was a good sign. He was learning again the human capacity for taking initiative. Perhaps there was nearly as much hope for the angels as there was for the rest of us.

"Yes, Mr. Corrigan, do you know?"

"Is that a citron, Pastor?"

"It is. It's a large yellow citrus fruit. The first citrus fruit, in fact, packed tight with vitamin C and cellulose and very good for you, but it tastes more bitter than a night in the Antarctic. The citron grows in the Middle East and North Africa and predates humans on this planet by quite some time. But this orange—which grows pretty much everywhere with a long-enough growing season—was an invention of man."

Murmurs. If Wesley had been here, he might have leapt to his feet and started quoting Scripture against his will. Thank heaven I did not have that urge anymore.

"God made citrons, and man took the citron and grafted and cross-pollinated and nurtured and grew until we had oranges and lemons and grapefruits and limes and tangerines and all sorts of derivative stuff that's been with us so long, we can't remember a time without it. Do you think the orange is better than the citron, Sarah?"

"I don't know." The little girl shrugged.

"What do you think, Mr.—" I strained my aging eyes toward the back of the big room. "Mr. Kent?"

"I think," the bespectacled man in the flannel shirt at the back said, "I think we improved on the citron for our own purposes, yes."

"I think so, too. Which is not to say that the citron—which may have grown in the Garden of Eden for all we know—was a bad idea. But you and I will take our vitamin C more reliably when it tastes a little less bitter going down."

I looked around. I loved this room. I loved the people in it. For the first time since I lost my Ellen, I loved my life again.

"We have cities to rebuild, my brothers and sisters. We

have a world that's waiting for us to mold it to our use. He gave us this lovely blue planet as surely as He gave us the citron. And He gave us the tools to see the imperfections and to make them better. Not perfect, but—for our own purposes, as our good Mr. Kent puts it so well—improved. So let us remember that when we make our choices—when we clone a grapefruit or repair a table or comb our hair or sit up late with a troubled friend—that here on Earth God's work must truly be our own."

And so the crisis passed. There was no grand celebration, though someday our children's children might set aside a day to mark the moment. Today, there is too much pain to forget, too much rebuilding to master. But there is faith here. So, though visions no longer haunt me, I must preach the lessons they taught me:

> A dream is not always a prophecy.
> The future, like history and intention and so much
>   else, is open to interpretation.
> And hope is brightest when it dawns from fear.

I closed, as I used to close when I'd been a young minister at my first pulpit, with the blessing of Aaron the High Priest: "The Lord bless thee, and keep thee. The Lord make His face shine upon thee, and be gracious unto thee. The Lord lift up His countenance upon thee, and give thee peace. Amen. Grace be with you."

CHAPTER 36

Ontogeny

Finally I got Jim Corrigan to go with me to Planet Krypton, the theme restaurant near Governor's Plaza. I had not been there since before all this, and I insisted that he could not fully experience it unless he was at least ostensibly in human form. It turned out to be a good day to go. Maybe Jim knew it would be.

"Look here," I said, waving the menu in his face. "A Spectre Platter. That's new. I'm sure of it."

"I wonder if that will help my career," he said. It was a joke—dry as dust but a joke nonetheless. This was another good sign. Apparently he'd had a rather impressive public career during my youth, even as an active and occasionally visible member of the old Justice Society for a while.

"Look at it this way, it's flattering to be remembered somehow," I told him.

The Spectre Platter was not really a meal at all, but a flavored rice cake with lettuce, tomato, and mayonnaise. Cellulose and empty calories, mostly. We both declined. We had a great time at Planet Krypton: took in the costumed waitpersons, made believe they flubbed our orders, pretended they were the real characters they were playing, and tripped them up with questions about ancient history, and so forth. This is not the way I generally find my fun—it was more like something I would have done with Wesley, actually—but my judgment as a minister told me that it was a fine prescription for someone as chronically starved for amusement as my friend Jim.

Then Superman and Wonder Woman walked in.

No one noticed, of course. Clark looked like a big middle-aged truck driver. Diana looked like she must have been his daughter. She turned more heads than the waitress in the Power Woman outfit, and of course this annoyed her. She would never outgrow that.

"Greetings, citizens!" the long-haired clueless kid in the Superman suit said to Clark Kent and Diana Prince. "Smoking or nonsmoking?"

"Be nice, Clark," Diana warned.

"Look over there," Clark said in that quietly commanding voice as I first noticed them. He was pointing at our table. Then they were coming over. "Diana, you remember Norman, don't you?"

"Of course. And is that you, James?"

"After a fashion," Jim Corrigan said.

"Clark," I said, quite flustered. He must think I go through life flustered. "And I'm delighted to meet you Miss, uh, Ms . . ."

"Diana's fine, Pastor."

I believe I was sweating. Ellen would be mortified. "What brings you here, of all places?"

"Meeting a friend," Clark said.

"Always a good idea to put this guy in unfamiliar territory." Diana smiled.

"Who? Clark?"

"No, our friend," she said. "Bruce. Need to work hard to keep him in line."

"Interesting seeing you again," Jim said. "We were just finishing up."

"We were just ordering another cup of coffee," I said, motioning for Jim to stay in his seat. I had no intention of missing this one.

△ △ △

"May I seat you, or would you like to go to the counter?" a smiling but firm young man dressed as the Blue Beetle interrupted.

"Seating us would be fine," Diana told the Blue Beetle, and laid a hand on Clark's arm. "There'll be three of us."

"Would you like to be paged when the rest of your party arrives?"

"I'm sure he'll have no trouble finding us." They sat at a table for four.

"This is awful, you know," were the first words Clark told Diana when they sat down. "Worse than I would have imagined."

"What do you mean? They gave us a menu right away. Want to order?" She was enjoying herself, and he found this perplexing.

"Don't you think this is . . ."

"What?" she wanted to know.

"Well, don't you find any of this unsettling?"

She looked around, and finally she managed to see the place through his eyes. "I was brought up differently from you, Clark." She smiled.

"What do you mean?"

"I grew up in an environment where it was the fashion among mortals to pay exorbitant homage to the gods. It's not a church, Clark, it's a restaurant. Relax."

"Where is he, anyway? He's never late."

"You're the one with the X-ray vision. Did you look behind the giant penny?"

"You didn't tell him, did you?"

"And ruin your moment? Who am I to deprive you of the opportunity to see the Batman surprised?"

"You think anybody else will recognize us? It's pretty crowded in here."

"This, from the man who kept his secret for years in a newsroom of all places, using nothing but a pair of glasses and a string of lame excuses. Are you all right, Clark?"

"I guess I'm actually a little nervous."

"Really? That might be better than seeing Bruce stumped."

"So you don't think anybody'll notice?"

"Us? Hardly likely. In the first place," Diana said, "you wrote the book on secret identities—"

"And in the second place," it was not Diana's voice, but that icy tone that seemed to come from all directions at once, "amid all this tawdry bric-a-brac, if we were fighting Dreadnaught and the Monster Society of Evil in full regalia, they'd all think it was some sort of floor show. Clark. Diana."

"There you are. How in the stars do you do that, Bruce?" Clark demanded. "You sneaked up on me. Me! Were you hiding behind a lead-lined potted palm?"

"Do you seriously think you would have noticed?" Bruce Wayne negotiated his significant bulk, his unwieldy titanium framing, and the overcoat that covered it all, among the bustling paraphernalia of this place and into the narrow chair as skillfully as a T'ai Chi master slices through a street riot.

"Good to see you under brighter circumstances, Bruce." Clark turned sincere and Diana just grinned. "How're the boys?"

"Dick's on the way to a full recovery. I believe I've convinced him to stick more to the nerve center in his future activities and leave off the running and jumping and swinging from ropes. He'd just as soon not end up with a cyborg skeletal system, too."

"And Xu'ffasch?" Diana asked.

"I'm leaving him to my gr— Uh," and he paused. Life held few uncertainties for Bruce Wayne, but relationships always seemed beyond his grasp. Just what was Nightstar to him? "To Dick's daughter. They seem to be getting on well. She's counseling him. Maybe he'll turn around yet."

"Really?" Diana and Clark said simultaneously, looking at each other.

"He's got a bit of a values problem, of course," Bruce said, "but he'll get over it, I think. He keeps talking lately about the proper disposition for the sort of enormous resources that he controls. That's what happens when you're raised by an isolated society. You end up a little brainwashed."

"You don't say," Diana observed, and Bruce ignored the irony. "There's always your example."

"How so?" from Bruce.

"You certainly use your resources in a responsible way."

"No." Bruce allowed a slight chuckle. "In Xu'ffasch's case we're talking about significant wealth. Not like mine."

"A billion here, a billion there." Clark sniffed.

"May I get you something to drink?" a waiter in the old Aquaman outfit with faux scales on his shirt asked.

"See?" Clark said. "He didn't sneak up on me. Milk, please."

"Water is fine," Diana said.

And Bruce ordered, "Coffee. Black. And keep it coming."

"We charge extra after the second cup."

"Fine."

"It's not the full price, but just—"

"Fine."

"We just need for you to know that—"

"I'm losing consciousness as well as interest waiting for my caffeine fix."

The waiter vanished.

"It used to be easier to strike fear in the hearts of the incompetent," Bruce snarled at Clark as a steaming mug of black double-roasted Java appeared at the table. It would be a few minutes before the milk or water got here.

"Maybe the costume had something to do with it after all."

Bruce looked around, caught sight of a thick young fellow

busing tables in a Batman outfit, nearly dropping a dish as a heedless patron stepped on his cape on the way out. "Maybe not," he said. "So tell me. Of all the burger joints in all the world, why'd you pick this one?"

"I didn't," Clark said.

"I did," Diana said, still smiling, still drinking in the mindless worship all around her. "I was curious. The atmosphere is elevating and humbling at the same time. Some of us can always use a little more humility."

"Kind of puts you on a pedestal, eh, Princess?"

"A little. And there's the humbling part."

"Excuse me." A man leaned over toward Bruce from a neighboring table. "Are you by any chance—"

"I am," Bruce said before the man had the chance to say . . .

"—using the ketchup? We've run out."

"Ah," Bruce said. "Be my guest."

Clark winked at the elderly white-bearded little minister a few tables away—at me. My friend was murmuring a blow-by-blow account of the conversation as it unfolded. I laughed. For a moment Bruce Wayne looked in our direction, too, and shrugged. Corrigan's back was to him.

"So I gather from your communication that we have business?" Bruce asked.

"Not business, really," Clark said.

"Some things to settle. News to share. We have not really spoken since Captain Marvel's incident," Diana said. "I think it's appropriate to start by remembering those sister and brother warriors who fell in battle."

"Of course." Bruce lifted his Green Lantern mug.

"To past friends," Clark said, and three drinks clicked among the three grateful survivors.

"Hi, I'm Robin," a girl in a yellow cape and green eye-shades said.

"Of course you are," the Batman said.

"Are you ready to order?"

"Steak," Bruce Wayne said. "Well done."

"Well," Robin said, "there's the Man of Beef, the Mongul Monstrosity, or could I recommend the Dynamic Duo? It's like surf and turf, only—"

"Steak," he repeated. "Well done."

"Yes sir."

"See? It isn't the costume," Bruce said to Clark, and Robin smiled, supposing he was referring to hers.

"I'll just have your giant turtle soup," Diana said.

"And for you, sir?"

"Do you serve anything like beef bourguignon?" Clark asked.

"We have Starro the Casserole," Robin said, reenergized. "It's got a special sauce that tastes a little like—"

"Fine," Clark said. "And maybe you could get us another bottle of ketchup."

"Yes sir. Ma'am. Sir," and she was gone.

Bruce leaned back and dropped his coat onto the back of his chair, revealing the titanium shoulder framing. Still, no one appeared to notice the trio any more than they noticed the Bronze Age wallpaper.

"So I don't recall anyone blowing up a federal building since last we spoke, Diana. Your remedial socialization program goes well?"

"Teaching. We call it teaching," Diana said.

"Absolutely," Bruce said. "I teach, too. But I still have to change the frequency on the inhibitor collars twice a day to keep the riffraff subdued."

"Even Luthor?" Clark wanted to know.

"Not so much. I caught him down in the cave twice last month trying to hack the computer. He sends his best."

"Really?"

"No."

"If the experience of the Gulag showed us anything, it's that students have to want to learn," Diana said. "Mine are getting there."

"Seeing most of your friends wiped out because of a stupidity you share with them is a fine incentive to learning, I've found." Bruce was slower than she to find charity. "The tactic worked wonders in the Gotham inner city during the drug revival about a generation back. I can't claim any credit for cleaning up that one."

"Perhaps some of the hard cases at your place would profit by a few months on our Island."

"I'll keep it in mind. And you, Clark? Still working at restoring the agricultural balance? The food supply seems back up. How irradiated is the soil these days?"

"I have no interest in growing house-sized zucchinis. As when we built the Gulag, the Ray and Jade have been a big help stripping the land of radioactivity." Clark smiled. "I expect the rest is a question of hard work and patience. I imagine you can relate."

"We're doing rather well in our rehabilitation efforts," Bruce said. "Fortunately I'm not laboring alone. I have been able to put several members of the Mankind Liberation Front to work in our ad hoc hospital. Vandal Savage alone is especially helpful, you should know. Fifty thousand years gives a man lots of time to figure out some pretty effective arcane healing tricks. Ever hear of using a hawthorne plant?"

"You mean to retard heart disease?" Diana asked. "The Amazons have been doing it for centuries."

"I'm sure," Bruce said. "Oh really, miss," he added as the steak arrived and Robin ducked away again, "that's not even remotely well done. Miss?"

She was gone. As Bruce called to her, Clark noticed the steak with his heat vision, and by the time Bruce looked down again, it was blackened around the edges and deep brown at the center.

Having Jim Corrigan to convey every word to me was better than using my own aging ears.

"Do I leave you the tip?" Bruce asked Clark. "So what's on your minds? Surely we aren't here just to compare résumés."

"Well." Diana paused as Bruce cut into his steak and Clark reached for the missing bottle of ketchup. "We have something to announce."

"You're pregnant." Bruce looked down, taking his first bite. He made a point of not looking up to note the inevitable flabbergasted looks on the faces of his old friends. In fact, halfway across the room when Jim murmured to me what he'd said, I dropped both a fork and a partial from my mouth.

"How did you—?" Diana asked. She tried again to complete her question: "How could you possibly—?" and could not.

"Observation," he said. "For an ageless Amazon of perfect physique, you've put on a pound or two. That was my first clue."

"Well, four or five actually, but who's counting?"

"And your hair's a little grayer and your skin's a little clearer."

"My skin is clearer? How is that possible?" She thought to be facetious, but in fact it did not seem quite possible. Her skin may not have been any clearer now, but it positively glowed.

"My best to you both. Congratulations on bringing another spit-curled demigod into the world. Sorry if I stepped on your dénouement, Princess."

"I don't believe it." Clark let his fork drop on the squeaky-clean, five-pointed plate that minutes ago had held a full portion of Starro the Casserole and half a bottle of ketchup. "How old do I have to get before I can stump you, Bruce? Always the detective."

"Well, let's see how well honed his escape artistry is these days." Diana's eyes narrowed as she leaned over the table toward both men. "Bruce, I want a commitment from you. I'd like you to be our child's godfather."

"What?" Clark said, just a touch astonished.

"Me?" Bruce responded. "I don't know what to say."

"Really? Then I win. The day is full of surprises." Diana

smiled and ordered dessert. "Apokolips pie," she said to Robin the waitperson. "Chocolate ice cream on the inside and dark chocolate cookie crumbs and chocolate chips on the outside. Yum. I love being pregnant."

"Make that three," Clark told Robin.

"I never order dessert," Bruce said.

"I know," Clark said, "but I'm always eating for two. Sometimes eight or ten."

"News to you too, I take it?" Bruce asked Clark.

"About your being the godfather? What isn't when it comes to her? When Diana runs out of news, she makes something up."

"Diana," Bruce said. "Where I come from, a godparent is the person who is responsible for a child's education, especially his spiritual education. Is that what 'godfather' means to you?"

"Well, yes, actually. We never really made much use of the concept, but I thought the range of this baby's influences ought to be as broad as we can make it."

"Hardly Athena's wisdom at work, Diana. My record as a parent isn't spotless."

"Your record as a man is pretty impressive," and she took Bruce Wayne's hand—took it firmly, the way a man might take a woman's hand.

"Diana," he said quietly. Finally, she'd found a way to move him.

"You're seeing Talia soon."

"Now you're the detective? How did you know?"

"As long as I've known you, Bruce, whenever I've touched your hand it's been solid as a rock. Not now."

The Batman blushed. I did not believe it either, but Jim Corrigan confirmed it. The Batman blushed.

Superman laughed.

"I'm meeting her at the airport in about two and a half hours. I thought seeing you two for lunch would be just the cold shower I needed."

"Surprise!" Clark said, and grinned.

"Bruce," Diana said, letting go his leafy hand, "I'll be the first to admit I know very little about fatherhood, but there are things you can teach our child that Clark and I simply can't. Things we would never conceive of. Doors you breeze through where our minds would not even think to wander. You're the least Earthbound person I've ever met, and that includes the red-haired guy over there."

"Now wait, Princess." Bruce looked in our direction, then held up his hand and put it down again lest it betray more. "This baby's got a father too. What do you think, Clark?"

"I think it's a fine idea."

"Yeah, sure, but we're of such different schools. Listen, Clark, for all practical purposes your word is law in every quarter of the planet—with the possible exception of Gotham—and you do it all by trust. I don't understand how you do that. I don't think I'll ever understand how, with all your power, you've still managed to define a life where you don't really need to use that power. I rely on fear and I always have. I've even done that with the partners I've taken into my home. Do you truly want a man like me in your child's life?"

"More coffee, sir?" a tall dark girl asked him. She wore an old Wonder Woman outfit, with the eagle breastplate.

"Oh, yes." Bruce Wayne smiled.

"Listen, Bruce," Clark said after a moment's thought. "Look at the lesson we just learned. Right now the scales of world power are balanced, but still too easy to tip. Our child, more than any other, will need the leavening influence of a mortal man—a moral man—whom we can count on. I've disagreed with your judgment from time to time, but never with your intentions."

"Never?"

"Never."

"Really."

"You're surprised? Could you not say that about me?"

Bruce was astonished at the thought. "How could I possibly ever doubt the goodwill of Superman? How could anyone?"

"Well, I feel the same way about you, Bruce. Why would that surprise you?"

"Because . . ." and Bruce Wayne wondered how to put this before he said, "because you're Superman, and I'm just a guy."

"Batman," Clark said through his last bite of his second Apokolips pie, "you are not just a guy."

Diana elbowed Clark in the ribs. If she hurt herself, it did not show. "It's settled, then?"

"The kid's mother is an Amazon," Bruce said, "and the father's a Kryptonian. You realize you've just handed me influence over the most powerful child of the twenty-first century."

"I thought you agreed rather quickly," Clark said, smiling. "Our child ought to have an actual human—an exemplary, mortal human—to serve as a moral compass. You're right about me, Bruce. Trust is the center of my world. I don't know if that makes me an expert on it, but I've thought about this a lot, and you're wrong about you. You're a man who deserves my trust. Our trust. Our child's trust. I can't think of anybody else, frankly, who does. Over all the years, despite our differences, there has never been a moment when I did not trust you."

Finally, Superman managed to flabbergast the Batman. Bruce Wayne rose to his feet and put both arms around Clark, who got up to return the embrace. Diana almost cried, but she was an Amazon after all. Robin brought the check, and by the time Clark and Diana looked down, it was clutched in Bruce Wayne's tight fist.

How did he do that? Clark wondered.

"So when do I get to see my godchild?" Bruce asked as he thumb-printed for the tab.

"About seven and a half months," Clark said.

"No, I mean how often?"

"I'm sure we can work out some sort of shared custody arrangement," Diana said as the register clerk in the Hawkman suit looked at the name that came up and gaped out from under his beak and headwings. "The baby shouldn't spend all its time in seclusion with us. After all, we wouldn't want the child raised by an isolated society of zealots."

"Touché," Bruce said. "The child of Superman, Wonder Woman—and Batman. Can you just imagine?" The aging Batman's voice filled unmistakably with wonder until he asked, "So have you given any thought to a name? Bruce is good."

Clark chuckled. "Bruce?" Clark looked around for a moment. He thought the Batman had pulled another of his disappearing acts, but he found his friend standing inside the door, idly staring at the two men getting up from their table across the room—the elderly little pastor and the tall redhead. There was no reason Clark and Diana needed to keep our presence from Bruce Wayne, other than the secret fun they had doing it. "Bruce? Maybe you'd like a lift to the airport?"

"Sorry," he said, "just wondering."

"About?" and I suppose if Bruce asked, Clark would tell him who we were, but he did not.

"Your personal torah," Bruce said. "Wasn't that what you used to call it?"

"Yes," Clark said. "Truth, justice, and the American way."

Diana took both men's arms and huddled against them as they walked outside into the light.

"Going to be quite a kid, that's for sure," Bruce said.

That night, we all dreamed.

ABOUT THE AUTHORS

❦

ELLIOT S. MAGGIN has written stories about his heroes—both real and made-up ones—since he was very young. He started publishing them at sixteen, when a boys' magazine accepted his time travel story about Winston Churchill and the Boer War. He has written at least five hundred comic book stories, including serving, on and off, as a principal writer of Superman comics from 1971 until 1986. He has written television, film, animation, journalism, speeches, and technical manuals, and designed software games. He is the author of two earlier best-selling Superman novels, *Last Son of Krypton* and *Miracle Monday*. *Kingdom Come* is his fifth novel.

Mr. Maggin has also raised horses, run for public office, taught at various high schools and colleges, and spent several winters skiing to excess. If he had not become a writer and still had managed to escape law school, he would probably have been a cowboy. He is the father of two and the husband of one. Like many of the characters whose company he enjoys best, he has grave primal doubts and knows very little for certain, but he essentially believes in everything. Even you.

MARK WAID has authored a broader range of well-known comics characters than any other writer in the history of the medium, having penned adventures for such comic book stars as Superman, Batman, the X-Men, Captain America, Spider-Man, and Archie. Mr. Waid also serves as a comic book historian and has fielded questions from such diverse sources as *Time, Variety,* the Library of Congress, and the Museum of Modern Art. He lives outside Philadelphia.

ALEX ROSS is an art school graduate and an ad agency survivor. His fully painted art has brought him critical acclaim and multiple awards, and has helped pave the way for the acceptance of other painted comics in the industry. His first major work was the best-selling, four-issue miniseries *Marvels* (Marvel Comics) in 1993. Alex Ross' next major project came in 1996 with the critically acclaimed painted series *Kingdom Come* (DC Comics); like *Watchmen* and *Batman: The Dark Knight Returns,* it is considered a seminal work in the industry. His most recent work includes *Uncle Sam* (Vertigo/DC Comics, 1997), on which he collaborated with writer Steve Darnall, and *Superman: Peace on Earth* (DC Comics, 1998), written by Paul Dini. Mr. Ross paints covers for many publications, including the monthly award-winning series *Astro City* (Homage Comics). The artist formerly known as "Sunshine," he lives and works in Wilmette, Illinois, a suburb of Chicago.

VISIT WARNER ASPECT ONLINE!

THE WARNER ASPECT HOMEPAGE
You'll find us at: www.twbookmark.com then by clicking on Science Fiction and Fantasy.

NEW AND UPCOMING TITLES
Each month we feature our new titles and reader favorites.

AUTHOR INFO
Author bios, bibliographies and links to personal websites.

CONTESTS AND OTHER FUN STUFF
Advance galley giveaways, autographed copies, and more.

THE ASPECT BUZZ
What's new, hot and upcoming from Warner Aspect: awards news, best-sellers, movie tie-in information . . .

**AVAILABLE AS A
TIME WARNER AUDIOBOOK:**

**KINGDOM COME
2 cassettes/3 hours
ISBN: 157042-5388
$17.00 U.S. / $22.00 Canada**